The Outlaw Hunter

by

Dave P. Fisher

DOUBLE DIAMOND

Washington

Dave P. Fisher

DOUBLE DIAMOND

Copyright 2014 by Dave P. Fisher
Double Diamond Books, Seatac, Washington
www.DoubleDiamondBooks.com

The Outlaw Hunter is a work of fiction. Though actual locations may be mentioned, they are used in a fictitious manner and the events and occurrences were invented in the mind and imagination of the author except for the inclusion of actual historical facts. Similarities of characters or names used within to any person – past, present, or future – are coincidental except where actual historical characters are purposely interwoven.

Double Diamond Books
Printed by CreateSpace, Amazon.com

To Life

Life is a journey, not a destination
Live it boldly and without fear
As for me
I refuse to tiptoe through life
only to arrive safely at death

Dave P. Fisher

To Doris—
May there always be a trail—

Dave P. Fisher

Books by Dave P. Fisher

The Poudre Canyon Saga

Where Free Men Gather
White Grizzly
The Men from Poudre Canyon
We Never Back Down
Shifting Trails

Individual Titles

Jury of Six
Trail Back to Eagle Rock
Zac Doolin's Gold
The Turning of Copper Creek
Virgil Creede
Beyond Raton
Bitter Grass
A Man for the Country
The Hanging of August Miller
The Outlaw Hunter

Short Story Collections

Bronc Buster – Short Stories of the American West

The Auction Horse (humor)

They Still Do That (cowboy poetry)

www.davepfisher.com

You need to rethink your life

"I'm calling you out, but you seem too terrified to move." He again waited as he was ignored and the laughter increased.

Eli wiped the biscuit through the meat juice on his mostly empty plate and spoke calmly without looking at the man. "Folks are in here eating their supper they don't want to see you bleeding on the floor. It's hard on the appetite and troubles the digestion. I think you need to go back to the bar and have another drink and rethink your life."

Standing up, Eli dug a silver dollar out of his left pocket and dropped it on the table. He moved out from the back of the table, ignoring the man standing in front of him. Laughter grew as he walked out the open door.

Eli walked to the edge of the street where he leaned against a porch post and waited.

Dave P. Fisher

The Outlaw Hunter

Chapter 1

The shack wasn't much, thin dry boards and a tar paper roof. The cracks in between the warped vertical boards indicated they had been nailed up green. It was a poor construction that only needed a good wind to blow it down. The saddled horses in the corral told him the two men he hunted were inside and that was all he cared about.

It wasn't his style to shout warnings or give the other man a chance to set himself up and deliver the first shot. In the outlaw hunting business, the man who delivered the first shot usually buried the man who didn't. He had yet to be the man who didn't.

Less than a hundred yards separated him from the shack as he lay on his belly looking down from a small rise. He thumbed back the hammer on the Sharps .50 and tucked the iron butt-plate into his right shoulder. Lining the sights up on the middle of the shack's flimsy door he squeezed off the shot. The rifle slammed back into his shoulder as the heavy bullet blew through the door, ripping the center plank into splinters.

He smiled at the effect and jerked open the rifle's breech, kicking out the spent brass and a plume of black powder smoke. He slid a new cartridge into the chamber and pulled the action closed. He watched the shack for several seconds to see what result his shot had on the men inside of it. He could see through the hole in the door and no one moved across it. Nothing happened.

Having delivered the first shot he was now willing to accept their surrender. He shouted down the hill in his deep, rough voice, "Charlie Monk and Buck Smith, you come out of that shack with your hands in the air." No answer came back to him.

The rusted and hole-riddled stove pipe stuck up out of the roof blowing smoke out along its length. He estimated where the stove was in the cabin and lined up the sights where he figured it should be. If it was as rusted as the pipe the idea should work. He fired and watched as the bullet tore a head size hole through the board and clanged into the stove. He fed in another cartridge and waited.

Smoke began to seep out of the cracks in the walls as the hole blown in the rusted stove released smoke into the shack. What remained of the front door swung open. A second later a man, gripping a pistol in his hand, bolted out of the shack in a crouched run. The man coughed continuously as he ran toward the corral where the two saddled horses waited.

Holding his position on the rise, he aimed the Sharps at the runner and shouted out again. "Charlie Monk, you drop that pistol and surrender." Charlie Monk fired two shots in the direction he thought the voice came from and jerked the corral gate open.

"I gave him a fair chance." He pulled the trigger and Charlie Monk slammed into the gate like he'd been blasted out of a cannon. The gate swung away leaving the man lying still on the ground.

He shouted back down the hill. "You're next, Buck, give up. It's easier tying you over a saddle than playing nurse maid to you all the way back to Pueblo."

Smith shouted toward the hill, "That all depends on who's talking.

"Eli Warren's talking and he's got a Sharps sighted on the third button of your shirt. If you want what Monk got, just stay right there."

Smith walked out of the cabin and into the open with his hands raised over his head.

Standing up cautiously, Eli Warren let the hammer down on the Sharps and headed down off the rise toward the man standing with his hands in the air. When he was half way to the outlaw Eli shifted the rifle to his left hand and pulled the Remington .44 out of his holster with his right. He held the big revolver in front of him as he closed the distance between him and Smith.

He pointed the revolver at Smith and thumbed back the hammer. "Pull that pistol out from the back of your belt. Make it with two fingers, I'm the nervous sort and might accidentally squeeze a little too hard on the trigger of this .44 if I get too scared."

Smith slowly lowered his right hand and placed it behind his back. He brought his hand back out to his side gripping the butt of a six-gun between his forefinger and thumb.

Eli gestured with his head to his left. "Throw it way over there, and I don't want to see a little sissy toss, *fling* it."

Smith tossed the gun into a bush several feet away and brought his hand back up to match the left still poised in the air.

"That was a good throw. Now, real slow pull your britches legs up so I can see what's in your boots."

Bending over slowly, Smith lifted his pants legs up over the tops of his boots revealing the handle of a knife.

"Same thing with the knife, toss it. I'd hate to have to shoot you after all this cooperation."

The knife fell next to the gun. Smith snarled at the man in front of him, "We done yet?"

"Empty out your pockets."

Smith rolled his eyes back and jammed his hands into

his hip pockets and pulled them out. A Barlow pocket knife fell out and landed in the dirt at his feet. "You want the cannon that's stuck up my rear end too?"

Eli gave him a cold look, "Funny. Sit down and pull off your boots."

"What! I ain't taking off my boots, damn you."

Eli frowned and shook his head, "Don't you curse at me, I don't like being cursed at. Do it again and I'll nail your nasty tongue to a pine tree."

"Why do I have to take my boots off?"

"Because you're going to be riding and won't need them. Because, you can't run far barefoot, and because I said so. Now, do it."

"Damn you, I won't."

"I said don't curse at me." With that Eli lowered the Remington and shot Smith on the inside of his right foot.

With a howl of pain Smith fell backwards onto his backside and grabbed his booted foot. He yanked the boot off; his eyes grew wide at the sight of the bloody sock. "You shot my foot!"

Eli showed no concern as he stared down at the man. "You can keep your boots on now, you won't be walking anytime soon."

Smith yanked the filthy sock off and examined his foot. The bullet had grazed the side of his foot. It was bleeding and painful but not seriously damaged. "You got something I can wrap around this?"

"Wrap that sock around it."

Tying the sock around his wounded foot, Smith glanced up at Eli. "You're a low down poor excuse, Warren. Look at what you did to Charlie, you bushwhacked him. That's not even fair."

"You're a fine one to talk about fair. How fair were you two coyotes to the people you robbed on those stages? Did you give that last stage driver and his shotgun man a fair shake when you killed them? I gave Monk a chance to give up, but he didn't take it. Don't expect any tears from me over him or you when you're swinging off a rope. Eli indicated the corral with a flick of his gun barrel, "Get over there and sit down against a post."

"I can't walk, you shot my foot."

"Then crawl over there," Eli snapped.

Smith got on his feet and limped to the corral and sat down with his back to a corral post. Eli wrapped a rope around Smith's arms and chest tying it tight to the backside of the post.

Leaving Smith tied and sitting in the dirt, Eli brought one of the saddled horses out of the corral and tied it next to Monk's body. Eli Warren was a big man, strong and muscled in the upper body. Standing over six feet tall his size alone was intimidating. He picked up Monk's body and tossed it belly down over the saddle. He tied the stirrups together under the horse and then tied the body down to the saddle's D rings.

Pulling the last knot tight Eli glanced at Smith, "I'm going for my horse, don't be running off."

Smith growled, "Oh, that's real funny, like I could run with my shot foot."

Turning toward the rise Eli walked over it to his tied horse. The blue roan turned his head to look at him and let out a huff of breath that fluttered his lips. Pulling the reins loose, Eli stepped into the saddle and rode back to the corral.

Smith was sitting head down in a dejected manner. Dismounting, Eli walked into the corral and led the second saddled horse out. He pulled the bridle off and replaced it with a weathered halter and lead rope that was hanging on a post. Removing the rope from Smith he ordered, "Get on."

"How am I supposed to get on with a shot foot?"

Eli pulled the Remington out and pointed it at him. "If I have to listen to you snivel all the way to Pueblo about your foot I'm putting a stop to it right here and now."

"Okay, okay, relax Warren, I'm going." Grabbing the saddle horn he stepped into the left side stirrup with his good foot and swung up into the saddle.

"Put your hands together over the horn." Smith obeyed and Eli tied his hands together around the saddle horn, then passed the rope through the saddle gullet and brought it up and tied it loosely around Smith's neck pulling him slightly forward. "You won't get far trying to control a horse with no bridle and tied like that so I suggest you ride along nice and not try anything. If you take off and the horse don't kill you, I will."

He tied the reins from the horse with Monk's body to the tail of Smith's horse. Stepping into the saddle, Eli picked up the lead rope to Smith's horse and set off to the north.

They were still a half day's ride from Pueblo when the sun began to sink behind the Great Divide. Picking a spot in a cluster of aspens, Eli rode into it and pulled the roan to a stop. He looked back at Smith who was half asleep swaying back and forth in the saddle. "We'll stop here for the night."

Untying Smith's neck and hands he studied the outlaw, he was looking pretty passive now. The bleeding had stopped on his sock-wrapped foot. It looked nastier than it actually was. "Get off the horse, Smith."

With an effort, Smith swung his right leg over the saddle and collapsed with a howl of pain as his feet hit the ground. Eli looked at him. "You might want to get rid of that one boot; it won't make it any easier to get around."

Smith glared up at him and pulled the boot off and angrily threw it away. "You plannin' on feedin' me?"

"Sure." Eli dug into his saddlebag and pulled out a hand-sized slab of dried beef and handed it to Smith. "Here, eat up. Now, sit with your back against that tree."

With a grumbled curse Smith slid backwards to the tree. Eli pulled the canteen off Smith's horse and tossed it to him. "You'll want some water with that."

Taking a coil of rope off his saddle Eli wrapped it twice around Smith's chest under his arms and tied it at the backside of the tree. Standing up he looked Smith over. "Looks like your foot stopped bleeding."

"It hurts like sin."

"Good, then you can contemplate your many sins."

"This ain't very comfortable." Smith squirmed against the tree.

"You want comfortable go to a social club in Denver."

Slumping back against the tree, Smith frowned and gnawed on the jerky and drank the warm water from his canteen. Mid-chew his chin fell against his chest and he began to snore.

Looking at the sleeping man Eli grumbled under his breath, "Good, if I had to listen to another minute of his sniveling I probably would have shot him." He untied Monk and shoved his stiff horseshoe shaped body to the ground. He then stripped the gear off the horses and staked them out to graze.

Building a small fire he set the battered coffee kettle out and poured water and coffee grounds into it. The smell of the coffee was drifting around the camp when Smith woke up and sniffed the air. "Any chance a condemned man can have a cup?"

"You got a cup?"

Smith jerked his head toward the saddles on the ground. "In my saddlebag."

Looking in the saddlebag Eli pulled out a dirty cup. He scowled at it, "Everything about you dirty?"

"Sorry, I flunked out of finishing school," Smith answered with a sneer.

Eli poured the cup half full and handed it to Smith who took the cup in both hands. Eli settled back down on the opposite side of the fire.

Lifting the cup up to his lips, Smith drank and studied the man across from him. "What made you become a bounty hunter, Warren?"

The image of his friend Huge O'Connor filled his mind. Eli looked out into the trees, "Got my reasons. What made you become an outlaw?"

"Got my reasons."

"Must be some pretty poor reasons to make a man want to become a robber and murderer."

"You're one to talk about being a murderer, look what you did to Charlie."

"That wasn't murder. I only kill men who have a gun in their hand."

Smith shrugged his shoulders with indifference. "I like being someone people walk carefully around because they know I'm dangerous."

Eli sniffed and chuckled, "You're not dangerous; you're a cold blooded killer. In the sea of outlaws you're a little-bitty fish, Smith. I pick up little fish along the way to pay expenses."

"So, what's a big fish?

"The Parson gang."

"The Parson gang, huh? Never run across them myself, but I've heard plenty enough. No lawman's ever been able to figure out where they'll hit next. What makes you think you'll find them?"

"Because I can."

Eli had enough conversation and stopped talking. The two sat across from each other in silence.

It was dark when Eli stood up from the fire and walked over to the saddles and pulled Smith's blanket off the back of his saddle. He walked over to Smith and tied his hands together. He then wrapped the blanket around him and tucked the ends into the rope on the backside of the tree.

"I sleep almighty light. I hear movement in the dark, I just naturally start shooting. I'd be a good boy if I were you and just sleep."

Bringing the horses in from where they were

picketed, Eli tied them to trees. Kicking out the fire, Eli disappeared into the dark and bedded down for the night. He put himself in a position with the horses between him and Smith, but where he could still see him between the horse's legs. He was one to wake often in the night and he'd be checking on his prisoner and relocating his bed each time he did.

Daybreak found Eli saddling the horses while Smith slept as he had left him. Poking the sleeping man with his boot toe, Eli called out for him to wake up. Smith lifted his head and groaned. He looked around and saw that the horses were ready with Monk's body tied down.

"I feel terrible," Smith moaned.

"Tough." Eli removed the ropes and stepped back. "Get up, let's go."

Smith struggled to his feet, he was stiff and sore from the position he'd been in all night. "Don't I get to eat something?'

"No."

Smith grumbled under his breath as he limped over to his horse and struggled to mount. Eli tied the man's hands and neck to the saddlehorn as before. He stepped into the saddle and rode out leading both horses.

Early afternoon found the grim parade moving through Pueblo toward the Wells Fargo office. Heads turned and people stopped on the boardwalks to stare. Reining into the hitch rail in front of the stage and banking office, Eli dismounted and walked through the door and up to the counter. Pulling the wanted poster out of his pocket with the descriptions of Monk and Smith he held it up in front of the bank man. "Got the two of them outside."

The bank man looked out the window past Eli and the wanted poster held up in front of his eyes. He cringed at the sight of the weary man slumped over in the saddle and the body on the horse behind him. He reached under the counter and brought out a sheet of paper. "Fill this out and we will mail you a check for the reward money."

Eli stared at the man, "I don't think so. You pay it right here and right now."

The bank man looked into the cold eyes of the big man and swallowed. "Let me talk to the manager." He stepped into an office and came back out with an older man dressed neatly in a suit and starched collar. He stopped in front of Eli.

Handing the wanted poster to the man, Eli said flatly, "Monk and Smith, got them outside."

The man nodded, "Let's have a look." They walked across the room and out the door.

The bank man looked up at Smith and then bent over to look in the closed eyes and rigid face of the dead man. The bank man didn't cringe or make a face when looking over the two. Eli could tell that this was a western man accustomed to the rugged ways of the country. "That's them all right."

"Of course they are," Eli answered. "I know what I'm doing.' He pointed toward the office, "Your man in there says you will mail me a check for the reward."

"That is our standard policy."

Eli's eyes narrowed. "Well, it's not my standard policy. I don't want a check that likely will never come. I want cash and I want it now."

The bank manager looked into Eli's eyes and saw the anger growing in his face. "Except I can make changes to policies if I choose to. Two-hundred dollars each. Come inside and I will draw your money."

Eli followed the man as he stepped behind the counter and counted out four hundred dollars, laying the bills out in front of him.

Eli watched as the bills were counted out. He picked them up and put the money in his hip pocket. "Nice doing business with you gents." He began to turn away.

The bank manger spoke before Eli turned. "If you would deliver that," he gestured to window, "to the

Sheriff's office I would be obliged."

Eli nodded and walked across the bank floor and back out the door. Several people had gathered around to stare at Smith and the body. Several boys were trying to sneak peeks at the dead man's face. When Eli stepped out, the adults unconsciously moved back a step as they looked at the tall man and his hard brown eyes piercing into them from his whiskered face.

One of the boys called out to him, "Did you shoot him, Mister?"

Eli looked down at the boy without a smile. "This is what happens when you are a bad boy and become an outlaw. Be good boys and mind your folks."

The boy's mouth dropped open and then he nodded, "Yes, sir."

Stepping back into the saddle Eli led the horses back down the street. He smiled to himself at the boy's reaction. He liked children; they were honest about things and came straight out with it. Most adults irritated him, but he liked youngsters. .

Reining in at the front of the Sheriff's office, a man wearing a badge came out the door and met him before he could dismount. He had a bulging belly from too many hours in the café and not enough in the saddle. He had a self-impressed look that Eli didn't like. The man glanced over the men and horses and then up at Eli with a disgusted expression. "Where are you going with all this?"

"To the sheriff. This is Buck Smith and what's left of Charlie Monk. I already collected the bounties from the bank. They're all yours now."

"What am I supposed to do with them?"

"Well, you might try putting this one in your jail," he pointed at Smith, "seeing how he's a wanted man and all. The other you can pass on to the undertaker."

"How do I know he's wanted?"

Eli shook his head and tossed the wanted poster down to him. "You ever see one of these? That's how you know. These two have been robbing stages and killing folks from Alamosa to Pueblo and you never heard of them? Go ask the banker, he knew them."

The two men locked eyes on each other for several seconds before Eli said, "Please tell me you're not the sheriff."

The man puffed out his chest, "I'm his deputy sheriffs out of town and *I'm* in charge."

Eli stared at the man. There were things he would have liked to say, but held his tongue. "Well, you tell the sheriff that you got Buck Smith and Charlie Monk. I'm sure he'll know what to do with them." He tossed the lead rope to the deputy who refused to catch it, letting it fall in the dirt. Eli reined his horse around to leave.

The deputy blurted out, "You're nothing but a dirty bounty hunter. I hate bounty hunters!"

Eli pulled gently back on the reins and looked over his shoulder at the man. "I'm an outlaw hunter; I hunt outlaws, not bounties."

The deputy scoffed, "But, you collect the bounties all the same."

"A man should be paid for his work." Eli gestured toward the lead rope on the ground. "You might want to pick that up before your prisoner walks away and then you can explain to the sheriff how you lost a half dead and a full dead man. Might prove embarrassing." He nudged the roan with his heels and rode away leaving the deputy staring angrily at his back.

Chapter 2

Eli rode down the street keeping the roan at a walk. He now had enough money to carry him for a while. His needs were simple; he wasn't much of a drinker and didn't gamble so there was no chance he'd blow through the money. Surveying the stores lining the street, a gun store caught his eye. He pulled the roan up and reined him over toward the store.

He stepped out of the saddle and walked into the store where the odor of new leather and gun oil met him. A gray haired man with a pair of spectacles balanced on the end of his nose was behind the counter. His concentration was on the hammer assembly of an older model Winchester rifle set up on a gunsmith's sawbuck.

Upon Eli's entry the man looked up and smiled. He made a quick assessment of Eli, taking in the worn butt of the Remington on his hip. He wiped the gun oil off his hands and removed the spectacles turning his full attention to the potential customer. "Now, you look like a man who knows his guns."

Eli gave a small smile back, "I know which end to point at the other man."

The gunsmith smiled.

Studying the rifles on a rack behind the counter Eli asked, "You happen to have a Winchester 1873?"

The man's faced brightened. "Just got a half dozen in day before yesterday. Yes, sir, that is one mighty fine rifle, 44-40 it is, powerful and accurate." The man turned from the counter and went through an open doorway to his back room and returned carrying a rifle.

Eli liked what he saw as the man handed him the rifle and he took hold of it. It was heavy and solidly built which was how he liked a gun. The gleaming hardwood forearm running halfway up the barrel and magazine tube felt good in his hands. He pulled down on the lever appreciating the smooth action. He closed it again. "How much?"

"Brand new like that, fifteen dollars. Expensive, but worth every penny."

"I'll take it. Give me a hundred cartridges for it as well. You happen to have a saddle scabbard to fit it?"

"Yes, sir." He went back into the back room and came out with a new leather scabbard. Eli could smell the new leather from six feet away. "How much all tallied?"

The man added the numbers on a paper pad, "Twenty dollars even."

Eli pulled the folded bills out of his pocket, peeled off the right amount and laid it on the counter. "Thanks." He picked up his purchases and headed back out the door.

The gunsmith picked up the money and watched Eli. He knew a dangerous man when he met one. Such a man didn't say much and the less conversation directed at him the better.

Opening one of the boxes of cartridges, Eli loaded the rifle magazine and leaned it against the porch pole while he mounted the scabbard on the right side of his saddle opposite the scabbard holding the Sharps. He was adjusting the scabbard's straps and buckling them to the saddle's D rings when he saw two men walk up and stop between him and the store.

One of the men laughed, "Why lookie here, brother, someone just left this brand new rifle settin' up here against this post. I think I ought to take it, seeing how it's just left here." The second man was younger and laughed as he watched Eli for a reaction.

Tugging on the last strap, Eli pulled the scabbard into

place and cast a sidelong glance at the two men. They were dirty and disheveled; they looked as ignorant as they sounded. The talker was wearing a holstered pistol that had worked its way around to the front of his right leg.

Eli warned in a low voice, "Leave that rifle right where it's at."

The talker put on a tough face as he shifted his pistol around to his right side, an action meant to intimidate. "I don't think you should be givin' folks orders on matters that don't concern you."

Eli reached for the rifle. "The rifle happens to be mine and that makes it my concern."

"What? You sayin' this here rifle is yours? I think it's mine, I done found it first, and now you're tryin' to steal it from me."

The second man grinned with half his mouth, looking simple minded. "Roy, my brother here, is a man you shouldn't oughta argue with, Mister. If'n he says that rifle gun's his, you'd best let him have it." His grin grew wider, "A feller could get hurt, you know what I mean?"

Eli pulled his arm back from the rifle leaving it against the post. He squared around to face the two men, as he did he slipped the loop off the hammer of the Remington. "What did you say?"

Both men froze as they looked back into Eli's cold hard eyes. The older brother laughed nervously, "We was just funnin' with yuh, Mister." Both men began backing up slowly. "No need to be grabbin' iron. It was just a joke."

"I don't like jokes like that. You just called me a liar. Where I come from, that's grabbin' iron talk."

Holding his hands out in front of him the man stammered, "I apologize, Mister. I was just funnin' with yuh."

"Then get out of here while I'm still in a forgiving mood."

The two men turned and ran down the boardwalk. Eli watched them until they were out of sight. "Idiots," he grumbled. Taking the Winchester up from where it leaned on the post he slid it into the new scabbard. He pulled the roan loose and mounted.

He wondered where he should head for now. He had no wanted men to follow up on and nowhere in particular to go. The last he'd heard of the Parson gang they were in Kansas. He thought about that for a bit.

The Parson gang had come to his attention a couple years back. The gang consisted of four men that pretty well rounded out the outlaw trade. They robbed banks, trains, stages, and stuck up freight wagons and travelers. They rustled cattle and horses, and were credited with several murders and probably more that no one knew of or could pin to their collars.

Each time he saw a new wanted poster for the gang the bounty had been raised. Cattlemen's Associations, banks, train, and stage lines had all pitched in for the bounties and it was up to twenty-five hundred dollars on each of their heads. A man could do a lot with that kind of money.

Maybe it was time to go back to his Uncle John's place. The more he considered the idea the more he liked it. He would head to the place that was the closest thing he had to a home and surprise the old man.

Riding south to the Colorado portion of the Santa Fe Trail, he took it headed east. John's cabin, which he had extended into a general store, was on the Trail where he had built it before there was a Boggsville or any other town in the area.

Arriving at John's store, Eli watched a man shuffle out the door carrying a bundle of goods that were deposited in a buckboard alongside the building. He reined the roan to the hitchrail on the west side of the building away from the front door and dismounted.

Eli stepped quietly through the open door and quickly scanned the room. There was no one inside except

John, who had his back to the door. The old man was arranging cans on a head-level shelf. Eli growled in low voice, "Don't turn around old man. Put your money on the counter and keep your mouth shut."

John slid his right hand down to the shelf below the cans and stood perfectly still. He spoke in a calm voice, "How am I supposed to put my money on the counter if I can't turn around?"

Eli growled back, "You figure it out."

In spite of his sixty some years, John Warren was still a quick man. He spun around, his right hand moving like a striking snake. The loud metallic click of a cocking hammer sounded in the quiet room as he pointed a revolver at Eli's head. "You're getting careless, boy. I could have had you dead right there."

Eli snapped back, "Careless? You want to talk about careless? I waltz in here and what do I see? Old man Warren with his back exposed to a wide open door. Talk about a target, why don't you just paint a bull's-eye on your back. You'd think an old trapper and wagon master like you would know better."

John thumbed the hammer down on the gun and replaced it on the shelf. He scowled at Eli as he made his way out from around the counter. Stepping up to his taller nephew he glared at him and then suddenly let out a whoop of laughter and enveloped Eli in a bear hug.

Eli laughed and returned the hug with equal intensity.

Stepping back John looked him over. "Well, I don't see any bullet holes, guess you survived another year. You're looking good, Eli, real good."

"I had a good teacher. You're looking pretty good your own self, old timer."

"Getting a little stiff in the joints, but a million nights sleeping on frozen ground will do that to you. In addition to a couple of Blackfoot arrowheads lost in my hide somewhere." John laughed that deep warm sound Eli associated with home. The laugh he had first heard that day a scared runaway stood at John's open door.

"Just fixing to close up. Let me do that and we'll go whip up some beef and beans." John crossed the room, shut and barred the front door.

John's original cabin adjoined the store addition with an inside door connecting them. As he headed for the door John grinned, "Got some of the good Tennessee stuff I got from a freighter who just happened to have an extra bottle that I parleyed away from him."

Walking through the door Eli looked the cabin over. Nothing had changed in the year he had been away. John grabbed a bottle from a shelf under the counter. Putting down a pair of glasses he poured whiskey into each. They sat at the table facing each other. "Tell me what you've been up to, Eli."

"Same thing, tracking down bad men."

"That's it, huh? A whole year gone and you can sum it up in one sentence. I thought I taught you how to articulate."

Eli smiled, "Let me work on that, Uncle John."

"You really like that sort of thing, don't you? Seems kind of like picking up rattlers with a blindfold on."

Eli held the grin and nodded, "Sometimes it feels like that. It pays a lot better than working cattle sixteen hours a day for a whopping whole dollar, though."

"Yeah, but those cows ain't laying for you, getting ready to kill you when you ride by."

"Oh, I don't know about that. I've encountered some mighty mean longhorns that *did* lay in wait to kill you when you rode by."

"Got me there, Eli, can't argue that one. Get any bad ones lately?"

"A couple wanted for robbery and murder down Alamosa way. Dropped them off at the sheriff's office in Pueblo."

John grinned, "Horizontal or vertical?"

"One of each. That old Sharps you gave me still can

fetch 'em. Speaking of, let me put my horse up and get my guns before some yahoo makes off with them." Eli left the room by the cabin's back door.

Leading his horse to the stable he looked around. The place still stood all alone on the Trail. Boggs had built his mansion two miles down the Trail and the town built up around it. The town had spread toward John's store, but stopped with a mile of open Trail between them. It hadn't hurt business though. Unsaddling his horse he took up his guns and saddlebags and returned to the cabin.

When he came back in he handed the 73 to John. "Look this one over."

John let out a low whistle as he took it. "I was thinking about getting a few in here to sell, hear a lot of good things about this rifle."

"Picked it up from a gunsmith in Pueblo. Haven't even shot it yet."

John raised one eyebrow as he looked at Eli, "Thought I taught you better than that. Plan on waiting until some outlaw is shooting at you to see if it even fires or the sights are true?" John shook his head and clucked his tongue, "Where did I go wrong?"

"Yes, sir, I consider myself properly chastised and hang my head in shame. How about right after we eat we go run a few shots through it?"

"Sounds good." John handed the rifle back to him as his tone turned serious. "I suspect it won't be long before you use it at the rate things are going. Criminal activity is on the rise around here."

"Everywhere," Eli replied. "Hear tell Las Animas City is getting the railroad and fighting Boggsville for the county seat." What's that going to do to your store?"

"Nothing. Being a mile out of Boggsville my trade comes mostly from the Trail, along with farmers and ranchers."

"A lot's changed since the day you and I first rode into this country. Not much here then, just us and later

Boggs and Powers down the way."

"Yes, it has grown up a bit since then. Say, you remember Cliff Adams?"

"Sure, we palled together when kids, as you should recall."

"I recall alright. You two tied a rope around the Adams' outhouse and tied the other end to a milk cow and set her on the run."

"Oh, you remember that."

"Cliff's pa was occupying the seat at the time and Cliff couldn't sit down for a week afterwards."

"And you made me cut ten-thousand cords of firewood for my punishment. You said that if I had enough time on my hands to cause mischief then I obviously didn't have enough to do."

"It was only five cords and you didn't cause any more trouble did you?"

Eli smiled at the memory. "I haven't seen Cliff in a few years. He was Boggsville City Marshal the last I talked to him."

"Cliff is now the County Sheriff. We had an election last fall and he won it hands down. Folks around here really like that man. He's got an office by the courthouse. You should go have a visit with him."

"I'll do that tomorrow. Meanwhile, I think you promised me some beef and beans. My stomach's starting to think my throat's been cut."

John stood up, "You haven't changed much, always hungry. I recall the day you came to my door in Independence, wasted away to skin and bones. You did nothing but eat for a solid week."

"I was hungry; it had been a long trip."

"That's what happens when you run away from home and home is in Virginia." John let go with the laugh.

It was good to be back, even though he knew he'd be moving on again. It was a pleasant thought, knowing you had a place to come back to where you were welcome. The older he got the more he thought about having his own place to come back to or maybe to never leave it. There was something to be said for roots.

Chapter 3

Doors were being unlocked and curtains pulled back in Boggsville businesses as Eli made his way toward the courthouse and Cliff Adams' office. He let the roan move at a lazy pace as he took in the activity around him. A small building, neat and freshly painted, sported a sign over the door that read 'Sheriff.' Dismounting Eli made his way to the door, turned the door knob, and walked in.

Cliff was standing in the center of the room, facing the door while sorting through some papers. Eli recognized a couple as wanted posters. "Anything in there for me?"

Cliff looked up and stared at the man across the room from him. "Eli!" Cliff grinned, "I'd say you're a sight for sore eyes, but that wouldn't be true, you're still as ugly as ever."

Eli smiled, "Let me return the compliment, oh ugly one."

The two men came toward each other and clasped hands in the rough and rowdy manner reminiscent of their boyhood days. Cliff stepped back, "It's been a while Eli, glad to see you're still in an upright position."

Eli looked around the office. "Sheriff, huh? You've come a long ways Cliff, congratulations."

"It's kind of funny. I was elected Sheriff of Greenwood County, and then last February they went and changed the name to Bent County. So, now I'm the Sheriff of Bent County. I'm likely the only lawman to have been sheriff of two counties at one time. It's not too tough of a job; we have a few hard cases drift in now and again off the Santa Fe, but it's mostly ranchers and farmers."

"Sounds pretty nice."

Cliff gestured toward the chairs at his desk. He poured out a couple of cups from the coffee pot on the stove and handed one to Eli. "I hear your name popping up every so often, you have a pretty wicked reputation."

"That all depends on who's talking. It's only wicked if you're an outlaw."

"True enough. If you're interested I've got a job for you."

Eli looked around the room, "I'll sweep floors, but I won't fetch your meals from the cafe."

Cliff scrunched up his face in confusion, "What?"

"If you're hiring a cleaning lady I'm just telling you what I won't do."

Cliff was quick to catch on. "Well, that's disappointing and here I thought I could get some papers shuffled and pencils whittled while a lackey runs for my supper."

"Sorry, but I have my standards."

Cliff laughed, "You haven't changed a whole lot. Better not let it out that you have a sense of humor it could ruin your reputation."

"I'll keep that in mind. Now, should you happen to have a wanted poster in those papers you're shuffling I might be interested."

Cliff leaned back in his chair holding his coffee cup in both hands. "No poster, but I do have a problem you might take care of for me. Four brothers named Yeager, wanted for a variety of crimes, but the Territory doesn't consider them enough of a threat to put a reward on their heads. They like to steal cattle and horses from the local ranchers so several of them threw in as a group to put a hundred dollar bounty on each of their heads."

"Why don't the ranchers run them down?"

"They don't have the time to chase all over the country looking for them; however, they are willing to pay someone who has the time. Frankly, I don't have the time either."

"Can't squeeze it in between the shuffling and whittling?"

"More like I can't squeeze it in between keeping Denver up on its mountain of paperwork and handling petty complaints from the electorate in town. If I had known how much paperwork and politics was involved in this job I might have had second thoughts."

"How will Denver feel about you opening your own outlaw bounty store?"

"Folks here have made it a local affair since Denver doesn't care. What they don't know won't hurt them."

"Fine by me. I don't care much for what politicians think anyway."

"Still holding a family grudge?"

Eli scowled at the memory of his power seeking overbearing father. "You grow up with corrupt politicians you end up with a grudge. Tell me more about these Yeager boys."

"The ranchers gave me the cash to keep for whoever brings them in. I know the ranchers would prefer a cheap burying to a drawn out court trial where they have to appear and provide evidence."

"So, it's dead or alive?"

"Preferably alive, but if they make a fight of it . . ." Cliff left it hanging at that.

"The Yeagers are local boys?"

"Pretty much, but they range out some. Clyde Yeager is the oldest and the meanest. He shot a gambler a couple months back in Las Animas City and lit out. People in the saloon said the gambler was cheating so it was considered justified, no one went after him."

Eli nodded his understanding. "Okay, I'll look into

it."

"Thanks. They might head down to New Mexico and be out of our hair. There's a land war heating up down in Colfax County."

"So, you think the Yeagers might hire out for the land war?"

"It's possible."

They both looked at the door as it opened and a skinny young man wearing a badge came in. Cliff looked at him, "Make the rounds, Lanny?"

"Yes sir, all the stores and offices are open and there are no problems."

"Go keep an eye on things."

"Yes, sir." Lanny walked back out the door.

Eli lifted a questioning eyebrow, "Your deputy?"

Cliff shook his head, "His father has pull with the county and his kid wants to be a lawman so they forced him on me. He's not much good so I keep him busy with petty stuff."

"Hope he doesn't get himself killed."

"Yeah, good thing we aren't Trinidad. He'd be dead already."

Eli didn't respond as he drank from his cup.

"Ever think of being a lawman, Eli?" Cliff jerked his head toward the door, "I could use a *good* deputy."

"You mean to be put on a chain, bound to jurisdictions and bureaucratic nonsense, and told what I could and couldn't do based on someone's influence, family, or wealth?"

"It was a stupid question wasn't it?"

"It ranks right up there," Eli grinned.

Cliff shook his head and laughed.

The two sat in silence for a minute before Eli asked, "Hear anything of the Parson gang?"

"You still looking for them?"

"At every chance."

"Good luck, they're a clever bunch. The last I heard,

a couple of weeks back, they robbed a train in Kansas somewhere east of Hays City. Their next target is anyone's guess."

"They've got to get lazy and fall into a pattern one of these days. I keep hoping they'll pull a robbery when I'm in the area and give me a hot trail. One good break and I'd have them."

"Big reward on their heads, make a man some sizable money."

"It would that. You had started to tell me about the Yeagers before that kid busted in here."

"Yeah, back to that. They come from one of those trouble making families the whole outfit is trash. Their old man got hung out in Nebraska for horse theft. There's Clyde, Mort, Ed, and Harry. They live out in the hills around here somewhere and come into town once in a while to drink and play cards. Except for Clyde killing that gambler there are no killings we can put their names on, although folks credit a few to them. It's mostly stock thefts."

"I'll see what I can do." Eli stood up, "I told John I'd give him a hand with some things today so I'd better head on back. He told me about your promotion so I figured it was a good reason to come over and see you."

Cliff put out his hand, "I don't know if it's a promotion or a curse, but I'm glad you came by. Don't be such a stranger; maybe stop by every two or three years." They shook hands and Eli left the office, promising he would come by more often.

Returning to the store Eli found a freight wagon pulled up in front of the door. John and the driver were carrying a variety of goods into the store. He tied off the roan and lent a hand until everything was accounted for. The driver pulled the wagon away leaving them standing in the store surrounded by bundles and barrels.

"You get to see Cliff?"

Eli nodded, "We had a good visit. I get the feeling

he's not too excited about the job though."

"He comes in once in a while, says it's part of his job checking on his citizens, but I know he's just making sure this old man is doing alright way out here away from town. He always manages to buy something."

"That sounds like him. He told me about the Yeager brothers and asked me, as a favor, to find them for him. Know anything about them?"

John hissed with irritation, "No good lot. Only difference between them and a pack of coyotes is coyote pelts are worth something. The last six months they've took to showing up here on occasion to buy tobacco or more likely to see if I have anything they can steal. I keep a gun handy when one of them comes around. I expect them to try and rob me one of these days."

"They sound like a pleasant lot."

"Yeah, so are scorpions."

Eli looked around him. "Let me put my horse up and I'll be back to give you a hand with all this."

Morning found Eli riding out toward the nearest ranch east of town. Asking some questions of the local stockmen about the Yeagers was a good place to start. Since he didn't have any other place he needed to be he could devote some time to helping Cliff with the Yeager problem.

A man met him in front of the ranch house as he rode up. The man's face was weathered and rough with a look of the Santa Fe Spanish to him. He wore a gun and looked like he could use it. "Can I help you?" His accent was Mexican, his tone more of a challenge than a question.

"I understand there's been some stock stealing going on by the Yeager brothers. I told my friend Cliff Adams I'd look into it for him."

Although the man eyed Eli with suspicion he was listening. "Who are you? I like to know who I am talking to before I tell my affairs to a stranger."

"Fair enough. Name's Eli Warren and I'm trying to get some information on the Yeagers."

The man's hard expression lightened. "I thought I knew your face. I saw you kill a man in Elizabethtown once."

"I've been there."

The man stepped forward and extended his hand, "Romiro Rios. Why is a man of your reputation looking for troublesome cow thieves?"

"Like I said, I'm helping a friend with a problem."

"Yes, we have a problem in the Yeager brothers. They steal a few cows here, a horse there. We will kill them if we catch them; however, I and my men do not have the time to go chasing all over the country to kill a few coyotes."

"That's how Cliff feels, he doesn't have the time or manpower to hunt them down, but I have the time."

"We will welcome your help."

"Know where I should start looking?"

The man waved his hand over the expanse of brown arid country. "A thousand places to hide in that my friend. Your guess is as good as anyone's."

"Thank you, Señor Rios, I'll see what I can do." Eli reined the roan around and rode away from the house.

He spent the day searching east and south of the Rios ranch while turning his thinking to that of an outlaw. Where would he hide if he was stealing cattle around here? There was a lot of country and it was understandable why Cliff and the ranchers couldn't devote any time to pursuing these two-bit stock thieves.

He rode the day out, returning to John's just before dark. The next day he covered the country north and west of the ranches. He talked to other stockmen, both sheep and cattle raisers, and got the same answers as from Rios. The brothers slipped, in stole what they wanted and then disappeared into the hills again. The end of the day found him no further ahead than the day Cliff told him about them.

The third day he stayed at the cabin trying to think out the problem. It was mid-morning and he was sitting at the table cleaning the dust and grit off the 73. While his hands worked, his mind prowled the surrounding country. It was the sound of a loud commanding voice that brought his attention back to the store.

He focused his listening to the store on the other side of the wall. A voice growled, "Hurry up old man. Get that cash box up here before I blow your head off."

Eli jumped out of his chair and went out the back door, levering a cartridge into the 73's chamber as he went. Pressing his back against the outside wall of the cabin he listened and then snuck a peek around the corner. Two horses stood ground tied outside the door as the shuffling of boots on the wooden floor sounded from the open doorway. Eli put the rifle to his shoulder and pointed it toward the horses and waited.

Inside the store John was looking down the bore of the robber's pistol and carefully following the orders being given. The robber's partner was behind him with his gun out watching the door. John was calm and watching for his chance to grab his gun and shoot the man in front of him. He dropped the steel cash box on top of the counter keeping his eyes on the man with the gun. The man grinned and grabbed the box. Both robbers turned their backs on John as they headed out the door.

As they turned John grabbed the pistol off the shelf and shouted, "Hey, you forgot something."

The man, cash box in one hand, gun in the other, stopped and turned around while his partner continued out the door. When he turned John shot him in the chest. The impact of the bullet pushed the robber backwards causing him to drop the cash box with a clattering of coins and steel.

The second man pointed his gun over his falling partner and fired a clumsy shot at John then turned and ran out the door. The bullet blew open a can of peaches that bounced off the shelf spraying liquid over the surrounding goods.

As the robber cleared the door and ran for his horse Eli sighted the rifle on him and fired. The bullet took the man in the neck spinning him around in a circle and dropping him lifeless to the ground. The man John had shot lay inside the store rasping out breaths through the hole in his left lung. As John looked down on him the robber gave a rattling long sigh and died.

Eli walked up to John, "Are you alright?"

John nodded, "Missed me, but made a heck of a mess in there. He looked out the door to the second dead man. "You wanted the Yeagers, well there's two of them."

"Branching out from stealing livestock."

"These are the same two that came in a few times before. Told you I always figured they were just getting an idea of what I had so they could come back and stick a gun in my face."

"Do you know which two these are?"

John shrugged, "No idea, just Yeagers is all I know."

"Guess I'd better take these two in to Cliff." He headed for the stable.

When Eli came back around leading his horse John had dragged the dead outlaw outside and was cleaning the blood off the floor. He had picked up the cash box and put it back in its place under the counter. Eli stepped past him headed into the cabin and came back out with his Remington buckled on.

John watched Eli as he threw the bodies over the saddles of their horses and tied them down. He next tied the reins of one horse to the tail of the other.

As Eli and John were standing by the horses a freight wagon rolling up from the south pulled to a stop in front of them. "Got a few things here for you, John." He stared at the bodies, "What happened here?"

"Yeager boys tried to rob me."

The freighter grinned, "Tried's the word alright. I saw Clyde and Mort Yeager on the Trail headed toward Cimarron yesterday." He gestured toward the bodies, "That would be Ed and Harry then."

"Well, at least Clyde and Mort are out of the country," John said.

"Unless they come back looking for their brothers," the freighter put in.

John shrugged, "I'm not worried about it if they do."

Eli mounted up and took the reins of the first horse. He left John and the freighter talking together in front of the store as he headed east on the Trail.

The townspeople were watching as Eli passed them with his grisly packstring. Dead men weren't a common sight in Boggsville so they drew attention. He pulled up in front of Cliff's office. Lanny hurried to the office from down the street and stopped not knowing what to say or do. His eyes bugged out as he stood gaping at the scene before him.

Cliff walked out of a saloon down the street. He narrowed his eyes trying to see what had stopped in front of his office. It took him a second to realize what he was looking at. He set a fast pace back to his office.

Cliff pushed his way through the gathering crowd. He looked into Lanny's face that was set in a shocked stare. He shook his head and then turned his attention to Eli. "What have we got here?"

Eli glanced around at the gathering crowd who were watching wide eyed and fascinated. "Yeagers."

The name was quickly whispered across the crowd.

Cliff walked alongside the horses and lifted the head of the first one, "This one's Ed." He walked to the second horse and looked at the face, "And Harry."

"Where do you want them, Cliff?"

Cliff poked the stunned deputy in the shoulder, "Wake up. Take them over to the undertaker. Tell him the county will pay him, but no fancy do-dads, just stick them in a hole."

The young man looked up with a nervous glance at Eli who was still mounted. He hesitantly took the reins of the first horse from him and led the horses down the street.

Cliff waved Eli to come in. Stepping off his horse, he followed Cliff into the office and closed the door. Eli jerked his thumb toward the outside, "That kid's not cut out for a lawman. He's going to get killed."

"I know, but his father has influence and wants him here. The commissioners agree with him. "

"They can all pitch in for his tombstone."

"I was breaking up a fight down at Soapy's when someone ran in yelling about dead men."

"Well, he wasn't wrong."

Cliff sat down. "So, how did you get them?"

"Actually, they came to us. They were trying to rob John's store. John shot the first one and I nailed the second one after he fired a shot at John and made a run for it."

"Can't say I'm sorry they're dead." He reached into his desk drawer and pulled out an envelope, opened it and counted out two hundred dollars and handed it to Eli. "There's still another two hundred in here for the rest of them. It's Clyde and Mort that's left and they're the mean ones."

"A freighter stopped by while we were trussing these two up. He said he passed Clyde and Mort yesterday headed for Cimarron."

"With any luck they'll get killed down there."

"I'm sure that would set alright with the ranchers."

"I got a telegram from Hays City, Kansas. Thought you'd like to know that the Parson gang robbed a stage carrying over ten thousand dollars of cattle buyers' money on it. That's two in the same area. You might want to head over that way and see if you can't pick up on them. They might be getting to that lazy part you were hoping for."

Folding the bills, Eli put them in his pocket. "I think I will. I'll see you whenever I get back."

Cliff came out from behind the desk and extended his hand. "Thanks for the help." They shook hands. "Make sure you stop by again."

Eli said he would and walked back out the door. A few people were still standing outside the office when he approached his horse. They stared at him and he heard his name whispered. He gave them a quick look over and mounted his horse riding out of town without a backward glance.

John met him at the store's front door as he rode up. "What did Cliff have to say?"

"That he was glad to have the problem dealt with, at least half of it." He pulled the bills out of his pocket, counted out one-hundred dollars and handed the bills to John.

John looked at him with surprise. "What's this for?"

"There was a hundred dollar reward on each of them. Cliff paid it, and since you accounted for one Yeager half the reward money is yours."

John chuckled, "Well, I can sure use it." He took the bills from him. "Thanks."

Eli looked down at the ground searching for the words. John recognized the look, "You'll be moving on again I suspect."

Eli nodded, "Parson Gang's active in Kansas. I need to head that way and see if I can't get on them."

"You're a restless spirit Eli; you go do what you need to do. Just make sure you come back to see me again." He reached out and gave his nephew a bear hug.

"Wear your gun Uncle John, the other half of those Yeagers might come around."

The old man smiled, "If I take them both do I get both rewards?"

"It's all yours. You just be on the watch and be careful."

"I'm an old mountain man and Indian fighter; I think I can handle it."

Chapter 4

Eli could smell the cattle in the Hays City stock pens before he ever saw the first building. The wind that blew across the Kansas plains never ceased and on it rode the smell of cattle. He liked the smell of cattle. He had ridden as a drover on a cattle drive to Montana in his earlier years and stayed on to work at the ranch. It was a combination of smells, sights, and dust favorably embedded in his senses.

Someday he wanted to build a nice house in the hills and raise cattle. Kansas was too flat to suit him and the Boggsville area too hot and dry with its sun scorched landscape. The mountains of Raton Pass and on up into the Canadian River headwaters is what he wanted. A good view of the Sangre de Cristo Mountains would be perfect. It was all possible if he could take down the Parson gang and get that ten thousand dollar reward. Maybe today he would get lucky, but he wasn't spending the reward money just yet.

He needed to talk to some of the local men about the Parson robberies. Such events always set tongues to wagging; however, the problem with that sort of information was how quickly it changed. He would have to sift through the stories to get the straight of it as most of the facts would be altered with each enhanced retelling. It was a starting place though and in the talk were always a few kernels of truth.

He needed a shave and a haircut, a clean appearance made people more willing to talk to him. Besides, barbershops were good places to pick up on the local topics of conversation especially if some of the old men were hanging around. He could try the saloons as well, but drinking men often gave the worst information. Enhanced storytelling mixed with liquor made for a poor combination. He would talk to the station master at the depot as well.

The day was growing late as he rode down the dirt street. The constant wagon traffic had packed down the dirt, but even so the wind kept the dust in the air. It had been years since he had last ridden through Hays, it was growing and the cattle trade was responsible for that. Only now the cattle business, and the national economy as a whole were crashing. He wondered how it would affect towns such as Hays who depended on cattle for their financial survival.

A few hard cases eyed him coldly as he rode past them. He met the eyes of one in particular as they held a mutual glare on each other. The man was a troublemaker as surely as if it were written on his forehead. It showed in his eyes that he was one who liked to push it. Hays hosted not only Texas cowhands, buffalo hunters, and plainsmen, it also attracted gunmen, gambling slicks, and trouble in all shapes and sizes.

A hand painted sign identifying a building squeezed in between a dry goods store and a drug store as a barber shop caught his attention. Three old men sat in wooden chairs in front of the building, all vigorously arguing over some bit of news. A large window gave him a view of the inside where the barber reposed in his chair while talking with another man seated across from him.

Eli pulled the roan up at the rail in front of the drug store and stepped out of the saddle. He scanned up and down the street before casting a quick glance at the old men. The old men stopped their argument and watched him as he was now of more interest than the previous topic.

One of them was studying him like he was trying to put a name to his face. The old man whose eyes so intently probed his face wore buckskins worn black and smooth on the thighs and elbows. He had a full gray beard and a wide brimmed hat with an eagle feather in the band.

A faded memory sparked in Eli's mind in regards to the old man who was plainly a buffalo hunter. He wondered if he didn't know him, but it had been years ago if he did. He walked past them and through the open doorway of the barber shop.

The barber jumped out of the chair. "Afternoon," he called out cheerfully. "Got a chair right here, no waiting."

Eli smiled and hung his hat on a wall peg. Taking a seat in the chair he settled back. "Looks like I walked in at the right time. I could use some of this buffalo hair taken off my head and feel clean shaven again."

The barber smiled, "Well, you came to the right place. I can take care of all of that for you."

Picking up a pair of scissors and a comb the barber started in on Eli's hair. He began to make the usual barber conversation. "Just passing through or are you with a drive?"

"Just passing through. Been a few years since I've been in Hays. What's new around here?"

"Same as the rest of the country, economy's going belly up. The cattle business has been bringing us some needed growth and money, but now cattle prices have bottomed out. No telling what will become of Hays now."

"Probably attract men you'd rather not have. It seems a bad economy brings the worst out from under their rocks. Like the bad characters I saw coming in."

"Oh sure. When money flowed like water around here the snakes slithered out from under their rocks for it. Now, with money tight the snakes have to work harder for it, but they still come for it." He chuckled, "No getting around the bad ones, but if you stay out of the rougher places you won't have any trouble. Although you look like a man who can handle himself."

"Heard some talk on the trail that an outfit called the Parson gang robbed a train around here. Are they some of that bad lot?"

The barber nodded as he clipped away at Eli's shaggy hair. "Now, that *is* a bit of big news. Bold as brass they were, used a rifle to pick off the engineer through the window, can you believe that? Just flat shot him dead. If not for the fireman stopping the train, it might have jumped the track and killed all those people."

"Must have been a pretty good shooter to hit him at train speed."

"Happened when the train was slowing down for the water tank a couple miles out of town."

The man in the chair opposite joined in the conversation. "There was money on that train, big money, and they knew it."

"Where do they come from?" Eli asked.

"No one knows where they come from," the man in the chair answered. "The Parson gang robs and kills all over the country. Bad business, no one is safe from that bunch."

The barber nodded, "Yeah, I heard they got a thousand in gold from the mail car."

""Nothing of the kind," the man in the chair shook his head. "It was thousands in cash."

Eli looked at the man seated across from him. "Anyone got an idea where they made off to?"

The man shook his head, "Don't know."

Running the comb through Eli's hair the barber added, "They robbed a stage carrying cattle money a couple weeks before that. Right outside of town! Bold as brass they are."

The man in the chair shook his head, "I sure hope they don't intend to set up shop around here. Why, with all the bad moving in these days they might feel right at home."

The barber nodded, "Too bad someone doesn't just shoot them all dead. We have the chance to have a nice town here and we don't need riff-raff and outlaws taking over."

The barber finished cutting Eli's hair and then pulled a white towel out of a pot of warm water and wrung it out. "Put your head on back and I'll put this on your face." He wrapped the cloth over Eli's beard.

The barber continued to talk about the town as he lifted off the towel and lathered Eli's face. He stopped talking as he concentrated on shaving the lather off. Taking the last stroke of whiskers off he wiped Eli's face with the damp towel. "There you go sir; you look like a new man."

"I feel about ten pounds lighter. How much do I owe you?"

"That's six-bits."

Eli stood up from the chair and handed him a silver dollar. "Keep the change."

The man beamed a smile, "Thank you, sir."

Eli pulled his hat down over his freshly shorn head as he stepped out the door. The three old men were still in the same chairs as he stepped up to the side of the roan and checked the cinch. He glanced over at the men who were looking at him, "How are you boys doing today?"

"Fair t' middlin'," answered one.

"Fine day ain't it?" said the second.

The man in the buckskins spoke in a casual tone, "Parson outfit went south after they robbed the train."

Eli studied the man. "Know that for a fact?"

"Wouldn't say it if wasn't. Saw 'em. I was out huntin' when I heard the shootin' out toward the water tank and saw what was going on. I bellied out on the grass so they wouldn't see me and watched. When they got done they went south toward Dodge."

Eli took in what the old buffalo hunter was saying and had no reason to doubt his story. "Seems I know you from somewhere, old timer."

"You were just a kid then, learning the ways from John."

A dim memory sparked to life in Eli's mind. "Red Buckner?"

The old buffalo hunter grinned, "'Cept, I ain't red no more, sorta went gray, Gray Buckner now-a-days." He let go a laugh.

Eli grinned back at him. "Thanks for the information, saves me a trip to the depot to ask them about it. How far out of town was it?"

"Follow the tracks east for about an hour, you'll see the water tank. Not many ride out that way so there might still be some tracks to follow."

"I'll head out that way. Good to see you again."

"Yeah, it was. Maybe you can run that bunch of murderin' coyotes to ground; no one else has been able to do it."

Eli stepped into the saddle. "That's the plan." Eli nodded to the men as he reined the roan back out onto the street. Behind him he heard one of the men ask Red, "Who was that?"

"Eli Warren," Red's voice came back. "He used to hunt buffalo with a friend of mine when he was a kid. Now he hunts bad men."

The last Eli heard was the questioner saying, "Yeah, heard of him. Friendly enough, but he sure is a mean looking feller ain't he?" The three watched him as he rode out of sight.

Eli rode to the tracks where they passed through the stockyards. Pulling the roan up he studied the sun as it hovered over the western horizon. He debated whether to set off on the trail or go back for a decent meal and start out at first light. It would be dark before he got to the place Red was talking about. He couldn't do much tracking in the dark. The gang already had a week on him, a few more hours wouldn't matter at this point. He turned back into town.

Riding down the street he remembered seeing a saloon coming in with a sign indicating it served food. He searched the line of buildings until he found the sign. Reining the roan in he tied him to a rail between a pair of bays. Walking to the open door he stepped into the saloon and quickly took in the room.

The saloon was a long, narrow room with a bar running the full length of the wall to his left and several tables with chairs lining the right wall. Men were lined up at the bar, some leaning, others standing upright, and more than a few listing to one side like a sinking boat. The more liquor they had in them the more they leaned or hung over the bar. The jovial ones were engaged in conversation while the brooders stared sullenly into a glass. Several of the tables were vacant.

The smell of beer, dust, and sweat hung heavy in the hot room. He never cared for long, narrow rooms cluttered with furniture and tightly packed in with men. He considered finding some other place when the smell of cooking meat made his empty stomach growl and convinced him to stay. He picked out an empty table close to the door and sat down with his back to the wall with a sidelong view of the door to his left.

A work-weary woman with strands of dark hair hanging in her face stopped at his table. She wore an apron that had once been white, but was now thoroughly stained with food and meat blood. Her manner was brusque reflecting her harried mood. Whether she owned the place or was hired help he couldn't tell. She told him a plate of beef and beans was the only thing on the menu so they didn't bother with one.

Eli said he'd have that. She nodded her acknowledgement and hurried away, but quickly returned with a large trail-drive-size coffee pot. She dropped a big metal cup on the table in front of him, and poured it full. She told him his meal would be to him soon and then walked away.

As he sat sipping at the hot coffee he studied the men in the room. They seemed the usual assortment of farmers, hunters, drovers, and non-descript drifters. There were more men squeezed shoulder-to-shoulder at the bar than seated at the tables. If there was trouble brewing in the room it would start at the bar from one of the brooders staring into his glass. Whoever it was would make his move when he finally had enough to drink to shut down what little common sense he had to begin with.

Eli wasn't disappointed at the heavy metal plate that was dropped on the table in front of him. There was a thick slab of beef, a generous load of beans, and a fist sized biscuit crowning the top. The tines of a fork were shoved in under the meat. He pulled out his knife and went to cutting the meat. He was half way through the meal when the anticipated trouble hunter at the bar finally reached the point where he lost his common sense.

A man pushed off the bar and straightened, lifting his chin into the air like he had finally made a decision. Eli spotted him as soon as he moved; there were certain things a man who lived by the gun learned to recognize. The man at the bar turned and looked directly at him. It was the same man he had seen when he rode in, the one he had locked eyes with.

Eli casually dropped a bite of meat on his lap, reached his right hand down to get it and slipped the loop off the hammer of the Remington in the same motion. He returned his hand with the piece of meat between his fingers to the table and continued eating while watching the man without appearing to do so.

The man moved unsteadily toward him and then stopped in the narrow walkway between the bar and tables. Eli continued to eat while the man planted his feet shoulder width apart and postured in front of him for several seconds. The man finally said with a taunting tone, "So you're Eli Warren. Hear tell you're some shakes with a gun, but I don't see anything special."

All conversation ceased at the challenge and the name. Men turned their heads, not only to see what was happening but just as much to figure out which way the lead was going to fly so they could get out of the way. Eli continued to eat and ignored him.

The challenger's eyes began to shift back and forth when he realized that he was being ignored. He shifted from one foot to the other and shouted, "Hey, I'm talking to you, *Eli Warren*!"

Eli swallowed and then drank from his coffee cup as if no one were talking to him. A few snickers of laughter sounded in the silent room. Eli's refusal to acknowledge him and the growing laughter began to push the man's temper. His face, already reddened from liquor, turned scarlet, as much from embarrassment as from anger. He raised his voice and shouted, "I'm calling you out, but you seem too terrified to move." He again waited as he was ignored and the laughter increased.

Eli wiped the biscuit through the meat juice on his mostly empty plate and spoke calmly without looking at the man. "Folks are in here eating their supper. They don't want to see you bleeding on the floor. It's hard on the appetite and troubles the digestion. I think you need to go back to the bar and have another drink and rethink your life."

Standing up, Eli dug a silver dollar out of his left pocket and dropped it on the table. He moved out from the back of the table, ignoring the man standing in front of him. Laughter grew as he walked out the open door.

Eli walked to the edge of the street where he leaned against a porch post and waited. The trouble hunter's pride had been badly damaged and he needed to rectify that. He would come. It was better to have it out now than wait until the trouble hunter bushwhacked him.

It was only a matter of seconds before the man burst from the doorway, his head turning back and forth as he searched for the man who had humiliated him. He ran out into the street squinting his eyes against the setting sun trying to find him. Several men followed him out curious to see what would happen while others watched from the doorway.

The man was forty feet away when Eli, still leaning against the post, spoke out loud enough for the man to hear. "Looking for me?"

The man spun around and glared hard at Eli. "You made a fool out of me in there."

"No, you made a fool out you in there. Why don't you just go home?"

Without another word the man jerked the Colt out of his holster and hammered three shots at Eli as fast as he could cock and fire the revolver. In his haste the shots missed their target.

Eli drew, took a quick aim, and fired as the man's fourth bullet zipped by his head like a hornet. The man died where he fell in the street, a bullet squarely between his eyes.

Men began to appear from doorways and step out into the street to see what the shooting was about. Some of the men who had been in the saloon and were watching from the door shook their heads and went back inside. The words, 'fool' and 'stupid' were heard as conversation resumed in the room.

Eli noticed one man remained outside of the saloon watching him. The man began to approach him, but stopped when the city marshal ran up to the dead man and looked down on him. "Who is responsible for this?" the lawman shouted into the street.

The watchers began to drift away ignoring the lawman's demand. Eli took a step toward him. "I am."

The lawman locked his gaze on Eli, "I don't allow gunplay in this town. Your story had better be a good one."

"I was defending myself. He tried to pick a fight in the room while I was eating my supper. I came out here; he followed me, pulled a gun and shot at me. Check his gun you'll find four spent cases." He reversed the Colt in his hand holding it butt out to the marshal. "Check mine, you'll find one."

"I don't need to check anything, what I say goes. I keep a tightly controlled. Town it's time for you to ride or go to jail."

"If your town is so tightly controlled then how come this drunken fool was packing a gun and trying to shoot me with it?"

"I don't need to explain myself, you have one minute to make a choice."

"Fine, I'm leaving, relax."

The marshal stood watching Eli as he mounted the roan and rode out of town.

Eli had reached the end of the buildings and was breaking out into the open prairie when he heard a fast running horse coming up behind him. He spun the roan around to see a man riding toward him. He pulled his gun and waited for the oncoming horse and rider. He saw it was the man who had been watching him in front of the saloon. The man pulled the horse to a sliding stop in front of Eli.

Eli glared at him, "Not the smartest thing in the world, racing up behind a man like that. It's a good way to get yourself shot."

The man moved his horse alongside Eli's and stared into his face. "Are you Elijah Warren who left Richmond, Virginia when he was twelve years old?"

Eli eyed the man suspiciously, a spark of recognition growing. "Yeah, I'm Eli Warren, why?"

"Because I'm William . . . your brother."

Chapter 5

Eli sat dumbstruck as he stared at the man. He could see reflections of his ten-year-old brother in the grown man's face and eyes. He didn't know what to say. The last thing in the world he expected to see again was any member of his family. Almost thirty years had passed since he had slipped out the bedroom window and headed west.

The two men said nothing for a full minute as they each studied the face of the other. At the same moment they extended their hands and clasped them tightly together. Eli broke the silence, "How long have you been out west?"

"Since just after the war. My wife and I, with our daughter, came out here in the summer of '65. We bought a farm a couple miles north of here. Bet you never thought I'd turn out to be a farmer."

"I never expected to see you again at all. You were the one thing I regretted leaving the most when I left that night."

William answered, "When I woke up that morning and you were gone I knew you had run away from the old man. Mother was devastated, but he didn't seem to care."

Eli snorted, "He wouldn't. The last thing he said to me was that I was worthless and would never amount to anything. I didn't fit into the mold he'd made for me."

William nodded, "I heard him say things like that to you a lot. The war took the arrogance out of him though."

Eli's expression grew grim. "Guess you were right in the middle of that war weren't you."

"More than you'd believe. Please, come home with me and meet my family. We have so much to talk about . . . please."

"Yes, I would like that."

"Good, this way." They turned their horses together and rode side by side into the growing night.

"Elijah, tell me what you have been doing all these years."

"When I left I made my way to Independence to find Uncle John."

William looked astonished, "You were twelve years old!"

"It took me six months, but I made it and when I told Uncle John that I was a family outcast like him he laughed and took me right in."

William nodded, "Father hated John. Imagine hating your own brother that much."

"John doesn't like him either."

"I take it Uncle John is still alive? I would like very much to meet him."

"Oh, he's still alive. Lives down in Colorado, runs a little store on the Santa Fe Trail outside of Boggsville. Remember all the awful stories the old man and the other relatives used to tell about him? What a disgrace to the family he was and all?"

William nodded, "I always wondered how much truth there was to them, or if it was just the rantings of spiteful relatives."

"None of it is true. Uncle John is the finest, fairest, and kindest man you will ever meet. He took me in and we've spent a lot of good years together. He taught me how to be a westerner, to trap and hunt. We led a wagon train to Oregon and we hauled freight on the Santa Fe Trail. Along with everything else, he taught me how to use guns and protect myself."

"He must have done a fine job of it. I was in the saloon having supper when all that commotion broke out.

When that man called out your name I almost choked on my coffee. I wanted to run right up to you then and there, but seeing that a fight was brewing I thought it best to stay back and wait until I could safely meet you."

"That was a wise choice."

"What was that all about anyway?"

"Just a man looking to pick a fight."

"And then you killed him in the street."

"That I did."

The two men were silent for a short while before William spoke again. "What do you do for a living now, Elijah?"

"Eli. I haven't gone by my full name since I got out here." He looked over at his brother. "I hunt outlaws."

"A bounty hunter?"

"An outlaw hunter."

The distinction was lost to William, yet the angry edge evident in his brother's voice when he said it indicated there was meaning behind the specific term. He thought it best not to pursue an explanation. "That man seemed to know you or your reputation anyway. He called you by name."

"I get that now and again. Some fool wants to make a name for himself."

William was silent for a minute before saying, "There was a time when that would have shocked me, but since my exposure to the war and its cruel realities, I'm not shocked by anything any longer. What I experienced during the war changed me. I've seen how depraved men can become when they think there are no limits on their behavior, how quickly a man can turn into a vicious animal."

"That they can."

They rode in silence for several minutes before William spoke again. "Mother wept for days when she found out you ran away, but she held out hope that you would come back."

Eli huffed, "If she was so concerned then how come she never came to my aid when the old man was raking me over the coals or giving me the belt?"

"She was afraid of him, too scared to cross him. You know what a tyrant and bully father was."

Eli's intense expression softened. "Guess I never thought about it from her side. As a child I only felt there was no support for me, that she hated me as much as he did. Maybe I can understand her position now."

"Yes, she was under his iron fist, but after you left she began to change, to lose her fear of him. She began to look at him with disgust and her words to him made it plain she hated him. He drove her boy away and she never forgave him for that. In a way I benefited from what you did. She grew stronger and bolder and she would defend me and the younger boys against him. Would you believe she actually once picked up the fireplace poker and threatened to hit the old man in the head with it if he struck me?"

Eli smiled slightly, "What did the old man do?"

"He backed down, shocked I believe."

"He always was a coward, most bullies are." Eli's smile widened, "Glad I was good for something."

William continued, "I was forced to go to law school. I hated it, but father wanted me to be a lawyer. He had political aspirations for me. I wanted to oversee the farm and our people working it. He said he had an overseer for that and no son of his was going to get his hands dirty. I came out a lawyer and hated every second of it."

"So you ran away and became a farmer."

"Not until the war had destroyed everything. Virginia fell in line with the Confederacy. In turn, the Confederacy claimed Richmond as their headquarters. Father, being the opportunistic politician that he was saw the Confederacy win the first major battles of the war. He was convinced the Confederacy would win. He joined the Confederate ranks and, because of his political position, they made him a Major and put him to work in the Richmond headquarters.

"He conscripted me into the Confederate hierarchy and put my law knowledge to work in Richmond. James and Arthur were little when you left, but they grew up. James joined the Confederate cavalry. Arthur believed in the sanctity of the United States and he joined the Union army. Arthur was killed at Fredericksburg, James died on the field at Gettysburg.

"Mother lost her mind when word came that Arthur was killed. When James was killed it was too much for her and she died soon after. Then the Union forces took Richmond at the end of the war and drove the Confederate forces and leaders out. As they fled, they tried to burn the city down. If not for the Union forces putting out the fires, they would have succeeded. In the process our mansion was burned to the ground, the fields destroyed by cannon fire, and the workers scattered.

"In the end the government of Richmond was restructured and men like father, who had turned against the Union, were out. You know how important his position, political power, and wealth were to him. He had lost absolutely everything."

William fell silent again. Eli looked over at him. "How did the old man handle that?"

William pointed his forefinger at his temple and imitated shooting a gun. "That's when I packed us up and came west. Kansas was good wheat country and I still wanted to be a farmer."

"Suicide sounds like something the old coward would do. I can't truthfully say I'm sorry about him, but I am sorry to hear about all the rest, especially mother and our brothers. I never got to know James and Arthur beyond being my little brothers."

"They were good boys. James followed the family ways, but Arthur was bold and independent . . . like you." William's voice steadily lowered as he spoke. "I was lost somewhere in between."

They rode the rest of the way to the house in silence. The lights shining from the windows guided them in. Riding around to the barn behind the house they stripped the horses and fed them before William led the way to the house.

William's spirits had picked back up between the barn and the house at the thought of introducing his long lost brother. He opened the door and walked in with Eli behind him. He could hear sounds coming from the kitchen. He called out, "Lillian, Carrie, I have someone I want you to meet."

A woman with blonde hair dressed in a simple gray dress came out of the kitchen followed by a skinny blonde haired girl who looked like her. The woman reached out and hugged her husband. Eli stood behind William with his hat in his hand feeling awkward.

She looked at Eli awaiting the introduction. Her eyes widened as she stepped back and looked directly into her husband's face, then back to Eli's. Eli was glad that he had gotten a shave and haircut that day. He didn't look like an unkempt tramp as he had before.

She looked back and forth between the men. "Don't tell me William." She put her hand over her mouth, "Oh my, is this Elijah, the brother you have always spoken of?"

William smiled, "How did you know?"

"Oh, the resemblance, it's remarkable. Anyone would know you are brothers."

"Yes, you can imagine my surprise when I found him in town. This is Elij . . . Eli."

Eli nodded to the woman, "Ma'am."

"Eli please, Lillian, this is the west, leave the formalities back east." She then reached out and hugged him. Eli clumsily returned the hug.

The girl was staring at him wide-eyed until William gestured for her to come forward. "Carrie, this is your Uncle Eli. He came out west a long time before you were born."

The girl stepped forward and shook his hand. Eli was surprised and impressed at the strength in the girl's handshake. "Pleased to meet you, Uncle Eli."

Eli smiled at her, "And I'm pleased to meet you, young lady. How old are you?"

"I am eleven; I will be twelve in January."

"I was eleven once, would you believe that?"

The girl giggled, "Everyone was eleven once, Uncle Eli."

He smiled at her as William invited him to have a seat in the front room. "You can stay for a couple of days, can't you? We've got a lot to catch up on."

Eli thought about the Parson gang getting a bigger lead on him. Then he realized how foolish the venture was, to follow a week old trail to possibly nowhere. It wasn't everyday he was reunited with his brother and he did want to renew the relationship between them. Maybe the gang would strike again in the area and he could get a fresh lead then. He nodded, "Sure, I'd like that."

Morning greeted him with a huge breakfast and William explaining about the farm and how the crops were doing. They had just harvested the winter wheat crop and would replant in a couple of months. He was raising a few head of beef cattle, not trying to corner the cattle market, as he put it, but only as a sideline to the wheat.

He took Eli on a ride around the two-hundred acre property. The ground was furrowed in neat clean rows. Cattle were grazing in an area fenced off from the wheat fields. William explained that he hired help during harvest and planting times, but other than that he worked the place himself.

Returning for the noon meal they sat up at the table where Carrie joined them. Eli had come to enjoy the girl's company. She was bright and a hard worker, nothing spoiled about her like the pampered privileged children back in Richmond had been.

"Uncle Eli, do you want to see my horse?"

"Sure, what kind of a horse do you have?"

"Papa says it's a sorrel because he is all red with a red mane and tail. He is very fast, too. I can ride him even at a full gallop!"

"You must be a true westerner if you can ride a horse like that."

She jumped up from the table and grabbed his hand, "Come on, let me show him to you."

Lillian spoke gently to her, "Carrie, don't be yanking on Eli like he's a stubborn calf. Let him have his meal." The girl gave her mother a disappointed frown.

She still had a hold of Eli's hand as he stood up. "That's alright Lillian, a horse like this one has to be seen to be believed." He winked at the girl who in turn burst into an ear-to-ear smile.

She led him to the barn and introduced him to her horse. "His name is Lightning, do you like that name?"

"I think that's a fine name."

They talked about the horse for a few minutes and then Carrie chattered on about other things, switching from one topic to another as children are prone to do. She then looked up at Eli, "What kind of work do you do, Uncle Eli?"

He hadn't expected the question, but accepted that it was one a child would ask. He considered it for a moment, how to tell a child that he hunted men. He wouldn't lie to her though.

"I chase outlaws, Carrie."

She gave him a puzzled expression, "Why do you chase them?"

"Out here in the west there are very few law officers, not like in Richmond where policemen are on every corner. Outlaws in the west have a lot of country to hide in when they commit their crimes. There aren't enough officers to find them and keep law and order in their towns at the same time. So, men like me help them by finding these outlaws."

Her expression showed a light of understanding. "You're a bounty hunter."

The frankness of the statement took him back a bit. "Actually, I prefer outlaw hunter. Do you know what an outlaw hunter is?"

"Oh yes, I read about them. They do exactly what you just said you do. Bounty . . . outlaw hunters bring bad men in dead or alive. Do you bring them in dead or alive?"

"Alive, when I can. If they surrender I bring them in and give them to an officer."

"What if they don't surrender? What if they try and shoot you?"

"Then, I protect myself."

"And you shoot them."

"Yes, sometimes I have to shoot them."

The girl pondered that for a few seconds. "I would shoot someone too, if I had to protect my life. Papa says it's okay to do that if you are defending yourself."

"Well, let's hope you never have to do that."

"Papa says you do what you have to do in the west."

Together they left the barn and returned to the house without further discussion on the subject.

By the end of the day Eli and William had completed their stories covering the last three decades and their friendship as brothers was solidified. Carrie adored her new uncle and was rarely far from him.

That evening he explained that he needed to get back to Boggsville to check on Uncle John. He told them of the Yeagers and the attempted robbery and that John's life could be in danger from the remaining brothers. The family understood his concern and need to go back, but regretted his leaving; Carrie especially didn't want him to leave, yet she understood.

Early morning found Eli saddled and ready to ride. He shook his brother's hand with a promise to return. The ladies hugged him and Carrie cried. As he rode slowly out of the yard Carric followed at his side making him repeatedly promise to come back. He assured her he would.

Arriving back at John's store, the first indication that there had been a problem was the front door being closed. Even in the fall John liked to leave the door open to allow the breeze to blow through. Tying off the roan alongside of the store, he pulled the Remington and walked to the door.

He stood outside the door and listened. Hearing nothing he pushed on the door, it didn't move, John had it barred on the inside. The sole window for the store was shuttered. Checking the stable he found John's black gelding head down, sleeping in the shady side of the corral.

.

Moving around the store to the living area, he peered in through the windows and saw no one inside. He turned the knob on the back door and the door moved inward slightly. Pushing the door open slowly, he stood back watching and listening. Sunlight streaming through the windows illuminated the single large room that made up the cabin. He saw and heard nothing from the room's interior.

He stepped in keeping the cocked .44 out in front of him. Looking first to his right where John's bed was he saw the old man asleep under his blankets. That was unusual as John was never one to take naps during the day. Convinced that the room was empty save for John, he holstered the Remington and stood over the old man who was lying on his side facing out into the room. John's breathing sounded rough as he inhaled and exhaled. On the table next to him was a pitcher of water, a glass, and remnants of food. Something was wrong with all of this.

Without warning John's eyes suddenly snapped open and he peered up at Eli. His voice was weak and his mouth smacked with dryness. He forced a grin, "Oh, it's you. I thought . . . ." He stopped mid-sentence and pushed his arm out from under the covers and laid the pistol he was holding down on the floor. "Good, your turn to watch, I'm going to sleep."

"Uncle John, what's wrong? What happened?"

John lifted the blankets to show he was shirtless with a wide band of white bandages wrapped around his mid-section. Dark spots indicated dried blood. "Yeagers came back."

Eli's temper instantly flared. At the same time he mentally beat himself for leaving, knowing there could be trouble. "When?"

"Give me some water and I'll tell you."

Eli poured water into the glass and helped John sit up enough to drink it. John laid back down and sighed, "That's better. A couple days back. They came in yelling about you killing their brothers and they wanted you. I told them you weren't here. They went to making all kinds of mean talk about shooting me instead. They didn't expect me to come up with a gun, caught them by surprise. I hit one and then the other shot me. I played possum and let them think they had killed me. The one I hit was yelling about getting him to a doctor so they took off."

"Who's been taking care of you?"

"A farmer came by in a wagon for supplies and found me. He patched me up and got me into bed. I told him to ride my horse and get the Doc and Cliff over here. He did, good man that one."

"The Doc got the bullet out, said nothing vital was hit, but I had lost a lot of blood. Cliff did some tracking and said they were headed south, probably back to that Colfax County business."

Eli swore under his breath, "I should never have left you alone."

"Eli, I came into this country alone. I was twenty the first time I took a Blackfoot arrow in the ribs. I crawled into a cave and laid there for a week drinking creek water and eating dried buffalo. A couple years later the varmints got me again, this time I had a cabin to hole up in. What I'm getting at is I don't need to be watched over; I've been in bad spots before and probably will again. So, don't kick yourself about it. I ain't exactly helpless."

Eli nodded, but it didn't make him feel any less guilty. "I'll stick around all the same until you're up on your feet again."

"You do that and those Yeagers will be too far ahead of you to ever catch up."

"I don't think so. They're mixed up in that Maxwell Grant fight. It's all going to center around Cimarron and Elizabethtown. They'll hang out somewhere between those two towns. A few questions in the right places and listening to some saloon talk and I'll find them."

"Okay, you know your business. I can't say I'd object to the help. Kind of hard getting around like this."

"I'll be here."

"The one I hit kept calling the one who shot me Clyde."

Eli frowned, "Clyde and Mort . . . they're both as good as dead."

Chapter 6

Eli remained with John helping run the store and doctoring the old man until he was back on his feet and able to handle affairs alone. Eli stood out in front of the store staring down the Trail thinking about Mort and Clyde Yeager. He had a score to settle with them and was getting restless to be about it.

John walked out next to him, "Time to go hunting?"

Eli nodded without answering.

"Best be at it then."

Eli glanced at John, "I'll be back."

Tension lay heavy over the town of Cimarron as Eli moved the roan slowly down the Santa Fe Trail, which also served as the town's main street. The fight over the land grant was painting its own picture. Men moved in groups ranging from pairs, to threes and fours, all armed and seasoned. Everyone was eyed with suspicion, especially strangers riding into the little New Mexico town. His understanding was that both sides were arming up.

It was difficult to tell which cluster of armed men belonged to which camp. It didn't matter since the danger could come from either side where a stranger was concerned. There was a fight brewing and any man who didn't have a reason to be in Colfax County was better off staying away.

He had never seen Clyde or Mort Yeager, but he knew what their dead brothers looked like. Brothers tended to resemble each other; he would be able to tell.

His first order of business in Cimarron was to learn who controlled each side of the fight. He heard Clay Allison led the property owner's side. Men like Clyde and Mort Yeager would join the land stealers side where they could run rough-shod over people and be paid to kill.

Eli acknowledged that he was a known man. There was no sense in trying not to be noticed, he would be. It would be assumed that a man of his stripe had come in to join one side or the other, but which side he had chosen was the question.

Eli knew he would be under scrutiny by both sides, but he doubted he would be challenged. Everyone concerned would be watching to see which camp he went into though. He figured to take advantage of the uncertainty and pretend that he wanted to meet up with Clyde and Mort; someone in their camp might set up the meeting.

The first place he hoped to find the information he sought was Lambert's saloon. At one point or another everyone in Cimarron hit Lambert's. Reining the roan over to the hitch rail he dismounted. Standing beside the horse he scanned the street in all directions and then casually strolled into the saloon.

The room was fairly full, he keened his listening trying to pick up on conversation, but the voices overlapping each other made for a nondescript din. Heads turned toward him and eyes followed him through the room. One man would speak to another and they would both look at him. He was sure there were wanted men in the room and each would be wondering if he was here for the war, or them.

He walked up to the bar and asked for a beer. He wasn't much of a drinker, but a man standing in a saloon with no drink looked out of place. He leaned his elbows on the bar and listened. The bits of conversation he was picking up were common talk, nothing dealing with the fighting or specific names. He casually turned and searched the faces for anyone who might bear a Yeager family resemblance. No one matched what he thought they should look like.

Eli's interest focused on a man entering the room. The man's movements were deliberate and he seemed directed toward a goal, not simply meandering in for a drink. He swiveled his head quickly right to left as if searching for someone in particular. The man's scouring gaze stopped on Eli at the bar and he walked toward him.

Eli had never seen the man before; however the man seemed to know him. That wasn't too unusual as a lot of men he didn't know knew him. The man stepped in next to him, ordered a beer and then leaned an elbow on the bar facing Eli.

Eli spoke in a cold tone, "Just lonely or do you want to say something to me?"

The man held a straight expression, "I'm not that lonely. I recognized you when you rode in."

"A lot of people recognize me."

"Which side are you lined up with?"

"Depends on who's asking and why, maybe I'm on my own side."

"I'm with the land owners and we could use a man of your reputation on our side. Providing of course you aren't already with the Santa Fe group."

Eli sipped from the beer. "Who's the Santa Fe group?

The man gave him an incredulous look. "You don't know?"

"This isn't my neck of the woods. Why don't you enlighten me?"

"The Santa Fe Circle, the outfit that took over Maxwell's Grant is running us all out. Figured you must be here to take a side."

Eli shrugged, "Maybe I have other business here."

"Then, you're not here to fight?"

"Nope."

"Are you looking for someone in particular?" The

man asked the question hesitantly.

"That's a little closer. Do you know two brothers, Clyde and Mort Yeager? Mort would be favoring a bullet wound. They would likely be lined up with this Circle you're talking about."

"Not off hand. Men come in here all the time, hard to tell when no names are said out loud."

As they stood together a man standing with a group of men turned his head to look at them. He left the group and marched directly up to them. He faced them and glared at the man next to Eli. "Get a move on Finch; don't be trying to hire every man that comes in here."

Finch stiffened as he glared back at the other man. "Move along your ownself, Cramer. I'm talking here."

Cramer ignored him and directed his attention to Eli. "Why are you looking for Clyde and Mort?"

Eli studied the man for a moment before speaking. He was obviously a hired gun who liked to push his weight around. The man rubbed him the wrong way and he took an instant dislike to him. "I don't care much for people butting into my conversations."

Cramer's eyes narrowed as he looked Eli over. "When a stranger asks about my friends, and I don't know who's doing the asking, I butt in."

Eli casually straightened his stance as he faced Cramer. "I don't know who you are either. Maybe I don't like people I don't know butting in."

The man puffed out his chest and hooked his left thumb over the buckle of his gunbelt. "Milt Cramer, now you know my name." He said it like Eli was supposed to know it and be impressed. "What's yours?"

"Well *Milton*, where can I find my old pals Clyde and Mort?"

Cramer stiffened at Eli's sarcastic emphasis on his name. He didn't like being made fun of. "You're coming close to getting yourself in trouble, mister."

Finch watched the exchange with a hint of humor on

his face. He couldn't believe that Cramer didn't know he was trying to push around Eli Warren. Then again, Cramer was dumber than a post and self-impressed with his imagined reputation. There was always the chance Warren would kill him and lessen the Circle's side by one.

"Save the tough act Cramer and answer my question. I'm supposed to meet with them here, so tell me where they are before I turn you upside down and shake it out of you."

Cramer's eyes flicked back and forth. He took in the broad shoulders and muscled forearms of the man. The man's hard eyes penetrated right through him. This man probably could turn him upside down and shake him.

Cramer took two steps back. "I'll check with them and see if they want to see you. Can't be too careful these days you know." He started to walk away and then turned back, "What did you say your name was?"

"I didn't."

Cramer nodded, "Okay, I'll talk to them. I'll meet you back here and let you know." He walked across the room and out the door.

As soon as Cramer went through the door Eli was on his tail. It was clear this Cramer wasn't too bright. He would go directly to where the Yeagers were holed up to ask them. All he had to do was follow him and take it from there. He stepped out the door to see Cramer pull his horse loose from the hitch rail across the street. He mounted and then headed north toward the river.

Eli stood in close to his horse and held his head down as Cramer passed him. Flipping the reins around the roan's neck he mounted and rode on Cramer's trail. He kept a good distance behind Cramer watching him when he could see him and following the shod tracks when he couldn't. Cramer only rarely looked back behind him as he rode up into the hills steadily climbing toward a destination.

An hour passed and Cramer's pace didn't slacken. His

trail led downhill toward a basin of pine and aspen trees shimmering with golden fall color. A creek wound through the basin and away to the east. A thin stream of smoke rose up out of the aspen grove. Falling back a ways Eli dismounted and snuck up to the crest of the hill where he laid down on his belly and studied the grove.

He watched for a minute or two before he saw Cramer appear from a low spot and walk his horse into the trees. He lost sight of him, but it was a safe bet that the Yeagers were at that fire. Eli took in the lay of the land around the basin. The best route in and out of the trees appeared to be the way Cramer had ridden in. Riding directly up to the camp was definitely the wrong thing to do, however, walking in would not be expected.

He decided to walk in on them and considered the necessary moves. If he shot from a distance they would have cover in the trees. In that grove they could hold him off and then slip away after dark. He needed to take them by surprise. The tables could turn on him very quickly if he gave them any wiggle room at all. He needed to do this fast.

He'd let them surrender if they had a mind to, but seriously doubted they would especially since they wanted him for killing their brothers. After what they did to John though he wasn't interested in taking prisoners. He moved back down the hill, mounted up, and headed in a roundabout way toward the place where he had chosen to go in.

He took his time getting into position on the hill above the camp. Tying the roan in a stand of sapling pines, he pulled the Winchester out of the scabbard and slipped the loop off the Remington's hammer. He moved down into the trees toward where he believed the camp to be located. He took each step deliberately being careful not to step on the dead branches that littered the ground.

He made a slow approach through the aspen. A steady breeze was blowing enough to keep the leaves rattling, covering any small noises he might make. The breeze blew toward him and he detected the smell of wood smoke and coffee. Drawing closer he picked up on voices, the men in the camp were arguing. He began to see movement ahead of him and then he had a good view of the men. Hunkering behind a big white aspen trunk he watched and listened.

One man was on his feet gesturing wildly with his arms and shouting at Cramer. A second man was sitting across the fire from them with his legs stretched out in front of him watching the argument. He assumed the one sitting was Mort and the bullet John had put in him had him stove up. The man standing and shouting at Cramer had to be Clyde.

He decided that Clyde was in the best position to shoot and had to go first. Mort might be slower due to his wound, but he wasn't banking on that assumption. He had no idea what to expect from Cramer. If Cramer played into it he could be second in line.

Easing the rifle around the tree trunk he thumbed back the hammer, put it to his shoulder, and fired a shot into the fire. The result was men jumping in different directions as sparks sprayed up over Mort. Mort wasn't so laid up that he couldn't move quickly as he hurriedly brushed the burning embers off his clothes. Eli levered another cartridge into the Winchester and walked out from around the tree moving toward the men.

He stopped at the edge of the fire pointing the rifle at Clyde. Clyde reacted before he could say a word. Jerking his pistol out, Clyde brought it up to bear on Eli. Eli pulled the trigger. The heavy slug took Clyde in the heart. He was dead when he hit the ground. Mort scrambled to his feet, grabbing his holstered gun as he did. Cramer stood back wide eyed, his hands away from his body, showing no fight.

Eli levered the rifle again and pointed it at Mort, "Don't do it, Mort."

Mort paused mid-move, "Who are you?"

Eli gave him a cold look, "Don't you know? You came hunting me and shot an old man because you couldn't find me."

Mort's face twisted into a hate filled sneer as he snarled, "*Warren.*" Mort completed the draw, thumbing back the hammer on the pistol as he brought the gun up fast. Eli shot him, levered in a cartridge, and shot him again. Mort fell three feet from his brother.

Levering in another cartridge Eli pointed the rifle at Cramer. Cramer threw his hands straight up in the air. "Don't shoot, I ain't doin' nothin'."

Eli looked at Cramer who was trembling with fear. "I've got no use for you Cramer, unless you want to play into this with your friends?"

"No, I'm out of it. I didn't know who you were back there."

"Now, you know. Here's some advice, get out of Colfax County, get out of New Mexico, in fact get off this planet. If you stick around and get a price on your head then I'll be coming after you. Now, throw your gun down on the ground and get out of here."

Cramer slowly pulled his gun out of the holster and dropped it on the ground. He turned around, grabbed the reins of his horse and threw himself into the saddle. He was hitting a gallop as he cleared the trees.

Eli looked at the two men who lay motionless on the ground. He wasn't about to pack their bodies all the way back to Boggsville to prove to Cliff that he had killed them. Not for two hundred dollars. Then again, Cliff was his friend and would no doubt accept his word that the Yeagers were dead.

He picked up the coffee pot that had fallen over from the first shot and shook it. There was a bit left. He poured it into a cup. An iron frying pan had slid to the side, the bacon that had been frying in it looked too good for his empty stomach to pass up. Pulling out his knife he picked up the slabs of bacon and ate them. Finishing the coffee he dropped the cup on the ground.

Looking at the bodies of the outlaws he whispered, "One for John, one for Huge." He kicked out the fire and headed back up the hill to where he had tied the roan.

Chapter 7

Eli rode out following the stream east. He had left the Yeagers where they fell.

He walked the roan along the stream through pine and aspen. It was near to October and the heart shaped aspen leaves were golden and shimmering like twenty-dollar gold pieces in the fall sun. He loved the high country and the soothing rustle of the leaves dancing in the cool mountain breeze. Breaking out into a wide green meadow he could see a series of beaver ponds below him widening out the stream.

The place was pleasant and restful. He decided to camp for the night and maybe loaf around for a couple of days in the beauty that surrounded him. The roan could use a rest and a belly full of good meadow grass. His own mind and body could use a rest as well.

Stripping the tack off the horse he picketed him in a patch of green grass and wild flowers. Moving back into the shelter of the white trunks, he built a fire and set his battered coffee kettle to the side of it. Unpacking his oversized saddle bags and bedroll he checked his provisions. Plenty of ammunition for all three guns, but the food was down to almost nothing. He stared in the flour sack at the slabs of dried beef in it and decided that if he had to make another meal of grinding hard beef between his teeth, he'd run through the woods screaming like a lunatic.

Then the small tin box that held a spool of fishing line and pack of fish hooks caught his eye. He looked at the placid beaver pond and the dimpling rings of feeding trout breaking the surface. Why eat old hard cow meat when he could stuff himself with fresh trout. Taking up the little box he headed for the pond.

He cut down an aspen sapling with his knife, trimmed off the branches, and whittled it down to a sixteen foot length. Five minutes of digging in the rich soil with his knife produced a half dozen worms and he caught a couple of bugs. Tying the line to the tip of the pole, he tied on a hook, baited it, and dropped it in the water and instantly had the first trout.

After a half dozen plump trout lay on the grass next to him he decided it was enough to make a good supper. He would catch some more tomorrow and feast again. There would be days when the twisted brown meat would look like a Kansas City steak, but today it looked like a piece of tree bark compared to the trout.

Darkness was closing in around him as he gathered the bones and remains of the trout he had eaten and buried them away from the camp. He walked down to where the roan was standing three legged, head down and sleeping. His belly was full and he was a contented horse. Eli pulled the picket and led him down to the water to drink. When the roan had drunk he took him up to the trees by his camp and tied him securely.

Putting out the fire, he moved back into the trees away from the camp and spread out his ground tarp. Wrapping in the blanket he lay down pulling the tarp around him and listened to the night sounds. The roan would warn him if anyone came around, but he felt that, for one night at least, it was safe to sleep. Still, out of habit, he removed the Remington from the holster and laid it under his hand.

The sun was streaming through the trees when he awoke the next morning. The air was taking on the chill of fall. He liked the feel of fall and the crispness in the air. It was also a reminder that winter was just over the hill. He listened and heard birds singing, they wouldn't be if there was anyone about. He flipped off the blanket and tarp cover and sat up, searching the area around him.

The roan's head was up and looking like he wanted back on the grass. Pulling on his boots, Eli stood up. Shoving the Remington back into the holster, he buckled the belt on and walked to the roan.

Untying the roan he led him to a fresh patch of grass and drove the picket pin into the ground. The horse did not hesitate and directly ripped out a mouthful of green grass. Eli looked toward the ponds and saw a herd of elk grazing at the water's edge. He wanted to stay right here forever. Maybe, he'd come back and do just that. A man couldn't wander forever, he needed a home. Here was a place he could live without any complaint.

Today he would loaf. Even ranch hands were given a day off occasionally; it had been some time since he had taken a day off and did nothing. He wasn't one to loaf for too long, he tended to get restless when idle, but once in a while it was a pleasant way to spend a day. He took up his homemade fishing pole and headed for the pond.

As he fished he considered his next move. He wasn't all that far from where the Parson outfit had last struck in Kansas. They moved in all directions, yet lately they seemed to be working Kansas a lot. He should head for the southwest corner of Kansas and see if he couldn't get lucky and be where they were for once. He decided to work his way east and then head up into Kansas toward Dodge.

An hour of fishing brought him another half dozen trout. Returning to the camp he built up a fire, dropped the trout in the frying pan, and listened to them sizzle. He leaned back against a tree trunk and thought over what he knew about the Parson gang. It was actually not much, just stories he'd picked up along the way.

The only one in the gang that was actually a Parson was Jude, the leader. Jude Parson had led a band of renegades dressed in Confederate gray during the war. They had grown accustomed to robbery and killing in the name of the war effort. They were a rag-tag collection of criminals who used the South's efforts as an excuse for their criminal behavior.

After the war they had no justification for stealing and killing. If they followed their old habits in a post-war country they would be branded outlaws, and if caught, hung. Regardless of the legal threat several followed Jude to the outlaw trail through Missouri and Arkansas until they were chased into Texas.

Eli smiled to himself when he thought of how Texans handled outlaws. Jude Parson had moved into the wrong neck of the woods. Texans didn't need law; in fact they preferred not having it as it slowed down their own process for dealing with outlaws. The Texans quickly reduced Jude Parson's gang to four.

The stories had them fleeing Texas up the panhandle into the 'Strip' or 'No Man's Land' as it was more commonly called. That bit of land that had fallen through the cracks of legal jurisdiction boxed in between Kansas, Texas, New Mexico, and the Indian Territory. It was here in this lawless section of country, that no state claimed, Jude Parson found a verdant pasture of opportunity. They could strike into Kansas, Colorado, and New Mexico and retreat back to hide.

That was the place they would go. Eli knew the reason no one could find them is because they disappeared into No Man's Land. It was there he would start his hunt.

Come the next morning he reluctantly packed up and headed east down through the valley. Eventually the trees and green valley opened up to flat dry land studded with sage brush and prickly pear. Scattered groups of cattle grazed on the sparse grass around him. There were no fences to indicate boundaries, but it appeared he had ridden down onto someone's cattle ranch.

As he rode through he saw more cattle and wondered

how many acres were on this ranch. He was uneasy riding on another man's range. He needed to veer more to the north and get off this ranch before someone shot him for trespassing. Looking to the east he saw three riders churning up a dust cloud as they loped their horses toward him. Cussing under his breath he whispered, "Too late."

He pulled the roan up and waited for them, trying to move away would make him look guilty, like he *had* been up to something. Just the same he thought, no one ever died from being too careful as he slipped the loop off the Remington's hammer. The three men pulled up in front of him and stopped. They didn't look happy to see him or friendly.

Eli made a quick analysis of the group. The rider in the middle was older than the other two and seemed in charge. The one to his right was a teen kid and to the left a man with an arrogant look to him. Eli met the middle man's eyes that suddenly took on the look that said he recognized him. "You realize you're on another man's land?" the older man remarked.

"I came down out of the mountains not realizing this down here was owned land. I saw the cattle and figured I must have come out on someone's spread."

"That you did. You planning on riding through?"

"That's exactly what I plan to do. I got on here by accident and have no plans to linger. In fact I'm trying to head up north hoping to be off the place."

The man nodded his acceptance of the statement. "Nothing personal, we've been keeping a close eye on anyone passing through. There's been a lot of rustling going on these days what with that rabble riding into the grant fight. We've also been having to run nesters and squatters off."

"I'm not a rustler or looking to nest, just rode onto a property I didn't know was here. I'll be moving on, if that's okay with you?"

The kid to the right butted in with a cocky smirk. "I

don't believe him Harley; I think he's scouting for his rustler friends. I think we should pull him off that horse and make him tell the truth."

The man to Harley's left agreed, "I don't believe him either." He looked at Eli, "This here's Grover Little's property, ever hear of him? He doesn't take kindly to trespassers like you."

Eli held the man's eyes as he took an instant dislike to him. "I said I was passing through."

"I think you're a liar."

Eli kept his hand on his hip an inch over the butt of the Remington where it had been when they rode up. His eyes turned to brown ice as he held them locked on Earl. "You want to ride on top the ground or be buried under it?"

Earl sat stock still, shocked by the cold tone in the challenge. He touched the tip of his tongue to his dry lips unable to form the words to answer.

Harley broke the stalemate. "Earl, you run your mouth too much. You both do. No one's going to bother this man at all. He said he's passing through and we're going to let him go on his way."

Harley turned his attention to Eli, "Ride on mister, head north and you'll be off the property in under an hour."

Eli nodded toward him, "Thanks." He then eyed the other two one at a time. "I don't like being threatened or called a liar, especially over a mistake. You're lucky you ride with a man who's got sense." He reined the roan toward the north and rode away from the trio who never moved as they watched him go.

Harley looked from one to the other of the two men with him. "If you two ain't the dumbest jugheads I've ever had the misery of working with. All we needed to do was tell him he was on Little's place and to get off and then leave it at that, but oh no, you idiots have to try and hoorah him. Dumber than a post, both of you."

With the threat removed Earl pulled his bravado back up. He smirked at Harley, "He was lying through his teeth."

The kid was clearly shaken. "You think so?"

Earl snorted, "Yeah."

"I thought he was going to draw on us," the kid said. "He looked like it, I swear." The kid pulled off his hat and wiped the sweat that had popped out on his forehead.

Earl snorted, "He's never killed anyone in his life. He was just bluffing, trying to scare us so he could get away."

Harley shook his head, "You jugheads really don't know, do you?"

"Know what?" Earl snapped.

"That was Eli Warren. Do you still think he was bluffing?"

Earl stared at him as his face turned a shade lighter. "How do you know?"

"I was down in Elizabethtown when some fool picked a fight with him. Warren killed him slicker'n spit, never even batted an eye. That's why I was trying to get him out of here fast."

The kid looked anxiously from one to the other. The look on Earl's face scared him. "Who's Eli Warren?"

Harley looked at the kid with disgust, "He's a man hunter, he kills men for a living. We're all lucky to still be alive. I won't be riding with the two of you again and I'm going to tell Prine that he needs to get rid of you both." He turned his horse and rode back the way they had come.

The incident put Eli in a foul mood. Pull him off his horse will they? That Grover Little they talked about would have had three less hands had they tried. Well, two less anyway, that Harley didn't seem to be playing in their game. His temper eventually began to cool down the farther he rode.

Shifting the reins, he moved the roan back to an easterly direction. He intended to ride through No Man's Land and into the Indian Territory if need be. If he was lucky he would hear something of the gang's movements or maybe even cut their trail. He had to be right, it all added up and fit too neatly. No Man's Land. It explained how they could just disappear like smoke.

He had ridden through the Strip several times in the past and had made acquaintances along the way. It wasn't his kind of country; it was too barren and lacking in water and mountains. The place held no interest to him other than to root out an outlaw.

He finally got off of Grover Little's ranch; the man owned a huge stretch of property. With the changing trends in the west and settlers coming in looking for land it was going to be hard for these land barons to hold on to it all. Eventually Little would start losing what he had. The days of getting away with running out and killing people the land barons considered nesters was coming to an end.

Eli spent the night on the New Mexico side of the border, and by the next mid-day he had moved into the western edge of No Man's Land. In the past he had a couple run-ins with Comanche, but they were supposed to be subdued now. That didn't mean a few young bucks wouldn't break away from the reservation and go hunting scalps. There wasn't much to stop them in country like this if they chose to do so.

He rode out the rest of the day not crossing the path of another man. He wasn't foolish enough to think that Parson would be out riding around seeing the sights. He needed to get where men were gathering and get them to talking about what they knew or had seen. If the gang was down here someone would know it.

He had a friend down here who ran a stop over house. It was an all stone building where a man could get a bowl of stew and hardtack for four-bits. Coffee, beans, and ammunition could also be purchased. No liquor was available as the owner didn't need a bunch of drunks causing trouble. A man could even throw his bedroll on the floor next to the iron stove if it was raining.

The owner's name was Dodger Belvidere, a name one could hardly forget. Dodger was a tough Welshman, a stone mason by trade. He had lived in an English sea town where he killed a man in a fight. The man he killed had influential friends and Dodger had none. Also being Welsh, a race the English despised, he knew his hanging would be arranged by payment to the right people.

As Dodger told it, he had no family or ties so he signed on to a ship bound for America. Once he reached New York he just kept moving west until he came to No Man's Land. Believing he was far enough away from the influence of the dead man's wealthy and influential friends he stopped and dug in.

Dodger had graying hair, a weather hardened face, and humor dancing in his brown eyes. He was a man with the bark on who packed a Navy Colt on his hip. Eli recalled a story of a would-be tough who demanded whiskey from Dodger. When told that no liquor was allowed in the house the man started to get mean and ended up with one of Dodger's .36 caliber bullets between his eyes.

Nobody was a better friend or worse man to have against you then Dodger Belvidere. He hoped Dodger was still around; he knew everything and everybody who passed through the Strip. He cooked up a pretty good pot of stew as well.

An hour east of Black Mesa brought Eli to Dodger's house. The building was a solid structure of stone walls with a thick sod roof. Dodger built it when the Comanche were still on the attack. He had said it was pretty tough for raiding Comanche to burn down a house made of stone and dirt. There were small glassless window spaces on each side covered by thick wooden shutters that swung to the inside. When closed there was a hole cut out that was big enough to see through while sticking a gun barrel out to shoot. The shutters were open today and no horses were tied out front.

Dodger was sitting at a table working on a cup of coffee with a hand of solitaire laid out in front of him. He looked directly at the door as Eli opened it and stepped inside. Dodger studied him for several seconds and then grinned, "I see you're still refusin' the devil the satisfaction of haulin' you in." His voice still held a strong Welsh accent to it.

Eli grinned back at him, "And I plan on doing just that for a long time." He gestured toward the cards, "You look pretty hard at it."

Dodger nodded, "I'd likely win once if the deck had all fifty-two cards in it instead of fifty, but that's where the skill comes in."

Dodger tossed the last card down and cussed, "Lost again." He looked up at Eli, "Takin' a little Sunday stroll through No Man's Land for the pleasure and beauty of the experience or seekin' to end the existence of another wayward soul?"

Eli remembered that Dodger had the heart of a poet and the sense of humor of a stage comedian. He liked to combine them both just to see the confused looks on people's faces. "You ought to be on the stage, Dodger."

Dodger spread his arms out wide, "And miss all this?"

Picking up the coffee pot from the stove Eli poured a cup and sat down opposite Dodger. He stared down into the thick black liquid, "Did you take your socks out of the pot before you made this?"

Dodger leaned across the table and looked in the cup, "Depends, what day is this?" He sniffed at it, "Hmm, guess not. Oh well, coffee should be chewy. What's wrong, gettin' finicky in your old age?"

"Sorry, I forgot myself there for a minute. Happen to have any of that stew around?"

"Just made some, you'll be the first one to try it."

Eli made a face, "Sounds like you're experimenting with a new recipe. What kind of meat is it this time?"

"You're better off not knowin'."

Eli nodded, "Sometimes that's best alright."

Dodger walked to the stove, filled a bowl with stew and pulled a couple of hard crackers out of a tin box. He put them on the table and sat back down. "Huntin' someone?"

Eli nodded, "Always. Trying to pick up a trail on the Parson gang. I've been keeping track of that bunch for a couple of years now and have an idea that they might be holing up down here. Figured I'd ride on through and see if I'm right."

"Sort of like that Cole gang, huh? I was here when they were, one or another of them stopped in once in a while. They behaved themselves while here, not bad sorts for outlaws."

"Until the army blasted them out of their Black Mesa fort of theirs."

Dodger chuckled, "Took cannons to do it."

"I'm wondering if Jude Parson wasn't part of Cole's gang. Everything seems to match up, both were Johnny Rebs, both were guerillas or bushwhackers of some sort, both running with a band killing, robbing, and plundering."

Dodger leaned back in his chair and scratched at his closely trimmed beard. "It's always possible, there was about fifty in the gang. Those the army didn't kill got clean away. One could have been Jude Parson, it's an interestin' theory, except his comin' out of Missouri rather blows your theory out."

"It was only a thought."

"Well, I've not seen anything of them around here. Haven't heard any talk about them either. If they are down here they're keepin' to low ground and not showin' themselves."

Eli frowned, "They're everywhere and nowhere, like to drive me crazy."

"I'll keep my ears open and the next time you ride by

maybe I'll have something for you."

Eli finished the stew and crackers in silence as he thought about his Parson dilemma. Eating the last he looked at Dodger, "Okay, what kind of meat is it?"

"Monkey."

"Monkey? There aren't any monkeys around here."

Dodger grinned, "Not anymore."

Eli looked at him, "I should just leave well enough alone shouldn't I?"

"I always find that's best, yes."

Standing up Eli handed his friend two quarters. "Guess I'll continue my Sunday stroll."

The two men shook hands. Eli left the stone house and stepped back into the saddle and kept moving east.

He rode for the next three days talking to anyone who wanted to talk and keeping an eye out. He was no farther ahead on his Parson hunt than when he left New Mexico. He was still convinced he was right though, they were hiding in the Strip.

Winter would soon be on them. He would spend it with John in the cabin helping him with the store. There wasn't much outlaw hunting going on during freezing temperatures and blinding blizzards. Even outlaws were smart enough to hole up until spring. He would make one last swing up to Dodge City and see what news there was of the Parson gang or any other outlaw activity and then head back to Boggsville.

Chapter 8

He was still a boy when he first ventured through the Fort Dodge area with John, hunting buffalo and slipping around Kiowa and Cheyenne war parties. The tribes took a dim view of the white man killing their buffalo. Now, they were on reservations and a town had sprung up.

He pulled the roan up at the railroad tracks that split Dodge City and looked up and down the tracks. There had been no city or steel rails when they first rode through here. When the railroad arrived what had been a couple of shacks on the prairie turned into a city. It had grown even more since the last time he was here.

The tracks were referred to as the 'Deadline', the border where all guns had to be checked if you planned on crossing over to the respectable north side of town. South of the tracks you could keep your gun on. Having as many enemies as he had parting with his guns was something akin to suicide. He had no reason to go north of the line anyway, the south side was where news of outlaws would be found.

Eli rode along the south side of the tracks until he spotted Hoover's store. He recalled Mort Hoover's make-shift saloon when it was the only building east of Fort Dodge. It wasn't much; the bar had a sod base with rough planks laid over the top. It was the place buffalo hunters and drifters stopped to have a drink.

Hoover's store now had an oversized false front and large painted letters boasting his name and the fact he sold wholesale wines, liquors, and cigars. Where it once had been the only building on the prairie it was now pressed in between the Long Branch saloon and a dry goods store.

Eli figured he should stop in and see how old Hoover was doing. He dismounted in front of the building, tied off the roan, and stepped into Hoover's store.

Mort Hoover recognized Eli immediately and shouted across the store, "Eli Warren! Long time since you've graced my fine establishment." Mort walked up to him and put out his hand. "How's that old bear bait uncle of yours doing these days?"

Eli shook Mort's hand. "John's doing well. He's still got that store outside of Boggsville. He got shot in an attempted robbery a few weeks back." Eli grinned, "But, you know John, it didn't slow him down for long. He managed to put some lead into one of them."

"Naturally. They catch them that did it?"

"It has been dealt with."

Mort looked at him with an amused expression. "Read 'em from the Book, did you?"

"Chapter and verse. They won't be robbing or killing anymore. Anything going on around here in my line?"

Mort shook his head, "Just the usual assortment of rowdies, hell raisers, and idiots. Which are generally one-in-the-same. Nobody passing through with a price on their head, not that I've noticed anyway."

"Hear anything about the Parson gang? They robbed a stage and a train up north toward Hays City not long back."

"Now that you mention it, there was some recent talk in regards to them. A freighter was murdered and robbed off to the west of here. His wagon, which included a case of rifles and several cases of ammunition, was cleaned out. Of course it's only speculation that it was Parson, no one actually saw who did it."

"They get the credit for a lot they don't do."

"Signs and all tend to match their style though."

"Sounds like someone plans on fighting an army,

which is interesting as I've been thinking lately about how much they resemble the Cole gang from a few years back."

"There is a resemblance, I'll give you that. What worries me is, figuring them for the coyotes they are, they might up and sell those guns and that ammunition to renegade Comanches. They've been making some noise down in the Staked Plains country."

"That's a scary thought."

"You ain't a-tellin' me."

"I suppose Parson will hole up for the winter now."

"More than likely, most outlaws do. Can't recall ever hearing of them doing anything during the winter."

"I was down in the Strip looking for them, no luck though. Since I was in the area I figured I'd head up this way one last time before snow flies and just see if there was any news on them."

"Sorry, I couldn't give you any good news on the subject. I'm glad you stopped by though; us old timers got to keep track of each other. Those of us, that is, who recall the days before the settlers poured in and it was just us and the Indians."

Eli grinned, "I'm not exactly in the old timer class like you and John."

"Close enough, you earned your place even if you are half my age."

Eli chuckled, "Okay, I'll accept the honor. Think I'll wander around town, pick up some supplies, and see if I can get myself into trouble."

"Now, you be watching your back out there."

"Always do. I'll give your regards to John." They shook hands then Eli went back out the door.

Returning to his horse Eli pulled the reins loose and mounted. Riding down the street he noted several new saloons mixed in between a variety of other stores and businesses. Reaching the end of the row he continued riding around to the back side of the buildings and down the alley behind them.

The shouts and boisterous laughter of men echoing down the alley drew his attention. He rode towards the sound and pulled up short in shock and disbelief. A small boy in ragged clothes was chasing bits of bread and food that three men were throwing at him. They were laughing as he snatched them up off the ground and ate them. Along with the laughter they were making barking sounds at him and whistling as if to a dog.

Eli's shock was instantly replaced with rage. He put the roan into a quick walk toward the men. Without slowing the roan, he rammed the horse's shoulder directly into one of the men knocking him back and against the building's wall. Pulling his boot free of the stirrup he kicked a second man in the head sending him sprawling in the dirt.

Eli shouted at them, "What's wrong with you men?"

The two men on the ground slowly rose to their feet as the man still standing stared at him. They didn't know him, but they recognized a dangerous man when they saw one. Blood was trickling down the forehead of the man who Eli had kicked. He wiped at it, "We was just havin' a little fun with the rug rat."

"Teasing a starving boy is *fun*?" Eli glared at the man who swallowed the lump in his throat. "Get out of here before I shoot the lot of you."

The men didn't argue as they turned and ran off down the alley.

Eli looked down at the boy who stood stock still staring up at him. His mouth was stuffed with bread and his dirty hands held a piece of meat and another chunk of bread. The boy's clothes were torn and were as dirty as the rest of him. His hair was shaggy and matted with bits of prairie grass and dirt in it. They were at the back door of a saloon; no doubt the men had come out into the alley and found the boy.

Eli stepped out of the saddle and slowly approached the boy who continued to silently stare up at him. He towered over the boy studying the youngster's gaunt features. Since the men had sandwiches, they probably got them from the saloon where a lunch had been laid out on the bar.

Tying the roan off to a post Eli turned to the boy and indicated the food in his hands. "Why don't you drop that trash, son." The boy looked at the bits of food unsure whether to let go of his meal or not.

Placing his hand gently on the boy's back Eli said in a soft voice, "It's okay, I'll get you some decent food."

The boy dropped the smashed, dirt covered food and allowed Eli to guide him toward the back door of the saloon. Eli opened the door and directed the boy into the saloon.

The bar was on the opposite side of the room, but he could see the plates of bread, meat, and boiled eggs set out on it. He brought the boy up to the bar, "Eat up, boy."

The boy's eyes widened as he looked at the food. He began to grab at the bread with one hand and the slices of beef with the other. From down the bar the barman shouted, "Hey you little whelp, get away from that, that's for paying customers." He rushed down the bar and raised his hand to strike the boy.

Eli stepped up to the bar and with a strong hand slammed a silver dollar against the barman's chest. The man stopped dead in his tracks and looked at Eli while rubbing the spot on his chest where the heavy coin had struck him. "There, I'm a paying customer, now get back there and wash your glasses."

The man glared at Eli, but said no more to the boy. He then bent over, picked up the coin and resumed his former position down the bar. The barman picked up a towel and glass while he cast a disgruntled look at the boy eating the food from the bar. He looked at Eli to find the big man staring at him as if daring him to do or say something. He diverted his eyes to the glass in his hand. The few men sitting at the tables were watching with interest.

A man leaning on the bar was smiling at the boy, "Little rag-a-muffin has himself an appetite don't he?"

Eli didn't comment as he called out to the barman, "You got any milk back there?"

The barman growled, "What do you think this is a Sunday school?"

Eli set a hard look on the barman. "I won't be asking again."

The barman swallowed and bent down toward the bar. Removing a small metal milk canister from under it he filled a glass with milk. He placed it on the bar and moved away.

Eli pointed to it, "That's for you son, eat all you want." Eli stood by and watched over the boy as he ate his fill. No one said any more to him. When the boy had finished Eli ushered him back out the alley door.

As they disappeared out the door a pair of seasoned, weather browned plainsmen sitting at a table were laughing at the barman.

Trying to save his pride the barman scowled and looked at the men. "Some psalm singing do-gooder. Probably spends all day in church."

The man at the bar laughed, "Not too many do-gooders sit in church with a .44 pistol buckled on. Good thing you shut up when you did."

Once back in the alley Eli looked at the boy, "Where's your folks?"

The boy looked up at him trying not to cry, but tears were welling up in his eyes.

"Are they gone?"

The boy nodded as he sniffed and wiped at his nose with the back of his dirty hand.

Eli untied the roan, and put his hand on the boy's shaking right shoulder. "It's going to be okay, you come with me." He led the horse as the two walked together in silence. Leaving the alley they walked around to the business fronts where Eli tied the roan in front of a mercantile store and took the boy inside. He told the store man to set the boy up with the proper size clothes and outfit him for the trail.

The boy watched as the man collected pants, shirts, and a variety of other items placing them all on the counter. Eli dropped a new hat on the boy's head, "Put that on the bill too." He picked a blanket and ground tarp adding them to the growing pile on the counter. On top of that he placed food supplies.

Eli handed the clothes to the boy and rolled his extra gear into a bed roll. Eli paid the bill, picked up the food and bedroll and walked out of the store. The boy followed carrying his new clothes. They next went to the barber shop where the boy's hair was cut and then he was set up with a bath.

Eli sat down on the steps of the bathhouse. "When you finish your bath put on the new clothes and come back out here." The boy nodded and went inside carrying his clothes while Eli guarded the rest of the outfit he had bought.

Eli thought about the boy as he waited. It was a rough life for an orphan in a country that had no provision for their care. There were orphanages, but they were little more than slave labor houses where more children were beaten or worked to death than were ever given homes. If not for Uncle John, that well could have been him scratching for survival at that age.

A short time later the boy emerged wearing his new clothes and walking timidly. He was wearing the hat and his clean face glowed under it. He stared at Eli not knowing what to expect next. Was he fed and clothed only to be turned back out to the prairie and alleys to try and survive another nightmarish day?

Eli stood up and studied him. The boy was on the small side, he seemed to be about ten years old, but his face looked older. "Now, that's a far sight better. You have a name, son?"

The boy had almost forgotten that he had a name; he had to think for a moment. He then spoke in a low voice, "Robert Slater, sir."

"Well, that's a mighty fine name, but let's shorten 'er down to Rob. That okay with you?"

Rob nodded, "Yes sir that would be fine."

"I'm Eli; you don't need to call me sir. Let's get you a horse, Rob."

"Am I going with you?"

"You'll be riding with me, if that suits you."

"Where are we going?" The question and the boy's expression indicated that he feared the worse.

"You're going to be my saddle pal and we're going to Colorado to winter with my Uncle John. Does that work for you?"

Rob smiled, "I would like that."

"Good, then let's rattle our hocks out of this town. Can you ride?"

"A little bit."

"No problem, you'll be an expert in no time. Let's head over to that livery. I see a couple of horses in the corral that should work out for you."

They looked over the horses for sale as the livery man followed them through the corral. Eli picked out a solidly built bay gelding and dickered a price with the man finally arriving at a sale. A little more dickering and he added a used saddle with attached saddlebags and a bridle to the horse.

Eli taught Rob how to properly saddle and bridle the horse. He gave him a quick talk on how to conduct himself around horses. They stowed his things in the saddlebags and tied the bedroll to the cantle.

Rob mounted the bay and followed Eli as they rode west out of town. He rode in silence wondering about this man. It was clear that he was someone other men feared by the reaction of the men in the alley and how he talked to the man in the saloon.

That night they camped in a grove of huge cottonwood trees beside the river. Eli showed Rob how to start a fire and make a camp. As night fell the air was filled with the sounds of crickets, frogs, and the occasional screech of an owl or nighthawk. Eli noticed that none of the sounds affected the boy who sat staring into the fire.

"They put me on a train." Rob broke the silence with the statement. Eli sat next to him and listened.

"Four men pushed their way into our house. My ma was real scared. They wanted our two horses and all the money Pa had. Pa gave them his money and then one of the men shot Pa and Ma both. I was hiding and they didn't see me, but I saw them. After they left I didn't know what to do. I walked to the house of some people who had been friends of my ma and pa and told them what happened. They said the men were renegades from the war. They said they would have the law go see my house and then sent me away; they wouldn't let me come in.

"No one around there wanted me. I heard people say they didn't want to be burdened with a kid who wasn't their own. They put me on an orphan train going west with a bunch of other boys and girls. I was scared and cried the first night. I had bad dreams about my folks being killed. The people on the train in charge of the kids said they would beat me if I cried again. So, I didn't, but I was still scared.

"The train stopped at towns where they made us line up and stand on the platform while people looked at us like they were trying to pick a milk cow. The other kids on the train whispered that we would end up on farms where we would be beaten and starved and worked to death. I was scared, but nobody picked me. I'm small for my age, I'm twelve, but look littler. I was glad I was small so no one would pick me.

"Then, the train stopped in this town and we stood out on the platform again. A man with a mean face pointed at me and said he'd take me. I jumped off the platform and ran as fast as I could and I just kept running. I hid behind a hill and hoped they wouldn't find me. They never did and then the train left and I was alone.

"I would sleep wherever I could, it was cold at night and I didn't have a blanket or a coat. So, I stole a blanket off a wagon and hid it where I slept. I found food where I could, sometimes I would steal food. I tried to find work, but no one would hire me. I'm small, but I'm strong. The town kids called me names and threw rocks at me and people made fun of me." He fell silent again.

Eli studied the boy as the firelight reflected off his weary face. He knew the boy needed to talk, to tell someone what had happened to him. "Sounds pretty tough alright. How long were you living like that?"

Rob shrugged, "A long time."

"Where did you come from?"

"Missouri. I hate Missouri and everyone in it."

"Well, you don't have to worry anymore."

Rob looked over at him. "Thank you for helping me and taking me with you. Will I be able to stay with you or are you going to put me on another train?"

"No more orphan trains. You can either ride with me or stay with my Uncle John. I do some pretty dangerous work and I wouldn't want you getting hurt."

"What is Uncle John like?"

"He's a wonderful, kind, and generous man. I ran away from home when I was twelve and walked all the way to Independence from Virginia to find him. He took me in like I was his own son and we've been pals ever since. He'll take you in too."

"What kind of dangerous work do you do?"

Eli could see that Rob was intelligent; being scared and hungry doesn't make someone stupid. The boy had been scared and wary, but now that he was fed and felt safe again his intelligence was resurfacing. He wouldn't lie to him. "I hunt outlaws."

Rob stared into the fire again. "Do you shoot them?"

"Sometimes."

"My pa had taught me how to shoot and hunt. I'm pretty good with a rifle." He then looked back at Eli and stared in his face for a long silent minute. "Do you kill war renegades?"

His thoughts went to the Parson gang. "If need be."

"Why did you start hunting outlaws?"

Huge O'Connor's tough Irish face drifted into Eli's mind. "I had a best friend once, his name was Huge O'Connor. One day he and I were set on by two outlaws, they killed Huge, shot him dead for no reason."

"What did you do?"

"I killed them both."

"You hunt outlaws to get even don't you?"

Eli thought back and remembered his vow to his dead friend to rid the country of outlaws. It was a tall order, but he would get as many as he could for Huge and the other victims of outlaws. He held Rob's intelligent eyes, "Yes, I do."

Rob continued to look into Eli's eyes as his boyish face became hard and stern. "Teach me how to hunt outlaws."

"There are better things to do with your life, Rob."

Rob immediately rebutted with, "Why didn't you do better things then?"

Eli was at a loss for words. The boy was no fool and had him fairly cornered.

Rob held Eli's eyes as he answered his own question. "Because they killed your friend Huge O'Connor that's why isn't it?"

Eli nodded, "It was, but are you sure that's what you truly want?'

"Yes."

"Because of your parents?"

Rob's bottom lip began to quiver as he fought back the tears. He nodded his head, "Just like you did for Huge

97

O'Connor."

Eli studied Rob's face and knew the boy would pursue this track whether he taught him or not. He could become a killer bent on revenge or a man trained for a purpose. Rob's future had fallen into his hands.

Eli nodded, "First you have to finish your education. A man who can't read, write, and know about the world around him is ignorant. You can't work against outlaws if you're as ignorant as they are."

"I went to fifth grade."

"Good. John and I will finish your education."

"And then you'll teach me how to hunt outlaws?"

"I will teach you the ways of men, in particular bad men. We'll see where we go from there."

Rob stared back into the fire his lips stiffened as he angrily growled, "I'm going to kill the four men who killed my folks, every one of them. I heard the men say the name of the man who shot my folks and I especially want to kill him. They said his name was Jude."

Chapter 9

A week had passed since Eli and Rob left Dodge City. Eli used the time they rode together to begin teaching his new apprentice. They talked of the western lands with Eli describing what he had seen and learned in his travels. They discussed history and talked of foreign countries. In between his school lessons Eli taught Rob about living on the land.

They often stopped and examined tracks. Eli pointed out the difference between the track of a ridden horse and one that was being led. He pointed out how every horseshoe track was like a man's signature; each one was different and could be traced to a specific horse and rider. They examined animal tracks with Eli explaining how following animal tracks in dry country can lead to water.

The lessons about men and their habits would come later. First Rob had to understand the land and all things connected to it. He had to know how to track before he could hunt. At no time did he talk about the Parson gang, in particular Jude Parson. He didn't want the boy focusing his efforts and will toward revenge. When he felt Rob was on his way to self-control he would tell him about his constant quest to run down Jude Parson and his murderous gang.

Rob had become comfortable enough with Eli and his new life to ride alongside of his teacher rather than drag behind like a puppy. He was an eager learner and listened well. He wanted to soak in everything Eli taught him as he realized how much Eli knew and how much he could learn from him.

A cold wind was blowing across the arid land as they rode into the eastern border of Boggsville. Eli reined the roan toward Cliff Adams' office and pulled him up. He glanced over at Rob, "Cliff Adams is the Bent County Sheriff. I collected a couple of outlaws I was after down in New Mexico. I'm going in here to collect the rewards from Cliff."

"Can I come in with you?"

Eli nodded, "Sure, you can meet Cliff. He's an old friend who we will be seeing more of in the future, so you might as well get acquainted."

The two dismounted and entered the office door. Cliff looked up from his desk, "Well, it's been a while since you set off on the Yeager trail, thought maybe you got lost." He tossed a questioning glance at Rob.

"I got Clyde and Mort down in New Mexico then took a side trip through No Man's Land and up to Dodge."

Cliff craned his neck looking out the front window at the horses tied out front. "You have them hidden somewhere?"

"I had places to go and dragging a couple of rotting corpses around the country with me wasn't part of the plan. I was hoping you'd take my word on it."

Cliff leaned back in his chair stifling a grin, "Well, I don't know, you being such a dismal person of poor character and all."

"And after all the nice things I've said about you?"

"Well . . .," He reached into the desk drawer and brought out the envelope holding the last two hundred dollars and laid it on the desk. "Okay, I'll trust you this once."

Eli took the envelope and put it in his hip pocket. "Thanks Cliff, you're a fine judge of character."

Cliff couldn't hold the smile back any longer as he

stood up with a laugh and shook Eli's hand. "So, you got rid of my Yeager problem. I owe you one, pal."

Rob had been standing behind Eli nervously taking in the mock exchange of distrust. Eli had said Cliff was his friend, but it didn't sound like it. Cliff then turned his attention to the boy. "Got a new partner there?"

Eli gestured for Rob to step forward. "This is Rob Slater. Rob this is Sheriff Adams." Rob stepped forward to shake Cliff's hand.

Cliff grinned; he was impressed with the boy as they shook hands. "Going to learn the trade, Rob?"

"Yes sir, but Eli says I have to have my education first. He says a man can't be as ignorant as outlaws. So, I'm just learning now."

"He's right you know, education is a fine thing and you will learn a lot from Eli."

"Yes sir, I know."

Eli tapped Rob on the shoulder, "Rob, go check on the horses and reset the cinches. We'll be leaving shortly." Rob turned and went out the door without a question.

"Fine lad you have there Eli." Cliff then narrowed his eyes as a hint of humor danced in them. "*Your* boy from some wild romance?"

Eli shook his head and laughed, "Hardly. I found him up in Dodge. He had escaped from one of those orphan trains and was about half starved. He'd been living as best he could for some time. He needed help and a place to belong."

Cliff grinned, "You're an interesting man Eli. You've got the nerve of a mountain lion; deadlier than a nest of diamondbacks, you go face-to-face with outlaws, then, you've got this huge heart that goes out to orphans. You are truly a paradox my friend."

The two were silent for a moment before Eli spoke again, "Rob's parents were murdered by Jude Parson and his gang."

"Did you tell him that you've been hunting them for

the last couple of years?"

Eli shook his head, "No. He wants me to teach him to hunt outlaws so he can kill Jude Parson someday, but I don't want him thinking about that. I want him to learn there is a lot more to life first."

"Sound reasoning."

"Anything new around here since I've been gone?"

"The railroad chose Las Animas over Boggsville. The County Seat will be moved to Las Animas City. The sheriff will be there, as will the courts and everything else that was once here."

"So, you will be moving."

Cliff shook his head. "I'll be resigning."

Eli's eyes widened in surprise. "Resigning? You're the best lawman this county ever saw."

"I appreciate that, but I have friends here; Ella has her friends and doesn't want to move either. I've got some money saved so I figure I'll buy a few acres and raise those cattle I talked about. At least I won't have to worry about someone shooting me. Ella especially likes that part."

"Have to keep your wife happy. You probably won't miss the politics."

Cliff snorted, "Not a bit."

"We can still get together and shoot the breeze once in a while. Talk about something besides outlaws for a change."

Cliff laughed, "I could get used to that. Coffee will always be on at the house."

"I'll be taking you up on that."

"I'm glad we could get this Yeager mess dealt with before I left office. The ranchers are singing your praises for getting rid of the first two. Now, they'll probably want to elect you sheriff."

"I think we already talked about that."

"Yes, you made your position clear on that one."

Eli grinned, "I'm not as diplomatic as you." He extended his hand to Cliff. "I need to be getting along."

They shook hands and Eli walked out of the office.

Rob was waiting patiently for Eli to come out. His coat collar was pulled up around his neck and ears and he was using the horses for a wind block. It was obvious he was cold, but he made no complaint. The two mounted and headed for their winter home.

Smoke was coming out of the store's stovepipe as well as the one above the living area when they rode around to the stable behind the cabin and store. They stripped the horses, fed them, and then headed for the store half of the building. The door was closed, but the shutter over the window was open reflecting the glass. It was getting colder causing John had abandoned his habit of keeping the door open for breeze. It was now more important to keep the inside warm.

Rob hung behind Eli, he was nervous about meeting John. There had been little in his life to make him trustful of people he didn't know. Eli had changed a bit of that thinking. Rob wasn't sure what to expect from the big rough man at first, but Eli turned out to be a good man true to his word. He hoped John would be as well; still he was going to be cautious.

Eli pushed the store door open and looked around inside the room. John was nowhere in sight; however, the door between the store and living area was open. Eli called out in a lowered rough sounding voice, "Hey, can a man get some beans around here?"

A gruff voice came from the living area, "Hold onto your britches, you can't be in that big of a hurry for beans."

Eli winked at Rob, "Well, I am you old coot, get out here and tend your store."

The sound of boots stomping across the floor drew nearer to the open doorway. John burst out into the room shouting, "I'll tend what I darn well please to tend you smart . . . ." He stopped in mid-sentence at seeing Eli.

He stood straight up and pretended to be mad. "Old

coot? You're wearing a gun you snot nosed kid, let's see if you can shoot that hawgleg as good as you shoot your mouth." Eli turned to face him.

Rob looked worried and watched. This couldn't be the nice man Eli had talked about.

The two men stalked toward each other and then John let out a roar of laughter and grabbed Eli in a bear hug.

John stepped back and looked past Eli at Rob, "Another stray nephew?"

Eli gestured for Rob to come up to them. Rob obeyed, but his expression was apprehensive. "Uncle John this is Rob Slater, my new apprentice. Rob this is Uncle John."

John could see the worry on the boy's face and was wise enough to see into the boy's eyes and realize there was fear and pain back down his trail. He put out his hand, "Welcome, Rob Slater."

Rob shook his hand, "Thank you, sir."

John understood his nephew's nature for helping those in need. It was the part of Eli Warren only he knew about. He had seen boys like Rob before and surmised that Eli had adopted an orphan. "We aren't formal here Rob, call me John or Uncle John if you prefer, but the sir isn't necessary. It is a fine display of manners though and not to be made little of."

Rob began to relax; Eli had been right about the old man. "Thank you, Uncle John." He liked the sound of that; he never had an uncle before.

"I was putting grub on the table when some big mouth yahoo come busting in here calling folks old coots and demanding beans. Now, I'll get back to my business and cut a few more steaks off the deer haunch and we'll be eating in no time flat."

It was growing dark as the three sat around the table finishing the supper John had cooked. John grinned at Rob, "He's got a healthy appetite that one does. You'll be bigger than Eli pretty quick you keep eating like that."

"I'm kind of small, Uncle John; I don't think I'll ever get as big as Eli."

"Size has nothing to do with it Rob. We got a saying out here, it's not the size of the man in the fight, it's the size of the fight in the man. I've known some small men that were tough enough to fight a grizzly bear and win. Kit Carson was no Goliath, but he had more guts than any ten men put together. You're doing just fine; don't be worrying none about your size."

They talked around the table some more until Rob fell asleep in his chair. John shook the boy's shoulder, "Rob, go throw your bedroll down by the stove there where it's warm. Tomorrow we'll build you a proper bed."

Rob smiled and left the table. He picked up his bedroll and spread it out on the floor. Pulling off his shoes he rolled up in the blanket and was instantly asleep. John studied the boy's young and innocent face. "Nice boy there. What's his story?"

Eli told him about finding Rob in the alley picking up the scraps the men were throwing to him and laughing. "I threatened to shoot them and they scattered like bugs."

John's mouth turned down angrily, "I *would* have shot 'em. There's no excuse for that."

Eli went on to relate the rest of the story including the part about Jude Parson killing Rob's parents. "He wants to learn the business so he can hunt down the men who killed his family."

"I don't blame him for that, but he is a bit young to be thinking about killing men."

Eli looked at the sleeping boy. "He's also too young to have gone through what he has and to see his parents murdered by a gang of animals that all need to be six feet under."

Hearing the stifled rage in Eli's tone John looked at Eli and read the anger in his eyes. "You going to teach him then?"

"If I don't someone else will or he'll go it on his own. If he's determined to have the scalps of Jude Parson and his bunch he will either get himself killed trying or become a senseless killer himself."

John nodded in agreement, "You're right. He can learn to hunt with purpose and discretion or turn into something no better than Parson."

"That's what I'm thinking. He asked me to teach him, I said he had to finish his education first."

John studied the sleeping boy for several seconds. "I'll help you, we'll teach him right."

Eli looked at Rob and then back to John, "Like you did for me."

Chapter 10

Rob had been with Eli and John a year and a half on the day he turned fourteen. He had grown and was packing on muscle from good meals, lifting and carrying for John, and hours of splitting firewood. His lessons in reading and studying world history had rounded his knowledge and understanding of the world beyond Boggsville. His lessons also included tracking, hunting and shooting. He was growing into a confident, thinking young man with a strong work ethic and a sense of responsibility.

As a gift for his fourteenth birthday, Eli and John gave him a new Model P .45 Colt with holster and belt. With the gun came specific instructions that he was not to wear the gun anywhere except when target practicing to learn how to use it. He was not to take it out shooting unless Eli or John was with him. The instructions were summed up by telling him that a pistol had one primary purpose as it was a poor hunting weapon, it was a tool for self-defense.

Rob sat at the cabin table as he inspected his new gun.

"You take on a mighty responsibility with that," Eli said."

Ron looked at him, "I know, it's not a toy."

"You don't wave it around to impress."

"Discretion," John put in. "You practice discretion at all times with it."

"I will," Rob responded with a serious expression.

That afternoon Eli took Rob out on the prairie and

the lesson in shooting the pistol began. Rob took naturally to handling the gun. Eli taught him to aim at the target using the sights and also how to shoot from hip level pointing the barrel like pointing a finger.

Rob asked how gunfighters used the quick draw. Eli warned him not to be thinking of the gun in those terms. Although Rob obeyed the instruction it was obvious to Eli the young man had a serious interest in handling the gun fast. Eli knew if he didn't teach him the proper techniques the boy would practice on his own and probably do it wrong and get hurt.

Eli agreed to teach him under the condition that he promised to never practice fast drawing with the gun loaded. It was too easy to shoot a leg or foot while learning as the hammer had to be thumbed back while the gun was coming up. When he was solid with the draw then he could practice with the gun loaded. Rob agreed and promised to do as Eli had said.

That evening Eli sat down at the table with John after Rob had gone to bed. John glanced over at Eli, "You realize that you haven't hunted an outlaw in almost two years?"

Eli considered that and nodded, "I guess I haven't have I."

John grinned, "You've become a father."

Eli raised an eyebrow as he looked at John, "You know something I don't know?"

John indicated Rob with a lift of his chin, "Yonder's your boy. You've poured yourself into his raising with little thought to anything else. Cliff's become a cattleman and he's never been happier. You might be approaching that fork in your road."

"What fork is that?"

"Between living on the trail hunting wanted men or settling down."

Eli nodded, "My thoughts have been in that direction lately, but I'm not quite there yet." Eli looked at Rob, "We have unfinished business."

"Jude Parson?"

"Yes. I've been getting him ready."

"He's fast approaching it."

"He's been talking more about hunting outlaws, but he's still too young to go out."

"Young men his age were the first drovers up the Shawnee and Chisholm Trails. He's fit to do a man's work and he figures he's fit to do a man's fighting."

"He's not there yet."

"Maybe you two need to hit the trail for a while and take him up a few notches in his training."

Eli looked across the table to John, "I was thinking about going to visit William, it's been neigh onto two years since I last was at his place."

"Sounds like a good idea. You have a brother that you need to keep up with. Too many things can go wrong in this country and you never know from day-to-day what will happen to folks we care about."

The next evening at the supper table the three were exchanging small talk. Rob had never developed into a steady talker; he thought much and considered all things as learning experiences. Eli had taught him that a man could learn more from listening to the conversations around him than he could by asking too many questions or talking. Rob was turning into a good listener.

Eli announced, "I think I'll ride on up to William's place for a visit. I haven't seen him in long time."

Rob glanced up from his plate at Eli, "Can I go with you?"

Eli looked at him and then back to John, "Can you spare your number one top hand here for a few weeks?"

"Sure. Rob's been working his tail off and never a complaint out of him. He could use a break and have some fun."

Rob looked at John, "I can stay if you need me to

Uncle John." His words said it but his eyes were pleading to go.

"I'll get by, you go on." John grinned toward Eli and then winked at Rob, "Besides, I understand there's a mighty pretty little gal over there that's just about your age."

Rob's face turned red, "I didn't know that."

Eli lightly smacked Rob's shoulder, "She's a sweet kid, you'll like her. No one is expecting you to marry her."

Rob's face turned a brighter red. He got up from the table, "Guess, I'll pack my gear. Will we be leaving in the morning?"

"First light be ready to ride. You can take your rifle, but leave the six-gun here. There are a lot of hard cases up that way and if they see you wearing a gun they'll figure you're fair game to pick a fight with."

Rob nodded and walked out the door toward the stable to bring in his saddlebags. John watched as the boy closed the door behind him. "That's a fine young man, you watch over him now."

"More than likely in a few years he'll be watching over me."

It took a week to cover the distance to Hays City and William's farm that lay to the north of it. Eli continued Rob's training along the way.

They rode into the Warren farm yard at mid-day. Stopping in front of the house they looked around, the house was quiet, but smoke was coming from the stovepipe. Suddenly the door burst open and a young woman burst out shouting, "Uncle Eli, Uncle Eli!"

Eli was surprised at how much Carrie had grown. He had expected she would, but he remembered her as a skinny little girl who anxiously showed him her horse. Now she was almost a woman; however, the girlish excitement in her eyes had not diminished.

She ran up to Eli and stopped beside the roan looking

up at him, "Are you going to stay for a long time this time?" She then lowered her voice and made a serious face, "Or are you hunting notorious *outlaws*?"

"I'll be staying a few days."

She jumped up and gave a cheer. It was then she saw Rob mounted on his bay hidden behind Eli. In her excitement she had failed to see him as her eyes took in only her uncle. She suddenly stopped her cheer and looked slightly embarrassed. She moved her head to the side to better see the young man who sat nervously looking back at her.

Eli smiled to himself over the reaction between the two. "Carrie, this is my friend Rob Slater. Rob, this is Carrie."

Both stared at each other for an awkward few seconds before Carrie stepped up to the side of the bay and extended her hand to Rob. "Hi, Rob."

He shook her hand and nodded shyly. At that moment Lillian came out of the house and saw Eli. She smiled, "Lands sakes all the shouting and carrying on out here, I thought we were under attack from Indians. Hello Eli, good to see you again."

She then looked at Rob, "And who is this handsome young gentleman?"

Eli looked back at Rob whose face had turned red. "This is Rob Slater."

Lillian smiled at him, "Hello, Rob."

Rob snatched his hat off his head, "Hello ma'am."

Lillian's smile widened, "And he has manners too. Come on in you two and rest, William will be in soon."

"Let us put up our horses and we'll be in." They dismounted and led the horses as Carrie walked beside Eli asking a steady barrage of questions. In between questions she was sneaking peaks at Rob who kept his eyes straight ahead.

Entering the barn Eli spotted Carrie's sorrel. "I see Lightning is looking well."

She then went into a long history of all the places she had ridden her horse. Rob pulled the saddle and bridle off his horse as Eli and Carrie talked. He was sneaking as many peaks at Carrie as she was at him, none of which was missed by Eli.

Carrie was the first to work up the courage to talk. "What do you think of Lightning, Rob?"

Rob looked up at her surprised that she was speaking to him. "I think he's a fine horse. You're lucky to have him."

Carrie beamed a smile at him and Rob began to relax his nervousness. The two made small talk as they walked back to the house. Eli let them talk as he quickened his pace to stay a few steps ahead of them.

Eli and Rob stopped on the porch to pour water into a basin and wash their faces and hands before coming into the house. Lillian had coffee and donuts on the table when they walked in.

Rob's eyes widened at the plate of donuts. He remembered his mother used to make them, but now that seemed like a distant memory overshadowed by the everlasting vision of her blood covered body lying on the cabin floor. He wasn't sure if he wanted to cry or feel good over the lingering memory of something as simple as donuts.

Eli saw the look on his face, "You okay, Rob?"

Rob quickly nodded his head, "Yeah, fine, a little trail weary I guess."

Lillian looked from Rob to Eli with an expression of concern. Eli in turned gave a slight nod and quickly blinked his eyes sending her the message that he would explain later. She understood and told Rob to hurry up and eat those donuts before they turned hard and she would have to hammer them out for horseshoes. His melancholy mood lifted at her light comment.

The sound of the opening door brought the steady clomping of work boots across the wooden floor.

William's voice sounded before he entered the kitchen. "Lillian, whose horses are those in the barn? That roan looks like my brother's broken down old nag."

William was beaming a smile as he entered the kitchen to see Eli feigning an angry glare. "Broken down old nag?"

"Like the rich snobs in Richmond used to say," William lifted his nose and spoke in a nasal tone, "that carriage is worn and dirty. I must have a shiny new one."

"I don't want my horse shiny, and carriages haven't much use on the trails I ride. Could you just see me riding up to some outlaws' camp in a shiny carriage?" Eli lifted his nose in the air and copied William's impersonation of the Richmond snobs. "Wait here driver, while I attend to these outcasts of society."

William grinned, "They'd shoot you dead on the spot."

"Heck, I'd shoot me dead on the spot if that was what I had come down to."

The two men then clasped hands and slapped backs. "I see you've been here long enough to drink my coffee and eat all my donuts," William said.

"Not all, there's a few crumbs left on the plate just for you." Eli picked a crumb off his shirt and handed it to William, "Here."

William laughed along with Carrie.

William then turned his attention to Rob. "Well, looks like the suitors are lining up for my daughter's hand already."

Rob turned bright red and Carrie blushed as well giving her father a gentle scolding. "What a thing to say Pa, you'll embarrass poor Rob to death."

"But, he's a fine strapping young gentleman, isn't he Carrie?" He put out his hand to Rob, "I'm William, Eli's younger, but more intelligent and handsome brother."

Rob shook his hand, "Rob Slater, sir."

"Sir! You see, he did come a-courting."

"Pa, really!" Carrie's blush deepened, but she was smiling slightly when she said it indicating that she did have an eye for the handsome young man.

The five of them were sitting around the table after supper drinking coffee and making conversation. Rob had said little, listening instead as he was prone to do. William turned his attention to him and asked, "Rob, how did you ever fall in with my brother?"

Rob cast a quick glance at Eli and then concentrated on the tabletop. "We just kind of hooked up in Dodge City."

William sensed it was a sensitive subject. He was about to turn the conversation in a different direction when Carrie asked Rob, "Where do your parents live?"

Rob continued to stare at the table top, "They don't." He then stood up, "Thank you ma'am for the supper. Think I'll go to the barn and turn in, I'm pretty tired." He turned and walked out of the kitchen and out the door.

The group sat in stunned silence. William coughed to clear his throat, "I think we stepped on some sensitive ground there."

Eli nodded. "I found Rob in Dodge City a couple of years ago. He had run away from an orphan train and was making do the best he could. He was starved, ragged, and scared. His parents had been murdered in front of him by Rebel renegades and the only help his neighbors would give him was to put him on the orphan train."

Tears welled up in Carrie's eyes, "Oh, how awful, and I brought it up. I feel so terrible."

"It's okay," Eli assured her. "He is learning to get past it, but it's still alive and every once in a while something brings it to the surface."

"Like we just did." William shook his head regretfully. "I should have been paying more attention; it is obvious he was orphaned."

"You had no way of knowing. He has to learn to ride

through it. He knows who the murderers are and the thought of finding them one day helps him get past pain."

"Who did it?"

"Jude Parson and his gang."

William showed surprise. "The same Parson you have been hunting?"

Eli nodded, "I haven't told Rob yet."

"Why not?"

He glanced at Lillian and Carrie. "There are reasons."

Lillian spoke from across the table, "That was a fine thing you did Eli taking him in like that and helping him."

"I couldn't leave him out there. He needed help." He hesitated and then added, "I've come to think of him like a son."

Lillian watched Eli. "I know it is none of my business, but how come you never married Eli? You would be a wonderful husband and father."

Eli shrugged, "My life has always taken me down a rough and dangerous path. That's no life for a woman." He then grinned, "Besides, I've never met one yet who would have me."

"I'm sure there are plenty who would, but I think you just like being in single harness."

"Probably."

William stood up and gestured to Eli, "Let's sit in the front room I've got a good bottle of bourbon I'll share with you."

As the men retired to the front room Carrie looked at her mother. "I need to go say something to Rob. I'll be right back."

Lillian understood. "Go ahead, and tell that young man that we have an extra room for him and Eli. He doesn't need to sleep in the barn with the animals."

The last light of the summer day was fading into a brilliant sunset when Carrie stepped into the barn. She called out, "Rob? Rob are you in here?"

A voice called out from the depths of the barn, "I'm

by the horses."

Carrie walked in to see Rob standing in front of Lightning's stall. He looked at her, "You have a nice horse."

She walked up to Rob where he stood by the stall and stopped next to him. "Would you like to go for a ride tomorrow? I can show you around the farm."

"Sure, I'd like that."

"Rob . . . I'm sorry I asked about your parents. I know my careless question hurt you."

"It's okay, you didn't know. I guess Eli told you what happened."

She nodded, "He did. I'm sorry for what has happened to you."

"Eli and Uncle John have been very good to me. They have taught me a lot."

"Are you going to be an outlaw hunter like Eli?"

Rob nodded, "Yes. One day I'll find the men who murdered my parents and I will kill them." There was no heat in the statement only the acceptance of the fact.

"I understand that and I don't blame you. Ma says for you to come in the house, there is an extra room for you and Eli. She doesn't want our guests sleeping in the barn."

Rob nodded his understanding. Together they walked out of the barn side-by-side and moved toward the house.

William was watching them out the window. "Looks like a friendship is growing there."

Eli looked out the window past him, "A good choice for both of them."

William continued to look out the window. "You're a good man Eli, not many would have done for Rob what you have." He paused for a moment struggling with what he wanted to say next. Then, he added, "If anything ever happens to Lillian and I, please take care of Carrie."

Eli frowned at him, "Don't talk like that."

William faced his brother. "If I learned nothing else from the war I learned how we all hang by the merest of threads. Anything can go wrong out here; you know that more than anyone. I will feel better if I know Carrie will be in your protective hands if anything does happen to us."

"Of course I'll watch over her."

"I want your promise."

"You have it."

"Good, now let's have that bourbon."

Chapter 11

Autumn returned to the New Mexico and Colorado Rockies as word spread up the Santa Fe Trail regarding the Colfax County War. Freighters who stopped at the store had stories about shootings, murders, and gunfighters lining up on both sides of the battle.

A freighter stood by the store's stove warming himself on a chilled cloudy day. John was busy checking his shipment when Eli walked in from a trip to Boggsville. The freighter nodded a greeting, "Afternoon Eli."

"Cold day, Jake," Eli replied as he stood next to the man taking in some of the stove's warmth.

"Hear about that Methodist minister that was murdered down in Cimarron Canyon?" Jake asked.

Eli shook his head. "They killed a minister?"

"Yup, man by the name of Tolby. His body was found in the canyon between Cimarron and Elizabethtown. Tolby had been an outspoken supporter of the land owners and opposed to the Santa Fe Circle. It's got the land owners fired up something fierce."

"I would imagine."

Jake glanced at Eli with a grin, "Fired up enough to put a three thousand dollar reward on the head of the murderer."

Eli looked over at Jake, "You don't say."

"Figured that might be of interest to you."

"Just might."

"Well, I've lolly-gagged around enough for one day, need to get on into Boggsville. Everything look alright

John?"

"It's all here."

Jake exchanged goodbyes with John and Eli as he left the store.

Still checking over his supplies John spoke without looking at Eli, "Suppose you'll be heading down to Cimarron."

"I have to think on it."

John chuckled, "Never thought I'd hear that answer out of you."

The rest of the day Eli considered what Jake had told him. By the end of the day he had decided to ride down and try and find the minister's murderer with the three thousand dollar price on his head. He knew it was a perilous time for a stranger to ride through that part of the country, but for that kind of money it was worth it.

He informed John and Rob that evening at supper that he was heading down to Cimarron to look for the minister's killer.

John knew Eli wasn't ready to hang it up yet. Deep down inside Eli craved the intensity of the hunt as much as to honor his vow to a man long dead.

Rob's expression turned anxious, "Can I go? Am I old enough yet to go with you?"

Eli shook his head, "Not on this one."

Rob's hopeful expression turned into a scowl emphasizing his disappointment. "How will I ever learn to hunt real outlaws if I never get out to do it? I can shoot and I've been practicing drawing the Colt every day."

"You're coming along well Rob, but I'm riding into a land war where every man is considered an enemy. It's going to take all the skills I have to stay alive down there. We didn't spend all this time teaching you only to have you shot in the back by some hired bushwhacker."

Rob's tone took on an angry edge, "Someday I'll go, right?"

"Yes, you will. You're not ready yet and someday you

will understand that." Eli decided it was time to talk about the Parson gang. "I want you ready when we go after the Parson gang."

Rob stared at him. "The Parson gang? Who are they?"

"They are a Rebel renegade gang of robbers and murderers who have been killing and robbing all across Kansas, New Mexico, Colorado," He looked Rob directly in the eyes, "And Missouri. Their leader is named Parson . . . Jude Parson."

The name did not immediately register in Rob's mind as he continued to meet Eli's eyes. Slowly his eyes widened with recognition, "Jude Parson. The Jude who killed my parents?"

"Yes, *that* Jude Parson. I was hunting Jude Parson for three years, up until a couple years ago when other things took precedence over the hunt. I intend to take the hunt back up and I want you with me when we go after him. This is important and I want you ready, that's why you can't come with me this time. Losing you down in Colfax County isn't part of the plan."

Anger filled Rob's eyes and tinged his tone, "How come you never told me you knew about Jude Parson?"

"Because I didn't want you focusing everything you were going to learn solely to use against him. You needed to have your thinking focused on learning to use these skills for their own merits and I think you understand that."

Rob considered that as he stared into Eli's eyes. He finally softened his angry expression and nodded his agreement. "Okay, I see that. There is actually a chance I can kill Jude Parson then?"

"I don't want you thinking about killing anyone. First, we have to find them. It's up to them at that point if there's gunplay or not. With someone like Jude Parson I expect we'll have to kill him as he'll never give up.

"You learn your lessons first. You have to be able to

find and out think them before you can confront them. If all you have on your mind is killing Jude Parson then you won't learn a thing. When anger and hate control a man's senses it makes him stupid and careless and he generally ends up the dead one. Do you understand that?"

Rob let out a heavy sigh, "Yes, I do understand. It's like you and Uncle John have taught me. Rule one, think. Rule two, confront. Rule three, kill only as a last resort."

Eli smiled at him, "Well said. Patience is the name of this game. You keep practicing with the Colt and be thinking of how to follow rules one and two. Rule three will create itself."

"One day we *will* go after the Parson gang?"

"Yes, we will."

"When?"

"When the time is right."

Rob's eyes narrowed, "And I'll be ready."

Eli headed south at dawn. His first stop was Trinidad to have a look at the wanted posters on the City Marshal's wall. Depending on the reception he received from the Marshal would determine his next step. If the mood seemed right he might ask about the problems in Colfax County. Information like that spread from lawman to lawman.

Trinidad had grown considerably since he was last through. It was becoming a city with new stores and houses lining the streets. The city still had its wild side which the decent citizens were determined to ignore. He didn't plan on staying long or hanging around the saloons listening. He was bound for Cimarron; this was only a stop hoping for some information.

Finding the Marshal's office, he dismounted and walked in through the door. A man with a badge on his vest was sitting behind a desk grumbling over some paperwork. His thick mustache hung over his top lip and moved with the muttered curses. He had the look of man who could walk into a saloon fight and clear it out double quick. The lawman turned his steel blue eyes up at the sound of the opening door and the two men sized each other up in an instant.

"Can I help you?" The lawmen held his eyes on Eli's.

"Maybe. I'm passing through on my way down to Cimarron, thought you might be able to give me the latest on the fighting down that way."

The marshal's eyes remained suspicious and cold, "Which side are you joining up with?"

"What makes you think I'm joining anyone's side?"

"Because I've been a lawman since who flung the chunk and you sure aren't headed down for church services. You're either a hired gun or a bounty hunter."

"I'm an outlaw hunter."

"Only outlaws have bounties, if you hunt one you're hunting the other."

The two men had not pulled their eyes off each other. "A man should be paid for his work," Eli said dryly.

"Most figure there's no difference between an outlaw and a bounty hunter."

"Some say the same thing about lawmen."

"And at times they're right. I can respect an honest bounty hunter, but never an outlaw."

"And I can respect an honest lawman. Honest men of both professions seem in short supply these days."

The marshal nodded his head slowly, "Amen to that."

Relaxing, the marshal's intense stare softened as he leaned back in his chair. "Colfax County is a powder keg with the fuse burned down to a nub. Nobody is trusted. It's gotten so bad a preacher got murdered. Now I ask you, who'd murder a preacher? A lawman named Cruz got hung for it; of course he might have had it coming."

"I understand there's a three thousand dollar reward for the killer of the preacher."

"Is that who you're looking for?"

"Among others."

"You can save yourself the trip; they pulled the bounty after Cruz was hung. They figured he did it and they had their man."

Eli frowned.

The marshal studied Eli for a minute and decided he liked him. His mustache hitched to the side of his face as he grinned. "No shortage of outlaws down that way though." He picked up a stack of papers from his cluttered desktop and sorted through them. He handed Eli several wanted posters.

Eli began at the top and looked at each poster in turn. When he reached the third one he tapped the paper, "I know one of the men on this."

The marshal reached out for the paper and Eli handed it back to him. "Oh yeah, Milt Cramer and Jethro Boxer. They've robbed a few stages, one not far from here. They're also suspected of murder, but no solid proof. The shotgun guard on the last stage robbed was shot dead. Cramer and Boxer are the likely suspects. We're hoping that one of the passengers or the driver can identify these two and will testify to that if we catch these men.

"Two of the robbed stages, prior to this third one where the guard was killed, had the same driver and guard. They didn't put up a fight like the last one and lived to say they recognized Cramer and Boxer. If we can pin the murdered guard to them we can hang them. On a separate charge they're also suspected of hiring their guns out to the Santa Fe Circle."

"I had a run in with Cramer a couple of years back. I told him to get off the planet."

The marshal handed the paper back to Eli, "Appears he didn't listen to you."

"Two hundred and fifty each makes it worth the ride and I believe I know right where to find them."

"If you do, there are a couple of stage lines that will be five hundred dollars' worth of grateful to get them out of their hair. And it does say dead or alive, they're not sensitive when it comes to protecting their assets."

Eli nodded, "Whatever it takes to skin the coon."

"It isn't like they aren't asking for it." The marshal paused for a moment, "I like to keep track of who's packing guns in my jurisdiction and would appreciate your name."

"Eli Warren."

The marshal nodded. "I thought so; the only bounty hunter who insists on being called an outlaw hunter."

"Why not? Men who hunt mountain lions for the bounty are called cat hunters, those who hunt wolves for the bounty are called wolfers. The emphasis is on the quarry not the bounty. It only stands to reason that a man who hunts outlaws would be called an outlaw hunter. Emphasis on the *outlaw*."

"Fair enough. You talk like an educated man."

"I went to school."

"A mighty fine one from the way you speak." The marshal stood up and extended his hand, "I'm Jack Clovis. I have a professional acquaintance, Cliff Adams, who used to be a Sheriff up north, he always spoke highly of you."

Eli shook Jack's hand. "Cliff's a good friend of mine, we grew up together. He turned in his badge and is raising cattle now."

"So, I've heard. I offered him a job down here when they moved the Bent County seat, but he refused it. He said he had enough politics and cows didn't argue with you or demand favored treatment."

Eli grinned, "Cliff hated the politics. He's doing better now and his wife is much happier with him."

Jack laughed, "Mine would be too if I got out of this job."

"Cliff used to keep me up on the outlaw activity and now I've lost that source."

"Any friend of Cliff's is a friend of mine. Any time you need help eliminating some of the outlaw trash around here just let me know."

"I appreciate that. Speaking of, have you heard anything new on the Jude Parson gang? I hunted them for neigh on three years and never got close. The last couple of years I've had other priorities, but now I want to take back up on them."

Jack shook his head, "Nary a word in some time now. I doubt they headed back to Texas and the neck tie party waiting for them down that way, they'll likely pop back up. Eventually they'll run out if luck."

"I want to be in the right place at the right time when they do."

"Don't we all. I'd trade in this badge for that kind of reward money and go to raising cattle myself."

Eli's grin turned into a smile, "And make your wife a happier woman."

Jack laughed, "Something like that."

"Think I'll take a little swim through shark infested waters. It was good to meet you Jack and thanks for the information."

"Stop by once in a while and I'll let you know the latest."

"I'll be sure and do that." Eli turned and walked out of the office.

Eli stood and looked up and down the street considering his next step. He was pleased with having made a friend in Jack Clovis and having a new source of information from a supportive lawman. He had made a few lawman friends here and there.

He acknowledged that most lawmen didn't care for him. As Jack had said they considered bounty hunters to be outlaws themselves because they took the law into their own hands without benefit of wearing a badge. To his way of thinking, if the field wasn't open to men like him why issue wanted posters and rewards?

His original intent was to track down the preacher's killer even though the facts and trail were slim to nothing. Cramer was a man he knew and he had a better chance of finding him, and where he found Cramer he'd find Boxer. Two birds in the same bush. Five hundred wasn't three thousand, but it was nothing to sneeze at either.

Eli recalled his last encounter with Cramer. He had warned the outlaw, now he would find out that Eli Warren didn't talk through his hat. He intended to start in Cimarron where he knew Cramer liked to hang around, maybe Lambert's saloon. Cramer was a simple minded thinker and might even use the same camp he had with the Yeagers.

Eli rode south out of Trinidad, crossed the bridge over the Purgatoire River and started climbing toward Raton Pass. Half way up the mountain he dropped off onto Dick Wooten's toll road. Dick Wooten met him carrying a Sharps .50. "Eli Warren, well it's been a month of Sundays since I laid eyes on you. How's my old trappin' pard, that uncle of yours?"

"He's good. Took a bullet in a robbery a couple years back, but you know him."

"Yeah, bet it didn't even slow him down a mite. I remember him taking a Blackfoot arrow and acting like it was a mosquito bite. Where you headed?"

"Cimarron."

"Oh, dangerous place right now with all the fighting and land grabbing. I was smart and got my land in writing from old Maxwell, a lot of others didn't. That Santa Fe crowd comes around here stirrin' up the pot and they'll get a taste of my old .50. I suspect you've a reason to be ridin' down into that hornet's nest?"

Eli grinned at the old man, "Let's just say I'm on a business trip."

Wooten chuckled, "Knowing you, it ain't banker suit and tie business."

Eli held the grin and handed the old man a two-bit piece for the toll. "See you when I ride back through." He moved the roan out along the road.

There was plenty of activity and movement on the

Santa Fe Trail so he stuck to it. There was less chance of catching a bullet in the back if he was traveling with others on the Trail. The factions would be watching to see who passed on by and who lingered. Those who hung around would be subject to a bullet and then the sides would argue who he belonged to.

The Trail took him into Cimarron. Lambert's saloon was on his left. Further down on the same side was the long low adobe stage station, and across from it was the old brewery which was now a gambling hall with a fresh coat of whitewash. Walking the roan down the street beside the stage station he let the horse drink from the water tank. As the horse buried his nose in the water Eli studied the new white washed building across the street.

After a minute he pulled the roan's head up out of the water before he drank too much and made himself sick. Water dribbled off the horse's muzzle as Eli turned him back to the main street. He stepped out of the saddle, tied the roan off to a rail and then walked across the dusty street to the double front doors of the new gambling hall.

He entered the building and quickly looked over the room that consisted of four plain walls and a ceiling. Several men were in the room sitting at tables playing cards or standing at the bar, they were men that obviously lived with their guns. He didn't see Cramer among them. He made his way to the bar where the barman met him. Eli nodded toward him, "This is new since I last came through, used to be a brewery."

"Henry Schwenk bought it a short time back. Changed it into what you see here. Men are calling it Schwenks, or Swinks if it suits them. What'll you have?'

"Beer."

The barman filled a glass and swiped the foam off the top with a table knife. He set it on the bar, "That's ten cents."

Eli dropped a coin on the bar. "I'm looking for a man name of Milt Cramer, know him?"

The barman looked uneasy. "Mister, I've got a wife and three kids I'm trying to feed. I keep my nose out of other folk's affairs. With the war going on around here men are getting shot for no good reason and I don't aim to be one of them. I just pour the drinks. I don't know or see anything. I think you see my position."

Eli studied the man for a few seconds. It was clear the barman was being honest with him and not trying to be smart. He was scared and had good reason to be. "Sure, I get it. Sorry, I asked." He downed the beer and walked out.

Pulling the roan's reins loose, he led him down the street to Lambert's, tied him off, and wandered in. He stood inside and looked over the men occupying the room. There was a range of men from freighters to hired guns all minding their own business. Tensions were at an exploding point in the county and the least slight or insult was going to result in guns drawn and men dying. Everyone was being careful with his neighbor to avoid trouble. Only a fool would start shooting off his mouth in a room like this.

He walked up to the bar and asked for a cup of coffee from the barman. The man poured a cup and left it on the bar without looking at him. He walked back to the end of the bar where he kept a watchful eye on the crowd; he was no greenhorn and knew what he was looking for. He noticed the man kept returning to a position at the end of the bar where he probably had a sawed-off shotgun under it, a weapon that would quiet down a fight in quick order.

The room was full and the bar elbow-to-elbow as Eli stood with his left side to it and watched the doorway into the room. He felt someone push into the bar behind him, the man who had been standing there began to object and then quickly turned quiet. Eli turned his back to the bar in time to see the man scurrying out the door. He looked to where the man had been standing to see Clay Allison standing there ordering a whiskey.

Without looking at him Allison said, "Kill anyone

lately, Warren?"

"About as many as you have."

Allison grinned, "That many huh? What brings you around, as if I had to ask?"

Eli looked at him, "Hear all kinds of stories about this place, preachers being bushwhacked, homes burned, folks shooting each other, outlaws with prices on their heads."

Allison tossed a glance at him. "Sides are lining up, gunmen on both sides. It's a good place to walk soft or choose a side." He tossed down his drink and gestured for another.

"I'm on my own side and I rarely walk soft."

Allison nodded and laughed under his breath, "About what I expected you to say. If you do decide to join a side just keep standing where you are now and you'll be on the right one."

"Hear tell you're leading the land owners."

"You heard right."

"What's the story on that lawman getting lynched?"

"Cruz Vega? Yeah, I heard about that. Seems the bunch that did it wore masks and no one knows who was responsible."

"Funny how that works."

"Yeah, funny. His uncle came in here accusing me of having done it. He tried that old 'fan your face with your hat' trick and pulled his gun on me when he did."

"I see you're still upright and breathing."

"I kicked the slats out my cradle the first time I ever saw that old trick. Two slugs, here and here," Allison pointed at two spots on his torso.

"I'm looking for a man name of Milt Cramer; he's on the *other* side."

"Yeah, I know who he is, used to run with Clyde and Mort Yeager. Their bodies were found up north of here some time back. Rumor had it a bounty hunter did 'em in."

"Can't be, a bounty hunter would have taken the

bodies with him."

Allison studied Eli's face, "Likely."

"You can't trust rumors you know. So, how about Cramer?"

"Cramer's partnered up with some Georgia goober name of Boxer. You can't miss him, he's got an eye that turns in like he'd been smacked up the side of the head with a shovel. They were with the Circle, but word has it they took the money to fight and then deserted. Those folks aren't too happy about that. Another word has it that the two of them have gone to robbing stages and travelers on the Trail."

"That's the word I've got."

Allison tossed down his drink. "Nice chattin' with you. If you change your mind look me up, we can always use another man that's good with a gun."

He watched Allison walk out the door looking neither right nor left. He was a man confident that no one would challenge him or block his path.

Eli finished the coffee and walked out of the saloon. It was growing dark as he stepped outside. Mounting up, he rode north out of town and into the hills where he would make his camp for the night. It was a long shot, but in the morning he would continue on up to the Yeager's old camp.

He put in a fireless, dry camp for the night and then resumed riding at dawn. He continued up into the hills out of the lowland cactus and into the pine. There was no trail to follow as he wound his way between the trees. The thick carpet of pine needles cushioned the footfalls of the horse as he kept a steady watch around him. He was hoping to find the two wanted men in the old camp; however, it was only a guess, they could be anywhere.

At the base of the hill where he had watched the Yeager camp before, he left the roan, pulled the Winchester from the scabbard, and worked his way up the hill. Nearing the top he lay down on his belly and crawled up to the crest. Peering over the top of the hill he looked down into the pine and aspen grove. There was no sign of activity. He wanted to see smoke from a campfire or horses, but the area was still. He lay there for another hour studying the area before deciding to go down into the grove and check it out.

Walking back down the hill, he mounted and rode around the hill and into the stand of white-trunked aspen. He kept the Winchester in his hand pointed forward, ready to use it if one of the men suddenly appeared. The grove was empty.

He began making a circle of the aspen grove, continually widening out making a spiral. There was nothing to show that the area was or had been used since the Yeagers. He frowned his displeasure, but acknowledged that it had been a long shot idea. He pondered on where to go next.

It was a big country, but men like Cramer had limited thinking. When they weren't committing some crime they tended to hang around a town. They wanted to eat without having to cook for themselves and at least one saloon where they could spend their stolen money on liquor, cards, and women. Cramer didn't strike him as the living in the woods kind except to hide out for a while.

A few years back he would have figured Cramer to hole up in Elizabethtown, but with their gold strike playing out the town was dying. It wasn't safe for Cramer or Boxer back in Cimarron if they had taken fighting money and deserted. Las Vegas was too far south. Jack Clovis had said they stuck up a stage near Trinidad which might indicate they were working to the north. They could head back for Trinidad thinking it was the safest place for them.

His best bet now was to follow the Santa Fe Trail back to Trinidad. He could talk to any stage drivers he met, they would know if there had been outlaw activity along their lines. He only needed one link to Cramer and he could take it from there. He needed a point to start from and if he kept his eyes and ears open Cramer would give it to him. He worked his way back to the Trail.

The next day he stopped at the Willow Springs watering hole for a rest. It was here the break he was looking for opened up to him. A stage was pulled off the Trail and stopped. The driver was intently working on a man lying out on the ground. The four passengers were out of the stage. Two women were crying while a male passenger spoke to them, apparently trying to comfort them. The second man sat on the ground looking shaken.

Eli rode up to the group. The women looked at him with frightened expressions. Their faces had tear trails tracking down through the dust on their faces. The man with them watched him suspiciously as he approached; he was wearing an empty holster on his hip.

The prone man was speaking while the driver held a blood soaked cloth against the man's chest under his shirt. Eli dismounted and walked up to them. The driver glanced up at him without comment.

Eli stood over them, "Is he going to be okay?"

The driver nodded, "I think so. He took a bullet through the collarbone and it went out the back of his shoulder. He's lost blood and hurting bad, but he should live."

"What happened?"

The driver jerked his head toward the Pass, "We got held up a ways back. They shot Mike here before he could get the shotgun on them. Took the mail pouch and some bank money, made the passengers get out and took what they had. I got Mike down here off the Trail to patch him up and then I intend to turn around and head back to Trinidad and get him to the doctor."

"Who robbed you, did you recognize them?"

He looked up at Eli, "I did that, they robbed me once before. It was that son-of-a . . ." he cast a quick glance at the women. "That skunk Milt Cramer and that cock-eyed partner of his. It was the cock-eyed one who shot Mike."

"Tell me exactly where it happened."

The driver glared at Eli, "You're sure nosy, are you a lawman or something?"

"Or something. I'm hunting Cramer and Boxer let's put it that way."

"Bounty hunter then. Well, I don't care what you do as long as you get that son…," he looked at the women again. "As long as someone puts an end to them. I hope you kill 'em both."

"So, where was it?"

"Half mile back, just before you start up the next hill. We had barely leveled out when they stopped us. They headed off to the west."

Eli turned back to his horse. "I hope your friend pulls through okay."

He mounted and moved the roan out onto the Trail. Whatever trail Cramer and his partner left it would be smoking hot and they'd be running their horses. This was the chance he had hoped for. He was sorry for the folks on the stage, and especially for Mike, but he'd take his breaks anyway he could get them.

The tracks from the stage were the last wagon tracks on the Trail. He kept one eye on the ground and the other to either side of the roadway. As the Trail began to rise up he found where the stage had been stopped with the stationary hoof prints of the harnessed horses in the dust where they had stood. Horseshoe tracks moved around the stopped stage and then a mix of the passenger's shoe tracks were beside the wheel tracks. Two sets of horseshoe tracks led off to the west, the horses were running hard and churning up chunks of dirt and digging deep into the ground.

He knew they would run for a short ways and then begin slowing down when they felt safe from any pursuit. At some point they would stop to go through the bags and lighten their load by tossing aside what they didn't want. He pulled the Winchester and followed keeping the roan at a walk. He stayed on the deeply dug tracks while watching the country around him and listening for any sounds that might belong to the robbers.

He was a quarter of an hour on their trail when the robber's horses were brought down to a walk. The tracks continued moving into the hills. Another ten minutes and he spotted the mail pouch on the ground alongside the tracks. The horses had been stopped and boot tracks were on the ground. He stayed in the saddle and looked the area over.

Letters were scattered in a circle where they had been pulled out of the pouch and thrown. The bank bag was a few feet away; it was open and looked flattened, as it would be if the money had been removed from it. A woman's traveling hand bag was turned inside out and lying opposite the bank bag, the contents strewn about. A second hand bag lay close to it in similar condition.

Tapping the roan with his heels he moved on past the spot. The tracks continued on at a casual walk. The two outlaws were confident their escape had been successful and no longer felt the need to hurry.

Another hour passed as the trail continued its plodding pace, and then Eli picked up the smell of wood smoke on the breeze. He pulled the roan up and listened.

The breeze was building into a steady wind that swayed the pine tops and rattled the leaves and branches. A weak branch broke loose from high in a pine and tumbled to the ground hitting other branches along the way. He glanced up into the sky as wisps of gray cloud began to take over the blue autumn sky. It was shaping up to rain. He knew late October storms could blow in cold and hard with thunder, lightning, rain and hail. He needed to get on the two outlaws fast or they would escape into the storm that would wash out their trail.

The sound of metal clanking on metal drifted to him at the same time a renewed charge of wood smoke blew through the trees. Dismounting he led his horse and moved in the direction of the sound and smoke smell while staying on the horse tracks. There was definitely a camp ahead.

Moving slowly, he let the layer of pine needles cushion his and the roan's footsteps while being cautious not to step on dry branches. The wind rattling the leaves and branches would help cover his approach. Keeping tree trunks between him and where he believed the unseen camp to be, he kept his eyes and head moving in all directions.

Another clank of metal and then the sound of laughter came through the trees. He knelt down on the ground and peered between the tree trunks hoping to see a movement. He saw nothing. Lying down on his belly he looked at ground level in the direction the horse tracks led. He spotted a flicker of flame and a puff of smoke. A man's boots moved between him and the fire a good fifty yards ahead. Tying the roan to an aspen sapling he moved off to his right and began making his way toward the camp.

Closing the distance to thirty yards, he lay on his belly and studied the camp. They had a coffee pot on the fire with steam spewing out the pour spout. Boxer was sitting cross-legged with the fire in front of him. Cramer was standing across the fire from him; he took a long pull from a liquor bottle and handed it across the fire to Boxer who took a drink as well. He handed the bottle back.

Eli liked what he saw, they were lazing around and half drunk. The last thing in the world they would expect to see was him walking into their camp. Between the liquor and their nonchalance he had the advantage. Shifting up to a squatting position he studied the camp for another minute. Boxer was to his right, Cramer on his left. Standing upright he thumbed back the hammer on the Winchester and moved swiftly into their camp.

He was all the way to the fire before the outlaws' liquor-fogged brains realized he was there. He leveled the rifle on Cramer's belly. "Didn't I tell you to get out of New

Mexico?"

Cramer gaped at him not believing what he saw. Boxer was less stupefied as his right hand slid swiftly under the bedroll beside him and came out with a long Arkansas Toothpick. As he cocked his arm back to throw the knife sidearm, Eli took a quick step forward and kicked the steaming coffee pot into Boxer's lap. The boiling hot contents flew over and between his legs. With a scream of pain he dropped the knife and grabbed at his legs rolling away from the fire.

"That was stupid," Eli growled at him.

Recovering from his shock Cramer lunged at Eli, his hands stretched out in front of him. Eli came down hard across Cramer's outstretched hands with the rifle barrel. As the barrel slammed down across the incoming hands he heard bones break. He followed the downward stroke by swinging the rifle's stock up and smacking him soundly in the face. Cramer fell to the ground with a cry of pain.

Eli stepped back to survey the damage. Boxer was rolling on the ground whimpering as the steam rolled off his pants. Cramer was lying on his side holding his oddly bent right wrist with blood trickling from a gash on his rapidly swelling chin.

Moving toward Boxer, Eli picked up the knife and threw it into the woods. He then unbuckled and stripped the gunbelt and holstered pistol from the outlaw and threw them out with the knife. He then walked around the fire to Cramer and pulled the pistol from his holster and threw it into a cluster of bushes.

Cramer came to his knees clutching his broken wrist, his face twisted in pain. "There was no call for that," he moaned.

"There was no call for him trying to knife me or you jumping at me either. I could have shot you both from the trees, but I was going to give you a fair chance to surrender peaceably. The warrant says dead or alive, and dead's a lot easier for me, so consider yourselves fortunate."

Cramer curled back his upper lip and snarled, "Someday I'll kill you for this Warren."

"Oh my, now I'm really scared." He planted his boot sole against Cramer's chest and shoved him backwards, causing him to twist and fall with a yelp of pain. "You're not in much of a position to be making threats." Eli reached down and ripped Cramer's boots off and tossed them into the fire.

"Hey, what do you think you're doing?"

"You'll be tied on your horse and won't need them. Now, sit there and shut your mouth before I make my job a lot easier by putting a bullet in your stupid head."

He walked over to Boxer and toed him with his boot. "Hey, take your boots off and throw them in the fire."

Boxer glared at him with all the hate he could muster. "No."

"Take them off or I'll burn them off with your feet still in them."

"You're a cruel man."

"Tell that to Mike, he'll have a crippled arm for life. Here let me shed a tear for you. Now, take them off or I'll burn them off."

Boxer leaned forward and pulled his boots off and lay back again wincing in pain. Eli kicked them into the fire.

Eli walked over to where their horses were tied. He checked the saddlebags and found three bundles of bills from the bank bag. Some jewelry, along with coins and bills from the passengers lay loose in the bags.

Cramer called out to him, "Why don't you keep that Warren and pretend like you never saw us. It's a lot more than the five hundred you'll get for us."

Eli ignored him as he continued his search. In one saddlebag he found a loaded pistol, probably the one that belonged to the passenger's empty holster, he threw it into the brush. He shucked the rifles out of each scabbard and threw them into the bushes as well. Satisfied that there were no more hidden weapons he pulled the horses loose and walked them over to where the outlaws were on the ground.

He pulled the cinches tight. "Mount up, it's a good seven hour ride back to Trinidad and I want to get started before this storm hits."

Cramer got to his feet and struggled to mount his horse while holding the broken wrist to his chest. Eli walked up to him and tied his good hand to the saddle horn and his broken arm against his body. He then pulled the end of the rope that bound his hand to the horn up and around his neck and pulled it down snug to the saddlehorn. "There, now don't run off."

Cramer growled, "This hurts."

"Tough, the life of a murdering outlaw isn't supposed to be a tea party."

He then ordered Boxer to mount. "I'm burned all the way up. How can I set a saddle?"

"Ride vertical or horizontal, pick one fast."

Forcing himself off the ground, the outlaw walked stiff-legged to the horse and then stood there trying to figure out how to mount with the least amount of pain. "I can't bend my legs enough to toe the stirrup."

Eli led the horse alongside the log Jethro had been leaning on. "Get on the log and then on the horse. Get funny and you're a dead man."

Boxer crawled up on the log and then pushed his leg over the horse and landed in the saddle with a hiss of pain escaping his lips. Eli looked up at him, "If you hadn't pulled that toothpick on me you wouldn't be in this fix."

"Can't fault a man for trying."

"Sure I can."

Eli tied Boxer's hands to the saddlehorn and tied a rope around his neck and through the saddle gullet. He led the horse up behind the one Cramer sat on and tied the reins of Boxer's horse to its tail. Eli kicked dirt over the fire and led Cramer's horse to where his was tied.

Mounting he led them out toward the Santa Fe Trail.

It was afternoon when they broke out onto the Trail and headed north. The unusual parade drew attention as they passed. Western men recognized what it was about and nodded with approval. An immigrant family in a wagon passed them. The man driving gaped in disbelief, his wife put her hands over her mouth in shock, and their children stared wide eyed.

One curious boy shouted out from a wagon, "Hey mister, are you going to hang them?" His mother quickly shushed him warning him not to talk to men that looked like that.

Eli looked at the boy as they passed. "No son, the law will do that."

The first drops of rain splattered down on the dusty road as Eli swung the horses onto Wooten's toll road. The old man met him at the toll gate. He stood in the rain and looked over Eli's prisoners. "Ugly collection you've got there Eli." He walked beside the horses and looked up into the face of each man. "Milt Cramer and Jethro Boxer, now there's a pair of sage rats to draw to. Taking them to Trinidad I presume?"

Eli took the opportunity to slip into his rain slicker. "They're a present for Jack Clovis."

Wooten chuckled through his bushy beard, "I like the way you've got 'em trussed up like that. You know if you was to tie a red ribbon around them they would indeed make a first rate Christmas present for Marshal Jack."

"They would at that. Got a red ribbon?"

Sorry, fresh out."

"Well, then I'll just deliver them with plain old hemp ribbons."

Wooten waved them on, "No charge for a civic minded individual such as yourself, Eli, keeping our fair country free from vermin and riff-raff. Tell that old wolf skinner John that I said hello."

Eli nodded, "I'll do that. You take care now."

"Watch your top knot, son."

Eli rode on as the rain pounded down harder. It was growing dark and he didn't want to be on the road any longer than he had to at night, but he was close enough to Trinidad to go on in.

Cramer shouted out in a hoarse voice, "Hey, what about me getting a slicker?"

Eli looked back at him, "You're going to get wet. Probably be the first bath you've had all year." Cramer grumbled and cursed under his breath.

Boxer remained silent. He rode with his eyes closed and bearing an expression that revealed his pain.

The sound of a rider moving up fast behind him caused Eli to turn around. He shoved his hand under the slicker and gripped the butt of the Remington. The rider, buried in a slicker and a hat pulled down tight over his ears, galloped on past. The rider did not look up as he blasted on by.

The lights of Trinidad were visible as Eli topped out over the hill above the Purgatoire River. He stopped the horses for several minutes to let them rest. Moving them out again he came to the bridge spanning the river. Halfway across he saw a mounted man waiting on the other side of the bridge. The man was silhouetted mid-trail and not moving. Eli pulled the Remington, holding it under his slicker.

He crossed the bridge stopping ten feet from the mounted man. The rain was driving down pouring off the front of his hat brim and blowing in his eyes making it hard to identify the man who sat on the horse in front of him. Eli shouted out, "If you're looking for trouble friend you've found it. I suggest you get out of my way."

The horse and rider moved forward until the horses' heads were even. It was then Eli recognized Jack Clovis' face sticking out from his scrunched down hat and pulled up slicker collar. "Hear tell you're bringing me a present."

"How did you know?"

"Rider came in with the message a while ago."

Eli grinned thinking that Wooten had given the message to the rider that passed them. "What we got here is one Milt Cramer and one Jethro Boxer, a little worse for wear, but breathing and ready for trial. They both need a doctor."

Jack glanced at the half drowned men mounted behind Eli. "Good."

Eli shouted through the rain, "They robbed another stage down by Willow Springs. Boxer here shot the shotgun guard, fellow name of Mike. He was looking pretty rough when I saw him, but the driver was going to get him back here to a doctor."

"He did. Mike's my brother."

"How's he doing?"

"Busted shoulder, lost blood, but it looks like he'll pull through."

Jack moved his horse up beside Cramer who was soaked and shivering. He shouted at Cramer, "Cramer, one of those stages you clowns robbed had Judge Jenkins' wife on it. She was pretty frightened over the whole affair and took ill, and you stole her heirloom family brooch to boot. Judge is mighty anxious to see you in his court. And you Boxer, we got a couple of witnesses that say it was you murdered that stage guard, and now you shot my brother. It'll be a rope for you and I will personally be happy to put it around your accursed neck."

"Come on up to the office Eli, we'll throw these two drowned rats in a cell and I'll sign the paperwork for you to collect the reward. There's a fire going and coffee on, the café's got hot food and the hotel has a bed waiting for you."

"Sounds pretty nice."

Jack laughed, "I told Judge Jenkins that you were coming in with these two and he said that a hot meal and a bed would be arranged for you on his bill. He was almighty grateful."

Eli grinned with the rain running down his face. "Some days it just pays to get up in the morning."

Chapter 12

The trial for Cramer and Boxer took place two weeks after the arrest and lasted a single day. Mike Clovis, with his arm and shoulder bandaged, gave his testimony. The witnesses to Boxer's murdering the stage guard from the previous robbery also gave theirs.

Eli was summoned to appear. He let Rob come with him on his return to Trinidad for the trial. Eli's testimony was the last to be heard against the two outlaws. The jury returned a quick guilty verdict to Judge Jenkins' approving smile. He sentenced Cramer to ten years at hard labor for robbery and accessory to murder, and Boxer to the gallows for murder.

Over the winter and into the next year Eli continued to seek out information in regards to Jude Parson and his gang. To his frustration nothing had been heard of them. It was as if they had fallen off the earth or quit the outlaw business, however, the reward for their capture dead or alive remained in force.

Eli and Rob spent a good portion of the summer searching for the gang. Dodger had heard nothing and believed they had retired with their wealth. No one in Dodge City had seen them, nor was there any barber shop or saloon talk about them anywhere they asked. It seemed they had reached a dead end in regards to the gang.

Now sixteen years old, Rob wore his Colt whenever he chose to. He had mastered the gun both in shooting and fast draw. Eli had seen few to match Rob's proficiency with the weapon, especially at his age. He was not only fast, but deadly accurate with a cool-headed attitude that accompanied his actions.

In the course of their hunt Eli and Rob worked their way up to Hays to visit William and his family. Rob and Carrie were now comfortable in each other's company and shared jokes and easy conversation. They took long rides together and it was clear that they were growing close. William and Lillian both had hinted that the two were a good match.

Returning through Boggsville after months of being away it was clear to Eli that the town was a shadow of its former self. Las Animas City had taken the county seat and it showed in the empty businesses that had moved to the city a few miles north. The sheriff's office was a vacant building.

Reaching John's store Eli was surprised to see three wagons stopped in front. Men were carrying supplies out of the store and loading two of the wagons.

Eli glanced at Rob, "What do you make of all this?"

"Business seems good for Uncle John."

They stepped off their horses and walked into the store. One of the men at the counter talking to John was Cliff Adams. Eli and Rob walked up to the counter and greeted Cliff with handshakes.

Eli looked at John, "What's going on here? You giving things away for free?"

John grinned, "What was bad for Boggsville was good for John Warren. The farmers and ranchers are coming here for their supplies rather than go the extra distance to Las Animas."

"Have you seen the town?" Cliff asked.

Eli nodded, "We just rode through it, looks like a ghost town."

"Almost is, but that's pretty common out in this country. One day you have a boom town, the next you have wind blowing through the empty buildings."

"Nothing lasts forever I guess."

Cliff grinned, "Some things do, like cattle."

"You're doing well then?"

"Great, in fact." Cliff looked at Rob. "I've got a good hired man, a Texas cowboy, but I could use an extra hand once in a while like for drives and that, interested?"

Rob glanced at John.

"Go ahead," John replied. "You could use a few dollars now and again I suspect."

Rob smiled and looked back at Cliff. "You hired yourself a man."

"Good. Come out in the morning, I've got a few days' worth of work I need help with."

"I'll be there."

Cliff finished his business and headed back home in his wagon.

The next three days Rob stayed with Cliff working the ranch. While he was away a letter was dropped off at the store for Eli. It was from the Bank Manager of the Las Animas bank. The letter explained that a prisoner, who was the arrested survivor of a foiled bank robbery attempt by two men, had knocked out a jailer and made off into the night on a stolen horse. The bank man was unhappy with the Sheriff's poor security and personally offered Eli one hundred dollars if he would bring the escaped prisoner in.

The next day Rob returned home. Eli handed him the letter and remained silent watching for Rob's reaction.

Rob finished the letter and looked up at Eli, "Are you going to do it."

"No, we are going to do it."

Rob grinned, "Let's go."

The next morning they rode to Las Animas City. They met with the bank manager who was elated that Eli had accepted his offer. He wanted the man behind bars not running loose. No outlaw was going to try and rob his bank and get off scot free. He wanted to serve an example to all other robbers to stay out of his bank.

They next went to the sheriff who refused to talk to them. Eli shrugged at the sheriff's refusal to help and they walked out of his office. Outside the office one of the deputies and a couple of men who had been with the search posse approached them. The group gave them what they knew. The prisoner's name was Art Johnson. He had knocked out the deputy on night guard and took his revolver. Johnson then rode out on a stolen chestnut mare. They admitted they were not trackers and had lost all trace of the prisoner.

The owner of the horse was among them and wanted Johnson hung for a horse thief if nothing else. He kept the horse in a rented stable and took Eli and Rob to it where they could get a look at the chestnut's tracks. The horse had been newly shod leaving detailed tracks in the dirt.

Eli studied the location of the jail and the stable. Picking the likeliest direction Johnson would flee they rode out and began to cast back and forth searching for the Chestnut's tracks. Once they had moved out away from the town where there were fewer trails to cause confusion Rob picked up the chestnut's tracks.

The tracks were dug in indicating Johnson was holding the horse to a gallop. The churned up dirt made for an easy trail to follow. A mile out and Johnson had brought the horse down to a walk. They stayed on the escaped man's trail and followed it into the low hills.

The trail led to an abandoned shack in a low spot between the hills. There was smoke coming from the shack's stovepipe. Keeping a safe distance they rode around the shack checking it out from all sides. A saddled chestnut horse stood alone in a small corral behind the shack. It all added up to their man being in the shack. Eli was reminded of Smith and Monk holding up in a similar shack.

Eli explained to Rob that there was a chance the

person in the shack was not their escaped prisoner. It could very well be someone who rode a chestnut horse that just happened by and decided to settle in, but the fact that the trail they had been following led right to the corral with a chestnut horse in it matching the description of the stolen horse pretty much cinched it.

Still, they had to be sure before they did any shooting. Western men didn't care how many outlaws were gunned down, but they wouldn't tolerate the shooting of an innocent man. Such a reckless act would put a rope around their necks. Any man who felt that he was under attack by two armed strangers was likely to start his own shooting thinking he was defending himself so they had to be sure.

They positioned themselves on a hill looking down at the shack. Eli stretched the Sharps out in front of him and shouted down to the shack. "Art Johnson, come out of the shack with your hands up."

They watched and listened, but nothing happened. Then, the dirty cloth covering the window moved slightly as if someone was peeking out from behind it.

Eli shouted out again, "If you're not Art Johnson we don't want you, so if you're not say so now. If it's you Art, we know what you look like so don't play any games. I won't tell you again. Come out or we'll fill that shack full of holes and burn it down on top of what's left of you."

They waited a full two minutes with no answer. Eli whispered to Rob, "If it was someone other than Johnson they'd be out by now identifying themselves. So, my bet is it's Johnson in there. Now, this is what we call the 'get his attention shot.' " He put a .50 caliber bullet through the upper hinge of the door. The hard report echoed against the sand covered hills. The door jerked and swung down on the lower hinge.

Eli and Rob both kept their attention on the shack.

Another minute passed and Eli shouted out again, "Last chance, Art, that rotten shack can't hold up against this Sharps."

A voice shouted from inside the shack, "I give up, I'm coming out."

"Throw your gun out first. I want to see it hit the dirt out front there."

"I don't have a gun. They don't hand out guns when you escape jail."

Eli fired a second shot. ripping the lower door hinge out of the wall and dropping the door to the ground.

Johnson screamed out in a panicked voice, "I said I'm giving up, what are you doing?"

"I'm not playing this game with you, Johnson. You took the jailer's gun, now throw it out here or all bets are off and I just drill the next one through your chest." The pistol suddenly came flying out the door landing in the dirt with a thud and a puff of dust.

"Step on out here with your hands in the air and kneel down in front of the shack and not where your gun is either."

The man walked out with his hands high in the air and did as he was told. Eli got up and walked down the hill toward the kneeling man. Rob walked several feet to his left side leading their horses. Eli circled Johnson checking him for other weapons. There were none at his waist and he wore shoes rather than boots where no weapons could be hidden.

Eli gestured toward the corral, "Get up and head for that horse."

Eli slid the Sharps back in his saddle scabbard and pulled the Remington, pointing it at Johnson. The outlaw struggled to his feet while keeping his hands up. Eli and Rob followed him to the corral. Johnson walked forward repeatedly turning his head to look at the two men behind him as if expecting to be shot in the back.

Johnson entered the corral and pulled the cinch tight on the horse. He then reached for the trailing reins.

Eli stopped him. "I'll take care of that. Get on the horse and be quick about it."

Johnson mounted the horse and sat with his hands on the pommel. Eli spoke to Rob without taking his eyes off Johnson. "Get your gun on him while I cinch him down to his saddle." He could hear Rob's Colt slip out of the holster.

Eli tied Johnson to the saddle in his usual fashion. Once finished, Eli picked up the reins and handed them to Rob as he took the roan's reins from him.

Eli mounted the roan and then took the reins to Johnson's horse back from Rob watching Johnson while Rob mounted. "I'll lead his horse, you ride behind him. If he gets loose or tries anything shoot him."

Johnson flicked his eyes toward Rob moving his head as much as he could. He studied Rob's firm expression and wondered who this kid was. He seemed too young for this business although he had seen plenty his age packing and using guns. He concluded that the kid wasn't anyone he wanted to test.

They took Johnson directly to the bank to show the bank manager that his robber had been captured. The banker came outside and smiled. He walked back into the bank with a brisk step, disappearing for a minute. When he came back out he handed Eli one hundred dollars.

The banker walked alongside them as they made their way to the Sheriff's Office. He looked up at Eli, "I want to make sure that lame-brain sheriff doesn't lose him again. I'll be giving him a piece of my mind regarding the next election as well."

Leaving the prisoner with the sheriff, Eli and Rob left without a word as the lawman took a tongue lashing from the banker. As they rode side-by-side out of town, Eli reached into his pocket. He sorted through the bills the banker had given him. He handed some over to Rob. "Here's your half."

Rob stared at the bills and then shook his head. "You don't owe me anything, Eli. After everything you and John have done for me, you don't owe me a *thing*."

Eli continued to hold out the bills, "It doesn't work that way, Rob. You and I are partners, we share the risk and we share the reward. Now take it before I shove it down your throat."

Reluctantly Rob took the money. "Thanks, Eli."

"That was an easy one, real easy. We'll get into some tough ones and you will for sure earn your half."

Eli then changed the subject. "It was good to see William again. Seems like you and Carrie had a good visit."

Rob grinned, "Yeah."

Eli smiled to himself. There was something growing between Rob and Carrie, but he didn't want to push it. "How is it working for Cliff?"

"Good. I like him a lot and he's teaching me about cattle, him and Luther. I swear Luther knows everything about cattle."

"Is Luther the hand Cliff spoke of?"

Rob nodded, "Interesting man. Has a lot of Texas stories."

"I'll bet."

"Cliff's going to drive a small herd to the train at Las Animas next week."

"Are you going to work that?"

"I told him I would."

They rode in silence for a spell before Eli said, "I'd like to settle down and raise cattle one day."

"I'll go into with you," Rob was quick to volunteer.

Eli smiled, "I'd like that. All we need is money."

"The Parson Gang money would do that."

Eli nodded, "That it would."

The next week found Rob riding behind forty head of Cliff Adams' cattle along with Cliff and Luther. Luther had a lined, weather-toughened face, knowing dark eyes that danced with mischief, and hair that was streaking gray through the black. He had been up the Chisholm Trail twice, and the Goodnight Trail into Wyoming the year before he hired on with Cliff.

The cowboy had taken a liking to Rob, seeing a quality in him equal to the men he once rode with in Texas. He was quick to answer the young man's questions and lend him a hand along with instruction in a slow patient drawl.

Luther took it for granted that Rob could handle the Colt he wore. Where he came from fighting with fists or guns was commonplace and at Rob's age you were fit to do a man's work, a man's fighting, and expected to do so. Among his crowd in Texas men all wore guns and they could handle them, the ones that couldn't were dead. The fact that Rob packed a Colt and rode with Eli Warren said all that needed saying about the young man.

The drive to the rail yard at Las Animas City took only half a day. They moved the cattle into a holding pen while Cliff went into town to find the man he had set the sale up with. Luther stayed horseback as Rob dismounted to reset his saddle. Luther wiped his calloused hand over his mouth. "Feeling a might dry, Rob. Think I'll go rustle me up a beer. You wanna' come along?"

Rob shook his head, "Eli doesn't want me hanging out in saloons unless I'm looking to find someone. He wouldn't take it too well if I did."

Luther nodded, "Well, you listen up to Eli, he'll teach you right. As for me," he chuckled, "I'm too old and too set in my ways to know any better."

Rob looked up at him and smiled, "Go ahead, I'll hang around here and wait for Cliff to come back."

Luther reined his horse around and headed for the line of buildings. Rob left the cinch slightly loose to give his horse some breathing room and led him to a water tank for a drink. He was holding the reins watching the cattle in the pen when two men walked up to the pen and looked over the cattle. Both wore guns and Rob didn't care for the looks of them as he continued to quietly watch them.

One of the men turned his attention to Rob. He

poked the second man with his elbow, they spoke together while looking at Rob. They began to walk toward him. Rob dropped the horse's reins and slipped the loop off the hammer of the Colt as he watched them coming toward him.

The man who had first looked at Rob pointed back at the cattle, "Those your cattle, boy?"

Rob walked away from his horse leaving him at the tank. "Might be, depends on who's asking and why."

"Smart little whelp, ain't yah? Well, smart pup, those brands are all run over our brand."

Rob continued to watch the two men. "How do you figure that?"

"Because I know my brand and I know running iron work when I see it. So, pup, we'll be taking our cattle back."

Rob glanced at the cattle and then returned his attention to the men, his expression showing no concern. He had spent the last four years copying Eli's look and stance when confronted with trouble. "What's your brand?"

The two weren't expecting the question and had to think fast which, appeared to be a challenge for them. "Box R," one of them shouted out.

"Box R? How can you run a Circle CA over a Box R?"

"Doesn't matter how you done it, you done it and we're taking those cattle back."

"I don't think my boss would like that very much, but if you think you can do it, well you just go ahead and try."

"You threatenin' me, boy?"

"Are you planning on taking those cattle?"

"Sure am."

"Then, I'm threatening you. Open that gate at your own risk."

"Think you're some kinda tough packing that gun

around do yuh, boy?" The man took a step to the side of his partner. "Let's find out." He poised his hand over the butt of his pistol.

Rob moved his hand to the side of the Colt. He had made this draw ten thousand times, but never against a man. Now, he would find out if he was fast enough as there was no backing down from here. He held a cold steady look on the would-be cattle thief.

The man's eyes shifted right-to-left, he was taken aback by the fact this kid wasn't scared or even nervous. He shoved away the mental warning to back off, telling himself this was just some stupid kid showing off. His hand grabbed the butt of his pistol, he was a thief and blowhard, but not a gunfighter.

Rob's hand snapped onto the Colt's familiar hardwood handle and he drew it clean. His gun was up, hammer back, and level while the man was still struggling to get his gun clear of its holster. Rob pulled the trigger. The man staggered back, his shirt front turning wet and red; he fell backward into the dirt staring wildly at Rob.

Taking advantage of the distraction, the second man drew his gun. Rob shifted the Colt's bore to the right as he thumbed back the hammer and shot the second man. The man fell to his knees and then went face forward into the dirt, his hand holding the gun stretched out in front of him.

Rob stood in silence looking down at the two dead men. He suddenly felt cold and shaky. He heard a voice behind him say in a slow Texas drawl, "That would be a plum big mistake mister, a plum big mistake." Rob turned to see a man standing behind him with a pistol pointed at his back. Luther was on horseback behind the man with his own gun pointed at him.

Luther went on, "You just drop that hawgleg and get on your horse and ride. Your pals bought into a packet they couldn't handle, best you not try or you'll be the guest of honor at a three-way funeral."

The man dropped the gun in the dirt and turned to face Luther. "He killed my friends for no reason."

"Oh, he had reason enough," Luther broke into a grin showing his several missing teeth, "And boy howdy, did you ever see such a fast draw in your life? Did yuh?"

The man looked back at Rob, "No, can't say I ever did. Who is he?"

Luther casually waved his gun toward the man, "Why, that's Rob Slater . . . he's Eli Warren's pard, if that tells you anything."

The man turned back toward Luther and swore under his breath. "Kid's poison with that six-gun, ain't he?"

"He is that."

"Guess, I'll count myself fortunate and haul my freight out of here."

"A right fine decision mister, right fine."

"Can I pick up my gun?"

"Nah, you'd best leave it right where it is. Seems you need a new line of work that doesn't require a gun. So, I'm going to help you onto the straight and narrow way, as the Good Book says, and have you ride out of here without it. You'll thank me in your prayers."

The man grunted his dissatisfaction, cast a look at Rob and then mounted and rode away.

A crowd of men were coming from the saloons and other buildings on the row to see what the shooting was about. They stared at the bodies and then at Rob who had remembered to reload and holster his gun. They began to talk low back and forth.

The sheriff came up behind them, "What happened here?" He looked at Rob, "I know you, you're that kid that hangs with that no account bounty hunter. Born troublemaker. You're under arrest, kid."

Rob clenched his fists ready to fight; no one calling Eli 'no account' and he had no intention of being arresting for defending himself. He remembered this lawman getting his whipping from the bank president. It became clear to him that the sheriff was looking for revenge.

"I don't think so," Luther cut the sheriff off. "Rob was rightly defending himself, I saw the whole thing. So, if you want to call me a liar you best have at it."

The sheriff glared at Luther and saw a dangerous man who would not stand still for being insulted. If he questioned his word there would be more gunplay. He realized his error in not making inquiries first, before bad-mouthing the kid. He turned his attention back to Rob. "Okay, what happened?"

Rob pointed at the two dead men. "They came up saying we had run over their brands on the cattle. They said they were going to take them since the cattle were theirs and we had stolen them. We had words and then they tried to kill me. I defended myself like Luther said."

This wasn't what the sheriff wanted to hear. He was sore about his embarrassment regarding the escaped bank robber and wanted to arrest Rob in retaliation. He also knew if he tried to arrest him under these circumstances the town wouldn't stand for it and he would have more trouble than he could handle. He snapped angrily, "Whose cattle are those anyway?"

Cliff came up to the group with the buyer beside him. "They're mine."

The sheriff turned sharply around, his face drawn down in anger. He stared at Cliff, "Seems I've seen you someplace, too."

"I used to have your job when it was in Boggsville."

The sheriff seemed to deflate and looked uncomfortable as he took in the angry faces surrounding him. "Oh yeah, Cliff Adams."

Cliff nodded, "That's right, and Rob works for me, and those are most definitely my cattle. Now, what is this nonsense about arresting my man?"

One of the men in the growing crowd shouted out, "Them two's Marty and Matt Rust, nothing but stinking cattle thieves and all around coyotes. If the kid says they tried to steal his cattle I'd sure believe him over a Rust." A round of voices agreed with the speaker.

Another voice shouted out, "Why didn't you arrest *them* when they were rustling everyone's cattle, instead of hoorahin' this kid? The kid did us all a favor. Go on back to your office." A second round of agreeing voices followed his.

A third voice shouted out, "You arrest that kid and we'll not stand for it."

The sheriff looked around and then back at the bodies. He had to get out of this spot and fast. In a loud voice he announced, "That's the Rust brothers alright. I'll send the undertaker out here." He turned and walked quickly back to the line of buildings.

The crowd began to break up and drift away. Those who didn't know who Rob was were told that he was Eli Warren's partner.

Luther dismounted and walked up to Rob. "I looked back before I got to the saloon and saw those two looking over the cattle, so I says to myself, Luther, if those aren't two of the shadiest looking characters and herd cutters I ever seen in my life then I've never seen any, and son I've seen a few. So, I rode back and spotted that one coyote sneaking up behind you to get the drop on you."

Rob sat down on the edge of the water tank, the color was coming back to his face and he had stopped shaking. "I'm sure glad you did."

"That was some mighty nice shootin', Rob, but you gotta remember to next time turn around and take a look behind yuh. Don't get rattlesnake vision and only see what's to your front."

Rob nodded, "Thanks, I'll remember that."

Chapter 13

Word of Rob's gunfight spread fast. Men were talking about 'that Slater kid' who rides with Eli Warren. Few actually knew the story behind the pairing of Eli and Rob so rumors, speculations, and fabricated stories bounced wildly about. One version said they were father and son with father teaching the son how to kill men. Others said it was nephew and uncle, while more elaborate tales had them as brothers similar to the James and Younger brothers. Whichever idea was presented, they all agreed that Slater was a fast gun who learned his business from one of the most dangerous men in the West.

By the time Rob finished his day with Cliff the story had beaten him home. He walked into the store to hear a rancher telling of the gunfight. Eli and John turned their attention from the man to Rob.

The rancher pointed at him, "That's the young man right there." The man glanced back at Eli, "Apple doesn't fall far from the tree does it? Well, gotta get on back home before the wife thinks I've run off."

The man hurried out of the store casting a quick approving grin at Rob as he passed him going out the door.

Rob turned to Eli, "Apple doesn't fall far from the tree? What does that mean?"

"A lot of people are coming to believe you're my son."

Rob shrugged, "That's okay by me."

"I don't mind either so I let them believe it."

John walked out from behind the counter. "Let's shut this place down for the night. I've had a kettle of venison stew on the stove all afternoon, ought to be nice and thick by now. Also got the Dutch oven buried out back full of biscuits and another with an apple cobbler in. Traded a man some tobacco for apples he had. Think you can eat any of that Rob?"

"That sounds fine Uncle John; I'm hungry enough for all of it."

John closed the door and dropped the wooden bar across it. He then walked across the store and through the inside door to the living area to tend the supper.

Rob stood silently watching John go through the doorway. He addressed Eli without looking at him, "I take it you heard?"

Eli nodded, "News spreads fast on the Trail. That rancher was in Las Animas before here."

Rob remained silent for several seconds and then looked Eli in the face. "Does it ever get easier?"

"Killing a man?"

Rob nodded.

"It shouldn't, but sometimes it does. I've become calloused to it, maybe that's bad, but I have. I've never killed a man though where it wasn't me or him. The answer to that question depends on a lot of things that each man has to answer for himself."

"How many times have you done it?"

"I don't count. Only men sick in the head count. That cutting notches on your gun is a tinhorn trick meant to impress."

"Do you just detach yourself from the dead men?"

"I look on it as 'they tried to kill me. I lived they didn't.' I give them a chance to give up and if they choose to shoot it out then it's on their heads. But, yes, I keep my emotions out of the job."

Rob nodded his understanding.

"Tell me what happened today."

"Two men tried to steal Cliff's cattle by saying we had run his brand over theirs. It was just me at the pens, Cliff and Luther had gone into town. We had words over the fact they were trying to steal Cliff's cattle. One of them was playing the tough and drew on me; he was pretty clumsy at it. I outdrew him and shot him. His partner pulled his gun and I shot him too. A bunch of the town men came up to look and they said it was Marty and Matt Rust, two cattle rustlers."

Eli nodded, "I know of them."

"The sheriff wanted to arrest me, said I was a born troublemaker and that I hung around with that no account bounty hunter. He made me mad and I was about to tell him something when Luther stepped in and spoke up for me and the crowd did too. He didn't arrest me, didn't want to buck the town I guess."

"Don't let it make you mad, a lot of people hate me. I don't even give them a second thought. They believe bounty hunters are the bottom of the barrel, but that's all right, I'm not asking them for anything."

"He still made me mad though." Rob paused again.

"Don't argue with the law, it won't get you anywhere."

Rob nodded.

Eli studied Rob's drawn face, "I take it there's more bothering you than the obvious."

Rob kept silent for a few seconds longer before speaking, his expression pained. "I made a big mistake today."

Eli waited patiently for the story.

"Luther saved my life. A third man from that outfit had snuck up behind me and was going to shoot me in the back, but Luther showed up and got the drop on him. He made the man throw down his gun and ride off. That was scary knowing I was that close to being killed all because I was careless."

"There's no easy way to learn those kinds of lessons,

Rob. Eventually you will learn what to do and not to do, but you never stop learning. Sometimes you miss something or the situation turns against you and that's when having a fast hand to a gun or a friend like Luther behind you saves your bacon."

"I learned that one well enough. It won't happen again."

"A smart man doesn't make the same mistake twice, especially if it's the kind that can get him killed."

Eli could see Rob was still struggling with something that he wanted and needed to say, "You know Rob, when I'm struggling with something I find it best to come right out and say it and clear my mind."

Rob looked at Eli with a hint of embarrassment. "Does it make me weak to feel bad about killing those men today? Even though they were outlaws trying to steal Cliff's cattle and then they tried to kill me? I still feel that I did something bad."

"No, that's not weakness; it's your conscience trying to settle with the reality that you took the lives of two men. They gave you no choice but to defend yourself, they brought the fight to you, not you to them. Sure, you could have run away, but in this country if a man runs from a fight he'd better keep running because he will never live it down and it will dog him forever. The thing you have to hammer solidly into your head is these men were criminals who would have killed you in a heartbeat."

Rob considered what Eli said before speaking again. "They had no reason to come up and start trouble with me, did they? They lied so they could steal Cliff's cattle and then when I said I wasn't going to let them do that they tried to kill me."

"That's the way outlaws are. Did any of the men from town try to steal the cattle or kill you?"

"No."

"That's because decent, honest men don't do that, only outlaws live that way. If you hadn't fought back where would you be right now?"

"Buried."

"I rest my case."

Rob stared at the floor in thought. "I'm starting to see how criminals are different than regular folks. It explains why Jude Parson could murder my parents and not care about doing it. It was like stepping on a bug as far as he was concerned."

"Outlaws don't care what they do to others."

Rob considered that for several more seconds. "That helps me to see what happened today in a different light and to feel a lot different about it."

"Now, you don't want to go around shooting first and talking second. You do want to give an outlaw a chance to surrender and let a judge take care of his punishment. Rule number three, shooting is the last resort, but if it comes to that, do it."

"That's what I did today."

"And you're alive to come home."

"That and Luther watching my back."

"Don't forget that. Just because the threat in front of you is eliminated doesn't mean there isn't another behind you" Eli studied the young man for a long moment. "Are you going to be okay about this?"

Rob looked at him confused, "About what?"

"About being an outlaw hunter, is this something you want to do, or not? It won't change anything between us if you choose to follow a different path. John and I will help you with whatever you want to do."

Rob stared into Eli's face as he searched his feelings. "If men like us don't step in where the law can't go and stop these killers and robbers then they win. They will go on destroying lives. Killing good, decent parents and leaving their children orphaned to survive by eating scraps. I want to be one of those men who stops them. I want to ride with you, Eli."

Eli met Rob's eyes. "Then you will."

Chapter 14

May proved to be a warm beautiful month after a long cold winter. Cabin fever had settled on Eli and Rob in the frozen dark days even though Rob had worked occasionally for Cliff to break the monotony. Business in the store was brisk between snow storms and dead at other times.

Mail into Boggsville was hit-and-miss due to the storms. Bags of mail were sometimes lost in transit between stage runs. The train brought mail into growing Las Animas City, but fading Boggsville was dependent on the stage lines whose runs were weather dominated. Rob had sent a letter to Carrie before Christmas but never received a reply. He wondered if she had lost interest in him.

Rob and Eli were rebuilding a portion of the stable that had suffered damage during the winter. Rob was staring out to the east.

"What's on your mind?" Eli asked.

"I sent a letter to Carrie last winter and never got a reply. I wonder if she found someone she likes better than me."

Eli sat down on a grain bin. "I doubt it. Not judging by the way she was looking at you last summer. Besides, you can't count on mail in the winter. She might never have gotten the letter."

"I hadn't thought of that." Rob looked at Eli, "Can

we go see them?"

Eli glanced at the back of the cabin and store. "I think John can spare us for a few weeks. He did fine without us all last summer."

Rob's face lit up, "Tomorrow?"

"Let's get everything done here first and then we'll go."

Rob laughed, "Then why are you sitting around. We've got work to do."

Eli laughed in return, "Spring, when young men's hearts turn to love."

Across the Kansas grass Eli and Rob could see the roof of the Warren house. Rob's heart quickened at the thought of seeing Carrie again. Drawing closer they could see a woman in the yard; however, it wasn't Lillian. The woman was washing clothes in a tub of wash water.

Eli and Rob looked at each other. "Who's that?" Rob asked.

Eli slowly shook his head, "Maybe a friend?"

"Washing clothes?"

Looking out across the fields they could see the green blanket of growing wheat. A couple of beef cows grazed in the pasture beyond the wheat. Eli turned his attention back to the house, "Something is wrong here."

Both men were nervous as they rode into the yard. The woman pulled her hands out of the water and wiped them on her apron as she looked at them. Eli stared at her before speaking. He tipped his hat, "Ma'am, is Lillian here, or William?"

The woman looked at him confused, "I don't know a Lillian or William. I'm Sadie Abernathy and my husband, Joseph, is in the fields."

Rob squirmed nervously in the saddle, his expression filled with fear. He looked round wondering if they had the wrong farm. It was like one of the crazy dreams he sometimes had where everything is wrong, you're lost and you struggle to find the right place until you wake up. This wasn't a dream though.

The woman looked at Rob and then back to Eli, "Is there a problem?"

Eli ran his hand over his whiskered jaw as his eyes cast back and forth. "My brother and his wife and daughter had this farm. We were here last summer and all was well with them . . . now you're here and they're not."

The woman put her hand to her mouth, "Oh my, how awful. I can imagine how you feel."

"How long have you been here?"

"We came from Illinois and bought this farm from the bank in April. Winter wheat was in the ground and cattle on the land. We asked the banker why the previous owners had left everything. The banker, Mr. James, said they were evicted due to owing back taxes and the bank resold the property to us."

Rob broke in, "Where did they go?"

The woman shook her head, "I am sorry, I have no idea. The house was empty when we arrived. I wish I knew what to tell you."

They could see a man walking toward them from the nearest wheat field. His pace quickened as he drew nearer. He was covered in dirt and sweat with the look of a hard working farmer to him. He glanced at his wife who showed no alarm as he stopped in front of them. "Can we help you with something?"

"Oh, Joseph, they came here looking for the previous owners." She gestured toward Eli, "His brother and family."

Joseph looked from his wife up to Eli. "Sadie probably told you we bought this farm from the bank."

Eli nodded, "She did, but what I don't understand is this back taxes business."

"Mr. James said they had defaulted on taxes and lost the place."

"Meaning no disrespect to you or your wife, Mr.

Abernathy, but my brother was a lawyer from Richmond, Virginia; he didn't make mistakes like that. I'm sure you bought this property in good faith, but my brother never lost this place over taxes. I'm going to have a talk with this Mr. James at the bank. Something isn't right here and I intend to find out what it is."

Joseph looked uncomfortable. "I hope you don't think we had anything to do with your brother losing his farm. We are completely ignorant of the previous owners or their affairs. We only know what Mr. James told us."

Eli shook his head, "No sir, nothing like that. I think some dirty business has gone on here by this Mr. James and that my brother's family, and you folks, have been taken advantage of. I will be getting to the bottom of this business."

Eli tipped his hat to the woman and reined his horse around and headed toward Hays. Rob fell in beside him. "What happened Eli? I don't understand."

"I don't either, but something happened here and it had nothing to do with owing back taxes."

Rob wanted to ask more questions as his mind swirled with anxiety and confusion. He knew it was childish to keep hammering Eli with questions that he had no answers for. Eli would get those answers though, he was confident of that. What happened to the family, especially Carrie? Where was she? His head buzzed with questions that he feared the answers to.

They rode the rest of way into town without speaking. They pulled up in front of the bank and dismounted. Eli's face was set hard and angry as he pushed open the door and walked up to a young man standing behind the tellers' window bars. "I want to talk to Mr. James."

The young man stared at him. He was looking into the face of a very irate and frightening man. James had told him to allow no one to bother him, but he wasn't about to tell this man anything of the sort. He glanced at Rob standing behind Eli and saw the same look on his face. He knew the caliber of men who occupied his town and when they looked like these two, you didn't argue with them.

"Yes sir, I will let him know you wish to see him."

"I know he's in here so tell him that he'd better not pretend to be out or I'll kick down that wall and drag him through it."

Eli was loud enough to draw the attention of the customers in the bank. They glanced at him. A few completed their business and got out of the building while others lingered to see what was about to happen. The thin walls around James' office didn't block out the angry words. He met the young clerk at his office door.

James was skinny with a long neck holding up a balding head with beady eyes that reminded Eli of a weasel He was dressed in an expensive suit, vest, and tie with a gold watch chain crossing the vest from pocket-to-pocket. He had the look of a snake oil salesman or a banker who would foreclose on his own mother. He slinked around the teller area and stopped in front of Eli flashing a false smile. "Can I help you…mister…?"

"Mr. Eli Warren."

The customers who were leaving stopped at the name and turned back to watch. This man sounded like he might be looking to tear James into little pieces. The idea suited them, as few in Hays had any love or respect for Franklin James.

James' face fell at the name.

"Yes, I bet you do know that name. How about my brother, William Warren? You know that name too, don't you? Don't you dare pretend not too."

James swallowed making his protruding Adam's apple bounce against the stiff collar as he frantically searched for a lie or an excuse. He never expected someone to show up and question the issue of the Warren farm. He understood the family to be isolated with no relatives to speak of. He chose to take a tack showing he was in control. "Yes, I know William Warren."

"What did you do to them? What's this nonsense about back taxes?"

"I am sorry, Mr. Warren, but your brother fell behind in his taxes and the bank took the property back. It was all perfectly legal."

"That's a lie," Eli snapped in the man's face. "First off, your bank had no claim to the property, it was paid for free and clear. Second, my brother was a lawyer. He didn't make stupid mistakes like failing to pay his taxes. Now, tell me the truth or I'll twist your head off that scrawny turkey neck of yours."

The customers stood with amused expressions.

James stretched himself up trying to look impressive and important, but only succeeding in making himself look like a scarecrow. "I am sorry Mr. Warren if you do not care for that answer, but that is the truth of it. The state of Kansas seized the property for failure to pay land taxes and gave it over to my bank to process the sale of the farm." James then took on a smug expression, "And there is nothing anyone can do about it."

Eli glared at the smug face. "Where is my brother and his family?"

"I have no idea; they packed up and left the country."

"I'm going to do some checking. It will be easy enough to prove your story or prove you the liar I know you are. When I prove you to be a liar and a thief, I will be back."

"Is that a threat?"

Eli leaned into James' bony, smug face and snarled, "No, you mangy dog, it's a promise."

James shrank back as the smug expression was replaced by fear. Eli caught himself before he punched the banker. Turning hard on his heels, Eli stormed out the door with Rob behind him. "Let's go to the marshal's office. He'll know what happened I hope it's not the same man I ran into a few years back."

Mounting up they rode down to the Marshal's office.

Eli was pleased to see the marshal was a different man than the one who had threatened to arrest him for the gunfight years before. This man had a friendly air about him. He greeted them as they came in.

Eli spoke in a concerned, civil tone. "I am looking into the disappearance of my brother and his family. They had a farm north of here and now someone else has the farm. The new owners have no idea what became of my brother and his family."

The marshal gave him his full attention. "Which farm would that be and who has it now?"

"Some folks named Abernathy have it now."

"Yes, Joseph and Sadie Abernathy. Good folks, they moved onto the place a short time ago. It had been the Warren place before they bought it."

"Had been? So, what happened to William Warren and his family?"

"Your brother, you say?"

"Yes, and his wife and daughter."

"I'm sorry, but as I understand it, your brother and his wife died of cholera during the winter. I'm sorry to break the news to you like this."

Eli stood stunned at the news. He tried to form his next question, but could only stand dumbstruck.

Rob broke in, "What about Carrie? What about their daughter?"

"I wasn't all that familiar with the family. The sheriff dealt with the bodies and property. I don't get much opportunity to know the farmers who live away from town. Let me think though."

The Marshal hooked his fingers over his cleanly shaven chin and thought of everyone he knew in town or of anything he had heard regarding the Warrens. Then, he remembered the girl who came to live with the Wilsons. "Would she be a blonde haired girl about your age?"

"Yes."

"That might be the girl the Wilsons took in. They own a dry goods mercantile and she's been working in the store and staying with them. I see her there whenever I go in. I never asked about her as I figured it was a family member and there were reasons for her being there that were private. The Wilsons are good people though and I'm sure they have treated her well."

Eli found his voice. "That banker, James, said my brother lost the farm to back taxes and moved away. He was given the property to resell and sold it to the Abernathys. I knew that was a lie, but how *did* he get his hands on it?"

The Marshal's eyes snapped open wide, "He told you that? The liar. I'll tell you what, that man slithered out from under a rock. He must have latched onto the property when they died and made up that lie to cover his theft and to justify reselling it. All he needed was an accomplice in Topeka to write the fake tax order. James is the most hated man in Hays and has a lot of folks over a financial barrel so they are afraid to buck him. He's a manipulating scoundrel, but he has the connections to keep his thievery appearing legal."

"Doesn't that farm legally belong to their daughter now?"

"It should, but if James and his government friends made it look like they lost it to back taxes . . ."

"It would go to the government for sale," Eli completed the marshal's thought.

"No matter what the truth is, knowing James, he's tangled it up with so many strings that it could be fought out in court for years and she would still never get it. If I had known about it, I might have been able to block him, but now it's done."

Eli growled, "Not all robbers use a gun."

"No, we all know that."

"Where was the sheriff during all this?"

"His responsibility ended with recording the deaths

and contacting the undertaker. The state would have stepped in at that point and dealt with the property, taking it out of his hands."

Eli's scowl deepened, "I suppose he has better things to do than ride herd on a crooked banker."

"Do you want to fight for the farm in court?"

Eli shook his head, "I wouldn't want to take the place from the Abernathys. It's not their fault and they seem happy out there. Besides, you're right, if James has it tangled up and he has friends in the government we couldn't win anyway. Maybe I could just choke the life out of James to make myself feel better about it."

"Stand in line, a lot of folks around here would love to choke him to death. We have a new bank being built in town and we can only hope they run him out of business."

"I want to go get my niece. Where do I find the Wilson's store?"

The marshal gave them directions to the store. Eli thanked him and him and Rob walked out of the office. Eli was shook up by the sudden news of William and Lillian's deaths. He stood staring out into the prairie that surrounded the town. Rob remained silent; he had come to love the people as well.

Several minutes passed before Eli turned to Rob. "Let's go get our girl."

They followed the directions they had been given to the front of the store. It was a neat place, an example of the kind of people who ran it. Eli and Rob stepped into the store and looked around. On the far end of the room Carrie was sweeping the floor, her face downcast and her eyes sad. She looked up and directly into the eyes of her uncle.

Carrie's eyes opened wide with recognition. She dropped the broom and rushed to Eli, wrapping her arms tightly around him she burst into tears. "Uncle Eli, I have prayed every day you would come and find me." He wrapped his arms around her as she cried.

Rob stood by watching, his face reflecting relief at having found her while at the same time feeling heartsick for her loss. She lifted her tear streaked face and looked at Rob. Letting go of Eli, she turned and wrapped her arms around Rob, he returned her embrace pulling her tightly against his chest.

A man, in his sixties, gray haired, and slightly stooped appeared from the back room of the store and watched them. His wrinkled face reflected kindness. The man asked, "Is it safe to assume that you are Carrie's Uncle Eli?"

"Yes, we just got here and learned the news."

The man put out his hand, "Roy Wilson, terrible what happened to her family."

Eli took his hand, "Thank you for taking her in and helping her."

"It's the least we could do. She is a fine young lady and a pleasure to the missus and myself to have in our home."

Carrie let go of Rob and wiped her eyes with her hands. "I want to go with you, Uncle Eli."

"Sure, of course. Go ahead and get your things together and we'll go."

Carrie turned to Roy, "Thank you so much for taking me in and helping me and being so kind to me."

"It was our pleasure, dear one. We are very sorry for what happened to your folks and the farm."

Carrie smiled at him, sniffed and wiped her eyes, "I'll get my things." She walked across the room and disappeared through the door Roy had come through.

Roy waited until she was gone and then turned to Eli, "That skunk James, man's lower than a snake's belly in a wagon rut. Steal the farm out from under the child like that. If anyone needs a good horse whipping and to be run out of town on a rail, it's him. I complained to the sheriff about it, but he said there was nothing he could do about it as it was a tax issue. Bah, tax issue, truth is he didn't want to bother, scared to rock the boat."

"I talked to the Marshal," Eli told him. "He was sympathetic, but it was out of his hands. James pulled off the theft and got away with it and there's nothing the law can do now without lengthy and expensive court proceedings. Even then it would be fighting a stacked deck"

Roy shook his head, "Just a shame, a wretched shame. Carrie spoke often of you and hoped you would come one day and take her home with you."

"Well, we're here now."

Several minutes passed before Carrie came back out of the room carrying a carpet bag. She hugged Roy, "Thank you again. I already said goodbye to Mrs. Wilson."

Eli once again shook Roy's hand and thanked him. He turned to Carrie, "Do you still have Lightning?"

She shook her head sadly, "He was sold with the farm."

"Well, let's ride out there and get him back."

"How can we?"

Eli smiled, "I met the people out there, and they seem like nice folks. Once I explain it all to them, I'm sure they will be happy to return him to you."

"That would be wonderful. I have missed him."

Together they rode out to the farm with Carrie riding double with Eli. Carrie stayed on the horse and cried as she looked over what had once been her warm and happy home. She thought of the loving parents she had shared it with.

Eli explained the whole affair to the Abernathys who received the information with compassion and a feeling of guilt. Eli assured them it was not their fault. He only wanted Carrie's horse back.

Joseph Abernathy hurried to the barn while Mrs. Abernathy spoke consolingly to Carrie. Several minutes later Joseph returned leading the sorrel saddled with Carrie's saddle. Carrie mounted her horse, thanked them, and they left the farm without looking back.

That night they camped close to Hays as Eli didn't want to travel far that day. Just after dark, Eli told Rob and Carrie that he had some business in town that he had forgotten to take care of and for them to stay in the camp. He rode away into the night. Several hours later he returned saying nothing of the business he had attended to.

The next day news spread throughout Hays of how the hated banker James had been beaten to within an inch of his life. He had been to the doctor and left town immediately after leaving everything behind. No one knew the details or cared where he had gone as long as he was gone. Businessmen and farmers alike all gathered together in the saloons to cheer his departure and to toast the health of whoever it was that had did to James what they all wished they could have done.

The marshal sat in his office knowing full well that William Warren's brother was Eli Warren. It was easy to put together that Eli had paid the hated banker a visit and no doubt given him his marching orders. After what the man had done to his brother and surviving niece he didn't blame him. He would have done the same thing himself.

Fortunately, with James gone there was no victim and nothing to follow up on. The marshal grinned remembering what James liked to say, 'And there's nothing anyone can do about it.' What goes around comes around.

Chapter 15

The three riders were a solemn procession trudging across the windswept Kansas prairie. A veil of sadness hung over the group, reflected in their silence and melancholy mood. Eli struggled with the loss of the brother that he had recently found after so many years apart from him.

The thought of how Carrie had been cheated out of her inheritance made him angry. If not for the generosity of the Wilsons she would have ended up like Rob, only for a girl her age it was far more dangerous. She could have been lost to them forever. He did not regret the beating he had given James; it was something long overdue. His final word to the swindler was a promise to kill him if he ever saw his face again.

Rob watched Carrie, but said little to her. He was uncertain what to say, the wrong words could cause more pain but the right words could heal pain, as he had been learning firsthand from the day Eli had found him in Dodge. He felt stupid and useless, too young and inexperienced to know how to deal with such a situation.

It was the second night's camp when Carrie began to talk about the events that had unfolded beginning the past winter. She told how her parents had fallen ill. Her mother had died first and then two days later, her father. She was terrified and didn't know what to do. The only people she really knew in town were the Wilsons because they had traded so much at their store. She went to them and told them what happened. They contacted the sheriff who dealt with the deaths and arranged the funerals. She said the sheriff had paid her little mind and she never saw him again after that.

After the funeral, the Wilsons invited her to stay with them, but she wanted to go home so they let her. She spent the first night sitting up crying at the emptiness of her home. There was food in the house so she could eat, but wondered what she would do after it was gone.

One day James, the banker, came out to the house and gave her a paper that said she had to leave the house. She read the paper that said something about back taxes owed and the bank was going to sell the farm. She argued with the man that it was her home, but he said the law said otherwise and if she didn't leave he would have the sheriff throw her out. She didn't know what to do so she left and returned to the Wilsons.

Eli ground his teeth as he listened and wished he had killed James, but concluded that what he had given him was better.

"Why didn't you write and tell me?" Eli asked.

Carrie looked at him confused. "I did, twice. The first time was in the winter and when I didn't received an answer I thought perhaps the letter never made it through. So, I wrote again a month ago. Then you came to the store for me and I knew the letter had reached you."

"Carrie, neither letter got to me."

Carrie stared at him, "How did you know then?"

Rob answered, "I sent you a letter, but never got a reply so we thought to come up and see."

Tears welled up in Carrie's eyes, "I never got it."

Eli explained, "We rode up to see if everything was alright and found the Abernathys at the farm. We talked to the marshal and that's how we found out you were at the Wilsons."

Carrie stared at the fire in silence realizing that Eli and Rob had shown up only by chance. The thought of her never seeing them again caused her to shiver in spite of the warm air. She began to cry again.

Eli put his arm around her shoulder, "You won't ever be alone again, I promise."

After that night Carrie began to feel better and look to the future. She also gained a deeper understanding of what Rob had gone through losing his parents. At first she wasn't sure which was worse, having your parents die in front of you from sickness while you watched, powerless to save them or see them viciously murdered. She concluded that Rob's experience had definitely been the worst. From that day a close bond formed between them.

John was standing in front of the store as they rode up. He looked them over with questions in his eyes. He gathered from the description he had been given that the girl was Eli's niece Carrie, but what had happened?

They dismounted and Rob volunteered to take care of the horses. He led them around the building to the stable behind it. Eli stood with Carrie who nervously looked around. She then followed Rob without a word.

John watched her and then looked back at Eli. "What happened?"

Eli gave him a quick rundown on the events; he told of the deaths, about James stealing the farm, and their finding Carrie.

John scowled in anger, "I hope you did that banker in because I sure would have."

"I took care of him."

They spoke for several minutes before Rob and Carrie wandered back around to the front of the store to join Eli and John. John put his hand out to Carrie, "Welcome, young lady."

She gave him a nervous smile and shook his hand. "Thank you. I hope I won't be a bother."

"Of course not, we've always got room for one more. Can you cook?"

"Yes."

"Good, I can use the help. If I feed these two

gunslingers one more meal of venison and beans they're like to shoot me." He winked at her when he said it.

The lightness of his greeting and joke eased her nervousness and she laughed. "I will help you, Uncle John."

He laughed with her. "It'll be a pleasant addition to have a pretty face at the table for once, instead of always staring at these two homely galoots."

She laughed again. John was truly everything Eli and Rob had said about him. She felt at home and safe for the first time since last winter.

They all followed John inside and through the doorway to the living area. John looked the place over. "Not really set up for a young lady's privacy, but I'm sure we can figure out something."

"Oh, anything would be fine, Uncle John."

"Let's see, Rob go out back and fetch some nails and a hammer along with a length of rope. We'll make a wall over there by hanging blankets over a rope. Won't be fancy, but it'll work."

Rob went out and returned with the items John asked for. They drove some nails into the walls and ceiling and then tied a length of rope to them. Draping blankets over the rope, they used clothespins to hold the blankets in place.

John stepped back and smiled at the construction. "There you go honey, fit for a princess. Wait a minute, we need a bed in there, can't expect a young princess to sleep on the floor."

"That's okay," Carrie quickly interjected, "I can sleep on the floor."

"Nonsense, I won't hear of it."

Rob spoke up, "She can have my bed. We'll move it in there, I don't need it. I would just as soon sleep on my bedroll anyway."

"That's generous of you, son."

Carrie looked at him and smiled, "Thank you Rob,

that is very kind of you."

Rob's ears reddened as he smiled back at her. "Oh, it's nothing."

John and Eli exchanged glances and grinned at each other.

Two months passed with Carrie fitting in comfortably with the family group. She was laughing again and was putting the pain of the past behind her, however, she never let Eli or Rob get far from her. Mentally she clung to them as her only family, afraid to lose them.

She worked behind the counter at the store helping John. She and Rob often took rides together where he taught her tracking skills and other trail knowledge he had learned. She also accompanied Rob once out to work cattle for Cliff.

It was then that a freighter came up the Trail from Cimarron and Trinidad delivering supplies to the store. He had a message for Eli from Jack Clovis about a group of three men who were robbing banks, stagecoaches, and anyone they could find. They were also leaving a trail of dead men from Las Vegas to the Colorado line, but little was known about them. Jack figured Eli might be interested in looking into it since it was out of his jurisdiction and there was a twenty-five hundred dollar reward for the three of them.

At supper that night Eli asked Rob, "What do you think, should we go hunting for those three Jack was talking about?"

"Well yeah, that's what we do, isn't it?"

"I'm all for it, but I didn't want to make the decision for both of us."

Rob grinned, "Twenty-five hundred dollars!"

"Yeah, but it won't be easy. No one knows much about them. We'll have to track them down and that could take some time. I guarantee you they won't come along peacefully. Knowing how that goes there will be gunplay."

Still grinning, Rob said, "I didn't figure to hand them a rose and ask them to the dance."

Eli laughed, "There won't be any roses, that's for sure. We can figure to be gone for weeks to maybe a couple of months. We'll start in Trinidad and work our way down to Las Vegas."

"Fine by me, but can we take a packhorse this time with food and our gear?"

Eli grinned, "Can't live out of saddlebags for a couple of months?"

"We did that all last summer, I like to have starved to death."

"Okay, it would be better alright, but you get to lead it."

"Fair enough."

As they talked Carrie listened nervously, she didn't want to be separated from Eli, and especially not from Rob. She knew she had fallen in love with Rob but she also feared losing the two most important people in her life. She loved Uncle John, but he wasn't Eli or Rob. She feared they would disappear or die like her parents and she would never see him again.

She finally worked up the nerve to say what was on her mind. "I want to go with you."

The talk ceased as they all looked at her.

"No, that's not a good idea," Eli said gently.

Carrie looked at him, "Please. I want to go with you."

Eli looked into the girl's sad eyes. From the very first time she had drug him away from the table to see her horse he had not been able to say no to any request she made of him, but this was different. "Honey, this is going to be dangerous and rough. We'll be sleeping out every night in all kinds of weather and there will be endless hours in the saddle. It will not be easy."

"I understand that," she countered, "but I want to be . . ." She glanced quickly at Rob and then back to Eli, "I want to be with you. I can take whatever comes and you know I'm not a complainer."

Eli read the worry in her eyes and understood there was the fear of losing her family again. "I'm sorry Carrie, it's too dangerous."

"Please, Uncle Eli. We are family and we have all been on the trail and camping out together." Her soft blue eyes pleaded.

The blue eyes almost swayed him, but he held firm. "No, Carrie."

Rob reached out and placed his hand on Carrie's. "Eli is right, Carrie. We're hunting dangerous men. We will come back, I promise."

Tears welled up in Carrie's eyes. She bit her bottom lip and nodded.

John listened to the exchange and knew that Carrie feared losing Eli and Rob. "I could sure use your help around here honey. What with the business picking up and all, and my rheumatis making it hard for me to get around. I know being stuck with a grumpy old man isn't much fun."

Carrie smiled through her tears, "You're not grumpy, Uncle John."

A sly grin crossed Rob's face. "Actually, I think Carrie, you need to keep an eye on Uncle John, what with Sally Benoit spending so much time around here and all."

"Sally *has* been coming around a lot lately," Eli joined in. "Seems odd to me that a widow would be so forgetful that she has to come in three times a week because she forgot sugar or coffee or flour or . . ."

"Okay, you two," John snapped, "don't be reading anything into it. The store she used to buy at in Boggsville closed and I have the next closest one to her, that's all. Besides she only comes in once a week, sometimes twice."

Rob looked at Eli, "He's keeping count, you notice that?"

"I did notice that."

"Tracks seem pretty clear to me, how do they look to

you?"

"Fresh as buffalo prints in wet sand. Old timer, Sally's set her cap for you, best send up the white flag and surrender."

"I don't know about that."

Carrie stood up and put her arm around John's shoulders. "I think Sally and Uncle John would be a wonderful match."

John smiled at her, "You think so? I guess I do kind of take a shine to her."

Eli smiled, "Then tell her, you old bachelor bull."

"Don't crowd me, I'm only tossing the idea around, just thinking about it."

"Well, don't think too long." He then looked at Rob, "A good woman only comes along once in a lifetime, don't miss the chance when she's right in front of you."

John scowled at Eli, "Don't you have some getting ready to do, matchmaker?"

"Yes, we do." Eli stood up from the table. "Come on Rob, we need to get our gear together." The two walked out of the cabin to the stable.

The next morning Eli handed Rob some money. "I want you to go up to Las Animas and buy that packhorse. Get one that will handle a pack without going crazy, but can still be ridden if we need to."

Rob took the money and put it in his pocket. "I'll go right now."

Carrie was standing by watching, "Can I go with you, Rob?"

"Sure, come on, let's get the horses." They walked away toward the stable talking and laughing.

John stepped up beside Eli, "How long you think before them two tie the knot?"

"Sooner than later I'd say."

The two stood together talking until Rob and Carrie came out leading their horses across the corral that was connected to the stable.

They mounted up and waved to Eli and John. Eli called out, "You be careful up there."

Rob knew what Eli meant. "Yes sir, the carefulest man in the world." They turned the horses to the north and rode away from the place.

John's eyes were on the pair as they grew smaller in the distance. "She's afraid of losing you and Rob. You heard it in her voice as well as I did. She might try and follow you, not out of disobedience but out of fear you won't come back."

"Maybe I should take her along to keep an eye on her."

"No, but I think this needs to be your last job."

Eli nodded, "I think so,"

Coming into Las Animas, Carrie looked up and down the streets. "Rob, can we walk along the stores just for a minute so I can look in the windows . . . please?"

"Well okay, but just for a few minutes. We have to stick to business and get back."

They tied their horses to a rail at one end of the street and walked along the storefronts. Carrie excitedly peered through the windows and commented on the different things she saw. Rob stayed to her right side so his gun was free from obstruction. Carrie looked in the windows and Rob watched the men around them.

As they walked men looked at Rob and commented to each other. He noticed that he was getting a goodly amount of attention. He suspected it was in regards to the gunfight. In between studying the windows Carrie began to pick up on the comments and stares they were getting. She stopped and looked around. "Why are so many men staring at us?"

Rob grinned, "Probably because they've never seen such a pretty girl in their lives."

She smiled at him, but didn't accept the answer. They

continued on their walk.

They were coming up on a saloon where two rough looking men stood in front watching them. Rob could see that one of the men was especially eyeing Carrie. He kept making comments to the second man who did not reply. Rob sensed trouble and kept himself between them and Carrie. As they passed the men the one who had been talking leered at Carrie while Rob glared at him.

Moving on past them, Rob heard the one who had been leering say to his friend, "I like blondes, I want that girl." The man began to step toward their backs when the second man put a hand on his arm and stopped him. "Don't, that's Slater." The man stopped in his tracks and didn't follow further.

Carrie didn't look at Rob when she asked, "What did that man mean by, 'that's Slater?' "

Rob wasn't sure what to say, but knew he couldn't start life with the girl he loved by lying to her. "The last time I was up here I was helping Cliff and Luther drive some cattle to the rail yard. Two men tried to steal Cliff's cattle, I stopped them. They tried to draw guns on me and I . . . killed them both."

Carrie stopped and looked at him, "Two men at the same time?"

Rob nodded, wondering what she would think of that. "Yeah, I guess so."

"No wonder everyone's looking at you and talking." They resumed walking. "Rob, I saw how that man looked at me and heard what he said. I also saw how he stopped at your name. I know I will always be safe with you." She took hold of his left elbow with both of her hands as she walked alongside of him.

Rob stood a little taller and felt pride swell in his chest. He smiled at her, "And you always will be, I promise."

"I know I will be for the rest of my life," she said softly.

Rob smiled at her, "Done enough window looking yet? We got a horse to buy."

The horse reminded Carrie that Rob and Eli would be leaving in the morning. She studied the ground at her feet as they walked toward the livery. "I will miss you, Rob."

"I'll miss you too, but we'll be back."

Carrie nodded.

The loaded packhorse stood beside the saddled roan and bay in the early morning light. Carrie fought back the tears as she hugged Rob and then Eli goodbye. Her eyes reflected near panic at the thought of being parted from them. Both Eli and Rob reassured her they would return. They then mounted and rode away from the cabin. Rob turned and waved. Carrie waved back.

Carrie walked back into the cabin with John. "I don't feel so well Uncle John I think I want to sleep for a while."

John understood her feelings. "You go right ahead. I'm going to busy myself in the store. Some of the ranchers and farmers like to come in real early."

Carrie slept for a couple of hours and then ventured out into the store to help John. Along after noon Sally Benoit parked her buggy outside. She walked shyly into the store. The elderly woman had her gray hair pinned up and was wearing a nice dress with a cameo around her high buttoned collar. Carrie smiled and greeted her knowing she had come to see John evidenced by how nicely she was dressed.

John greeted her with a beaming smile. "Can you stay for a bit Mrs. Benoit and help me with these books?"

Sally smiled, "Certainly, Mr. Warren."

Carrie whispered to John, "I am still feeling a little ill, I would like to lie down again."

"You do that. I can handle the store and we will be doing some bookwork."

Carrie smiled and walked back into the living area.

She slipped in behind her blanket wall and sat on the bed thinking. Eli and Rob had been gone for hours now. Eli had said they were riding down the Trail headed first for Trinidad. She wondered how far they had gotten by now.

She was feeling the panic rise up in her knowing that Eli and Rob would disappear like her parents. She just had to be with them. The call of a familiar voice sounded in the store. It was one of the freighters John got his deliveries from. The man announced that he had a big load for John.

Carrie tiptoed across the cabin floor and peeked into the store. John and the freighter were busy bringing supplies in. Sally was sitting on a stool studying the account book. Carrie made up her mind. She quickly changed into her riding skirt and rolled some clothes and personal items into her blankets. She left a note on her bed telling John she had left to catch Eli and Rob and then slipped out the back door.

Hurrying to the stable she quickly saddled her horse, tied the bedroll over the cantle, and led him outside. She led the horse far enough away from the cabin to be out of hearing when she mounted and kicked the sorrel into a gallop down the Trail.

She knew that Trinidad lay on the Trail, all she needed to do was stay on it. Eli and Rob would go to Sheriff Clovis' office. As she rode she remembered what Rob had taught her about tracking. They had used their own horses' tracks for study. She looked at the dirt covered Trail and spotted the tracks to Rob's horse. If nothing else, she could follow those tracks.

John's legs and back were giving him spasms of pain when the last of the supplies were put away. He sat down by Sally and wiped a blue bandana across his forehead. "I must be getting old Mrs. Benoit."

"You worked very hard, you should be exhausted."

John shrugged, "A little. He turned his face toward the living area. "Carrie was feeling poorly, I should check on her." He stood up stiffly and limped across the store.

Entering the living area he didn't see Carrie and figured she was still sleeping behind her blanket wall. "Carrie," he said in a low voice, "are you okay in there?"

No answer sounded from the small area behind the blankets. He repeated the question with no answer. He hesitated opening the curtain and peeking in. It was improper and if she was in there, he would be deeply embarrassed.

He limped to the open doorway, "Mrs. Benoit, could I get your assistance please?"

Mrs. Benoit left her stool and walked to where John stood in the doorway.

John gestured toward the blanket wall, "Carrie's little room. I'm not getting an answer from her. Would you peek in there and see how she is?"

"The poor child, is she ill?"

"In a way. Eli and Rob left for New Mexico today and Carrie is very upset about being parted from them."

"I see," Mrs. Benoit answered, "a little bit of missing her young man."

"There's a lot more to it than that."

Taking the few necessary steps across the room, Mrs. Benoit parted the blankets slightly and peered in. She turned her head toward John, "She is not there."

"What!" John's voice sounded panicked. He pulled the blankets apart and stared at the stripped bed. Seeing the note he picked it up with growing apprehension. He read it and groaned.

"What does it say?"

John dropped his arm to his side and hung his head. "She went after Eli and Rob."

Mrs. Benoit put her hand over her mouth. "Oh my. She will not be safe alone."

"I need to go after her."

"Can you ride in your condition?"

"I'll ride alright. Could I trouble you to close up the

store for me?"

"Yes, I will take care of it. Go and find that child. It will be dark soon."

John headed out the back door for the stable.

Chapter 16

Carrie alternated between walking and galloping her horse to gain ground on Eli and Rob. They would be riding at a slow pace and she knew from the trip they made from Kansas that Eli liked to make his camps early so the horses could be grazed and then tied securely before nightfall. She was confident about finding them.

On occasion she could make out one of the tracks from Rob's horse mixed in with other tracks from horses and wagons. She had heard enough talk to know the Trail led right through Trinidad so there was no reason for them to leave it. Coming on a northbound stage stopped at the top of a long hill resting the horses she asked the driver if he had seen two men riding south.

The driver studied her with concern. "I see a lot of men ride past me. Should you be out alone like this?"

"I won't be when I find those I am looking for."

"What do they look like?'

She described Eli and Rob.

"I did pass a pair of riders like that about an hour ago."

"Thank you," Carrie said and then kicked her horse into a jog headed down the hill.

Eli pointed to a grove of trees a short way off the Trail with good grass for the horses. "We'll make camp there."

They reined off the Trail and into the trees where they broke down the pack and unsaddled the horses. Rob built a fire while Eli staked the horses out in the grass. He returned to the camp and gave Rob a hand with a meal.

Rob grinned as he sliced bacon, "I like that pack horse already."

"Getting soft in your old age? Prefer fried bacon over hard tack and dried beef?"

"If that's soft, then sign me up."

Standing up, Eli watched a freight wagon rolling slowly by. He recognized the driver was Jake. He called out him.

Jake turned to look at the man who had called him. Seeing it was Eli he waved.

"Come on into camp," Eli shouted to him.

Pulling up Jake called out, "Was looking for a camp spot for the night. This one looks as good as any, got good company and I can smell the coffee from here."

Eli gave Jake a hand unhitching the team and staking the horses out to graze. They made their way to the fire where the battered coffee pot was bubbling and spitting coffee out the spout. Rob had bacon and pan bread cooking. They poured cups of coffee and sat around the fire talking.

After they had finished the meal Jake walked over to check his wagon while still light enough to see. He looked back at the Trail and received a shock. He called back over his shoulder, "Eli, better get over here."

Eli looked at Jake and then to the Trail. He froze and then uttered, "Oh, no."

Rob turned around. "What is it?"

Eli pointed at the Trail. Rob narrowed his eyes against the setting sun looking to where Jake stood talking to a rider. "Uh, oh," he whispered.

Eli walked briskly toward Jake where he stood with Carrie, who was still mounted. Eli fought down his anger reminding himself that the girl had problems to overcome. Patience was needed here. "Carrie, what are you doing here?"

"I . . . I'm sorry I disobeyed." She began to cry.

Eli's heart softened to her. "Come on into camp. We'll have to decide what to do with you."

Rob stepped up beside Carrie and put his hand on her arm, "Don't cry, it'll be alright." He took ahold of the sorrel's bridle cheek strap and led the horse to the camp. Eli and Jake followed.

Carrie dismounted as Rob took the horse. Carrie hung her head not wanting to meet her uncle's eyes. "I was afraid to lose you." She wiped tears from her cheeks.

Eli put his hand on her shoulder, "Does Uncle John know you left?"

Carrie nodded, "I left him a note."

Eli looked at Jake, "Knowing John, he'll come looking for her."

Rob staked out Carrie's horse and returned to the fire. "Come on and sit Carrie, there's still food."

Carrie sat down and quickly ate the last of the bacon and bread.

"We'll have to take her back home," Eli said to Rob.

"I don't want to go back," Carrie said in a low voice. "I want to be with you."

"We talked about this Carrie," Eli began to raise his voice and then stopped.

Rob gestured for Eli to step away from the camp with him. They walked into the growing darkness out of hearing range. "Eli, if we take her back we lose two days."

"Then, we abandon the hunt."

"And let those outlaws continue their killing? I think Jack was counting on us to do this. Besides, we can use the reward money, we're all about broke."

Eli was silent as he debated the issue in his mind.

"Having her along shouldn't be a problem," Rob continued. "The land war is over, the hired guns are gone. We can set up camps and have her stay in them."

"How is leaving her in a camp supposed to keep her safe?"

"Give her the shotgun you stuck in the pack."

Eli scowled, "No, it's too dangerous for her to be with us."

"I know that and you know that," Rob lifted his chin toward Carrie who sat staring into the fire with a look of dejection. "She doesn't know that."

"Doesn't matter, she goes back."

"And how will you keep her there? It's plain she is determined to be with us."

"John will just have to keep her there."

"How? Lock her in? Chain her to her bed? She's scared of losing the only family she has. I know how she feels, Eli. For the first few months I was with you I was scared to death to lose sight of you. I believed if I did I would end up back on the orphan train. She's afraid to be back alone. I got over it, she will too, but not yet."

Eli stared in Rob's face.

"We need to keep her with us."

"No."

"She'll follow us again. We got real lucky this time with her finding us. Next time we might not be so lucky and something bad will happen to her. If she's with us at least we know where she is."

Eli inhaled and tightened his lips in a stern grimace. Then, he let out the pent up breath. "It's against my better judgment, but I have to agree you. She will do it again and next time who knows where she will end up."

Rob smiled at persuading Eli. "We have to get word to Uncle John that we have her. Do you think he'll keep riding until he finds her?"

"He'll ride until it's too dark to see. He knows it's futile to search in the dark and he will go back home. In the morning he will set out again."

Rob looked at the camp. "Jake will start out early, we can have him pass on the message to Uncle John."

"We can do that. Jake might meet him on the Trail and can turn him back."

Eli studied Carrie sitting forlornly at the fire. He loved the girl like his own daughter and understood the fears she harbored. He had promised William to protect her and right now the best way to do that was to keep her in sight. How they would manage the hunt would have to be ironed out one day to the next. They returned to the fire.

Carrie turned her face halfway up toward Eli and waited tentatively.

Eli hunkered down across the fire from her. "What will you do if I take you back home?"

"I don't want to go back. I want to be with you," she answered in a soft voice.

"You will follow us again won't you?"

Carrie only looked at him and gave no reply which, in itself was Eli's answer.

"Okay, you stay with us so we can keep an eye on you. You have to do everything I say though and no arguing, understand?"

Carrie smiled, "I promise I will."

Eli stood up and looked at Jake.

"I'll give John the message," Jake said anticipating the request. He then chuckled, "You expected less from a Warren?"

The three sat in Jack Clovis' new office drinking coffee and having a friendly visit. He had been elected Las Animas County Sheriff. His office was still in Trinidad, but two streets over from his old City Marshal's office.

Jack found it interesting that Eli's little family of orphans kept growing. It said something about the man, the one underneath the stories and reputation.

Jack leaned back in his chair holding the cup between his hands and got down to business. "When the reports about this gang arrived here I thought of you and sent up the message. Not much is known about them except they bounce across jurisdictions creating a legal tangle, but that has no effect on you. If anyone can shut these men down it's you. There are three men, they're being called the Bandit Band, and yes, I know it's a silly name, but no one knows who they are yet. They just popped up a couple months back and went on a crime rampage."

Jack put his cup down and looked up at the ceiling as he ticked off the band's crimes on his fingers. "Let's see, three stage holdups between Willow Springs and Cimarron, another above Las Vegas, their latest big robbery was a bank in Santa Fe. On top of that are at least a half dozen highwayman-style robberies against lone travelers scattered from Colorado to Las Vegas. Four men, to date, have been murdered in the robberies." He brought his gaze back to Eli, "And that's only the ones I know about from the reports."

Eli raised an eyebrow, "All this was in the last two months?"

Jack nodded, "Three actually, but yes, they're busy boys."

"Like beavers with guns. Have you seen any kind of a pattern in the crimes?"

"Witnesses report the men wore kerchief masks over the bottom halves of their faces, but the limited descriptions are all the same. That's how we know it's the same men. The three robbers all had dark skin, two had black hair, one had gray hair and appeared to be older than the other two. They had Spanish accents. Sounds like they're Mexicans, likely fresh up from Mexico."

"Who's putting up the reward money if no one knows who they are?"

"The affected stage lines, and the Santa Fe bank kicked in as well. In fact the bank is holding the money. The names might not be known, but the individuals should be identifiable by the witnesses once they are caught."

"True. A rag over the mouth doesn't hide all that much."

"We've gotten convictions on such testimony

before."

Eli thought over the information. "Sounds like Las Vegas would be a good starting point."

"Be careful, the law down there is every bit as bad as the outlaws."

"It's been a while since I've been down there and it was bad then, sounds like it hasn't changed all that much."

Jack frowned, "It hasn't. If you do get these men take them to the Sheriff in Santa Fe, he's a friend of mine and he's the one who knows what there is to know about the robberies and murders. Do not take them into Las Vegas. I wouldn't put it past the marshal there to arrest and hang *you* and turn his friends loose."

"What if they're dead?"

"Then definitely don't take them to Las Vegas. I have a friend, Mick Baxter in Las Vegas, tougher than whalebone and smart as a fox. You can't miss him. He used to be a bare knuckle fighter and a good one too. He tends bar at Close and Pattersons now, he's always got his eyes and ears open. Tell him I sent you, he might have some ideas about this Bandit Band."

"I'll be sure and do that. Speaking of bandit bands have you heard anything at all about the Parson gang?"

"No, and that's strange. They were active all over the country but nothing for a couple of years now. If they had been caught I'd know it, if they had been shot to pieces in some town it would be all the talk, but nothing. Maybe they just took their loot and retired."

Eli looked disgusted, "I was hoping to get that ten thousand. Is it still in effect even if they retired and are now living normal lives?"

Jack nodded, "Absolutely. They still committed those crimes and murdered people, the law still wants them."

Rob broke in, "Maybe we're looking in the wrong places. Maybe they've done like the scalawags and carpetbaggers in the south and put on business suits and are robbing people like that Banker James did. They made enough on their robberies to set themselves up in a safe business."

Eli stared at him as he thought. "You might be right. Why risk getting killed in stick-ups when they can make more working a crooked business."

"Like the eastern crime syndicates do," Jack added.

Rob looked at Jack, "Exactly, what else would explain their disappearance?"

"Let me look into your idea from that angle," Jack said. "I think you might be onto something here." He grinned at Eli, "You've got a real good thinker on your crew."

Eli laughed, "You're not telling me anything I don't already know. It's like I told John, one of these days he's going to be watching out for me instead of me for him."

Jack smiled toward Carrie, "And now you have two to watch over you. You can't go wrong."

Eli smiled at Carrie who was blushing slightly at the attention. "Looks that way. In the meantime we've got bandits to hunt down."

They all stood up and shook hands with Jack. As they were filing out the door Jack said, "Eli, a word alone."

"Sure."

"We'll wait outside," Rob said as he and Carrie left the office.

Jack waited for the door to fully close. "Is that a good idea having that young girl along?"

Eli shook his head, "Probably not. Problem is that she's my niece and her parents died. Since then she's very attached to me. She's afraid to lose me too."

"She couldn't wait with your uncle until you got back?"

"That was the original idea except she followed us. She's a good girl, but is afraid to lose sight of her only family."

Jack nodded his understanding. "So, by keeping her under your wing you know where she is."

"Yes." Eli hesitated a second and then added, "This is going to be my last job."

Jack's expression showed surprise, and then he nodded, "Right. You have a family to worry about now."

Eli glanced back at the closed door, "Guess I found something more important to do with my life. My war against outlaws can't go on forever."

"Even for the Parson gang?"

Eli's eyes narrowed as he looked back at Jack, "For them I'll make an exception. I owe that to Rob."

"I understand. Next time I see you maybe I'll have some information on that idea of Rob's."

"We'll be sure and stop by when we ride back this way."

The third day out of Trinidad found the trio riding into Las Vegas. They had stayed on the Santa Fe Trail riding with Eli in the lead, Carrie next leading the pack horse, and Rob bringing up the rear. In this manner both men were free to defend the group if set on by robbers while at the same time keeping Carrie safe between them.

New buildings and businesses had been added to the town since Eli had last ridden through several years back, but behind the false storefronts it was still the same town with the same problems. Saloons filled up the spaces in between the other businesses with outlaws and long haired gunfighters drifting in and out of them.

Eli pointed out Close and Patterson's Variety Hall, "There's where we find Jack's friend." They pulled their horses to a stop.

Eli turned to Carrie, "Take the packhorse back to the store we passed and get the supplies we need. Rob and I will be in there," he pointed at the Hall. "We will meet you at the store."

Carrie nodded and turned her sorrel back down the street. Eli and Rob watched her as she rode away leading the pack horse.

"Let's make this quick," Eli said. "The sooner we get the information we need the sooner we can get Carrie out of here."

They stepped off their horses and tied them to a rail. They entered the Hall and stopped just inside the door to study the place and see what kind of men were in it. Men were lined up at the bar, sitting at tables drinking, playing cards or both. There were businessmen in suits and trail dirty range riders mingled together. A few girls in revealing dresses were busy working the men to buy drinks which they would get a small commission for selling.

Eli and Rob drew attention as they walked toward the bar. They were being sized up by the crowd, especially Rob whose age made him the object of study. Eli hoped to be done and out before trouble could start.

Rob looked over the room as they moved across it. One man in particular was eyeing him, a dark skinned man with a heavy black mustache. His white teeth gleamed as he grinned, watching Rob from his seat at a table. The man was well dressed and sported a red vest with a chain across the front of it with white objects dangling from it. Two other men sat at the table with him and a bottle was between them.

Eli reached the bar with Rob standing back from it and to his left. The barman stood at the far end of the bar pouring drinks. He was a big man heavily muscled, but unlike overly muscled men who were slow, he moved easily. His face was scarred and his nose wider than normal across his face. This had to be Mick Baxter.

He moved down to where Eli stood and stopped in front of him waiting for his request. "Beer," Eli spoke the single word.

The barman looked at Rob, "And you?"

"Nothing, I'm just waiting for him."

"You're taking up room at my bar, kid."

Rob looked at him, his eyes steady and showing no fear. "No I'm not, I'm standing back here."

The barman shook his head and poured the beer. He set the glass down on the bar, but before he could turn and leave Eli stopped him. "From Jack Clovis' description I'd say you're Mick Baxter."

The big man stopped mid-turn and looked at Eli. "You a friend of Jack's?"

Eli nodded, "He told me to look you up."

"Yeah, I'm Mick. If you're a friend of Jack's that's okay by me. What do you need?"

"Three Mexicans who like to rob stages and shoot people. No one seems to know their names, but Jack thought you might know who they were."

Baxter studied Eli for a full minute, and then said in a low voice, "You Eli Warren?"

Eli nodded and then gestured with his head toward Rob, "My partner, Rob Slater."

Baxter turned his full attention to Rob, "From Las Animas?"

Rob looked at him, "Thereabouts."

"Word moves up and down the Trail."

He then returned his attention to Eli. "Jack wired me, said you might be by. Those three you're looking for are hiding out on a ranch up by Wagon Mound. It's the Rodriguez place; the old man and his two sons. They're a tough lot, don't take it easy on them."

"Depends on how they want to play it."

"Guns is how they'll play it, trust me."

Carrie reached the store only to realize that Eli had forgotten to give her money to make the purchases with. She turned her horse and rode back to the place they had parted. She dismounted and tied the pack horse to her saddle horn and the sorrel to a post next to Rob's bay.

She walked up to the door of the saloon and stopped. She wasn't sure if she was allowed to go in. She debated the action. It didn't say it was a saloon, it said Variety Hall, which meant it should be alright for her to go in. If it was a saloon she would know not to go in, but a variety hall meant it was like a theater and Eli never said she couldn't go in, only that they would meet her at the store.

She decided she would go in and quickly get the money from Eli and then go right back out. She would only be in there a minute, that should be alright. She drew in a breath and let it back out and opened the door. The smell of stale hot air, dust, and tobacco smoke hit her full in the face. She blinked, stunned for a second by the air.

The room was not brightly lit, but light enough to see everyone in it. She stood just inside the door in her light gray riding skirt and her blonde hair tied back in a ponytail. Men in the room stopped what they were doing to look at her. A couple of the women turned and studied her with shocked expressions that asked what a young girl like her was doing in the place.

She spotted Eli and Rob across the room talking to the man behind the bar and hurried toward them. Rob's eyes grew large as he saw her coming. He jabbed Eli with his elbow and gestured at her. Rob began walking to meet her just as she passed the man in the red vest.

The man reached out and grabbed her by the wrist, "*Hola* pretty girl, come and sit with me, have a drink."

Carrie pulled against the hold he had on her wrist, "Let me go."

The man stood up, his grin widening as he held her wrist. "You and me, we can do some other things you will like."

Carrie pulled her wrist out of the man's grip at the same moment Rob reached her. The man cursed at her and tried to grab her again. In a rage Rob slammed his work hardened hands into the man's chest, sending him flying backwards into his chair. He hit the floor hard as the chair crashed out from under him. The room fell dead silent.

Carrie stood in shock as a woman in a blue dress walked quickly up to her and took her hand. "Come with me honey. Those two young bulls are about to kill each other and you don't want to be in the middle." She led Carrie across the room away from the two men. Tears filled Carrie's terrified eyes.

Eli watched the two men and all those around them. He saw Carrie led away by the woman and knew she was safe for the moment. His focus was on the brewing fight between Rob and the red-vested man.

The man lay on the floor, momentarily stunned by his hard fall. He shook his head; the grin was gone replaced by a look of anger and hate. He stood up and dusted off his vest and sleeves. He spoke English with a heavy Spanish accent. "You have made a very big mistake. Are you her man? After I kill you I will show her what it is to have a man. I know I would like her, at least once."

Rob held his ground and snarled, "Keep your dirty hands off my girl."

The man's grin returned, "I will have more than that on her after I kill you." He flicked the gold chain across his vest with his finger making the white objects bounce. Rob snuck a quick glance at the objects, they were human teeth.

"Every time I kill a man I knock out one of his teeth and put it on my chain, there are twelve; your tooth will be number thirteen." He pointed at the end of the row of teeth, "Yours will go right here. You gringos don't like the number thirteen, you think it unlucky. It will be unlucky for you I think, *niño*."

Rob studied the man; he wasn't more than a few years older than himself. His black eyes had a mesmerizing wild look to them, like those of a crazy man. Rob shifted his eyes away from the man's eyes down to his hands and the gun on his hip. Eli had taught him to check the eyes, but it was the hands that would kill you. You had to concentrate on the hands, not the eyes. He did that now.

The man in the red vest was obviously savoring the moment, taking Rob's action of shifting his gaze down and off his eyes as a sign of fear and weakness.

Less than a minute had passed from the time the man climbed up off the floor, made his little speech, and went for the pearl handled six-gun on his right hip. Rob saw the hand move and acted decisively.

The two men cleared leather in a blur of movement. Since Rob had been looking at the man's gun hand when he first twitched it Rob's draw was a split second quicker. He had the .45 up and spitting the first burst of flame. The man with the pearl handled gun doubled over like he'd been kicked in the stomach. He half straightened and pointed the gun at Rob, his face twisted in shock and pain. Rob thumbed back the hammer and shot him again. The pearl handled gun hung from a lifeless finger for a second and then fell at the same rate as the body. A pool of blood was spreading across the wooden floor from under the dead man.

With his gun still out Rob looked around to see if anyone else was a threat. The faces he saw surrounding him were blank with shock, there wasn't a sound in the room as the haze and acrid smell of the black powder smoke hung in the air around him. He looked back down at the dead man, took the few steps toward where he lay and pushed him over on his back with his boot toe. "I guess thirteen was *your* unlucky number, *niño*."

Carrie ran back across the room and wrapped her arms around Rob. "I'm sorry," she sobbed into his shirt. "I didn't know."

"It's okay, don't cry."

Eli stood with his back to the bar and facing Rob. He surveyed the room making sure there was no one else trying to play into the fight. Baxter leaned across the bar and spoke to the back of Eli's head, "I'd heard about that kid killing the two men in Las Animas in a standup gunfight, but this was amazing. Do you know who that was he just killed?"

Eli spoke without turning, "Obviously a fast gun with a reputation from the look of the blank faces in this room."

"Antonio Ortiz. Reputed to be faster than Clay Allison and Ben Thompson rolled together. But, I guess not faster than Rob Slater."

"I've heard of Ortiz." Eli glanced back at Baxter, "Thanks for the information about the Rodriguez outfit."

He walked toward Rob and Carrie. "Let's get out of here."

Every eye in the place was on Rob as he walked across the room with his left arm around Carrie and still holding his Colt in his right hand. Men began to move toward the body of Antonio Ortiz shaking their heads and talking in low tones. As they were going out the door they heard a voice speak above the others, "That was Rob Slater, the Las Animas gunfighter."

Chapter 17

Within the hour every man in Las Vegas knew that Rob Slater, the Las Animas gunfighter, had killed Antonio Ortiz in Close and Pattersons. Men were making their way to the Hall to see for themselves and to hear the story from those who witnessed it.

The purchase of supplies was put off as the three quickly left Las Vegas. They rode in silence toward Wagon Mound before finding a grove of trees to make camp in for the rest of the day and night. They stayed busy unpacking the horse and setting up a camp. Carrie put together a supper while Eli filled a coffee pot and set it on the fire.

As they settled beside the fire Rob moved in close to Carrie and put his arm around her. "Are you alright?"

She shook her head. "No, I am not alright. You were almost killed and it was my fault."

"I was *not* almost killed and it was *not* your fault. That man had no business grabbing you and scaring you like he did. He got what was coming to him."

Eli watched them considering what Rob had developed into and he was barely seventeen. He had rarely seen anyone get a revolver into action faster and to beat a gunhand like Ortiz to the draw and kill him was a feat. He had taught the boy well, but Rob's ability had gone far past his as a gunfighter.

Rob continued to hold Carrie close to him. "Why were you coming into the saloon, Carrie? Woman never go into saloons, it's just not done."

"I didn't know it was a saloon, it said Variety Hall, I thought it was a theater, and there were women in there," Carrie answered in a low voice.

Eli frowned, "They are a different kind of woman, but we don't need to go into that. What possessed you to go in there?"

"I got to the store before I realized that you had forgotten to give me any money to buy the things with so I went back. I thought that it would be alright to go in just to get the money from you and go right back out."

Eli shook his head. "That was stupid of me. You're not at fault here, Carrie. If I had given you the money you would never have gone in there. From now on though don't go in saloons for any reason, okay?"

She gave him a weak smile and sniffed. "Okay."

They finished their meal; Eli poured a cup of coffee and leaned back against a tree. "Do you know who that was you outgunned back there, Rob?'

Rob shrugged, "Some fool who liked to scare girls and collect the teeth of people he killed. He looked crazy to me."

"His name was Antonio Ortiz; he was, up until today, one of the fastest guns around. He killed all those men in gunfights, I doubt he back shot any of them."

"He wasn't that fast. He just liked to tell himself he was."

Eli shook his head, "No, Rob, he *was* that fast. I've seen a few gunfights and been in my share. I've seen men move a gun like a striking snake and Ortiz was one of those. Only, you were faster."

"I was watching his gun hand like you taught me to do, when he moved it I drew."

"You did the right thing. Ortiz had a reputation, now you have yours and his."

"Is that good or bad?"

"Both. A reputation like that will get you into and out of a lot of situations. It will make troublemakers back off and you can end up with fewer problems. The other side is there's likely to be men looking you up wanting to try your hand. You will have to be careful."

"I won't let it go to my head. I don't aim to be strutting around like that banty rooster back there jingling my collection of teeth at people. Knowing I can do it is enough. I will walk away from any fights I can. I don't have to stand there and shoot it out with every fool that wants to see if he's faster. Then again, if it comes down to defending myself or any of us, it's good to know I'm fast enough to do it."

"I'm glad to hear you say that. A reputation like that in the head of someone your age can be a terrible thing. It puffs them all up inside and they start thinking they're bigger than they really are and go to pushing their weight around. You start picking fights and you won't live to see twenty."

"Don't worry about me Eli; I had two of the best teachers in the world. I won't disappoint you."

"I'm not worried about being disappointed in you; I'm worried about keeping you around to take care of me in my old age." Eli laughed.

Rob laughed with him, "You're too darn ornery to ever grow old. Old age will be too scared to come around you."

"Old man time catches up with all of us, it's simply a fact of life."

The rest of the evening was spent planning out the strategy for rousting the Rodriguez outfit out of their hideout. It was decided that they would keep this camp and have Carrie stay in it. They would scout around, find the ranch house and study the movements of the men in it. They didn't want to rush into a risky attack. They would watch the place for a few days and go from there depending on what the bandits did.

Eli pulled the short-barreled 12 gauge shotgun out of the pack along with a box of brass shotgun shells. He sat down next to Carrie and instructed her on how to load and handle the shotgun. He took her out away from the camp and the horses. Here he taught her how to tuck the stock snuggly between her elbow and waist and had her shoot it. When satisfied that she could handle the shotgun they returned to the camp.

At first light Eli and Rob saddled up and made ready to ride out to find the Rodriguez place. Eli instructed Carrie to stay in camp and not leave it. He watched her load the shotgun and made sure she remembered all she had learned about handling it. He told her to keep it by her at all times, she was not to leave it somewhere she couldn't get at it quickly. Still apprehensive about leaving her alone, however, realizing it was how this would have to be done, they rode off.

Carrie busied herself about the camp finishing chores before sitting down on a blanket to read a book she had rolled in her blankets. The shotgun was on the ground beside her. After a few minutes of reading she found herself nodding off and falling asleep in the warm sun.

She was awakened by the sound of approaching horses. She opened her eyes expecting to see Eli and Rob, instead it was two strange men. They stopped a ways back from the camp and spoke between themselves. She didn't like the looks of them; they were dirty and rough. A shiver of fear went through her as they stepped off their horses and walked toward her.

They stopped a hundred feet from where she sat and leered at her with evil grins. One of them said, "We saw your smoke and figured to stop by for coffee, and low and behold we find you. We saw you in the Hall yesterday with all that blonde hair."

Carrie held her place on the blanket. She fought down her fear and forcing strength into her voice answered, "You better leave me alone. If you were in there yesterday you saw what happened to the last man who touched me."

The man laughed, "But your boyfriend ain't here, is he? You're all alone, but you ain't alone no more though." He took a step forward.

"I'm warning you," Carrie shouted at him, a slight tremor entering her voice. "Leave me alone!"

"We will, after we get what we want from you."

The two men moved toward her slowly enjoying the stalk. They wanted to see the girl's fear. What they didn't see was the shotgun next to her on the blanket. Their attention was focused on her and they were confident they would meet no real resistance.

Carrie knew the men had no intention of leaving. She also knew what they had in mind. Choking down her fear she grabbed the shotgun. Standing up, she pulled back both hammers, tucked the stock between her waist and elbow, and pointed it at them. "I said leave me alone." The warning came out in a higher pitch then she wanted and it made her sound desperate and scared.

The men laughed as they shifted apart. putting several feet between them. The man had spoken before said, "Now, you ain't gonna shoot us sweetheart, just put that down and we can have some fun." They closed to within thirty feet of her and kept coming. If they rushed her she'd never have a chance. She remembered listening to what Eli had once told Rob, that when you need to shoot don't hesitate, shoot.

When the twin bores were centered on the mid-section of the first man she pulled the rear trigger. The gun kicked back against her and belched out buckshot and blackpowder smoke sending the man spinning backwards and throwing him hard to the ground. Without hesitation she shifted the barrels to the other man, who stood frozen in place staring at her his face blanched white with fear. She pulled the forward trigger with equal results. The two would-be attackers lay unmoving next to each other on the ground.

Dave P. Fisher

Carrie held the shotgun and stared at the bodies. Her ears were ringing from the two blasts and her hands trembled until she could no longer hold the heavy shotgun. She laid the gun down and continued staring at the bodies. She wanted to cry, but didn't. Her stomach felt like she wanted to be sick. She sat back down for several minutes clearing the wild rush of emotions out of her head.

Eli had said to reload right away, she remembered that. She stood back up on shaking legs and went to the packs on the ground. She found the box of shotgun shells and grabbed up two of them. Returning to the blanket she sat down and picked up the shotgun. Breaking it open she pulled out the spent brass shells and slipped two loaded ones into the barrels and closed the gun.

She held the gun across her lap and watched all around her. The dark lumps in the grass that were the bodies of the two men were in front of her. She was no longer sleepy. Suddenly she realized what Eli had been trying to tell her about how dangerous it was for her out here. She had almost gotten Rob killed and now she had killed two men. If she had stayed home as instructed none of this would have happened, but she was here now though and must see it through. She would never disobey Eli again.

She was thankful for the shotgun and Eli's instruction. If not for it she might be dead now or wishing she was. She had defended herself. She felt a surge of courage and strength well up inside of her. Her shaking stopped and she no longer felt sick to her stomach.

Holding on to the shotgun she picked up the blanket and book and moved further back into the trees. Spreading out the blanket she sat back down. She laid the shotgun down beside her and tried to read the book, but found it hard to concentrate on reading as her eyes were continuously leaving the pages to search the country around her.

Eli and Rob spent most of the day trying to find the Rodriguez ranch with no success. They knew it had to be close. There was a scattering of adobe and wood framed houses throughout the area. Some places were grazing cattle while others had crops growing. It could be one of them or it could be nestled into the hills and not noticeable unless you knew exactly where to look.

They had pulled off to the side of the Trail to discuss the situation when a man rode abreast of them. He was well set up on a smooth stepping black horse. He wore a short jacket in the Spanish style, black pants that flared at the boot, and a wide brimmed hat that was somewhere between a Mexican sombrero and a John B. Stetson. He was armed with a pistol and a rifle. He looked to be in his fifties and, all in all, cut an impressive figure.

He pulled the black to a stop beside them. His lips formed a smile under a carefully trimmed mustache streaked with gray. He spoke with a slight Spanish accent, "Gentlemen, you look lost."

Eli smiled back, "Not lost, trying to find someone's ranch."

"My name is Domingo Garza, I have had my rancho here for many years, as it was my father's, and his before him. I know most everyone who comes and goes. Who do you look for?"

"The Rodriguez ranch."

The smile fell from Garza's face as he studied them with hardened black eyes. He remained silent for a moment before speaking. "The Rodriguez house is near, as to a ranch it is not one. They make a pretense of raising cattle, but cattle is not their business." He studied them for another moment. "You seek them for a visit?"

Eli studied Garza in return; he was obviously a well-to-do rancher with a long family tradition and not one who would run with outlaws. He decided to be straightforward with him. "No, we are not interested in visiting them. They are criminals and we are hunting them."

Garza nodded, "I like that. I like an honest man who speaks out. There are too many who lie and are dishonest today. They play children's games of deception and I have no use for them. I will tell you about the Rodríguez. Come with me to my home, it is close and we can talk of this over a glass of wine."

"Thank you, Señor Garza, that is generous of you. I am Eli Warren and this is Rob Slater."

Garza nodded in response and rode along the Trail. They followed him to a single track trail that spurred off of the Santa Fe and down into a green valley. His house was big enough to be seen from a distance and could hold John's store and cabin in it three times over and still have room to spare. They arrived at the huge adobe house and dismounted. A man hurried out to take Garza's horse. "Miguel, my friends will not be long as they have important work to attend to, but feed and water their horses please."

The man grabbed up the reins of all three horses, "Si, patron."

"Come in and sit where it is cool Mr. Warren and Mr. Slater."

They followed him into an inner room with leather covered furniture. The air was noticeably cooler in the room than it was outside. A different man came to Garza as they sat down. "Wine please, for me and my friends." The man quickly hurried out of the room.

"Now gentlemen, you seek the Rodriguez men. Let me first tell you a bit about them. These particular men moved in only three months ago, their property borders mine. There is a Rodriguez family on my mother's side from Mexico, some are still down there, others are in the Santa Fe area. This family of Rodriguez were all banditos in Mexico and they have changed little since coming north. Those that have moved in next to me are from that family.

"As I said, they make a show of raising cattle. If they are cattlemen they are the worst cattlemen in the world as they are always gone and rarely seen working their few old cows. They are reclusive and do not socialize, they come and go at will. I know because I have my vaqueros keeping an eye on them as I know they are not to be trusted. My men tell me of their movements.

"There have been many robberies since they moved here. Several coaches have been robbed and men murdered and robbed on the Trail. A bank in Santa Fe was also robbed. There is no doubt in my mind that these men are responsible. There are three of them, two sons and the father, all of them bad men."

The man returned with filled wine glasses on a polished silver tray. Eli took one from the tray as it was offered to him and took a sip. "Sheriff Clovis in Trinidad is a friend of ours, he told us about this new gang that has been on a crime rampage between Colorado and Las Vegas. We came down here to find this gang and learned that the Rodriguez men were the ones we sought."

"You are not lawmen?"

Eli shook his head, "No."

Garza nodded, "So, I would think you are hunters of such men, am I right? Thus, your term, 'hunting' them."

Eli nodded, "You are."

"There is then a bounty on their heads?"

"There is."

"Mr. Warren, excuse me for saying this, but you are well spoken and seem an educated man unlike other men I have met in your profession. You do not seem the kind of man to be a bounty hunter."

"A man does not have to be ignorant or ill educated to be an outlaw hunter; he only needs to care about ridding the country of outlaws."

Garza smiled, "And collecting the bounties."

Eli smiled in return, "Are you paid when you sell your cattle?"

Garza laughed, "A man must be paid for his work, I understand. The better you work, the better you should be paid, true?"

Eli smiled without further comment.

"Ride to the west border of my property and you will see an adobe house against a hill, that is their house. They are away from it at present as my vaqueros have informed me, no doubt on another robbery. You should go have a look while they are gone."

Finishing their wine Eli and Rob stood up. Eli extended his hand to Garza and they shook hands. "Thank you for your hospitality Señor Garza and for the information."

Garza then took Rob's extended hand. "My vaqueros tell me that you killed Antonio Ortiz, that you are a very fast man with a gun. Antonio Ortiz was a bad man; he killed a beloved cousin of mine."

Rob nodded, "I am sorry for your cousin, Señor Garza."

"Be careful young man, a fast gun is good to have; it can also be a very bad thing."

"Yes sir, I will be."

A young girl walked through the room and smiled at them as she passed.

"My daughter Julita," Garza said.

Eli saw here an opportunity to put Carrie someplace safe. The fight in the Hall seemed to have given her an understanding of why he was hesitant to have her with them. She would have another girl her age to be with and hopefully be willing to stay until he and Rob finished this Rodriguez business.

"Señor Garza, if I may presume upon your hospitality, my sixteen-year-old niece travels with us. Her parents died of cholera and she is now in my care. At present she is alone in our camp. We do not like the idea of her being alone out there all day. Would you mind if she stayed here in your care and safety until our business is completed? I realize it is a presumptuous request as you do not know us."

Garza waved his hand in the air. "It is not presumptuous to wish safety for our children. No young girl should be alone in this country, it is far too dangerous. Bring her here tomorrow morning. Julita, I am sure, would appreciate the company."

"That is very generous of you Señor Garza, thank you."

"It is a small favor that I can grant you. Ridding us of the Rodriguez banditos so my men can tend to cattle instead of watching them is a much greater favor. If they had stolen even one head of my cattle we would have killed them, but they have not, we have no reason to. You do and I wish you success."

Eli and Rob left the house and were met by Miguel holding their horses. They thanked him and rode out of the ranch yard.

They rode west through Garza's ranch until they reached his border. On the land next to his was a scattering of cattle. As Garza had said, they were not good beef cattle but a mix of everything put on the place for appearances sake. They moved onto the Rodriguez property and found the adobe house as described.

The ranch was only a front for the men's outlaw activities. People who knew nothing of cattle would consider them legitimate ranchers and not suspect them of being the bandits that were responsible for the rash of robberies and murders over the past few months. Men who knew cattle could see what was going on.

They scouted around the property looking for the best vantage points for watching their movements. At present there were no horses in the corral next to the house which fit in with Garza saying they were gone. The house was closed up and no smoke came from the stove pipe sticking out of the roof.

They climbed the hill next to the house which gave them a good view of the front, back, and east side of the house. Eli instructed Rob to stay on the hill while he went down to have a quick look around the place and maybe get in the house. He rode down the hill figuring if they suddenly showed up while he was at the house he would make some excuse about passing through and looking for water.

Riding around the house Eli found the door to be made of thick wood with a heavy padlock holding the door closed. The windows on all four sides were sealed from the inside with wooden shutters. There was a back door that was as heavy as the front and didn't move when he pushed on it. The house was a fortress that could not be successfully attacked.

Riding between the back of the house and the corral he spotted a blackened circle on the ground where a fire had been made. Studying the black ash he saw what appeared to be a piece of canvas bag. Dismounting he dug it out of the ash; it was a piece of a bank money bag. They were burning the stage and bank bags to get rid of them. It was a good bet they were out robbing something else right now. He headed back for the hill where Rob waited.

He told Rob about the piece of money bag that lent proof to their having the right men. He described the house and how there was no way they could get them out of it if they dug in to fight. They decided to head back to camp for now and come back in the morning and start watching for them to return. They hoped an opportunity to catch the three outlaws would present itself.

It was late afternoon when they approached the grove of trees that hid their camp. Rob was first to spot the saddled horses grazing out from the camp, he was instantly alarmed. They rode quickly toward the camp and almost ran over the stiff corpses lying in the brown grass. Eli stepped out of the saddle to check the bodies. "They've been hit with buckshot."

Rob looked into the trees and saw no movement. He shouted out Carrie's name and kicked his horse forward. Jerking back on the reins he brought the horse to a skidding stop in front of their lean-to tarp tied to the trees. Carrie jumped out from under the tarp and ran to him.

Rob leapt off his horse and caught Carrie in his arms, she clung tightly to him. Rob asked anxiously, "Are you alright? What happened here?"

Carrie answered, "Yes, I'm alright."

"We saw the bodies, what happened?"

Eli walked up to them leading his horse. He said nothing as Carrie stepped back from Rob and explained.

"They came this morning." She pointed out toward where the bodies lay, "I was sitting out there reading a book, I had the shotgun with me like you told me to. They said they had seen me in the Hall and they said some other things. I told them to leave me alone, but they wouldn't. They said they were going to . . . you know . . ."

Eli cut her off, "We know what they were going to do, you don't have to say it."

Carrie nodded, "I warned them to leave me alone, but they kept coming toward me. I pointed the gun at them and they laughed at me. I was frightened . . . I shot them both."

She hugged Rob again. "I was so scared, but I defended myself just like you and Uncle Eli taught me to."

Eli put his arm around her, "You did just right."

Carrie lifted her head and looked at him. "I had no choice."

"No, you didn't."

"Did you find the men you were looking for?"

"We know who they are and where they are living. They weren't there so we'll go back tomorrow."

Carrie's eyes flashed a second of concern before she nodded, "I'll be okay here."

"You won't be staying here. We met a fine Spanish gentleman with a big ranch who said you could stay in his care and safety until our work is finished here. He has a daughter your age who would enjoy your company."

Carrie's eyes widened, "But, I . . ."

Eli cut her off, "No, Carrie. What happened yesterday and today should convince you that it is not safe for you alone and you can't go where Rob and I go."

"But, I want to be with you."

Eli took Carrie's hands and looked kindly into her face. "You are not going to lose us. I know you are afraid of that, but you don't need to be. You need to be safe."

"If I go there will you come back for me?"

"Of course we will. We would never abandon you."

Rob put his arm around Carrie's shoulders, "You can't lose me that easy."

Carrie showed a slight smile, "Well, that would be alright I guess. Who are these people? How did you meet him?"

"They are Domingo and Julita Garza. He knows the outlaws, they are relatives that he does not claim. He was very helpful in directing us to their hideout."

"Will you leave me there for long?"

"Only until we catch these men and then we will be back for you."

"I will miss you."

Rob pulled her in close and hugged her, "Don't worry we'll be back for you."

Chapter 18

The three rode into Domingo Garza's ranch yard early the next morning. Miguel was quick to meet them with a smile and warm greeting; they returned it to him in kind. Domingo made his way out the doorway with sixteen year old Julita walking gracefully beside him. She had alert black eyes that matched her shining raven hair.

"Welcome again Mr. Warren and Mr. Slater, I am pleased to see that you have brought your lovely niece to share the hospitality of my home."

They all dismounted, Eli stepped up to Domingo and extended his hand which was warmly accepted. "Thank you Señor Garza. We are all friends here, please call me Eli."

Rob then shook his hand, "Rob, please, Señor Garza."

"Then you may call me Domingo. Men of valor and action should be friends, yes?"

Eli smiled and nodded, "Yes."

The two girls stepped up to face each other. Julita extended both her hands out to Carrie. "I am Julita, welcome to my home. I am sure we will have much to talk about."

Carrie took her hands, "Thank you for having me, my name is Carrie."

Domingo gestured toward Miguel, "Miguel, please take care of Señorita Carrie's horse."

Eli asked, "Can we leave the pack horse and pack as well? We plan to travel light."

"Of course. Miguel, the pack horse as well." Miguel bowed slightly and led the horses away.

Domingo turned to his daughter, "Julita, would you please take Carrie inside and make her welcome."

Julita understood that her father wished to discuss matters she should not be privy to. She smiled and ushered Carrie into the house.

"I have some very good news for you gentlemen. One of my most trusted men only last night returned from Santa Fe where he was conducting business on my behalf. He was in my cousin's cantina and the three Rodriguez men were in there drinking and waiting. There is to be a stage coach with gold on it leaving Santa Fe in two days bound for Las Vegas. He believes they are waiting for it so they can follow and rob it."

Eli smiled, "That *is* very good news."

"If you ride across the hills you can be there by tomorrow. If you take the Trail it will be a much longer ride. You will find my cousin's cantina on the south end of the plaza. His name is Jesus Sanchez, tell him I sent you and he will feed you. It is not elegant, but his food alone is worth the ride."

"We had best get to it then," Eli said. They shook hands with Domingo and mounted up.

Rob looked around for Carrie. As they were turning the horses to leave Carrie ran out of the house and up to the side of Rob's horse. She reached her arms up and he lifted her up to him and they embraced. He let her gently back down.

Carrie stepped back, "You be careful, Rob Slater and you come back to me in one piece."

"Don't worry I will."

She looked at Eli. "Take care of him, Uncle Eli."

He smiled at her, "More than likely he'll take care of me. Don't worry we'll be back."

They reined their horses around and left the ranch yard. Domingo turned his attention to Carrie and smiled,

"They are good men on a mission. If there were more such men we would have no outlaws or banditos to contend with."

Julita stepped up beside Carrie, together they watched Eli and Rob ride away. "Is Rob your young man?"

Carrie hesitated for a second unsure how to answer and then nodded her head. "Yes, he is my man."

"You are very lucky; he is a handsome and brave caballero. The vaqueros talk of how he saved you from Antonio Ortiz and then killed him; they are very impressed with him."

Carrie did not answer as she stared out the way they had gone.

"To travel with two such handsome and brave men, you are fortunate indeed."

"Yes, I know." Carrie turned to her new friend, "Do you have a young man?"

"Yes, he lives in Santa Fe; we are to be wed in the spring. Father says it will be a fiesta grande like none has ever been. I will want you to come."

"I would be happy to come, thank you."

"Let us go, we have things to do." Together the young women returned to the house.

Eli and Rob pushed hard through the day finally stopping when the horses started to stumble from exhaustion. They made camp a half day ride out of Santa Fe. They could have pushed themselves on through the bright full moon night; however, the horses were worn down and needed to graze and rest. They would continue on in the morning.

They reached Santa Fe mid-afternoon of the next day. They rode through the town that was a mix of adobe and lumber framed buildings. Spanish influence dominated the town that had begun as a Pueblo over two hundred years before when Governor Don Pedro de Peralta moved the capital of The Kingdom of New Mexico to Santa Fe.

They found the cantina of Domingo's cousin, Jesus. Leaving their horses tied in front, they went inside the adobe structure. The room was bigger inside than the outside suggested. It was large enough to hold two long tables with benches to each side and a scattering of single tables with chairs. The room had a pair of glassless windows that allowed light to enter, candles burning on the tables provided additional light.

The room held an equal mix of Anglos and Mexicans. A low murmur of voices hung in the air as the occupants looked up from their drinks and food to watch them. They lived in dangerous times and unknown men always called for study.

Eli and Rob sat down facing each other at the end of one of the long tables. In this manner they could watch the other's back as well as the open doorway. A Spanish man of fifty-some years, with his sleeves rolled up and wearing a food stained apron wrapped around his waist, moved quickly up to them. He smiled, "Señors, would you like to eat or drink? My tequila is the best north of Mexico and my food the best anywhere."

Eli smiled back, "We were told to ask for Jesus Sanchez."

"And you have found him amigos." He placed his hand on his chest; I am Jesus Sanchez, owner of this fine cantina. Who sends you to me?"

"Domingo Garza said you served the finest food in all of Santa Fe."

"Oh yes, my favorite cousin. He is too kind in his praise, but he is mistaken, my food is not the best in Santa Fe, it is the best in the world." He laughed good naturedly, "You are friends of Domingo?"

"We are."

"Then, the meal is on the house. Friends of my favorite cousin who he has sent to me eat free in my cantina." He then leaned in close to Eli, "But, do not tell anyone or my cousin will suddenly have many friends he never knew he had wanting to eat free and then I will become a poor man very quickly."

"We know what you mean; your secret is safe with us."

Jesus smiled broadly and disappeared into the back kitchen. In a matter of minutes he returned carrying two plates heaped with food. A young woman carrying a glass of beer in each hand followed him. Jesus set the plates down and the girl set the glasses next to them.

"Amigos, this is my daughter, Benita."

Eli and Rob tipped their hats to her and said hello.

"Eat until you explode." Jesus laughed and father and daughter walked back to the kitchen.

They ate with little talk between them. It had been a long ride on scant rations and they ate like it. Finishing off the last of the food they both leaned forward resting their forearms on the table. Eli looked at Rob, "Domingo wasn't exaggerating, that was the best food I ever ate."

Rob grinned, "Better than dried beef and hard tack? You must be getting old."

"Don't get smart, kid."

Jesus returned to the table and smiled, "You must have liked it."

Eli grinned, "You were right my friend, that was the best food in the world."

"Do you want more?"

Eli held up his hands, "No, any more and I *will* explode. Jesus, can you sit for a minute?"

He sat down next to Rob, his eyes meeting Eli's. "You wish to know something, yes?"

Eli leaned forward and spoke in a low voice, "Domingo told us of his bandito relatives, the Rodriguez, a father and his two sons. One of Domingo's men told him they were in here yesterday. We are looking for them."

Jesus leaned in and spoke in an equally low voice, "They are my relatives as well. Very bad men. They are up to no good, I believe."

"We believe they plan to rob the coach with the gold leaving here tomorrow for Las Vegas."

Jesus studied Eli and then glanced over at Rob sitting beside him. "You look like men who hunt such men."

"We are hunting them, yes."

Jesus shifted his eyes to his right. "See the table in the corner with the three men sitting at it?"

Eli casually glanced in the direction indicated. He saw three Mexicans, two young, one older. They had a bottle of tequila on the table and half-filled glasses. "Yes."

"That is them, Montes, and his worthless sons, Paco and Frisco. They think because we are relatives they should eat and drink on me for free, I tell them no. They think their guns will scare me, I am not afraid I make them pay. They do not like it, but they pay. Be careful amigos they are dangerous."

"Do you know when the stage with the gold is to leave town?"

"I understand it to be the ten o'clock stage tomorrow."

Eli glanced at Rob who nodded his agreement to the unspoken idea that they would be ready for it.

"They are relatives, but a bandito is a bandito and all are bad, we do not claim them. In my family, and my cousins' families, we are honest men who work for our living. In Mexico, the Dons hunt banditos like coyotes, the vaqueros kill them so they come up here to make their trouble. If you kill them it is good for all of us." He stood up and left the table.

Rob looked across the table at Eli. "That was easy."

"It pays to know the right men. The Mexicans don't share information with many people, especially Anglos. If Domingo and Jesus didn't like us we would still be nowhere."

"Why don't we just take them when they leave here?"

"We have nothing to physically connect them to the other robberies and murders. They can't be arrested or taken into custody for eating in a cantina. It boils down to their word against the knowledge of their relatives, that won't hold up. We have to catch them actually robbing the stage."

"So, do we follow them or the stage?"

"I would prefer to keep an eye on those three so we don't lose track of them. If we do lose track of them we will follow the stage as they probably left ahead of it to set up an ambush somewhere down the Trail."

They got up from the table and began to walk out, Jesus stopped them. "Amigos, where are you spending the night?"

Eli shrugged, "We hadn't thought about that yet."

"My sister has a casa across the plaza; she sometimes rents a room for the night for a bit of money to help. It is very clean, no bugs or scorpions. If you stay there I can send my son to give you a message of any moves they make." He flicked his eyes toward the Rodriguez men.

"Gracias, we will go see your sister."

"Good, her name is, Ynez. Oh, and one more thing, her husband Tomas is a jealous man and good with a knife, be sure and tell them I sent you."

Eli grinned, "Glad to know that. We will be perfect gentlemen."

They crossed the plaza and knocked on Ynez's door. When she answered it they introduced themselves to her. Tomas stood behind her; he was a big man who looked like he could lift a freight wagon single handed. He watched them suspiciously with no hint of friendliness in his face until they said Jesus had sent them. He then relaxed and became hospitable and showed them to a room.

The first morning light found Eli and Rob up and getting ready to leave. A hard knock shook their door; Eli opened it to see an ominous looking Tomas filling the doorway. The first thought that came into Eli's mind was that he didn't do it whatever it was.

"My nephew brought a message from Jesus for you. "The Rodriguez have gone down the Santa Fe. They left only a few minutes ago."

"Gracias, Tomas."

"Ynez has breakfast, come and eat." Tomas turned to leave and then stopped. "Montes is a bad one. He will try to kill you, he will not surrender."

Eli was not surprised that Tomas knew of their purpose as the Mexican families shared information with each other.

Rob looked at Eli with the question on his face as to what they should do next.

Eli looked back at him, "Right now we go have some of Ynez's breakfast and then we follow the stage out. I'm sure the Rodriguez have gone ahead to set up an ambush so there's no sense in us getting in a hurry until the stage leaves."

Tomas led the way to the kitchen. He spoke over his shoulder, "You are not like other Anglos. I have come to hate the Anglos as they look down their noses at the Mexican and try to take our homes and overrun the land grants the Dons have held for hundreds of years. But, you are decent Anglos, Jesus and Domingo like you that is good enough for me."

Eli answered as they walked, "We appreciate that, Tomas. We're always happy to make another friend."

They sat and ate with Ynez and Tomas, three children sat at a smaller table next to the big table. The children were all under ten years of age, silent and well mannered. The family was poor, but proud.

At the end of the meal Eli asked what they owed for the room. Tomas said they owed nothing as they were friends. Eli didn't want to step on their pride, it was obvious though they could use the money and Jesus had said Ynez lent out the rooms for money to help them get by.

"That is very generous, Gracias" Eli said. "He then

looked warmly at the children as he pulled some folded bills from his pocket. "You have very nice children and as a friend I wish to give a gift for them." He laid the money on the table.

Tomas and Ynez accepted the money as it would have been insulting to the giver to turn down a gift. "Gracias," Ynez said in a low voice.

Leaving the house Eli and Rob went to their horses in the stable behind it. They saddled and rode toward the stage station for a look. The stage that would be carrying the gold was being hitched to a fresh four horse team by the hostler. Two men were standing by holding rifles, a third had a shotgun.

"There won't be any passengers on that stage," Eli commented. "We'll ride a ways down the Trail and wait for it to pass."

They rode out of town until they found a spot off the Trail to watch from. They settled back in the shade of some trees to wait.

Eli explained to Rob what he believed the Rodriguez would do. They would have an ambush set up; no doubt scouted out ahead of time. When the coach approaches, they will shoot the armed men on the outside. They will shoot the passenger area full of holes to kill whoever is inside, but they won't shoot the driver as they need him to stop the coach.

Rob's expression was troubled, "Can't we do anything to prevent all those men from being killed?"

Eli shook his head, "We have no idea where they have the ambush set and won't know until the shooting starts. If we follow too close the guards will think we intend to rob them, if we ride with them we will be killed in the ambush."

Rob frowned, "We have no choice then do we?"

"Unfortunately, no. We can try to help, but it will happen fast, only seconds are needed to load the coach with lead. In the end they will kill the driver and then make off with the gold leaving no witnesses. The best we can do is get to the shooting fast and hopefully save someone."

"How do you want to do this once the holdup takes place?"

"I will throw down on them with my Winchester from this side of the Trail; you flank them to the south side with your rifle and we start shooting into them."

Rob nodded his understanding. "No sense in wasting time trying to make them surrender."

"It won't be a surrender situation. Just kill them."

Two hours passed before the sound of the rolling stage wheels were heard. As it passed they counted a shotgun guard next to the driver, a man with a rifle on the top, and another man hanging a rifle barrel out the side window from the coach's interior. It carried no passengers as Eli had predicted.

Mounting up Eli and Rob rode alongside the Trail, staying upwind of the coach's drifting dust trail. They passed a few wagons and riders headed into Santa Fe, but for the most part the Trail was quiet. An hour and five miles passed uneventfully when suddenly the hills resounded in a volley of rifle fire.

Kicking their horses into a gallop they topped a small rise that looked down on the Trail. A hundred yards below them the stage was stopped with one of the wheel horses dead in the traces. Three mounted men with their faces covered, two on the driver's side, and one to the opposite side of the coach held guns on the driver who had his hands in the air. A man could be seen lying on the top of the coach and another was in the Trail behind the coach.

The driver turned toward the boxes and bags on top of the stage and picked up a canvas bank bag.

"Change of plans." Eli shouted as he pulled the Sharps out of the scabbard. "As soon as the driver hands over that sack, the one who isn't handling the gold will shoot him. I've got that one; you take the lone man on the other side of the coach."

While still horseback Rob pulled his rifle and levered in a cartridge. He shouldered the rifle and took aim at the lone robber opposite the driver. The driver let go of the obviously heavy bag into the hands of the man closest to him while the one behind him lifted his pistol to shoot him in the back of the head. The report of the Sharps boomed against the hills and the man with the pistol somersaulted over the head of his horse, slamming into the side of the stage.

Rob's rifle barked and the robber in his sights gripped his side and slumped over in the saddle. Levering in cartridges and steadily firing down on the wounded robber, Rob's rifle took its toll dropping the man to the dirt. He was appreciative that they had taught their horses, like the cavalry, to stand still under gunfire.

The man that had taken the bag had it resting on the saddle pommel in front of him. He spun his horse around wildly trying to find out who was shooting. Spotting Eli and Rob on the hill he spurred his horse away from the coach holding the bank bag down with one hand.

Eli quickly dismounted and sat down on the ground. He tucked the Sharps tight against his shoulder, rested his elbows on his knees, and drew a bead on the fleeing robber. The fleeing rider managed to put three hundred yards between him and Eli before the Sharps boomed. It took a full second before the man stiffened in the saddle and slid off, bouncing several times before skidding to a stop in a cloud of white dust.

Eli slid the Sharps back into the scabbard and mounted. Together he and Rob rode down to the coach as the driver turned in the seat watching them come toward him. Rob stepped off his horse next to the man lying in the road and rolled him over on his back. "He's still alive."

Eli rode up next to the coach and looked at the driver. "Are you okay?"

The driver released a pent up breath as he pulled a red bandana from his back pocket and wiped his forehead with a trembling hand. "I sure thank you men. I thought I was a goner for sure."

"You almost were."

Eli dismounted and checked the man inside the coach who was piled up on the floor between the seats. He called out to the driver, "This one's dead, took one in the head. How about the man on top?"

The driver had climbed up on top and was checking the unconscious man. "He took two, he's breathing though."

Eli checked the outlaws they had shot. They were the ones Jesus had identified as Paco and Frisco Rodriguez, they were dead. He walked back to where Rob knelt next to the man on the ground. Together they picked the wounded man up and put him on the coach seat.

Eli pointed at the dead horse, it had been dragged by the lead horses before the coach could be stopped. "Get the harness free of that horse so the coach can move."

As Rob and the driver worked at unhitching the dead horse, Eli mounted and kicked the roan into a gallop toward the outlaw who couldn't escape the long reach of the Sharps. Checking the man he found him to be the gray haired, Montes. The heavy slug had struck him between the shoulder blades and took out most of his chest as it passed through. Backtracking he found the bank bag. Stepping down he picked it up and then rode back to the coach.

Eli rode up alongside the coach and dropped the heavy bag on the top. "Better get these men back to Santa Fe and a doctor. Tell the Sheriff we'll be bringing in the bodies and that they're the Bandit Band, he will know what that means."

The driver looked out to where the last outlaw lay spread eagle in the dust. "That was quite a shot." He climbed back up on the seat and gathered the reins. Turning the coach around he put the horses into a run back to Santa Fe.

Eli turned to Rob, "Let's get their horses and load these up."

Two of the horses were grazing a short way from the where their riders lay. Rob collected those while Eli went after the last horse, knowing it would have run for a ways. He followed the tracks of the hard running horse. He rode for half an hour before finding the horse where the dragging reins had hung up in a gnarled bush stopping it.

Returning with the horse, he stopped and loaded Montes' body over the saddle and tied it in place. He led the horse back to where Rob waited with the dead men's horses. He helped Rob load the other two bodies onto the horses and tied them in place. Tail-tying the horses together, they headed back up the Trail to Santa Fe.

They were almost back to town when they were met by the sheriff riding with four men behind him. They pulled up in front of Eli and Rob with the men spreading out blocking their way. The Sheriff looked at the bodies on the horses and then studied Eli and Rob. "Walt told us what happened. Seems like a strange coincidence how you happened on the robbery like you did. Almost makes me think you knew something about it."

Eli looked the man in the eyes, "And you didn't?"

"What exactly is that supposed to mean?"

"You have this Bandit Band running loose, and a coach known to be carrying thousands in gold, didn't you suspect they'd show up trying to steal it?"

The lawman glared at him knowing the statement was true and that he should have been on top of the situation. "I suppose you did know?"

"Suspected."

"Why didn't you come to me with that information?"

"There's twenty-five hundred reasons."

"Oh, bounty hunters," the sheriff scowled. "I could arrest you for withholding information regarding a crime."

"We didn't know there would be a crime, we followed a hunch."

Eli gestured with his left thumb over his shoulder, "Regardless of what we knew or didn't know, there's your mysterious bandits that have been pulling all the robberies and murders around here."

A younger man sitting behind the sheriff was shifting anxiously in his saddle like he was anxious to say something. Finally he came out with it. "I think you should arrest them, sheriff, until we find out about this. If you ask me I think they were in on it."

Eli gave the young man a hard look, "If we were in on it then how come we stopped the robbery, helped the wounded, and gave the gold back to the driver? We could have easily finished off the driver and left with the gold."

The sheriff snapped angrily over his shoulder, "Jordie shut up I'm doing the questioning here." He returned his attention to Eli, "What makes you so sure about these being the bandits? No one knows who they are."

"The local people, the Mexicans knew. This is the Rodriguez family, the old man and his sons, bandits up from Mexico. Domingo Garza told us they had moved in next to him a little before all the robberies started. He knew who they were. He figured they were the bandits responsible for all the robberies and killings here lately."

"If that's true, why didn't they come to me and say so?"

"Take a look around you. The grant wars, Anglos taking over; they have no reason to trust you or any Anglo for that matter, so they keep what they know to themselves."

"You look pretty Anglo to me, why did they trust you and not me?"

Eli shrugged, "I guess because we made friends with Domingo Garza and he told the others we were all right to talk to. They're a hard bunch of men unless they like you."

"And they like you?"

"Guess so."

The sheriff frowned and reluctantly agreed. "Yeah,

there's a lot of mistrust between us."

"Jack Clovis knew they had to be around Santa Fe or Las Vegas. That's why he aimed us down this way to find them."

The sheriff's eyes locked on Eli. "You know Jack Clovis?"

"He's a friend. He said we should contact you if we find these men because you were the only honest lawman in the area."

"Jack said that about me?"

"He did."

"What are your names?"

"I'm Eli Warren and this is Rob Slater."

The sheriff's face showed recognition at the names. "I've heard of you, you've got a reputation. I can't honestly say I've ever heard anything bad about you though, except that you're death on outlaws." He shifted his attention to Rob. "Are you the Las Animas Slater who killed Antonio Ortiz in Las Vegas?"

"That was me."

Jordie sneered at Rob; it was plain to see he fancied himself a tough man. He remarked with a snide tone, "I heard Ortiz never had a chance, that this kid just shot him while he was sitting at a table minding his own business."

Rob looked directly at Jordie. "Well, you heard wrong, but anyone can see you're brainless so I'll take it into account that you run your mouth like the scours because you're just plain stupid."

Jordie stiffened, "You can't talk to me like that."

"I just did, what are you going to do about it?"

Jordie's eyes shadowed with fear while he tried to keep up a tough face. He liked to talk and act tough, but there wasn't anything tough about him. He moved his hand closer to his gun like he was trying to scare Rob.

"I wouldn't do that," Eli cut in, "you'll never clear leather. Rob will have you loaded down with lead before you can say boo."

The sheriff snapped angrily, "That's enough."

One of the men to the right of Jordie was wearing a deputy badge. He broke in, "Sheriff, you had better send Jordie back home before his big mouth gets him killed." The deputy looked directly at Jordie, "My brother was in the Hall when the fight happened. Slater flat beat Ortiz to the draw and killed him in a stand up fight. So stop trying to act tough, you never saw the day you could stand in any kind of fight."

Jordie clenched his jaw in anger, his face turning bright red. He was humiliated and sore about being called down and scolded like a child.

The Sheriff spoke back over his shoulder, "I never asked you along Jordie, you jumped on the band wagon. I don't need or want your big mouth, now go home before I arrest you for interfering with a peace officer."

Jordie jerked his horse's head around and kicked him into a gallop away from the group and his humiliation.

The sheriff looked at Rob, "I appreciate your self-control, most men would have blown him out of the saddle."

"I only draw when pushed into it. I wasn't there yet."

The sheriff continued on. "Okay, where were we? Oh yeah, Walt said you came out of nowhere and shot these men in the middle of their robbing the stage. They had already shot the three guards and were about to shoot him when you nailed the one. Is that how it went?

"That's how it went. They were pointed out to us yesterday. When they left town this morning we followed the coach figuring they had an ambush set up somewhere on the Trail. If you still doubt us you're more than welcome to wire Jack and ask about us."

"That won't be necessary. I believe you about Jack. On top of that we have Walt's story to tie it all together. Let's get these bodies into town and have a couple of the bank folks who were robbed have a look at them. Then, we'll settle up on the rest."

The group rode back into town drawing a good deal of attention from the people they passed. Children ran to look and men watched and spoke amongst themselves as to what happened. Walt's story about the robbery and its end result was already spreading.

The people at the bank came out and looked over the dead men. They were unsure until the sheriff pulled the dead men's kerchiefs up and covered their faces from the nose down like they were wearing masks. At that point they all agreed that these were the men who had robbed them.

Eli and Rob followed the sheriff to the undertaker's where the bodies were left off. Then, they returned to his office where the sheriff signed the paperwork that would clear the way for them to collect the reward.

They left the sheriff's office and returned to the bank where the reward money was held in an account. After making small talk with the bank manager, they pocketed the money and walked out of the bank. Standing in the street they looked around. Eli suggested they go and have a meal at Jesus' cantina, which was an idea that appealed to Rob.

Jesus met them at the door, "I heard you got them. The driver has already told all of Santa Fe the story of how you saved him, the wounded men, and the gold. He told of your long shot to kill the last one trying to get away."

Eli nodded, "It went something like that."

"Please, come in and eat."

They followed him inside and took seats at one of the single tables. Jesus brought them plates filled with food and beer the same as before. As they ate, Walt entered the door in an excited manner, spotted them at the table, and hurried over to where they sat.

"They said you were in here." He thrust out his hand to each of them. "I sure would be proud to buy you fellas a drink."

"Thanks," Eli replied, "but we're in good shape here.

You're welcome to sit down and join us."

Walt pulled out a chair and sat down. "I want to thank you for saving my bacon back there. Looks like Sam and Ray are going to pull through thanks to you. Hear tell you're Eli Warren and Rob Slater, I sure couldn't have asked for a better pair of guardian angels."

Eli grinned, "I don't think guardian angels shoot outlaws."

"Maybe not, but I'm sure saying my thanks for you two showing up like you did."

Walt's expression turned serious as he turned to Rob. "Jordie's over at a saloon across the plaza getting himself drunk and talking bad about you. He's going on about how he's going to show everyone that you're nothing. Jordie's got a big mouth, and he's yellow as corn to boot, but like my old pa always said, a coward is more dangerous than a brave man. You can trust a brave man to face you, but a coward will shoot you in the back. You be careful with him."

Rob held a stoic expression. "We'll be heading out pretty quick and I'd just as soon avoid him. When he sobers up he'll think better of it."

"Maybe, but watch yourself all the same." He rose from the table, shook their hands again and left the cantina.

Rob continued to eat as if the warning had no effect on him. He cast his eyes up at Eli, "Figure I can avoid that idiot?"

"We'll try, but if he calls you out you'll have to deal with him."

"I don't want to shoot a big mouth drunk."

"He might not give you a choice. If you run into him you'll have to play the hand as it's dealt in whatever way you see fit. Whatever you do, don't drop your guard thinking he's all mouth. A drunk talking tough, especially one who's had his pride stomped into the ground, will draw on you just on principle thinking he's saving his pride. If you're not ready, he'll kill you no matter how slow he is."

"Let's ride out of here now while he's still talking himself up."

They got up from the table and thanked Jesus for his hospitality and said they would give his regards to Domingo. He smiled at that and wished them well and invited them to come back again which they agreed to do.

They walked outside and mounted up. Reining their horses into the street they began to leave town. As they passed a saloon Jordie ran out and drunkenly began shouting at Rob, calling him a coward and a liar and challenging him to come down and fight. Eli could see Rob's jaw starting to clench as he was losing his temper and the ability to ignore the man.

"Watch it Rob, don't let your temper get the better of you. Keep your head."

Rob unclenched his jaw and took a breath. He reined his horse around and rode him right at Jordie. Jordie stood stock still staring at him as Rob rode the horse directly into him.

Jordie stumbled clumsily out of the way. "Hey, watch where you're going with that horse."

Rob kept pushing the horse into him, backing Jordie toward a water tank. The bay had developed into a good cow horse from working with Cliff's cattle. Whichever way Jordie moved the horse was ahead of him. In his drunken confusion Jordie kept backing up trying not to be stepped on by the horse. He bumped the back of his legs into the water tank and fell into it with a resounding splash. He cursed and floundered in the water splashing wildly with his thrashing arms.

Rob dismounted as a crowd gathered on the street to watch. Rob grabbed a hold of Jordie's shirt front and yanked him out of the tank. Rob slapped him hard across the face with his open palm and then backhanded him on the return swing. Blood dribbled from Jordie's split lips as he awkwardly stood, stunned by the blows. Rob yanked Jordie's gun out of his holster, flipped open the gate and dropped the shells out of it onto the ground as Jordie drunkenly watched. Thumbing back the hammer Rob slammed it against the tank snapping the hammer off the gun and dropped the gun in the tank.

He finished by giving Jordie a hard shove landing him back in the tank with a splash. "Now sober up." He remounted and moved the horse down the street. He could hear the crowd laughing behind him.

Eli moved in next to him. "Nicely done. The town will be talking about that for a long time. They will also be saying how the gunfighter Rob Slater didn't shoot a drunk, which wouldn't have gone over very well with the town or the sheriff. You made a bigger impression with what you just did."

"I didn't see a need to kill him, not over words. All he needed was to be slapped around a bit and have his gun taken away before he gets himself killed."

"He'll never live it down."

"Good, maybe he'll leave the Territory. Now, let's get Carrie and go home."

Chapter 19

Carrie rushed out of the Garza house when she heard Miguel talking and Eli's voice answering him. She grabbed Rob in a bear hug, laughing with glee. "I expected you to be gone much longer," Carrie said excitedly.

Rob laughed, "I can leave again and come back later if you want."

"Don't you dare Mr. Slater, I'll hunt you down myself if you do."

Releasing Rob, Carrie moved over to Eli and gave him a hug.

Julita walked out of the house and watched them. Carrie took the few steps back to Julita and put her arm around her shoulders and ushered her toward Rob. "Rob, this is my friend, Julita."

Rob tipped his hat, "Hello, Julita."

Julita held a sly smile, "I have heard much about you."

"I'm not sure if that's good or not."

Carrie broke in, "All good, I promise. Julita is going to be married in the spring and we are invited to the wedding. It will be a *fiesta grande* like none other." The two girls laughed at Carrie's using the same words Julita had used earlier.

Rob smiled, "Well, that sounds fine. Congratulations, Julita."

Eli stood by watching and listening to the young people talk. Carrie's hint to Rob was wide enough to drive a train through. He wondered if Rob caught it, however, it seemed to go right over his head.

Domingo joined the group, greeting Eli and Rob with handshakes. "I have heard that your mission was successful."

Eli gave him a nod, "Yes, it was."

Domingo glanced at the young women, "Let us go inside and we can talk of it."

Domingo led Eli and Rob into the main room where he invited them to sit. "Your success is good news. I did not appreciate having banditos for neighbors, even if they were relatives."

Eli gave him a complete accounting of the attack and deaths of the Rodriguez men. Domingo's vaqueros had brought word to him of the encounter, however, they did not know all the details. He was pleased to hear what had actually transpired.

Domingo offered his hospitality to them for the remainder of the day and overnight. He wished to learn more about his new friends. They gladly accepted as they wanted to learn more about him as well.

The evening was spent in good conversation and food. They learned that Domingo's ancestry reached beyond Mexico and into old Spain. The ranch he now held had been granted to his great grandfather when the land was still under Spanish control.

Domingo had no concern about New Mexico becoming a territory of the United States or its becoming a state. He did worry about the move to have all Spanish land grants revoked and taken from the present owners with the property being divided among the new settlers. He was in the process of taking legal measures to protect his property in advance of any challenges.

Eli assured him that if he needed to have fighting men to back him that he only needed to call and he and Rob would be right down to help. He appreciated the offer, but felt that he could resolve the problem through the legal process by securing a United States title to his ranch.

At the end of the evening Eli and Rob were escorted to a room for the night. The room had a lamp lit on a central small table. Eli looked the room over, "I could live in a house like this and get mighty used to it."

Rob looked around as well, "Yeah, it'd be pretty nice. Raise cattle and build something permanent." His lost home and parents never ceased to be a dull ache in his chest.

As they settled in Eli pulled the wad of folded bills out of his pocket and peeled off half and handed them to Rob.

Rob took the bills reluctantly. He was still having trouble accepting half of the reward money from the man who had done so much for him. He separated several bills and handed them back to Eli. "You put up the money for the supplies and pack horse you need to take your expenses out first."

Eli took the money and studied Rob for a second. "You did pick up on the hint Carrie threw at you earlier, didn't you?"

Rob looked at him blankly, "What hint?"

Eli grinned, he had called it right. "'Julita is getting married in the spring and we are invited.' That hint." Eli gave him an expression that asked, 'do you catch on?'

Rob looked confused. "That was a hint? I thought she was just telling me that." He paused for a few seconds in thought, "What would that be a hint about?"

Eli chuckled and lightly shook his head. "Carrie wants to marry you. She would never say it as it's not a woman's place to propose. So, what do you plan to do about it?"

Without hesitation Rob answered, "Marry her of course. I thought she knew that."

"She can't read your mind, Rob. Women like to be told how you feel about them. She isn't supposed to carry a crystal ball around in order to know what you're thinking. When it comes to marriage a woman expects to be asked."

"How do you know so much about women?"

"Experience my boy, experience. I was young once too, you know."

"How come you never got married?"

"Almost did once, until at the last minute, the woman I was engaged to suddenly up and moved in with a slicked up gambler."

Rob gaped at him, "You're not serious. She moved in with another man?"

Eli nodded and chuckled, "Actually, she did me a favor by letting me know what she was before I made the mistake of marrying her. As it turned out, she had an eye for every man she saw and she wasn't just looking, if you know what I mean."

"What happened then?"

"The gambler ditched her one night. The last I heard he was headed down the Missouri on a riverboat bound for the Mississippi, probably ended up in New Orleans. She had the gall to come back looking for me after he left her. I didn't want anything to do with her after I found out what she was. She wouldn't leave me alone though, dogged me like a hound. I got ahold of my pal Huge O'Connor and we took off for Colorado on the double. I guess I've been a bit gun shy ever since."

Rob laughed, "Where was that?"

"Montana. I've never been back since, scared I'd run into her, I guess." He laughed.

"I guess you and Huge O'Connor were pretty thick, huh?"

Eli nodded, "Yeah, best friends. We were drovers on the same outfit driving a herd into Montana, then stayed on to work the ranch. He warned me not to marry that woman, said she was bad business. He laughed and said 'I told you so' when I told him why we were headed for Colorado."

Rob knew Huge O'Connor was a subject Eli tended

to skirt around. He returned to the original discussion about Carrie. "I do want to marry Carrie. So, I guess I need to tell her, don't I?"

"That would be a good idea. I'd like to see you two together. When, we get back home I want you to take Carrie on the train to Denver. Let her buy some new clothes, eat in a couple of fancy restaurants, and let her have some fun. She's had a hard go of it."

"I'll do that."

"Buy yourself a dress suit as well. You need to dress up once in a while, especially going to a fancy wedding like the Garza's, and for your own wedding. A man ought to dress decently once in a while; he doesn't always have to be covered in trail dust looking like a ragged tumbleweed."

Rob smiled and stared at the floor slightly embarrassed by his ignorance. "Thanks for explaining to me about Carrie." He then looked up at Eli, "Thanks for everything Eli. I don't know what would have become of me if not for you."

Eli was at a loss for words; he looked at Rob and nodded absently. "I guess you're the son I never had and I'm proud of the man you turned out to be."

"I'm proud you think so, Eli."

Eli coughed nervously and changed the subject. "I liked the way you handled Jordie back in Santa Fe. Most men would have shot him even though he was talking drunk talk. You showed a lot of common sense in what you did. You topped out looking like a man in charge of himself. You disproved his claims that you were a coward, while at the same time putting him in his place."

"You taught me that shooting was the final step. If shooting can be avoided that's how it should be done. I was only following the advice of my teacher."

"Let's get some sleep so we can head north tomorrow first thing." Eli blew out the lamp and lay in the dark thinking about what Rob had said to him. It was time to settle down. Rob and Carrie needed roots and a place to call home, and he was tired. It was time to let Huge's spirit rest in peace.

He examined his thinking and realized that he had started to change the day he took Rob out of that alley. Then, the tragedy with William and Lillian, and Carrie looking to him as her only hope. Her running away to follow him into danger because she feared losing him solidified in his mind what he must do.

Rob and Carrie needed him; no one had ever needed him before. Such a thing changes a man's perspective on a lot of his ingrained ideas. He knew he had rounded a bend in his life and was a rapidly changing man.

The next morning they rode away from the Garza ranch. Keeping to their traveling pattern of Eli in the lead, Carrie in the middle leading the pack horse, and Rob bringing up the rear, they headed north.

With the Garza ranch house behind them Eli turned in the saddle and spoke back to Carrie and Rob. "We're going to take a break. I think we've all earned some loafing time. I'm going to take you up to a spot I found in the mountains."

Carrie smiled excitedly, "Oh that would be wonderful. What does it look like?"

Eli planted the image of the country in his mind. "God's country. A stream beavers have dammed into pools, pine, aspen, green grass. It's a paradise."

"I can hardly wait to see it."

"We can fish or sleep or stare at the mountains, anything we want for a few days. Get away from everyone for some peace and quiet."

Rob agreed, "It has been a crazy spell. I could use some peace and quiet."

Eli led them away from the Santa Fe Trail and northwest toward the distant Sangre de Christo Mountains. They continued to climb in elevation leaving the cactus behind and moving up into the aspen and pine.

The air was cooler and filled with the smell of pine rather than dust. They dropped down into a valley of green grass with a stream running across the western-most part of it. The still beaver ponds reflected like sapphires in the sun.

Eli waved his hand around him, "This is it."

Riding across the meadow they stopped where Eli had last made his camp. Here they broke down the pack, picketed the horses in the grass, and settled in.

The breeze fluttered the green heart shaped aspen leaves and swayed the tops of the pines. They could smell the water from the stream and ponds. It was a good place and Eli knew they needed to stay right here forever.

There was grass and water for stock. It was low enough in elevation that the winters wouldn't be severe, yet high enough to be above the heat and dirt. He could build a house here and just run some cattle. He didn't need to run a million head and be a millionaire, just enough to live on.

Rob brought in an armload of dry wood and got a fire going. Carrie watched his every move. Eli smiled to himself, thinking 'now there is a woman in love.' When Rob had the fire going he set a pot on for coffee as Carrie set about making supper.

As they sat by the fire with the sun setting Eli spoke his thoughts. "I could live up here forever. I wonder who owns this valley or if it's land owned by the Territory."

Carrie sighed, "It is so beautiful and peaceful here. I could live here too."

The spreading sunset reflected off the aspen leaves casting a golden glow over the valley. A beaver glided across a pond leaving a V in its wake as a herd of elk, headed by a huge bull, moved out of the trees and began to graze. The screech of a night hawk capped the natural wonder of the scene.

Eli pointed to a level area halfway up from the bottom of the valley. "Right there would be the spot for a house. There's a good view, shade trees, and high enough above the valley floor so it's not wet in the spring."

Rob filled his coffee cup. "So, how do we find out who owns it?"

"Up here I would guess its government land. This is not part of the old Spanish grants. There should be a land office in Taos that would have that information."

"When we leave here let's head down to Taos and find out."

"I'm not sure how much it would cost or how much acreage is available. It could be out of our price range."

"We've got over two thousand dollars between us right now."

"You hold onto your money, you're going to need it." He flicked his eyes quickly toward Carrie, a move only Rob caught.

Eli sat silent for a long while thinking about the possibility of owning the property. If the Parson gang hadn't disappeared that reward would buy it. He wondered about the gang and the discussion they had with Jack Clovis before they left Trinidad. Maybe they had gone into some kind of business and could still be found. Jack had said no matter where they were or what they were doing the law still wanted them and the reward money would still be on their heads.

The next day Eli and Rob began to explore the valley. One of the first things they discovered was piles of old dried cow manure throughout the area. Eli scanned the country around him. "Someone has run cattle up here at one time, it's been a while though."

Rob frowned, "Does that mean someone already owns it?"

"More likely someone is using it figuring it as free range. A lot of big ranchers run cattle on government land. Some are good about understanding they are only borrowing it while others act like it belongs to them."

He recalled running into those riders east of here several years ago. He tried to remember the rancher's name without success. What he did remember was the one named Earl. He remembered Earl because the man stuck in his craw the way he was trying to show how tough he was and bragging about how they ran out the nesters. Which meant a nester was anyone who settled on land his boss claimed, whether he owned it or not.

This land baron might be the one running cattle up here. It would be a good summer range if it was an exceptionally dry year down below. He might lay claim to this valley even if he didn't own it.

They returned to camp for supper. "What did you find?" Carrie asked.

"Good country all around," Rob answered. "Someone has run cattle up here at one time."

Carrie frowned, "Someone already owns this?"

Rob shrugged, "Eli doesn't think so."

Eli put in, "I think a rancher from down below ran some cattle up here during an especially dry summer once. From the sign it was a while back."

Rob smiled at Carrie, "Did you have the relaxing day you wanted?"

"Yes. I read a bit, took a nap, walked along the ponds."

While they were eating Eli spotted a lone rider crossing the valley from the south. He was passing by until he looked up and saw their smoke and turned toward the camp. They watched as the man drew closer.

Rob tensed, wondering if this was the land owner and he was going to kick them off. He glanced at Eli who was keeping his attention on the rider without seeming to be alarmed or on guard. Rob decided that he was simply keyed up from the past week and didn't need to suspect everyone of being an enemy.

The man pulled his horse to a stop outside the camp. "Evening," he said in a friendly manner. He tipped his hat to Carrie, "Ma'am." Carrie nodded back at him.

Jerking a thumb back over his shoulder the man

explained, "I've a place south of here, like to come up here and do some hunting now and again." He eyed the coffee pot, "Thought I'd stop and pay my respects."

Eli studied the man and decided he looked honest and really was hunting game and not trouble. "Step on down and have a cup."

"Thanks, that's mighty neighborly." The man stepped off the horse and walked up to the fire. Carrie handed him a cup.

He thanked her, filled the cup and sat down across the fire from Eli. "Good elk hunting up here. I take one once in a while for table meat. Locals call it Beaver Valley because of the beaver dams."

Eli nodded, "Appropriate name. We've seen a few elk today, including one big old bull."

"Yeah, they're up here. You live around these parts?"

"Up north. We were down to Santa Fe on business and now heading back."

"There was some fireworks down that way recently. A gang of Mexican bandits tried to stick up a stage carrying gold and got shot to pieces for their efforts. Word has it Eli Warren and his partner, that Slater kid, did the shooting. Now, there's a pair I wouldn't want to get on the wrong side of."

Rob stiffened wondering if this man was something other than what he claimed to be. If he turned out to be hunting them he would kill him where he sat.

Eli poked a stick into the fire with his left hand keeping his right close to the holstered Remington, a move not missed by Rob. "They're probably alright with decent folks," Eli said casually.

"Yeah, could be. People like to talk up things more or worse than they really are. I don't know anything about them except what I've heard. I prefer to draw my own conclusions, Warren and Slater are probably a lot better than what's said about them."

The man drank from his cup and looked up into the

trees. "Sure do like it up here."

Eli watched him. "I do too. I've been through this valley before and thought we'd spend a few days taking it easy before heading home."

"Nice place alright. Government land, you know."

"Is that a fact? I wouldn't mind owning it."

"I'd buy it myself except I don't have much extra cash. You can go on down to the land office in Taos and find out. Only hitch to it is Grover Little figures he's got claim to it."

The name rang the memory bell in Eli's head, that was the name Earl was throwing around, Grover Little.

Rob asked, "If it's government land how can Little lay claim to it?"

"Same as he lays claim to everything else he wants. He owns a big spread east of here and thinks he's God. Pretty much of a land hog. He has his men run off everyone who tries to settle around here. He tried to throw his loop too wide down my way and I put a bullet into one of his riders. They never came back."

Eli grinned, "I guess if someone else owned this valley he'd be out of luck wouldn't he?"

"He'd still try to ram his way through. He's getting on in years and is afraid to lose what he's got or thinks he's got."

"'Or *thinks* he's got,' is right. He doesn't own this so if I want to own it I can."

The man studied Eli for a moment, and then looked at Rob, and back again to Eli. "Little would try and run you out anyway."

"'Try' is the word."

They all sat silent for a pair of minutes. The man finished his coffee and stood up. "If you buy this property would you mind if I still came up and hunted once in a while?"

"You're welcome; just don't shoot that big bull, I'd like seeing him around."

The man put out his hand. "It's a deal. Name's Hank Young, hope we'll be neighbors."

Eli shook his hand. "I hope so too. I'm Eli Warren, this is my niece, Carrie, and Rob Slater."

The man froze in mid-shake staring at Eli and then he burst out laughing. "Oh yeah, Little is about to hit a stone wall. I sure hope you get it."

"We do too and I'm anxious to meet Grover Little."

"You move in up here and you will, and I'd like to see it when it happens."

Chapter 20

The idea of buying the property was discussed long into the night. All were in agreement that they would want to live in this valley and build a permanent home for all of them. The decision to ride down into Taos in the morning and check with the land office was unanimous.

Mid-day found them all in the land office eagerly looking over a platted land map of the area with the agent. The agent agreed that the government was willing to sell land to new settlers. The area they wanted took in a section and a half making up one-thousand acres. The selling price would be three dollars an acre. One-fourth of the purchase price could be put down and the remainder paid off on an agreed upon term.

The three stepped away from the map on the table and put their heads together for a quick discussion. Eli ran the figures in his head. "He would need seven hundred and fifty dollars down. I've got that and more in my pocket right now, what do you think?"

"I've got almost that much on me too," Rob said. "It's for all of us so let's split it fifty-fifty like we do everything else."

"Okay, that would leave enough between us for materials to build a small house on it."

Carrie listened and then broke in, "I don't have anything to put in."

Rob smiled at her, "You don't need to, I'm taking care of us."

She stared at him with hope and excitement in her

eyes. Rob looked into her blue eyes, "I want to marry you Carrie and build this place for us."

The girl's eyes lit up and a smile burst across her face. "Oh Rob, I want that too." She wrapped her arms around him and they embraced.

The land agent stood off to the side watching them with an amused smile.

Rob handed the money to Eli who in turn handed seven hundred and fifty dollars to the agent. "Sir, you just sold a section and a half of land. Let's wrap up the paperwork."

Ownership of the land was put into Eli and Rob's names. Carrie's name would be added along with Robs when they were married and shared the same name. They walked out of the office in possession of the land. The deed itself would stay with the land office until it was paid off in full.

The ride heading back to Boggsville was filled with conversation regarding the prospects for their new home. At the first night's camp plans were made and diagrams for a house were drawn in the dirt. Cattle would have to be purchased, a small herd at first as their money would be limited. They would build a quick cabin to live in until the house could be built.

As they talked around the fire Carrie stopped and asked, "What about Uncle John; won't he miss all of us? He will be alone and he's getting too old to be alone."

Eli answered, "We'll invite him to come along, but knowing him he will want to stay with his store. He has friends and regular customers who depend on him and he knows it. Besides, it would kill him to sit around and do nothing, he has to have something to keep him busy and the store does that."

Rob grinned, "Don't forget about Sally. She comes in and looks at him like a moon struck calf."

Eli laughed, "Seems that's what we were talking about before we left wasn't it? I wouldn't be a bit surprised if the two of them don't hitch up together and run the store."

"Sally is a wonderful old soul," Carrie added in. "Old folks need someone to love too and being a widow I'm sure is difficult. I think it would be wonderful if they married."

"In that case, he's probably anxious to be shed of us," Rob added with a laugh.

They all laughed and felt that the question of who would care for John was answered.

Eli turned serious again. "Okay, our money is limited so we'll have to go at it slow and build. The first priority is to pay off the land, we can't lose the land."

Rob stared silently into the night thinking.

Eli turned to see what Rob was staring at. "You see something out there?"

"No. I was thinking about the Parson gang. If we got them we'd have all the money we need."

Eli studied him without speaking. "That would make all the difference alright. Just as long as it's about bringing down the criminals and the reward, not revenge."

Rob slowly shook his head. "I left anger and revenge behind. After you told me how living for revenge eats a man up inside and rules his actions I decided that wasn't how I wanted to live. If I find Jude Parson I will take care of old business, but it's no longer an obsession."

"That's something you learned a lot earlier than me," Eli said solemnly.

Rob turned his eyes to Eli. There was a lot in Eli's past he didn't care to talk about. It involved his old friend and living for revenge. How many outlaws Eli had killed he would never know nor did he care to know. He had watched the anger in Eli slowly ease out of him over the years, much like his own had.

Eli continued, "We'll talk to Jack on the way in and see if he's learned anything on Parson going into some criminal business. I believe you're on to something there with that idea, it explains a lot and accounts for their disappearance."

"In the meantime maybe we can get on some other outlaws and take those rewards," Rob said.

"This was the last job," Eli said flatly.

Rob looked at him surprised. Carrie showed relief.

"Why?" Rob asked.

"It's time." Eli looked from Rob to Carrie. "There are some things more important to me now."

"Does that include Jude Parson?"

"No. We will go after him providing we ever find him."

Rob gave a relieved sigh. "I was hoping I wouldn't have to hunt them alone."

"You won't."

Rob glanced at Carrie who was showing apprehension in her expression. He wanted to get off the subject of man hunts. "I did like the Garza house and the feeling of settling down to a place like that didn't you?"

Carrie smiled at him, "Yes, very much so."

"I've never had roots deeper than topsoil," Eli said. "John's was the only home I really ever had and it was only a stopover once I was grown. "There's a lot to be said for roots, deep ones."

Carrie spoke in a low voice, "Pa used to tell me that your father was an awful person. That you ran away from home because of how he treated you."

"It wasn't a home, it was a prison. I ran away and in a lot of ways I've been on the run ever since. Now, I want a home and I want the two of you to have roots in Beaver Valley. A place where your children can always come back to and call home."

Carrie stood up and walked around the fire to Eli and sat down beside him. She wrapped her arms around him. "Thank you, Uncle Eli."

They stopped in Trinidad the next day and met with Jack Clovis. He was relieved to know that the mysterious

Bandit Band was dealt with and would no longer be a problem to him or anyone else. As to the Parson gang he had learned nothing. All the lawmen he had contacted had the same answer; nothing had been heard from the gang in a couple of years.

Two days later they arrived back at John's store. They took the horses around to the stable and stripped the gear off of them. Rob and Carrie volunteered to rub them down and feed them while Eli went in to check on John. The front door was open letting in some fresh air.

John was behind the counter when Eli stepped in. John looked at him, "Heard you ride in. You have Carrie with you I assume."

"Yes, she and Rob are tending to the horses."

"She scared the daylights out of me disappearing like that. Then, I ran into Jake on the Trail and he said you had her."

"Long story. She was scared."

"Figured as much. The word's up and down the Trail about you two shooting the Rodriguez boys to doll rags. So's the word about Rob killing Antonio Ortiz. It's big news." John grinned, "So, anything out of the ordinary happen down south?"

Eli grinned as he shook his head, "No, pretty dull stuff, nothing exciting."

Rob and Carrie walked in the front door at the same time Sally Benoit walked out of the back living area carrying an accounting book.

"John," she began, "I've been going over these figures and . . ." She stopped and looked at Eli and then Rob and Carrie. "Oh my," Sally stammered for words, "I am sure this looks very improper. I'm not . . . we're not. Oh, my," Sally whispered again as her faced reddened with embarrassment.

Eli looked back at Rob and Carrie who were stifling smiles. "Do you see anything improper here?"

Carrie and Rob spoke at the same time, "No, nothing,

nothing improper at all."

Sally blushed a deeper red.

John snapped at them, "Alright, you bunch of grinning coyotes give the poor woman a break. She's just helping me out with some arithmetic. For all the education I have, I still can't master anything with numbers attached to it. Mrs. Benoit used to be a school teacher and can run down a column of figures like a cat running down a mouse. She is simply assisting me."

Still blushing Sally turned to John, "I should be going." She laid the book on the counter. She tossed an embarrassed glanced at Eli and then Carrie as she made to pass the girl heading out the door.

Carrie reached out and put her hands on each side of Sally's shoulders. "Please stay Mrs. Benoit; we know nothing improper has gone on here."

Sally looked into Carrie's warm smiling face, "You are such a sweet child and so pretty. You remind me of my daughter who I have not seen in many years."

"Thank you, what a nice compliment."

Eli moved next to John, leaned in and whispered to him, "Why don't you marry the poor woman. That's what she wants you know."

"I've been thinking about it."

"Thinking about it? Get on with it man!"

John called out to Sally, "Mrs. Benoit, Sally, stay and we will all have supper together."

Carrie was still standing by her, "Yes, please stay."

"Yes, Sally stay." John echoed Carrie's request. "Let's close up the store and get supper finished up for these trail weary and dirty travelers." He frowned at the three, "A little soap and water might be in order all around for the three of you."

John crossed the room and dropped the wooden bar across the front door. "Shall we, Mrs. Benoit?" John held his elbow out to her.

Smiling at him, Sally answered, "Thank you, Mr.

Warren," She took his arm and they disappeared through the doorway into the living area.

Carrie smiled, "They are so sweet."

Eli grinned, "I guess that resolves the problem of who takes care of Uncle John."

They all sat around the table making small talk in between the scraping of silverware on plates. In the midst of the meal Carrie apologized to John for running off and scaring him and causing him to search for her. Sally acknowledged that she had given them quite a scare, but all was forgiven.

When they finished eating Carrie beamed a smile and announced, "Rob and I are going to be married."

Sally squealed with delight, "How wonderful."

John reached across the table and shook Rob's hand, "Congratulations."

As the excitement and congratulations waned Eli told John about the land they had bought in New Mexico. He felt nervous when he told John they would be moving out of his house and down to the new place. He wondered how John would take it; they had been together for so long.

John smiled at him, "We've come a long ways together, son. I recall the day you came to the cabin in Independence, a tired, starved kid standing at my door. I recall you said something about us both being black sheep of the family and so you came clear from Richmond to find me."

"I remember and I can never thank you enough for all you have done for me and all you taught me."

"You thanked me the day you took up an orphan and did for him what I did for you, and then you picked up a second one. You're a good man Eli and I'm mighty proud of you. All things come to an end, so don't feel bad. These young folks are starting a new life together, they need their own place and you have to put down roots someday."

Eli felt relief at John's acceptance of the situation.

"We aren't that far, we can still visit."

"You had better; especially with the train breaking through from that direction it won't be a week long ride anymore."

John looked at Sally and grinned slyly, "Since I'm finally getting the kids out of the house, how about you and me tying the knot and running this store together?"

Sally's smile lit her entire face, "Yes John, I think that is a fine idea."

A round of hand shaking, hugs, and laughter went around the table again.

Rob turned to Carrie, "How would you like to take the train to Denver for some shopping? You can buy some new clothes and Eli thinks I should have a suit. We can eat at a fancy restaurant or two and have a good time. I'm flush with cash right now; you had better take me up on this once in a lifetime opportunity."

Carrie squealed with excited delight. "Oh, that would be so *wonderful*. When can we go?"

"We can take the train out of Las Animas tomorrow."

Chapter 21

John and Eli drew from the formal training of their early years in Richmond to teach Rob and Carrie how to conduct themselves in the big city and at well-to-do restaurants. Carrie already knew what to do as her mother had taught her the proper manners they had once used among the elite of Richmond. Rob grudgingly accepted the napkin on the lap and attempted the refined table skills. He thought it a lot of foolishness, yet was willing to do it in order to save Carrie embarrassment.

Eli had also given them specific instructions to stay away from the Holladay Street area, as that was the worst part of the city. The best places were on Larimer Street. There were also four train depots in the city so wherever the train let them off they would probably have to pay a rig to take them to a hotel on Larimer Street.

In the morning Carrie put on her best dress and did up her hair in the fashion of a mature woman. Sally had been insistent the night before that a decent woman did not ride a horse in her best dress. She came back to the store and drove them to the Las Animas train depot in her buggy. She would also pick them up at the appointed time. Arriving at the depot, Carrie and Sally embraced and she and Rob thanked her for the ride.

Carrie couldn't believe how fast the train was moving across the land. It was two-hundred miles to Denver and the conductor had proudly boasted that they were traveling at twenty-five miles per hour and could actually travel faster on the flat stretches of track. It amazed her that they could cover twenty-five miles in a single hour; a horse could only cover three to four miles in that time. At this rate they would be in Denver in eight hours.

Arriving in Denver, Rob had to pay a man a full dollar to drive them to a good hotel. He attributed the high price to Denver being a gold strike city and an outfitting point for all the gold towns around it. Stepping into the lobby of the hotel, Carrie was taken in by the grandeur of the hanging lights and draperies around the windows. It was the finest place she had ever been in.

Together they stepped up to the desk; a man in his late twenties was standing behind it. His hair was slicked down and parted in the middle and his mustache was neatly trimmed and waxed. He wore a suit with a high stiff collar and tie. Holding his chin up, the man looked downward at them with a haughty expression.

Rob didn't care for the man's demeanor, but allowed that the sour look was due to his being choked to death by the collar and tie. "We'd like two rooms," Rob said in a friendly tone.

The man looked at them with a smile that reminded Rob of the banker in Hays who had stolen Carrie's farm. "Are you a married couple?"

"No, that's why we want two rooms."

The man looked Carrie up and down in a manner that made her uncomfortable. "Two rooms? This is Denver. Anything goes here; no one will know the difference. If I was with a woman that looked like this I would only want one room so we could . . ."

Rob's friendly expression instantly turned dark and deadly as he glared hard at the man. He pushed back the right side of his jacket, and rested his thumb over the forty-five on his hip. He made sure the gun and gesture were plainly visible to the clerk. The young clerk's eyes widened as he clamped his mouth shut mid-word.

Rob's voice was a low growl, "Go ahead, finish what

you were going to say, we could what?"

The clerk's chin lowered as he stared at the gun and then he swallowed making his Adams apple jam up against the tight collar. His voice was strained as he tried to maintain control of his pride, "This is not the frontier. This is Denver. We do not carry guns here."

"I'm not from Denver, I'm from the frontier and we carry guns. Now, I want to hear what you were going to say?"

Sweat broke out on the clerk's forehead as he stammered, "Nothing, I was not going to say anything."

Rob moved his hand off the Colt and dropped the jacket back down. "Good, I'm glad you weren't going to say anything. For a minute there I thought you were going to say something I wouldn't like."

The man nervously swung the register around and handed Carrie the pen, "Please, ma'am sign in, I have two rooms for you on the third floor. Are side-by-side rooms agreeable to you, sir?"

Carrie signed her name and then Rob signed his. "Yeah, side-by-side is fine." He stuck the pen back in the holder and glared at the man who avoided his eyes.

The clerk nervously set two keys down on the counter and involuntarily took a step back putting distance between him and Rob.

Carrie began to walk toward the stairway as Rob lingered at the desk a moment longer. He leaned in toward the sweating clerk, "If you ever run your eyes over my girl like that again I'll blow your head all over this room."

The man stared at him wide eyed and terrified. He was unable to speak and could only nod his head in acknowledgment. Rob turned and caught up to Carrie.

As Rob and Carrie went up the stairs the clerk's legs suddenly felt weak and he sat down. Pulling out his crisp white handkerchief he wiped the beads of sweat off his brow. An older clerk with gray hair who had been at the far end of the desk helping another customer had overheard the exchange.

He walked over and looked at the sitting man. "How many times have I told you you can't talk to people like that out here? Maybe you could get away with that in New York City where you came from, but you try that out here and someone will beat your ears down around your ankles or shoot you."

He spun the register around and looked at the names. He laughed. "Rob Slater."

The younger man stared at the older clerk, "Who is Rob Slater?"

"He's a gunfighter, a very deadly gunfighter."

"Him? He was just a boy."

"They don't make boys out west, they make men. Age means nothing here."

"How do you know about him?"

"Because in this country we discuss gunfighters like people in New York discuss prize fighters. Everyone knows who they are and what they have done. It's a different world out here from the one you've known so you had better learn to bridle that bad mouth of yours and keep your eyes off another man's woman or head back East before you get yourself killed." The man turned away from him and returned to his work.

Carrie stifled a smile while attempting to look serious as they walked up the stairs. "I don't think showing your gun to that rude man was what Eli and John had in mind when they were teaching us how to behave in the city."

Rob feigned an innocent look, "I was just standing there and my hand accidentally hung up on my jacket and my pistol just happened to be there. I was only asking him what he was going to say. I was being polite."

"Rob Slater, you big fibber, you know darn well you were trying to scare that man."

Rob grinned, "I did more than scare him, he probably had to go change his drawers."

Carrie playfully slapped his shoulder, "What a thing

to say." Unable to hold back the smile she laughed, "But, you are probably right."

They walked up a few more stairs and Carrie asked, "What was that last thing you said to him while I was going toward the stairs?"

"I just thanked him and told him to have a nice day."

"Hmm, I'm sure you did."

They arrived at their rooms. Rob handed Carrie a key and affectionately put his hand on her arm, "Get rested up and we'll go down and have supper in that restaurant I saw off of the lobby. How about five o'clock?"

"Yes, that would be fine." Carrie gave a quick look up and down the hall and then gave Rob a quick kiss. "I love you."

"I love you too. I'll knock on your door at five." He watched as Carrie unlocked her door and closed it behind her. He entered his room once confident that she was safely inside.

At five o'clock Rob knocked on Carrie's door. She opened it and stepped out into the hall. She had smoothed her dress and brushed out her hair and reset it. Rob held out his arm, "Shall we, the future Mrs. Slater?"

She took his arm, "Why, thank you Mr. Slater, you are so gallant."

Together they made their way down the stairs. As they passed other people who were moving up the stairs the men tipped their heads to Carrie and offered cordial greetings. Rob in turn bowed his head to the ladies he passed.

Arriving in the lobby, they passed the desk with the young clerk who quickly found work elsewhere when they passed. Stepping through the entryway into the restaurant they were greeted by a man who escorted them to a table, pulled out a chair for Carrie, and seated her.

A second man came and asked if they would care for wine with their dinner which they refused. He then handed them each a menu and left the table. Rob's eyes widened and his jaw fell momentarily slack as he looked at the prices on the meals. He was glad he had the majority of the remaining reward money with him as it looked like he would need it.

Having made their dinner choices they gave their order to the waiter and sat back. Carrie's eyes roved around the room taking it all in from floor to ceiling. In her distant memory she seemed to remember being a very little girl in a house that looked as elegant, perhaps it was her grandparents' from the stories her mother had told her about Richmond.

Rob watched her knowing she was in awe of her surroundings, he hoped she was having a good time. He was yet to be impressed with the elegant trappings, but had no intentions of spoiling the event for Carrie. When the dinners came the man placed them on the table, first to Carrie, and then to Rob. He told them to enjoy their dinner and left.

Rob stared at his plate; there was far less on it than he had expected. Accustomed to the places they sometimes ate at on the trail with plates overflowing he had anticipated a loaded plate especially for the price. He looked across the table at Carrie's plate, it was the same, however, she seemed pleased with the meal.

Carrie smiled at him across the table, "Don't you think this is all so wonderful, Rob?"

Rob nodded and forced a pleasant smile, "Pretty nice alright."

Carrie continued to study everything around her as she contentedly ate her dinner.

Rob's empty stomach growled at him as his mind protested the skimpy dinner. Hoping the meal was still coming and maybe this was simply one of those appetizers John had said fancy restaurants served. He discreetly studied the other diners and what was on their plates. He concluded that he had the whole thing. He smiled at Carrie and finished the plate off in a matter of minutes.

After the dinner they took a walk along the street and looked at the buildings and the steady movement of people. Carrie was fascinated by the city, its buildings, and people. Rob felt closed in and crowded, he preferred wide open land around him or the lofty view of mountains. Brick and glass didn't interest him. Finishing their walk they retired to their rooms with plans for Carrie to shop for clothes the next day.

In the morning Rob suggested a café for breakfast that he had seen on their walk. Carrie agreed and they walked down Larimer Street and entered the café. It was neat and they were met by a man who spoke with a heavy Italian accent. The breakfast was more to Rob's liking and he felt ready to take on a day of letting Carrie shop.

Leaving the café, they began the process of moving from one store to another. Carrie looked over the many choices in dresses and various clothes. By noon Rob was dragging his toes on the walkways, yet all the while keeping up a cheerful front for the girl he loved.

As they walked past a store that offered men's clothing Carrie reminded Rob that he was supposed to buy a suit. They went in and looked over the suits and talked to the man inside. The tailor explained the different styles and what fashionable men were wearing. There were styles from basic broadcloth suits to silk. Rob picked out a simple broadcloth jacket and trousers with a white shirt and black tie.

Carrie wanted to return to one of the first stores they had visited as she preferred the dresses she had seen there. Rob was wishing he could have ridden a horse up and down the streets as his feet were hurting from so much walking on hard walkways and streets. Making their way back into the store the floor lady met them with a smile. She looked knowingly at Rob, familiar with the exhausted pained expression on his face, and brought him a chair. His thanks to her was heartfelt.

Carrie tried on different dresses with the lady making

a fuss over her in each one. She finally picked out two that she liked that were practical styles. A blue dress, meant only for special occasions, held Carrie's eye although she returned it to the lady with a resolute sigh.

Carrie walked over and stood by Rob as the lady went into a backroom to wrap the two dresses. He whispered to her, "What about the blue one, it really made your blue eyes stand out. I liked that one."

She leaned in to him, "These dresses are so much more expensive then I had expected and the blue one is twice the price of the others."

"Carrie, *everything* in this city is expensive, let me worry about that. Do you like the blue dress?"

Carrie sighed, "I love it, but the price is too much."

"Take it; you can wear it tonight to dinner."

Carrie's face brightened at the prospect of having the dress. "Are you sure?"

"I'm sure. Go tell the lady before she sells it to someone else."

They walked out of the store with Rob carrying the paper and twine wrapped bundles stacked in his arms. Once back at the hotel he left Carrie to try on her new clothes and he went to his room, pulled off his boots, and landed soundly on the bed with a groan. He had about all the big city he wanted. Carrie was having a good time though so he would continue to keep up a brave face. He concluded that hunting outlaws was far easier than shopping.

The next thing Rob heard was a steady knocking on his door. He opened his eyes and stumbled toward the door. He opened it to see Carrie standing in the hall. She laughed, "Hello, sleepy head, I wore you out today didn't I?"

"No, I was just, umm, resting."

She smiled at him knowing he had fell into exhausted sleep. She also understood he was doing this for her making her love him all the more for it. "When do you want to go to dinner, I am going to wear the blue dress and you must wear your suit."

"We can go now. I'll knock on your door in ten minutes."

Carrie laughed, "Maybe you can be ready in ten minutes I will need a little more time than that. Make it thirty minutes."

Rob nodded sleepily, "Okay, thirty."

Carrie returned to her room and Rob shut his door and stared at his reflection in the mirror. He had shaved that morning so he still looked clean. He poured some water in the basin and washed his face and then got into his new suit. He was glad the tailor had showed him how to tie the tie as he had no idea how and would have just knotted it on like a kerchief.

Standing in the stiff suit he felt uncomfortable. Still, he had to admit he did look good all dressed up. He straightened the tie, took a deep breath, and left the room.

Shrugging his shoulders he fussed the jacket and stiff shirt into a tolerable position. He knocked on Carrie's door. It swung inward and his mouth dropped open as he stared at her. She was beautiful in the blue dress with her blonde hair done up and pinned at the back of her head.

She beamed a smile at him, "Do you like it?"

Rob stammered for words without success, all he could do was stare at her. He finally found his voice, "You're beautiful."

She stepped out of the door and closed it behind her. With a mischievous grin Carrie pushed back the right side of Rob's unbuttoned suit coat. "Just checking."

"For what?"

"To see if you were wearing your gun."

"The coat wouldn't button with it on," he grinned at her. "So, I tucked in the back of my waistband."

Carrie reached out and patted the back of Rob's jacket. She laughed lightly, "You fibber. Shall we?" She took his arm and they walked down the stairs.

As they passed through the lobby men's heads turned to look at her. They did their best to sneak a discreet look at her; however several received jabs in the ribs from their wives who in turn marveled at the girl in spite of their chastisements on their husbands.

Rob and Carrie were seated at a table. They ordered and then sat back talking as they waited. Rob couldn't take his eyes off of her and decided the money spent, and his enduring the city, had been worth it.

Rob eventually started looking around the room at the other diners. His gaze passed over a table one down from them where four well-dressed men sat drinking wine and talking. Suddenly a memory broke loose in his mind and he returned his gaze to the four men and stared hard at them studying their faces. He knew them from somewhere. He searched the visions in his mind; he especially had a strong sense of remembrance about the man sitting in the position that directly faced him.

With startling clarity the spark of memory fanned to flame, the man facing him was Jude Parson. The man was slightly changed, several years older, and dressed like a millionaire, but not so much Rob could not see him standing over the bodies of his parents with a pistol in his hand. One man had his back to him; however, the two whose faces he could see came into focus, it was the whole gang. There wasn't a doubt in his mind who he was looking at.

Carrie saw the change come over Rob's face and turned in her chair to see what he was staring at and then looked back at him. "Rob? Are you alright, you look pale, are you ill?"

Rob leaned across the table and motioned for her to lean in closer. "The second table behind you," he whispered, "the four men, it's the Parson gang. Jude Parson is facing me."

Carrie's expression turned startled, she glanced over her shoulder at the table and the men sitting around it. She turned her head quickly back before they saw her looking at them. "Are you sure?"

"Yes."

She looked back at Rob with worry. "You aren't going to confront them in here are you? Please don't."

Rob shook his head, "Of course not, but I am going to find out where they came from."

As the waiter who served Parson's table passed by Rob lifted his hand to catch the man's attention. The waiter came over to the table. "May I help you, sir?"

Rob put on his best front and made sure to pronounce all his words. "Those four men at that table, they look familiar I believe they did some business with my father, I am not certain though. If they are the ones I would like to go to them and say hello; however, if I am mistaken I will look the fool and disturb them unnecessarily. Could you tell me their names?"

The waiter glanced at the men, "Oh yes, Jason Pierson and his *business associates*." His tone was disdainful. "They used to run a . . .," he glanced at Carrie, "a questionable business on Holladay Street. They have since moved to Central City and opened a gambling hall called The Glory Hole."

Rob feigned disgust, "Those are definitely *not* the men my father did business with. Thank you for saving me from embarrassment."

"You are quite welcome. Will there be anything else, sir?"

"No, you were very helpful, thank you again."

The waiter walked away and Carrie leaned toward Rob. "It's not them."

"Oh, yes it is."

"But his name is Jason Pierson."

"Think about it Carrie, how close is the name Jude Parson to Jason Pierson? It's a false name. He certainly isn't going to go by Jude Parson with a ten-thousand dollar reward on all their heads. Trust me that face is seared into my brain."

Carrie nodded her understanding. "I see. What are you going to do?"

Rob smiled at her. "Nothing. We are going to eat dinner and enjoy this last evening in Denver. There's a play I thought you might like to see."

"I've never been to a play."

"Me neither, it'll be a new experience for both of us."

"I was actually referring to them," she tilted her head slightly toward the gang. "What are you going to do about them?"

"Nothing right now. I know where to find them."

Carrie studied Rob, she knew him all too well. "And then?"

"Eli and I will go and pay a visit to The Glory Hole in Central City."

Chapter 22

The first words out of Rob's mouth when they walked into John's store were, "I found the Parson gang."

Eli was moving flour sacks for John. He stopped and stared at Rob in astonishment. "You found the Parson gang? All of them? Where?"

"We saw all four of them in a restaurant in Denver. I learned that Parson is going by the name of Jason Pierson and they are running a gambling hall in Central City."

"You're certain it's them?"

"A little older and heavier, dressed like millionaires, but it's them. I could never forget those faces."

Eli stared down at the floor in thought. "We have to let Jack Clovis know we found them. We need him to send us a telegram verifying the warrants are still active and the rewards still in force. He also needs to send us any descriptions he has of them and have other law officers send us telegrams regarding crimes that happened in their jurisdictions. We will need all that to prove who they are. We will also need the telegrams to prove our case whether we take them dead or alive. The Central City law will want proof.

"There's no time to waste, I'm riding for town to send off the telegram to Jack and get this rolling. I will stay in town until I get all of the telegrams back we will need." He rushed out the door and ran to the stable.

Sally had picked Rob and Carrie up at the depot as promised. She and Carrie had exchanged a steady flow of conversation involving all Carrie had experienced in

Denver. Rob had remained silent as his mind mulled over the turn of events involving the Parson gang.

Sally stood in the store dumbstruck by the sudden flurry of talk between Rob and Eli and Eli's sudden dash out the door. Sally looked at John, "What is the Parson gang?"

John was staring out the door at Eli's rapid retreat. "Long story. I'll explain it to you later."

John turned to Rob and Carrie, "Well, other than that, how was Denver?"

Carrie excitedly told him every detail she had already given Sally. She unwrapped the paper around the dresses and showed them to John and Sally. John smiled and made approving comments. Sally oohed and ahhed at the dresses.

Rob poured a cup of coffee and sat down, grinning at Carrie's excitement. He was feeling good about finding Jude Parson. At last they would be brought to justice, or the graveyard, whichever course the outlaws chose to pursue. The reward money would pay off the land and set them up in the ranch.

Eli returned the next afternoon. Jack had wasted no time in contacting his peers. Law officers from Colorado, Kansas, and New Mexico responded to him verifying that the Parson gang had committed crimes in their jurisdictions and were wanted by the law.

Rob anxiously met Eli outside as he rode up. "Well?"

"I have to ride to Trinidad. I got a wire back from Jack saying he had a stack of telegrams to give me from officers. Judge Jenkins is issuing fresh warrants for each of them. They could be mailed up here, but I want to make sure I have them in my hand."

"I'll ride with you."

"No, I'm taking an extra horse and riding hard. I can be back here in three days. I want you to go to Las Animas and buy us tickets for the train to Denver. Then, get ready to go."

"So, what's the plan? They have become businessmen with alias names. How do we get at them?"

"I will figure that out on my way to Trinidad and let you know when I get back. I've still got some daylight I'm leaving now. Throw some food in a sack for me and fill a canteen. Tell John I'm borrowing his black."

A quarter of an hour and Eli was riding down the trail with John's black gelding in tow. John was standing beside Rob watching Eli disappear down the Trail. "The final job," John remarked. "Can't say I'm sorry."

Rob glanced at John, "Why is that?"

"Because it's eaten up a lot of his soul. When we led wagon trains together and trapped alone in the mountains he wasn't like that. He was restless, which is natural for a young man, and took the job driving that herd to Montana. When he came back he was filled with rage and a killer's heart."

"He said something about letting Huge rest in peace. Eli never did say much about that, do you know the story behind it?"

John shook his head. "Not much, only what Eli was willing to tell me. Eli met Huge on that drive. They became saddle pals, thicker'n bees in a hive from the sounds of it. They were heading back to Colorado together when one night in their camp two outlaws tried to rob them and steal their horses. They flat shot Huge down for no reason. Eli killed them both and charged headlong into a vendetta against outlaws. He said he planned on killing every outlaw in the country. Lord, how he hated them."

"He made a sizable dent in their population," Rob commented.

"But, he never knew a day of peace since then. Always on the prowl. Always seeking revenge for Huge."

"He told me not to live for revenge because it ate you up. He's made comments in regards to not learning that lesson early on. I guess it must have worn him down."

"It did. In time he went at it as a business rather than revenge, but he never passed up a chance to kill an outlaw."

"He took some in alive though."

"After a while he did, yes. He really started changing when he brought you back here. Then, when he picked up Carrie he saw his world as more than killing outlaws. You two became his purpose for living a better life."

Rob was silent for a minute before saying, "I guess that's why he encouraged me to marry Carrie and plant roots. He never wanted me to live for the purpose of killing Jude Parson."

"That's why he never told you about his hunt for the Parson gang until you were solid enough to handle the quest with discretion."

Rob turned to walk back into the store. "One final job and then we settle down."

Three days after he rode out Eli returned riding the black and leading his roan. Both horses and rider were dust covered and trail weary. Rob walked out of the store to meet him. Eli leaned out of the saddle and slid exhausted to the ground. Rob caught him and steadied him.

Rob chuckled, "You're getting to be an old man."

"A crabby, hungry, tired old man. Watch it kid."

"I'll take care of the horses go on in and be crabby at John." Rob led the horses back to the stable.

By the time Rob returned to the store Eli was sitting at the cabin's table drinking coffee and eating. He appeared to be in a better mood. Carrie was talking to him, her soft voice always calmed Eli down when he was wrought up.

"Did you get the warrants?" Rob asked.

Eli gestured to an oilskin pouch on the table. "Take a look."

Rob opened the pouch and pulled out a dozen telegrams and four tri-folded papers. He began reading the wires. All were from law officers stating that the Jude Parson gang had committed, robbery, murder or both within their jurisdictions. He opened the warrants and read them."

Eli grinned, "Judge Jenkins designated you and I as official servers of the warrants."

Rob glanced at Eli, "They say dead or alive."

"He didn't flat out say it, but the judge's inclination was leaning toward the former."

"Only one has Jude Parson's name on it the others are blank where the name goes."

"The names of the others are unknown. We will write the names in when we take them."

"Okay. Did you come up with a plan?"

"I did. We go to The Glory Hole dressed in our suits presenting ourselves to Jude Parson as businessmen, crooked businessmen. We get to Jude and I tell him that my son and I have a business proposition we would like to discuss with all of them in private. We get them together in a back room and they can either walk out or be carried out."

Rob looked skeptical, "That sounds a little too easy."

"Sometimes a simple approach is less suspicious to people like Parson than an elaborate plan that makes them wary of what you are up to."

"What if they have the law in that town bought and paid for?"

"With official warrants and all those telegrams of confirmation? No lawman who wants to stay out of prison would dare to buck that."

"Okay, we want to get them boxed in. What if they do get suspicious that it's a trap and we can't pull them all together?"

"They have been out of the robbery business for years now. You said the waiter told you they had a business in Denver for a while, now they have this business in Central City. It's been long enough for them to believe their past identities have been forgotten and not trackable back to them. They're feeling confident in their new lives and money is their major interest. If we dangle a big enough dollar sign in front of them they'll bite like a trout."

"That makes sense. When do we leave?"

"We ride to Las Animas in the morning. Did you get the tickets?"

"I did. Everything is ready to go."

"We take the train to Denver in the morning. We'll board our horses in Las Animas and rent horses when we get there. We ride to Central City. I want to be horseback and not dependent on a stage in and out of there."

Carrie sat quietly across from Rob, the conversation scared her. These were murderous men with no conscience or regard for life and she feared what could happen to Rob. Now, that they were to be married she looked at his work in a more frightening light. She had hoped they could begin the ranch soon and he and Eli would no longer ride away to hunt dangerous men.

Rob stacked the telegrams and returned them to the pouch. He got up from the table and walked outside. He stopped and looked toward the distant mountains as Carrie moved quietly up next to him. He smiled at her.

She slipped her hand into his and squeezed it. "Do you have to do this?"

He looked at her, "You mean go after Jude Parson?"

She nodded and bit her bottom lip.

"Yes, it has to be done." He turned and looked her full in the face. "Carrie, these are men who have rampaged across the country murdering as they pleased. They murdered my mother and father. Shot them down like they were nothing for the few dollars they had and a couple of horses. Yes, I want to do this."

He paused as an intense fire built in his eyes. "And yes, I want to look Jude Parson in the eyes and kill him. If that makes me a bad man then I accept that, I'm a bad man." He shifted his glare down at the ground with his jaw clenched.

They remained silent for several seconds as they stood together. Carrie wiped away a tear that trickled down her soft cheek. "I understand." She placed her fingers under Rob's chin and lifted his head so she could look in his eyes. "But, you had better come back to me, Rob Slater."

"I will. I promise."

Eli and Rob rode into Central City two days later. The town had suffered a massive fire several years before that wiped out most of the business district. The previous wooden constructions had been replaced with rows of tall red brick buildings. The city was active due to several big gold strikes surrounding it. They rode up and down the streets until they came to a two story brick structure with a gaily painted sign on the front reading *The Glory Hole*.

Eli and Rob exchanged glances that reflected their mutual satisfaction in having finally run the Parson gang to ground.

Rob's expression of satisfaction evolved into one of cold stone as he stepped off his horse and spun the reins around a hitch rail. "Let's finish this."

Eli followed suit. The two of them stood facing their horses and each covertly slipped a sixth cartridge into his gun.

Eli stepped around the rear of his horse so the two of them were between the horses. "Okay Rob, I know how you feel." Eli pushed his fingertips into Rob's shoulder causing Rob to half turn and look in his face. You have to follow my lead if we want this to work. You go jumping out half-cocked and we'll both get killed."

"I know. I want this to work too, I'll keep myself under control."

"Make sure you do."

Rob studied Eli's stern face and matching tone, he

couldn't recall Eli ever speaking to him in this brusque manner. It sunk in how important this was to Eli, he had hunted these monsters for years and now they had them cornered. Eli didn't want to lose this one chance because he acted like a vengeance wracked fool.

"I know this is as important to you as it is to me Eli. I won't ball it up."

Eli nodded as they stepped out from between the horses and up to the door. They stepped into a room that was elaborate in all details. Tables, waxed and buffed to a brilliant sheen, gleamed under the light thrown off by hanging oil lights bearing painted globes. A polished bar ran the length of the back wall with a full length mirror reflecting the bottles and glasses stacked in front of it. A painting of a barely clad woman hung over the mirror.

Men sat at tables throwing money down to sharply dressed card dealers. The barman was busy pouring drinks while women, painted and rouged, worked among the customers selling drinks and themselves. Eli spotted at least three thugs meandering around the perimeter of the room closely watching every player and drinking customer.

Eli caught the attention of one of the thugs and made eye contact with him. The heavily muscled man swaggered toward him. He posed in front of Eli in a manner meant to intimidate him. "You want something?"

Eli held the man's eyes without the hint of the fear he knew the thug expected to see. "We want to see Jason Pierson."

"Mr. Pierson doesn't see anyone unless he asks for them."

"He'll see us."

"You don't hear so well I guess," he spoke slowly as if to a child, "Mr. Pierson does not see anyone."

"Tell Pierson I want to see him or he can go out in the street and shovel up a new thug."

The man glared at Eli and raised his fist to throw a punch. Rob's hand moved down and in an instant had his cocked Colt pointed at the end of the man's nose. "Now, my father asked you politely to get Jason Pierson out here. I'm not so polite, get him."

The thug's eyes narrowed, glaring at Rob as he held his clenched fist in the air. He debated as to whether the kid look would pull the trigger or not. His dilemma was settled when he was abruptly dismissed.

A man in a tailored suit stepped up to them. "Go back to work Fogerty, I'll take care of this."

Fogerty held his glare on Rob, who glared back at him over the Colt.

"*Now*, Fogerty!" the sharply dressed man snapped.

The thug turned on his heels and stomped angrily back across the room to where he had been previously standing.

The man studied Rob with approval. "You have a fast hand with a gun, we might be able to use a man like you."

Rob holstered the Colt. "I work for myself."

The man looked from Rob to Eli. "I am one of Mr. Pierson's associates, can I help you?"

Eli coolly met the man's eyes, "My son and I have a proposition to discuss with Mr. Pierson and all of his associates. I understand there are three of you who work with him."

"What kind of proposition?"

"The kind I want to discuss with him in a room that doesn't have so many ears listening in. It represents a great deal of money and I know Mr. Pierson is always interested in large amounts of money."

"How much money?"

"Let's say enough to make listening worth his time."

"Why come to us?"

"Word has it that you are men who use what you have to get what you want. My son and I are much the same, we get what we want; however, there are times we seek out cooperative partnerships with men in our line of business."

"Exactly what is your *line* of business?"

"Making money by interrupting the cash flow of others."

"What are you offering?'

"Let's just say we have what we need to bring this association to an acceptable conclusion and we need all of you to agree to make that happen." Eli cast a quick glance around the busy room, "I'm not answering any of you questions or going into detail in here though."

The man studied Eli for a long silent minute. He wasn't about to admit that he had no idea what this man was talking about. He was tempted to tell the two to leave, yet if he was talking big money, and they lost out because of him, Jude would take it out of his hide. Jude was the one to make decisions on this sort of thing.

"*Come on*," Rob snapped at the man. "Make a decision or are you just a lackey who can't make decisions?"

The man's face reddened as his eyes blazed into Robs. "Your son has a hot temper."

"He's young and headstrong, like we all were at one time." Eli smiled, "We only need a few minutes of your time, and unlike my son, I believe you are a man in power here. Trust me it will be worthwhile."

Rob held a stern expression, but inside he was nervous hoping taking this tack would keep the man from walking away. He had waited a long time for this and the meeting Eli was trying to set up was on the verge of falling through.

The man shifted his eyes from Rob to Eli, "Alright, come with me." He led them across the gambling floor to a single closed door. He opened the door and ushered them in.

The room was large and lavishly decorated. Paintings hung from the walls, a large ornate desk with a comfortable chair behind it was in the center. A silver cigar box was on the desk along with a decanter of brown liquor and several glasses. There was a second closed door in the back wall of the room.

"Wait here while I gather Jason and the others. Go ahead and have a seat." He went out the second door.

They remained standing. Rob whispered, "So far so good."

"I thought we were about to lose him until you kicked his pride in the pants."

"I figured that would do it. He pictures himself important here and didn't want us to know he's just one of Jude's boys. I took a chance on getting tough with him. It put him in a position where he had to do something or look weak."

"Watch every move they make. I'll start like this is a real deal and then open the ball. When I do you'll know it and I want you ready. If it goes to shooting, we're in tight quarters with them and we could all end up dead, so don't miss."

"I never miss, I was taught by the best."

They waited a quarter hour before the door opened again and the same man led the way through it. Behind him filed in three men. Rob knew the faces and the last man in was Jude Parson. Parson took a seat behind the desk while the others stood spread out behind him. Eli made a quick mental calculation and decided the two on his left had to go first. Rob would know what to do with the one on his side and Parson.

Parson leaned back in his chair and studied them with suspicion. "I am Jason Pierson; my associate says you have a proposition for me; however, his judgment is at times flawed. First, let me tell you right up front I do not appreciate being summoned like some common servant so this had better be well worth my time or you will very much regret my inconvenience."

Eli looked Parson square in the eyes, not impressed by his practiced eloquent diction. He had hunted this man for years without ever laying eyes on him and now he sat four feet away from him. "That is not a very polite way to start a relationship. I had hoped we could all be friends."

Parson gave him an irritated scowl. "I think you are wasting my time. What are you anyway, a drummer? A salesman trying to sell me something, you certainly lied your way in like one." He rose up out of his chair. "Den, have Fogerty teach these bums a lesson and then throw them out into the street."

"I wouldn't do that, Jude."

Parson froze in mid-move and snapped his head around to look at Eli. "What did you call me?"

The three men with him jerked to attention and began to move their hands closer to their bodies.

"Jude, Jude Parson. What, you've been going by Jason Pierson for so long you forgot your real name? Just because you put on a hundred dollar suit and wax eloquently doesn't change what you are. By the way, there's still a little Missouri in your speech."

Parson's eyes flicked back and forth trying to think of something to say. He shook his head, "You're loco, I ain't never heard of any *Jude Parson*."

Eli grinned at him, "Careful there Jude, you lapsed back into your old speech pattern."

"I have no idea what you are talking about."

"Dead or alive Jude, the warrants are still in effect for all of you. In fact I have four fresh ones hot off a judge's bench. Either way is fine with us. Walk out of here or be carried out, it's your call."

Parson took on a smug expression, "You can't connect me, a legitimate businessman, to Jude Parson. Nice try."

Eli smirked, "Because all the witnesses are dead? Won't work Jude, it's over, you've run out of luck."

Rob spoke up, "I can connect you. I saw you when you came to our farm in Missouri and murdered my parents. I'm a witness and that's enough to bring you in, and there are other witnesses and when they are all rounded up, you'll swing."

Without a warning Parson grabbed the liquor decanter and threw it at Rob. As his arm drove forward, his body momentum was heading for the back door. The other three men pulled their guns.

Rob had been watching Jude's twitching hands when he grabbed the bottle. He ducked the thrown bottle clearing the Colt as he dropped to one knee. Two shots whiffed the air where Rob had been standing. He shot the man in front of him, one slug to the heart.

Eli drew and in an instant put two bullets into the torso of the man to his left. As he ducked down the man in front of him fired a shot that broke a lamp over Eli's shoulder showering him with oil. Eli emptied his gun into the man who stripped the contents off the desk as he fell across it and slid off.

Rob burst out of the room on the heels of Parson. He could see the man disappearing around a corner in the long hallway. He followed the hallway as it wound back into the main gambling room.

Parson tore into the room pulling a red velvet curtain off a doorless entry as he ran through. Parson shouted at Fogerty to stop the man chasing him as he wove his way through the tables and across the room.

As Rob ran into the gambling room the thug rushed at him in an attempt to block him. Rob snatched up a chair and slammed it into the big man's ankles causing him to scream out in pain and fall. He saw Jude swing open a door, rush through it, and slam it shut behind him.

Rob burst across the room and kicked open the door without breaking stride. Pieces of door latch exploded into the landing at the base of a stairway leading to the second floor. Taking the steps two at a time Rob topped out on the stairs to hear slamming and shouting.

Catching his breath he made a quick scan of the area at the top of the stairs. He looked down a short hallway to see Parson at the end of it cursing violently and trying to beat down the padlocked door that led to the outside stairway on the rear of the building.

Rob holstered his gun and approached Jude at a slow, deliberate walk. Parson turned around pushing his back against the locked door his eyes wild with fear. "Come on kid, give me a chance. I'll make you a rich man, you name it and it's yours. You can walk out of here a rich man. What do you say kid?"

Rob watched Jude through cold passionless eyes unmoved by the outlaw's pleas. He remembered Parson's merciless manner when he was demanding money from his folks and what he was going to do to them if they didn't give it over. They gave him what they had and then he shot them anyway and grinned about it. Now, here he was a trapped coward bargaining for his life. It was disgusting.

Rob's tone was low with a steel edge to it. "I've wanted to look in your eyes and blow a hole in your belly since I was twelve years old. You've murdered your way across this country for years, showing no mercy to anyone. Now, here you are begging like the yellow dog you are. You're wearing a gun Parson, the only way you leave this hallway is in a box."

Parson's panicked voice coming out shrill, "Come on kid, *please.*" Even as he said it Parson knew this was no kid, but a man with emotionless, obsidian eyes that would kill him. He made a desperate draw dragging his gun out from the shoulder holster hidden under his suit coat.

Rob's hand flashed like that day in Las Vegas. He felt the .45 buck in his right hand and saw the impact of the bullet on Parson's white shirt front. He thumbed back the hammer and shot him again, and then a third time. Parson's gun slipped from his fingers as he slid down the door leaving a blood smear on the white paint and a hole where one of the bullets had gone through. He let out a rattling breath and died.

Rob stood looking at the lifeless form of the man he had carried a hatred for since that day in Missouri. He had finally done it, looked the murderer in the eyes and killed him. Jude Parson was finished. Rob turned around to see Eli standing behind him.

Rob spoke calmly. "He begged for mercy. He begged like a dog." Rob looked back over his shoulder at the dead man, "And I shot him like one."

Chapter 23

Rob looked over the valley as the land rolled out before them. It was lush in green grass, bordered on three sides by hills of pine and aspen with the eastern end opening out to the desert below. The snow-fed stream flowed from the east side of the mountains curving to the south as it cut across the upper portion of the valley. It had been a brutal summer in the lower country and even the high country felt the effects of no rain, still the beaver ponds never went dry even in this dry summer.

Throughout the valley cattle grazed or lay half asleep methodically chewing. The bold W/S on each animal's hip was evidence of the ranch's growing success. It was prime grazing land and the envy of any cattleman.

Two years had passed since the day in Central City when they finished off the Parson gang. Rob reflected on his killing Jude Parson and never to this day regretted doing it. They had taken the reward money and paid off the land, bought lumber for the house, stocked it with cattle, and still had seed money for the future. They hadn't hunted a wanted man since.

Rob shifted his weight in the saddle and glanced over at Eli. "Quite a picture, isn't it?"

Eli only nodded as his eyes beheld the scene before him.

Rob studied him. A scattering of gray hair showed at his temples under the brim of his sweat stained battered old hat. The hat had been a light gray color when new, but there had been a lot of miles, sun, and snow on it since then. He recalled a time when Eli was a fire breather, his name alone struck fear in the black hearts of outlaws. Now, he was an aging man, content to be at peace and look over his land.

Eli shifted his eyes toward Rob and caught him looking at him. He grinned and pointed down from their position on the hill, "Better view down there, son."

Rob grinned back, "You're not that pretty to look at. Just thinking back."

"Don't think too much; you manage to get yourself into trouble every time you do."

Rob turned his gaze back to the valley and pointed down into the aspen at a herd of elk making their way out to the meadow. "There's that big bull again, bet his horns weigh a hundred pounds and he's ten years old."

Eli watched the elk. "He's like me, gray in the muzzle and fought out. He hopes to take it easy and live out his days without a pack of wolves taking him down."

"I think we left the wolves behind."

Eli watched the sun spread the last glow of day across the western mountains. "Funny thing about wolves, you never know where one will show up."

Eli reined the equally aging roan around and spoke with a hint of humor, "Best get back before Carrie throws our supper out."

They turned together and headed back to the house. Riding along, Rob's thoughts drifted. He remembered the first time he saw Carrie and thought she was the prettiest girl he had ever seen. Then her parents died, that banker stole her farm, and she came to ride with them. They had gotten married before they moved here from Boggsville.

Riding into the barn, they stripped the saddles and bridles off the horses and turned them into the corral with a couple forks of hay and headed for the house. The lamplight glowing through the curtained windows made for a friendly welcome. Eli spoke in the growing darkness, "Looks right homey, doesn't it?"

"Yeah," Rob answered, "right homey."

Carrie opened the door at their approach spilling a beam of light onto the ground. She took Rob's hand and kissed him lightly on the lips and smiled. The baby she carried was just starting to bulge the front of her dress.

She closed the door behind them as Eli looked at Rob with a mock angry father expression. "Mister, I saw you sneak a kiss from my niece, just what are your intentions?"

Rob went along with the joke and took on a serious expression. "Yes sir, I admit it, I done kissed her, so I figure to make an honest woman out of her, marry her, and give her baby my name."

"That's fine then." Eli unbuckled his gunbelt and hung it from a peg by the door.

Carrie laughed, "Okay you two, sit and eat or I'll throw it out."

With a nod toward Rob Eli grinned, "See, told you."

Grover Little scowled as he surveyed the brown stubble that passed for grass on his range. The rainless New Mexico summer had been cruel to the land. The waterholes had degraded into cracked hollows in the dead ground. The river was dry except for a series of stagnant holes surrounded by quicksand that claimed the thirsty cattle as they attempted to reach the last water.

The cattle were rapidly losing weight and looked more like walking skeletons than the beef animals they had once been. Every pound shed represented lost income to Grover Little. Enough lost and he would be ruined. His foreman, Lew Prine, sat on his horse next to him and waited.

Without looking at Prine Little barked an order in his usual manner. "First light tomorrow move three-hundred head up into Beaver Valley. Then rotate herds, 300 at a time, in and out of there."

Prine paused for a moment without answering. Little sensed that his foreman was questioning his order and turned his head and snapped, "Is that a problem for you?"

"Beaver Valley is owned by the W Slash S now; we can't move stock onto that range anymore."

"I'll move my stock wherever I blame well please. I always ran my cattle up there during the drought years. I control everything in this country and that includes the valley."

"You used to use the valley, but the situation has changed. You can't take over another man's property."

Little's ears began to turn red with anger. "It's a nothing two-bit outfit squatting on my range. I ran off other squatters, I'll run them off too."

Prine was a man of honesty and integrity. He had followed his boss's orders in the past pushing nesters off the range figuring they had no right to just take over another man's land. Now, he was being told to do exactly what they had been attacking others for doing. His honor was worth more than his job and he refused to agree to the action.

"This is different Mr. Little, those people own the valley. They bought it, they're not squatters. Times are changing."

Grover Little was a man with no bend in him, he was stubborn and self-confident. When he wanted something done he expected it done. He wasn't accustomed to having his orders questioned or dealing with a matter he couldn't force to his will. The fact that the valley was now legally owned and he no longer had any right to use it, was a twist he was unsure how to handle.

Prine continued, "If we move cattle onto that property we'll be trespassing. At best it will get the law on us, at worst it'll turn to a shooting affair."

A hint of reason squirmed its way into Little's angered thoughts. He had to admit there was some validity to what Prine was saying. He wasn't worried about the law; he was too wealthy for them to try anything with him. On the other hand starting a shooting war wasn't what he wanted either; there were no winners when it came to a range war. He knew the old ways of controlling large tracts of land were no longer overlooked as in the past, but he wanted that valley.

"Fine," he snorted. "Tomorrow ride up there and make them an offer to buy them out."

Prine nodded, "Yes sir."

Little glared at him, "Make sure they understand it's in their best interest to sell out."

"And if they don't want to?"

"I'll have Milt and the boys pay them a visit." He turned his horse and rode away.

Prine watched him go until he was out of sight. He shook his head, understanding that anyone who had bought that valley wasn't going to sell it. Little would push it and if the new owner was a tough man it would end with blood on the grass. He knew Little was bull-headed enough to push it, he also knew the man was wise enough to know when enough was enough and back off. He hoped to reason with that side of him before men died over land and cows.

First light found Lew Prine knocking on the door of the Beaver Valley house. Eli, Rob, and Carrie were eating breakfast getting ready for the day's work. They all glanced at each other. Carrie walked to the door, opened it, and looked at him.

Prine removed his hat, "Morning ma'am, sorry to disturb you. My name is Lew Prine. I'm foreman for Grover Little, could I have a word with you folks for a bit?"

Carrie remembered what their neighbor, Hank Young had said about Grover Little that night they were camped in the valley, how he would eventually be around for the valley. Hank had been up to visit a couple of times since they moved in and had on occasion mentioned some problem Little was causing a settler or small rancher. Little had never been to the valley since they had bought it.

Neither had he shown himself to be friendly or a neighbor of any kind. All of this did not set well with her in regards to Prine's unexpected visit.

She stepped aside and invited him in. He thanked her and looked across the room to where the two men sat at the table. The hard eyes of the older man penetrated him, he knew right then they would never sell and if Little pushed these men someone would die. Still, he had to follow his orders and make the proposition to them.

Carrie gestured toward the table, "This is my Uncle Eli, and my husband, Rob. This is Mr. Prine, from Grover Little. He would like to speak to us."

Eli stood and shook his hand, as did Rob. Eli gestured toward a vacant chair, "Have a seat. Care for some coffee?"

"Thank you, I would."

Carrie brought him a cup and filled it from the big metal pot. He thanked her and stared at the tabletop. He felt like a fool sitting there, these men weren't weaklings and the proposition he was being forced to present to them echoed in his head like the limping gait of a lame horse. He resented having been sent here in the first place on a fool's errand. He decided not to treat these men like greenhorns and tell them the truth.

Lew looked across the table at Rob, he was young, but there was toughness reflected in his face. A younger version of the older man. He then turned to Eli. "First off, I have to tell you I feel foolish for being here so I'm going to be straight up with you. I'm sure you're familiar with Grover Little and all his holdings. He used to summer his cattle in Beaver Valley during drought years like this one. Water's about gone on his range and he wanted to push three hundred head up into this valley like he used to, but I reminded him that you now own the property. He wanted me to do it anyway; I was able to convince him he couldn't do that to another man's property." He stopped and studied the two men for a reaction. Rob's eyes were narrowing with growing anger, Eli held a poker face and remained silent.

He continued on. "Little sent me here to ask if you would be willing to sell out to him." He turned silent again.

Eli shifted forward in his chair. "First off, Mr. Prine we are not interested in selling, not now, not ever. Second off, I am well aware of Grover Little's tactics in dealing with people he considers nesters, so what does he really intend to do?"

Prine felt embarrassment as he said, "If you don't sell, he'll try and drive you out."

Eli leaned back in his chair and grinned, "How does he plan to do that?"

Eli's grinning over something that scared most men made Prine nervous. "He keeps some men on the payroll for such jobs. Have you ever heard of Milt Cramer? He was a hired gun in that Maxwell Grant business some years back. He's a hand with a six-gun."

"Milt Cramer!" Eli's whole face lit up as he burst into laughter. He looked at Prine, his eyes dancing with humor. "I'm not laughing at you, Mr. Prine, but you go back and tell *Milton* that Eli would love for him to come around. He'll know what you mean."

Prine studied Eli. Most men froze at the mention of a visit from Milt Cramer, but this man merely laughed it off. He obviously knew the gunman and had no reservations about calling him out. Little would be biting off way more than he could chew if he pushed this man.

Without moving, Rob spoke in a cool tone, "You don't seem like the driving people out type, Mr. Prine. So, you being his foreman, how do you feel about this? You can speak openly to us."

With a shake of his head Prine looked directly at Rob. "I've had this job for over ten years and I'd like to keep it, but I'll have no part in stealing a man's land that he's legally bought and paid for. I'll admit I've run off some nesters who didn't have any legal ground to stand on. This is different, you do."

"Is that the only reason, because of the legal ground?"

Prine held the young man's hard eyes for several seconds before speaking. "No. I don't cotton to any of it anymore. Little has pushed his weight around in the past and thinks he still can, times are changing and he has to change with them, we all do. I ride for the brand, always have, but I'll quit before I join up with the likes of Cramer to ride against you."

Prine felt a strong sense of embarrassment as he stood up to leave. He thanked them for their time, turned around, and began walking to the door. He stopped and looked back at Eli. "And it's not because I'm afraid of you."

Eli looked soberly at the man. "I know you're not, Mr. Prine, you seem a man of integrity and decency."

Prine nodded, "Name's Lew." He half turned to leave then looked back at the men, "Who should I say owns this land when I see Little?"

Eli held the steady look. "Warren and Slater."

The pieces fell into place. Eli . . . Eli Warren, the outlaw hunter and Rob Slater the gunfighter who killed Antonio Ortiz. He nodded his understanding. Little had no idea what he was getting himself into, but he would be sure and explain it to him. He walked out closing the door softly behind him.

Carrie sat down at the table. "What should we do, Uncle Eli?"

"I think we should take the fight right to him," Rob answered. "Don't give him time to get set."

"No." Eli took a drink from his cup. "We do that and we become the aggressors and the law will be on Little's side. We wait and see if he's a lot of hot air or if he really means what he says. We have to let him make the first move."

Rob argued, "Letting him make the first move might

get us killed."

"Us making the first move could get us hung if we are the aggressors and kill someone. This calls for patience and keeping a sharp eye out."

Carrie frowned, "Hank told us what Grover Little has done to people he considers nesters. Why won't he do that with us?"

"Because we're not nesters and those were simple farmers who didn't have the skill or heart for a fight. They were easy victims for a man like Little. I doubt he ever took on someone who fought back."

Carrie thought about that. "You are probably right. Remember when Hank said he put a bullet in one of Little's men and they never bothered him again."

Rob nodded. "You're right, and Carrie's right too, he won't stand and fight."

Eli looked at him, "We can't make the first move, but on the other hand we can't assume he won't. He's managed to hold all that land for a long time by force. He might very well push the issue."

Rob thought on that for a second. "It's a touchy situation isn't it?"

"It is that," Eli agreed. "We will have be on the alert."

"What if he does attack?"

Eli's expression hardened, "Then, we have every right to fight back, and we will."

"We might have a friend in Lew Prine though. A friend in the enemy camp could be helpful to us. He seemed like an honest man."

Eli nodded, "He did seem a decent sort." Eli took another sip from his cup as he thought. "We'd better stay close in for a day or two and see what happens."

Three days passed and there was no sign that Little was going to make good on his threat. The ranch work was backing up, forcing Eli and Rob to ride out and get back to working the cattle. Eli left Carrie with instructions to keep the shotgun handy and if anyone came around hunting trouble to give them a warning and then shoot them if they pushed it.

Rob was concerned about leaving her alone without being sure of Little's intentions. Eli reminded him of what happened to those two men who came into the Wagon Mound camp thinking she was helpless. It made Rob feel better, yet if they attacked in force Carrie wouldn't be able to hold them off. They decided to check back on her every few hours.

It was mid-afternoon when the six men rode up to the house. They stopped and lined their horses across the front of it. One of them called out. "Hello the house, Grover Little's got a message for you."

Carrie leaned the shotgun against the wall just inside the door, opened it and stood in the doorway looking at them. "What do you want?" Her tone was not friendly.

"We want to talk to the man of the house, not some wisp of a girl. Is he in there hiding behind your skirts?"

Unseen to the riders Carrie moved her hand to the left and laid her fingers on the double barrels of the shotgun. "You can talk to me or turn around and ride. Speak your piece and be quick about it."

The men looked at each other and laughed. "You're a right smart little girl, ain't you? Okay, short and sweet, you've got one day to get your squatter tails off Grover Little's land."

"We own this land, bought and paid for. So, you ride on back to your boss and tell him that. We are not squatters and we won't be going anywhere."

The speaker turned angry, "You'll leave and be quick about it."

Carrie pushed her chin out defiantly, "Or *what*?"

"Or what? How about this." He turned to a rider on his right. "Earl, shoot out those windows."

Just as Earl pulled his gun and pointed it at the window, Carrie brought up the shotgun and cocked back both hammers. Holding the gun hip high and pointed at Earl she shouted at him. "You fire one shot and I'll blow you clear into Mexico."

The man froze in mid-motion, uncertain what to do next. He wasn't sure if the girl was bluffing or not, but the shotgun was directly on him and she didn't look like she was bluffing. He looked back at the leader with the question in his eyes as to what he should do.

Without taking her eyes off the man with the drawn gun, she addressed the leader. "He gets the first shot and you get the second, but I'm sure you will all get some buckshot when it spreads out. You wouldn't be the first men I've killed. Like I said before, you better ride."

Only a fool argued with a shotgun held in the hands of someone who wasn't afraid to use it. "Okay, you got it over us now, but there'll be another time and we won't be announcing ourselves then. You tell that yellow-bellied coward hiding in the house there that Milt Cramer will be back for him."

"I'll be sure to tell him, now get."

As a group, the riders turned and rode away. Carrie waited until they were far enough out and fired a shot directly over their heads so that the buckshot would rain down on them without doing any more than sting. A second behind the shotguns roar she saw them duck and yell out. Their horses jumped at the stinging lead pellets and bolted into a mad gallop causing the riders to grab onto their saddles to keep from being thrown. Carrie grinned at the show. "That'll warn them," she whispered.

It was only a few minutes from the shotgun's blast to the time Eli and Rob pounded into the yard at a hard gallop. Looking around as they rode, they pulled the horses to sliding stops in front of the house. Carrie was still outside holding the shotgun. "What happened?" Rob shouted as he ran toward her.

"We had a visit from six of Grover Little's riders. They said we had one day to, as he put it, 'get your squatter tails off Grover Little's land.' "

"What was the shot?"

Carrie giggled, "One of them, some fool named, Earl, was going to show me they meant business by shooting out our windows. The shotgun made him reconsider and he decided not to. I just dusted them a bit to hurry them on their way. You should have seen their horses take off with them trying to stay on." She burst out laughing.

Eli looked around, "I had a run in with a man named Earl down this way a long time back, I'm sure it's the same man. Did they say anything else?"

"Yes. They were convinced the *man of the house* was hiding inside, too scared to come out. The one who seemed to be the leader said his name was Milt Cramer and to '*tell that yellow-bellied coward in the house*' that he would be back."

Rob looked at Eli, "I thought Milt Cramer was in prison."

"He got ten years. His sentence must have been shortened between then and now."

"Well, I guess he didn't get any smarter, he's right back to his old tricks."

Eli glowered, "Looks that way, don't it."

"Uncle Eli, he also said that next time they wouldn't be announcing themselves. I'd take that to mean they will attack without warning. If that's the case one or all of us could be killed."

Rob was trying to hold his anger in check. "I think that time has come to pay Little a visit."

Eli frowned, "As far as I'm concerned that was the first move, we can have a free hand now."

"Let's shove it down his throat," Rob snapped.

Eli turned the roan with Rob jumping into the saddle and following.

Grover Little's house could be seen for a half mile out. The house was big, two stories and freshly painted white. A covered porch wrapped around the front and one side. The house and grounds spoke of his wealth. Where most people would have been cowed by the appearance of Little's power, Eli and Rob could care less. They stopped their horses where the steps led up to the front door.

Eli called out, "Grover Little, we've come to talk to you. Have your butler announce us and get out here."

A man hurried out of one of the barns and half-ran up to them. "If you want to talk to Mr. Little, why don't you go up and knock like a civilized person?"

Eli glanced at the man, then returned his attention on the house. "Because I'm not civilized, and because he just sent his hired guns to my place to threaten us. I'm not interested in having tea with him. So you can either go up there and tell him that Eli Warren and Rob Slater's here to talk to him or you can get back to the barn and mind your own business."

The man's face blanched at the names. "Lew told us you owned Beaver Valley now."

"He told you right. Your boss seems to think he can waltz on up and take it, we're here to tell him otherwise. Now, get him out here."

The front door opened and a man with at least ten years on Eli stepped out onto the porch. His face was weathered and hard with a thick gray and black mustache covering his upper lip; his slate-blue eyes were frigid and steady. "Here I am; you want to talk? Let's talk about you getting off my range."

Eli set his elbow on the saddle horn and leaned toward him. "Since I have a deed with my name on it, and Rob's as well, how do you figure it's your range?"

"It always has been."

"Well, it's not anymore. You keep your cows off and if your hired guns come back threatening us, I'll send them back to you tied over their saddles. And, if anything happens to my family or property, I'll be coming back here and shoot you right on your own porch."

If Little was intimidated or concerned it didn't show.

"I don't take threats kindly."

"Neither do I. You can push a bunch of farmers around, you push me and I'll bury you."

The two men held their ground glaring into each other's eyes. Little knew he didn't have a leg to stand on, still he was too set in his ways and stubborn to give in or show weakness. The man was right, but he wasn't about to let him know it. "We'll see who buries who; now get out of my yard."

"We'll go for now, consider yourself warned, you send that scum around again and we will be back." With that they turned their horses and rode away from the house.

Rob glanced back over his shoulder to see Little still standing on his porch watching them. "Think he'll send them back?"

"He'll send them back. I stepped real hard on his pride and he favors himself a big man. He'll want to show us who's bull of the woods around here."

That evening a lamp had been burning in the Beaver Valley house for less than an hour when the crash of breaking glass and gunfire exploded through the main room. The shots rolled over each other so steadily the number of shooters couldn't be determined. They all went to the floor at the first spray of glass. The windows on the front of the house were gone in seconds, the curtains shredded and on the floor. Carrie's few and precious knick-knacks and glass figures on a shelf opposite the windows shattered in the volley of bullets. A few bullets hit the heavy cast iron stove and ricocheted dangerously about the room.

Eli lay on the floor and violently cursed Grover Little, vowing to make good on his promise to kill him. He could see that Rob and Carrie were uninjured. He snatched the lamp off the table.

Rob was making his way to Carrie when the whine of a bullet off the stove ended with Carrie's scream as the bullet tore across her upper arm. The floor under her was quickly covered in blood. Rob yanked a towel off the kitchen counter and wrapped it tightly around her arm to stem the bleeding. He covered her with his body as she lay on the floor breathing heavily and wincing against the pain.

Eli blew out the lamp and shouted, "Get her in the bedroom."

The first volley of gunfire lasted only seconds, it was followed by individual shots being fired every several seconds to keep them from getting to the windows and shooting back. Eli duck-walked his way through the broken glass to the wall under the empty window panes.

Rob helped Carrie to the bedroom and crawled back into the room. He sat against the wall and watched the empty windows from the interior of the darkened room.

Eli spoke in a low voice, "Rob, don't shoot back, let them think they got us. It'll get quiet for a bit and then they will sneak up to see. Anyone pokes his head in one of these windows, blow it off."

Rob propped his back against the wall. His six-gun was in his hand ready to raise and fire. Eli stayed where he was thankful that he was able to get the lamp blown out before it was shattered and caused a fire. Even in the dark he could make out the destruction in the room, it fired his anger and he renewed his vow to kill Grover Little, along with Cramer and that Earl character.

The shooting stopped and silence fell heavy over the night. With their eyes now adjusted to the dark they could make out motions from each other. Eli pointed toward the windows, "Pay attention," he whispered.

Several minutes passed before the first clumsy footfalls were heard approaching the front of the house. Both men cocked back the hammers on their guns and pointed them toward the windows. The top of a head down to the eyes slowly rose up from the bottom of a glassless frame. Here it paused peering into the dark room, the head rose further up until it was framed in the opening.

Rob and Eli fired at the same time; the head disappeared followed by the thud of a body hitting the ground. Several shots rang out in rapid succession, the bullets slamming into the walls of the house.

As quickly as it began the shooting again stopped. Time moved slowly as they waited and listened. A scattering of rifle reports sounded. Eli and Rob exchanged confused looks realizing the shooting was not directed toward the house.

The night returned to silence until the sound of a walking horse could be heard approaching the side of the house. The horse stopped and then a familiar voice shouted from outside. "This is Lew Prine, are you okay in the house?"

Eli shouted back, "Stick your head in the window and find out."

"I'm not with them. I just drove them off, guess they didn't expect to get shot at from behind."

"How do I know that?"

"Because you have my word on it. I'm coming in the front door, don't shoot me."

The door opened slowly as Lew Prine pushed it open and peered into the dark room. The first thing he made out was Eli sitting against the wall to his left with a gun pointed at him. A glance in front of him revealed Rob's silhouette against the wall in the same position. He held his hands out in front of him.

Eli and Rob held their positions until Prine entered fully into the room and they were confident he was alone.

Eli watched him, "Are they gone?"

Prine nodded, "Yes, I left one lying in the grass and the others headed out. You can light a light now, it's safe."

Eli lit the lamp sitting on the floor next to him. "Who was it?"

"I'm not sure, Cramer's my guess." Prine looked around the shattered room and shook his head, "Lord, I'm sorry."

Eli swore and got to his feet. "Little sent them. I told him flat out if he did I'd be back to shoot him." He began to cross the room for the door.

"It wasn't Little," Prine said quickly. "I know because I was with him."

Rob got up and joined them in the middle of the room. "He sent them earlier today."

Prine agreed, "He did, except Cramer was under orders to only scare you, they were not to pull any rough stuff. I found out he had sent them after the fact. When I did I told Little flat out to his face he was a pig-headed fool and that he'd better make peace with you fast or he could find another foreman."

Rob left the room to see to Carrie while Eli continued to question Prine. "How did that go?"

"He blustered a bit and then finally admitted that he had made a mistake in sending them. He sent me up here to make sure nothing had happened. That's how I happened to get here when I did. Little can be jackass stubborn, and at times a fathead, but lately you can talk sense into him."

"So, you're saying this second visit, the attack was all Cramer's idea?"

"Definitely. It wasn't under Little's orders I know that for a fact. Cramer and his bunch never came back to the ranch this afternoon or he would have been told to back off."

"Where can I find Cramer?"

"He likes Cimarron. He probably headed there."

Rob led Carrie out of the bedroom supporting her as she slowly shuffled along. Her face was drawn and pale. He had her sit down at the table.

Prine looked at her and the blood soaked towel around her arm. He moved quickly toward her and began to unpeel the wrap. "Let me take a look at that."

Carrie winced in pain and gave him a questioning look. "Are you a doctor?"

"Of sorts. I was assigned to guard the medical tents during the war and ended up spending more time helping the surgeons patch up wounds than guarding. I learned a lot."

Prine glanced at Rob, "There is a medical pack in my saddlebag, go get it and I'll take care of this." He smiled at Carrie, "Don't worry Mrs. Slater I'll do a good job."

Rob hurried out and ran back in with a green canvas pack and handed it to Prine. They watched as he expertly cleaned and dressed the wound. He smiled at Carrie, "You're lucky it only cut a groove out of the back of your arm, had it been the front you would have a far more serious wound. As it is you will have a nasty scar, but it should heal clean."

Carrie smiled at him, "Thank you."

Rob looked at Prine. "Thanks for coming up to help, and thanks for taking care of my wife."

"It was the least I could do." Prine turned toward Eli, "Are you going after Cramer?"

"Wouldn't you?"

"Do you know Schwenk's?"

"Schwenk's Hall in Cimarron? I've been there."

"So will Cramer."

Eli turned his attention to Carrie who looked pale and weakened by her wound. "You need to go to bed and sleep and let your body rest so it can replace the blood you lost. It's important for the baby."

"I know I do, but first I want to know what we are going to do now."

"*I* am going to ride to Cimarron and deal with Cramer. *You* are going directly to bed and Rob is going to stay here with you."

Rob's head snapped around sharply, "You're not going without me."

"You need to be here with Carrie."

He was suddenly torn between his loyalty to Eli and the knowledge that he would need help, and the protection

Dave P. Fisher

he owed to Carrie. He stared at Eli for several seconds trying to decide. Carrie broke in and settled the question. "I'm not that injured and you will need Rob with you."

"I can handle it," Eli argued stubbornly.

Rob took a step closer to him. "It's not just Cramer. Carrie said six men came to the house; two are laying out there so that leaves four and I'd lay money they will still be together. So, you're not just taking on Cramer, you're up against four killers. You need a second gun."

"I handled Cramer before, he's nothing."

Rob's temper flared as he argued. "Look, I'm not letting you go alone and get shot to pieces. Maybe you can handle it, but even you will have trouble against four men. I'm not letting you go alone and that's final dammit!"

"You don't need to do this; you *need* to take care of your wife."

"No, I don't *need* to do it. Just like you didn't *need* to pick up that starving kid in Dodge, but you did. Now, that kid is not letting you go alone and he can be just as stubborn as *you*."

Eli scowled at him for several seconds as Rob mirrored the look. Eli's eyes softened, and then he sighed, "Guess, I taught that kid too well."

"You got that right."

Prine stepped into the conversation. "Rob's right, there's four of them and they're a back-shooting dirty lot. You hit the trail right now and you'll be there in the morning. I'll stay here and make sure Mrs. Slater gets to sleep and stand watch over her through the night."

Eli looked at Carrie, "Are you okay with that?"

"Yes. I agree with Rob, you can't do it alone and if they are not stopped they will be back."

Eli looked at each face and then nodded. Sticking his hand out to Prine, he looked him in the eyes. "I won't be forgetting this." They shook hands.

Eli turned to Rob, "Let's finish this."

The sun had been above the eastern horizon for an hour when Eli and Rob crossed the bridge into Cimarron. A freight wagon rolled slowly along the main street, its squeaking wheel hubs echoing across the quiet scene. Businesses were still closed with only a few people walking between the buildings and along the side streets. A man was passed out alongside a building with a dog sniffing at his head.

As they rode past Schwenks the door opened followed by a man throwing a bucket of soapy water out into the dusty street. He glanced up at them as they rode by and then disappeared back inside the whitewashed building.

Eli's eyes shifted from side-to-side taking in everything and missing nothing. He spoke without looking at Rob, "Cramer might not be here yet he's likely sleeping off his drinking somewhere and won't show up for a while."

Rob's gaze swept the street around him as he rode. "Probably."

"Let's get some breakfast and then we'll come back and find us a place to sit back and watch."

Turning around, they again passed Schwenks. Eli motioned toward the Barlow Sanderson stage station to their right and across from the saloon. The building was long with a porch roof running its length and benches under it and against the wall. "We'll come back and sit in the shade under that roof and wait for them to show. We can have a good view of the place from there."

Pulling up next to the St. James, they tied off their horses and went inside to the small dining room where breakfast was being served. An hour later they were riding back to the stage station.

The stage was in front loading passengers and taking up the area they intended to sit in. They watched Schwenks closed door as they waited for the stage to move out. More activity was showing on the streets as businesses began to open their doors. Schwenks first customers of the day were going in.

The stage pulled out leaving a cloud of dust in its wake. Tying their horses off to the hitch rail, Eli and Rob settled back in the shadows on a bench and waited. They made small talk, but spent most of the time in silence. Eli was sure that Cramer didn't know the house he shot up was theirs or he never would have done it.

Rob remembered the trial that sent Cramer to prison and his partner to the hangman. Unless he had changed a lot while in prison he should recognize the man.

The heat of the summer day grew in intensity as the sun reached its mid-point in the sky. Rob walked the horses over to a water tank and let them drink. Returning he sat back down next to Eli and waved a fly out of his face.

The long night with no sleep and the warmth of the day was taking its toll on Rob. His head bobbed up and down on his chest as he drifted in and out of sleep. Eli's years of hard living had given him a flint-like edge allowing him to go for long periods of time without sleep. He was wide awake and studying each passing walker, rider, and wagon.

It was past noon when Eli spotted two men riding alongside each other up the dusty side street toward Schwenks. One of the men looked familiar. He studied the man, added a few rough years to his face and recognized Milt Cramer. Both men dismounted at the back corner of Schwenks and stood there talking. Eli elbowed Rob causing Rob to spring up instantly alert.

Eli spoke low without taking his eyes off Cramer, "There he is."

Rob focused his attention in the direction Eli was looking. He saw the two men and recognized, Cramer from the trial. "How do you want to do this? The other two could be inside already we have no idea what they look like."

"We haven't lived this long by being careless. Let's assume they are and they'll be coming out to join their friends. I would like to keep this outside to avoid getting innocent people hurt."

"Then, we should do it now while they're still hanging around out there."

Both men rose to their feet in a casual manner so as not to draw attention. They crossed the street as if heading for the hall's doors. Rob broke off and drifted up the street so he could cut back and flank the two men without their knowing he was there. Eli shifted his direction toward Cramer rather than the doors. He was forty feet from them before Cramer's attention was drawn to him.

Cramer stared at Eli with irritation in his eyes; he didn't like men walking up to him. The second man was now looking at him as well. With their focus on Eli neither had seen Rob taking a position on their blind side.

The look in Cramer's eyes began to change as he wondered why he knew this man. Suddenly, full recognition dawned on him and he knew the man coming directly at him was Eli Warren.

Eli stopped twenty feet from the two men, his cold brown eyes holding no sign of friendliness. "Fancy meeting you here, Cramer."

Cramer's eyes flicked from right-to-left. "What do you want with me? I've got no bounty on my head. You stole six years out of my life, they about worked me to death. Ain't that enough for you?"

"I didn't steal those years out of your life; you did when you took to robbing stages. If we could have pinned any of those killings on you it would have been a rope alongside your pal, Boxer. You got the better end of the deal."

The second man was looking from Eli to Cramer and back again. Eli glanced at him, "Earl, isn't it? Long time since we last met."

Earl stared at him, "Am I supposed to know you?'

"You tried running me off Grover Little's land once and threatened to teach me a lesson."

"I've run a lot of people off his land, you're nothing special to remember."

Eli did not respond, but held his attention on Cramer. "I see you're no smarter than you ever were. Prison didn't teach you a thing."

"It taught me that I owe you and, if you recall, I swore to kill you if I ever got the chance."

Eli laughed, then commented with a sarcastic tone, "You mean if you ever got a chance at my back."

Cramer scowled at Eli. "I don't think you looked me up to renew old friendships, what do you want? I haven't robbed a thing since I got out."

"Maybe not, but you're still hiring out your gun."

"That's a lie, I've gone straight."

"I happen to know you work for Grover Little." Eli then lifted his chin toward Earl, "And running with coyotes, there's two more around here someplace. Six of you rode in and shot up my place, but only four of you ran away."

Cramer's eyes grew big and he touched the tip of his tongue to his drying lips. His mistake was taking root in his mind and he was getting scared. "I don't know what you're talking about."

"Sure you do, you shot up a house last night, someone Little put you on to."

Cramer was growing more nervous by the second as sweat began to trickle down his cheeks. Earl took a step back and lowered his hand to his pistol.

Eli turned his eyes to Earl, "I wouldn't do that." He then motioned with his head toward Rob. "Behind you."

The man slowly turned his head to see Rob standing forty feet off behind his left shoulder. He eased his hand away from his gun.

"That's better, not many can outdraw Rob Slater."

Earl stared a second longer at Rob and bounced his

Adam's apple in a hard swallow.

Cramer shouted at Eli, "I never shot up no house."

Eli ignored the denial. "You and your tough gang threatened my niece and then in your wild shooting you wounded her and curse a man who would shoot a pregnant woman. Cramer, I'm about sick of running into you."

Earl swore under his breath. He now remembered trying to scare this man years ago and being told it was Warren and how lucky he was to have lived through it. Now, he was facing him on equal ground and all because Cramer ignored Little's orders and went off on his own to shoot up Eli Warren's house.

Earl put his hands in the air as he backed away from Cramer. "It was all his idea to shoot up that house. Little had said not to do it."

Eli heard boots moving in the dirt behind him and knew they belonged to the last two men from Cramer's party. His muscles began to tense for the shooting as he shifted to his right so he could see the newcomers out of the corner of his eye. He decided he'd shoot Cramer first, Rob would get Earl and then they'd do the best they could with the two who were now on his left quarter.

Cramer grew cocky with confidence. He smirked, "You're boxed in Warren, I guess you'll have to walk away empty handed . . . if we let you walk away at all."

"I'll walk away when you're all in the dirt."

When it happened it was in the blink of an eye. Cramer's hand went down for his gun. Eli expected it and his draw was a full second faster, the bullet slammed into Cramer's chest. Not waiting to see what effect the shot had, Eli jumped to his left closing the distance between him and the nearest man behind him. He fired directly into the man at the same instant the man's gun fired across his face, the flash and powder residue sent a sharp burning pain through his eyes Blinded, he fell to the ground. He could hear a rolling burst of gunshots that continued for a fast few seconds and then it was quiet.

A strong hand was suddenly under his arm, lifting him up to his feet and making him walk, as his eyes watered and burned. He could hear running feet all around him. Then, his face was in sun heated water and it was being splashed into his eyes. As his vision cleared slightly he could make out that Rob was holding him over a horse tank splashing water into his face. He stood up and looked around through blurry vision to see four bodies on the ground.

"You get them all, Rob?"

"You killed Cramer. He went down like a pole-axed steer and never got up. You got one into the man behind you, but he was still on his feet. That Earl, who was giving up, tried to take advantage of the situation and pulled his gun. I took care of him. The two that came late to the party didn't know I was with you. They figured you were easy meat being down like you were. They got educated the hard way."

Eli grimaced at the pain in his eyes, "Glad you came along. Good thing I taught you to be so stubborn."

"You've got some powder burns on your face, can you see at all?"

Eli nodded, "Burns like sin, but I can see a little better now."

"That bullet came mighty close to taking your head off."

A crowd had gathered around to look at the dead men. Some voices threw questions out as to what happened, others who had seen the fight relayed the story. It had all happened, first shot to last, in less than half a minute, but by the time the story made the rounds it wouldn't resemble the real events at all.

Eli's vision remained blurry as Rob guided him back to the stage station and their horses. Eli sat down on the bench under the roof, while Rob dipped his kerchief in the horse tank and handed it to him. Eli held the cloth against his closed eyes until the burning subsided a bit. He started to feel better. Rob watched the streets for any problems arising from the shooting. Men were looking at them, pointing and talking; however, no one approached them.

Eli stood up and handed the kerchief back to Rob. "Now, I'm going to pay Grover Little a visit."

"Lew said that Little didn't have anything to do with this. I believe him Eli, Lew's not a liar."

"Yeah, Lew's a good man alright and because he is, he rides for the brand. I would expect him to defend his boss."

Rob stood in front of Eli. "Even that Earl said they weren't supposed to do anything, it was Cramer's idea."

Eli remained stubborn, "But, if Little hadn't put them up to it in the first place nothing would have happened."

"Okay, he did open the ball and I was all for shoving it down his throat. I'm seeing it different now. We need to give the man a chance to say his piece before you up and shoot him. Lew helped us, and Carrie, we owe him that much if nothing else."

Eli nodded, "Fair enough. Little can talk and then I'll shoot him."

Rob knew it was futile to talk to Eli when he was wrought up like this. "We'll cross that bridge when we get to it. Right now we need to get out of this town. Let's get up into the hills and camp for the night. We can go on in the morning; it'll give your eyes a chance to rest."

"Okay, I want both of my eyes open when I shoot Grover Little."

Rob sighed, "Lord, you're stubborn." He helped Eli get mounted as a wagon pulled up to the four dead men.

Putting their horses into a quick jog they headed toward the bridge. The city marshal passed them riding toward the scene of the shooting. Once he was behind them they crossed the bridge and kicked the horses into a gallop.

The sounds of hammering and sawing could be heard before Eli and Rob broke out of the trees and got a full view of the house. They had been discussing how they were going to rebuild and replace all the expensive broken windows. It was going to be costly and the glass would probably have to be brought in from Santa Fe where the original windows were purchased and carefully brought up in a wagon. If they were lucky a store in Taos might have glass. The thought had put Eli in a sour mood. Now, they wondered at the sounds.

Breaking out of the trees, they stopped their horses and studied the house. A buckboard and several saddled horses were in front of it and men were busy putting in windows and hauling boards into the open doorway. Eli stared, "What the heck?"

They rode on down to the house. Lew Prine stepped outside at the sound of the horses. He looked up at them, "Find 'em?"

Eli looked around at the activity. "It's been dealt with."

Prine didn't have to ask, he knew what that meant.

Both men stepped off their horses. Eli stood dumbstruck watching the activity. He moved his head and squinted against the sunlight reflecting off the fresh wood window frames and the new glass two of them held. His eyes still hurt, but his vision was almost normal again.

Prine grinned, "Bet you're wondering what's going on here?"

Eli nodded, "I guess so."

Prine called back into the house, "Mr. Little, would you come out and explain to these two gentlemen what's going on here?"

Eli's expression turned angry as Grover Little stepped out of the house. Little's face was still stern, yet there was a resigned look in his eyes. "I'm overseeing the rebuilding of your house. I only had enough glass at my place for two of the windows, I placed an order for more out of Trinidad and will have workmen put it in when it arrives by freight wagon."

Carrie walked out behind Little. Her arm was wrapped and her complexion had returned to normal, she looked rested. "I know, Uncle Eli, I was just as surprised. This morning, Lew and Mr. Little pulled up with the wagon and these men. The wagon was filled with glass and lumber and they started right into work. Isn't it wonderful?"

Little continued on, "I know you don't like me Warren, and I can't say I blame you. I'm responsible for this and I make good on my mistakes. For the record, I never sent Cramer out to do this. He's a loose cannon and I lost control of him. If you haven't kill him already, I will. Times are changing Warren, and I need to change with them. I figure it's time I made myself a neighbor to those around me, instead of an enemy."

Little turned toward Prine, "I'm heading back to the house. You make sure everything gets done here. No one comes back to the ranch until it is." He began walking for his horse.

Eli watched his back as he walked and then called out to him. "Mr. Little, I'm badly in need of a cup of coffee, care to join me?"

Little stopped in his tracks and turned his head to face, Eli. "Is it strong enough to float a bar of steel?"

"Is there any other kind?"

Without a word Little headed back to the house and then stopped in front of Eli. "If I had any friends, Warren, they'd call me Grove."

Eli put out his hand, "My friends call me Eli."

The two men shook hands. Eli spoke as they went into the house, "It's been a mighty dry summer Grove, let's see what we can do about getting your cattle up on some of this Beaver Valley water."

Chapter 24

The year was 1940 and it was Carrie Slater's eightieth birthday. Her six children, their children, and their children, four generations of Slaters had come to the Beaver Valley ranch house to celebrate it. She was showered with hugs, kisses, and presents from her loving family.

Soon the women went to the kitchen to prepare dinner and the men gathered in the living room to discuss baseball, President Roosevelt, and the war in Europe. Carrie sat alone in her comfortable chair and looked around at her home. How long it had been since they first rode into this valley and when they built the first house. The house had increased in size over the years to accommodate a growing family and the changing times.

She sighed and rose slowly from her chair. Her Rob had been gone three years now and she dearly missed him. She made her way to the room Rob called his office and bear den, she felt closer to him in there. Half closing the door, she sat down in his chair and studied the walls.

Rob had hung Eli's old Sharps .50 and the Winchester on one wall. Rob said that a man never came into that room that didn't try to buy them off of him; of course they were never for sale.

Next to the rifles hung a photograph Rob and Eli had taken together in 1900. They were both in their suits looking very stern and handsome. Rob wanted to have the photograph taken to show they had made it into a new century. It was a good thing he did because Eli died the next year. She remembered how hard she cried and that Rob had disappeared in the barn for a long time before coming back out with his eyes red and swollen. She knew he had been weeping, but was too proud to let her or the children see.

There were old wanted posters tacked up on the wall, including the one for the Parson gang. The paper was yellowed and cracking now. So many years had passed.

Her mind wandered back over the years. She recalled the first time she met Eli, she was eleven and he looked rather scary, but he spoke so kindly to her and was so nice she immediately lost her fear of him. Then there was the day he showed up at their home with Rob, a handsome boy with wavy brown hair and brown eyes.

She could only vaguely remember the faces of her mother and father, but she still felt the horror of their deaths and the fear of what was to become of her. There was the kindness of the Wilsons who took her in. She recalled the day Eli and Rob came to their store to take her with them. She wrote them a letter after she and Rob were married and went to visit them once on the train.

Eli and Rob had taken her to Uncle John's. She could still recall how kind the old man was to her and how he teased her. She still regretted causing him such worry when she ran off to follow Eli and Rob. John lived for ten years after she and Rob married and moved away to Beaver Valley. Sally went soon after him. She cried when she got the word John had passed away and Eli rode off into the woods alone and was gone a long time.

She lingered on the warmth of the love she had felt for all of them and how important they had been in her life. She thought of Rob and how brave and handsome he had been. She saw him again in Las Vegas when he pushed Antonio Ortiz over the chair and the tension in the room when the two faced each other, their hands hovering over their guns. She could still hear the shots echoing in the room.

There was the woman in the Hall that had led her out of harm's way. She smelled of perfume, she was gentle, but her eyes looked tired and sad. She later learned what Eli had meant about her being a different kind of woman. It didn't change how she felt, she still held a warm spot in her heart for her and hoped her life had gotten better.

Then they bought the land she still lived on today and how Grover Little had sent his men up to run them off. Grover later became a good friend and spent a good deal of time visiting. He was a widower, a lonely man she could tell.

Rob never did tell her what had happened in Cimarron when he and Eli went after Milt Cramer. Later she had heard the stories that were being told of the gunfight, that Rob had saved Eli's life when he was temporarily blinded. They had expected repercussions from the law, but nothing ever happened.

A smile spread over her face as she recalled far more good times than bad. The trip they made to Denver before they were married. She knew that Rob was not enjoying it as much as she was, still he kept up a good face because it was important to her. He was always so considerate of her.

The day she and Rob married, the birth of their first son and the three boys and two girls after, all remained as bright as the day they happened. There was Julita's grand wedding and how they were still best friends to this day. She and her husband had inherited the Garza ranch.

The amazing inventions of the twentieth century like men riding in automobiles and flying through the sky in airplanes, who would have ever thought such things were possible? Electricity and telephones that made it possible for her to talk to Julita whenever she chose to. Simply amazing.

Motion pictures were something to behold, she had gone to a couple with her daughters who adored them. Her son took her to one once that was called a 'western'. The men in it were all pretty with powder and rouge and neatly ironed clothes. These were not the western men she had known wearing their dust-caked rumpled clothes for days on end. She didn't care for westerns.

Writers were calling the years gone by the 'old west' or the 'wild and wooly west.' It was all history now and they made a big commotion about it. She never thought of any of it as historical, they were simply living in the times. Men carried guns and sometimes fought with them. Hays, Trinidad, Las Vegas were just towns like any other.

She had lived in a time that was now considered a part of American history. It was an era that would never be repeated. Now it was a whole new era, yet, for all the grand inventions and the awe of the changing world, what beat strongest in her heart was the memory of the two men she loved most in this world, her husband and her beloved uncle. A tear rolled down her wrinkled cheek as she thought of them.

The sound of the door creaking open brought her back to the present. She looked to see a small boy's face staring in at her. "Are you all right, Great-Grandma?"

She wiped the tear off her face. "Yes dear, I'm all right. Just remembering, like old people do sometimes. Come in, don't be afraid."

The boy timidly stepped through the door. As he looked at the walls his eyes grew huge, "Wow."

Carrie watched his fascinated expression and smiled, he had wavy brown hair and brown eyes and looked like Rob. He was one of her several great grandchildren, the grandson of her first son they had named Elijah. She had yet to meet this boy.

"Is this Great-Grandpa Rob's room?"

"Yes, he spent a good deal of time in here."

"Are those guns real?"

"Those belonged to my Uncle Eli. He and Rob were best friends."

"Grandpa talks about Eli; he said he was an outlaw hunter and the bravest man he ever met next to Great-

Grandpa, Rob."

He squinted at the yellowed wanted poster, "Who was the Parson Gang?"

"A gang of very dangerous outlaws who robbed and killed people."

"Was that back in the old west?"

"Well, I guess that is what they call it now, but it wasn't old to us then. It was at the end of the 1870's."

"Who are the two men in the photograph?"

"That is your Great-Grandpa Rob and my uncle, Eli."

The boy looked closer at the photo, "They look pretty tough alright. Grandpa says Great-Grandpa Rob was a gunfighter." It was a statement and not a question.

Carrie smiled at him, "I don't think we have had the pleasure to meet yet."

"My name is Robert Slater, Great-Grandma," he stuck out his hand and they shook hands.

Carrie continued to smile, he was named after her Rob and he even looked like him.

"I have a question Great-Grandma, was the old west for real?"

She looked confused at the question. "I'm not sure what you mean, Robert."

"We live in Minnesota where my father works. My teacher said that the old west wasn't real, that there were no outlaws or gunfighters, and men didn't really have shootouts. She says it's all made up for the cinema and radio programs.

"Grandpa says she's full of it, that she was probably one of those dim-wit twenties flapper girls and didn't know a manhole from a prairie dog burrow. Father says she is wrong, but Mother says to respect my teacher. You lived in the old west, is my teacher right or wrong?"

"Robert, your teacher is very mistaken. What they are now calling the old west was very real. Men did fight with guns, and there were many outlaws, and the men who tracked down the outlaws were very brave. Your grandfather would remember some of those times."

"Did you ever see a real gunfight Great-Grandma?"

She thought back to that day in Las Vegas and could so vividly see the events that froze her world for those terror filled minutes. "Yes, I did . . . once."

"Was it like in the cinema?"

"No, it was much more frightening."

"Grandpa says the old men in Las Vegas still talk about the day Great-Grandpa Rob outdrew Antonio Ortiz and killed him. Was that true?"

"Yes, it was true . . . I saw it happen."

The boy looked at her wide-eyed, "Wow!"

"So, Grandpa *is* right, it was all real."

"Tell you what Robert, why don't you sit up here with Great-Grandma and I'll tell you a true story of a young girl, a handsome young man, and a brave and good man everyone called The Outlaw Hunter."

About the Author

Mountain men, Voyageurs, pioneers, and explorers make up the branches of Dave's family tree. His mother's side was from Canada where the men plied the fur trade in the Canadian wilderness. Others moved down into the wilds of Northern Minnesota and established trading posts among the Chippewa.

On his father's side, his natural grandfather died out West while working as a telegrapher for the railroad. His step grandfather, born in the 1800's, was Blackfoot Indian from Montana. He was a hunter and horseman who brought a great deal of Old West influence into the Fisher family.

As a lifelong Westerner Dave inherited that pioneer blood and followed in the footsteps of his ancestors. Originally from Oregon, he worked cattle and rode saddle broncs in rodeos. His adventures have taken him across the wilds of Alaska as a horsepacker and hunting guide, through the Rocky Mountains of Montana, Wyoming, and Colorado where he wrangled, guided and packed for a variety of outfitters and the National Park Service.

Dave weaves his experience into each story. His writing, steeped in historical accuracy and drawing on extensive research, draws his readers into the story by their realism and Dave's personal knowledge of the West, its people, and character.

He has near to 500 fiction and non-fiction works published. Included are 19 western/adventure novels and short story collections, 70 short stories, and inclusion in 18 anthologies. He is the first, and currently the only, writer to win the *Will Rogers Medallion Award* three times. In 2008 for Best Western Fiction, in 2013 for Best Western Humor, and 2014 for Best Western Novel. Nine of his short stories have earned Reader's Choice Awards.

You can learn more at: www.davepfisher.com

From Double Diamond Books

Zak Doolin's Gold

Spence Logan finds himself being drawn deeper into a maze of secrets involving a blue eyed girl, a man on crutches, and a murderous woman all hunting for a dead man's trail to gold.

Chapter 1

Spence Logan sized up the situation around him and it wasn't looking too good. He was a stranger, in a make-shift saloon, in a two-bit little hole in the desert. He had come in looking for a drink, not trouble. The little voice in his head had told him to ride on by. Having always been one to follow his sudden whims and ignoring the little voice, often to his detriment, he followed this whim and now he wished he hadn't.

The four men who surrounded him were a dirty, raggedy lot. They slowly circled him like wolves, while three other men in the room smiled and watched. A pair of giggling women completed the crew. He cast a quick glance at the women and shuddered, he couldn't recall the last time he had seen such ugly females, he wondered if they were actually human or crossed with some kind of domestic livestock. A man would need to have been a long time in the desert, sun struck, and very drunk to ever be attracted to one of them. He returned his attention to the men.

He hadn't liked the look of the bunch the minute he stepped through the doorway. As their attention turned to him, he had slipped the loop off his Colt. For a brief moment he considered turning right around and getting back on his roan. That idea was cut short when a big man, who was more fat than muscle, came up behind him from the outside and blocked the door cutting off his escape. Well, since he was there, he might as well go on in and have that drink. Showing the white feather at this time, or trying to run away, would serve about as much good as running from a grizzly and with the same results.

He knew exactly what he had walked into and he cussed himself for being a blind fool. He also promised to listen to the little voice next time. He was prime for the picking and these people, if you could call them that were the pickers. It was becoming clearer by the minute that they were accustomed to robbing, and probably killing, anyone foolish enough to stop in their little hole.

After being hemmed in by the fat man, the next best move was to walk right in like he owned the place. He had made it halfway across the packed dirt floor before three of the men got up from different corners and came toward him; the fat man completed the set as they surrounded him. He concluded that he was definitely in a bad spot, but then he'd been in bad spots before and he was still in an upright position.

The four men began to pace around him on a slow mindless path. Eight feet separated them from him as they circled; he could smell the whiskey and stench of filthy bodies from across the space. They grinned at him as they moved and he couldn't help but notice that they all had the same facial features, droopy eyes and slack jaws with their mouths hanging open. They were sizing up to be a herd of lunatics, he'd seen lunatics and crazy people before and these certainly fit the bill. He was betting they were inbred to boot. He had been moving his feet just enough to keep his eyes on all of them as they circled. After a minute the game was becoming tedious and it was time to change the rules.

No one in the room had yet to speak to him; they just grinned and watched with an occasional laugh coming out of a tobacco-drooling mouth. Stopping his movements, he locked eyes with a bony, loose-jointed character who seemed to be the leader. "You plan to keep waltzing in a circle until you wear a rut in the floor or what?"

The man's grin widened as his eyes reflected his lunacy, but their slow methodic walk around him never changed.

Spence found it interesting the things a man notices when he had to really concentrate on something. The bony one had a head that was a tad lopsided on the left side, he'd trimmed his beard with a dull knife, and he had one blue eye and one brown like a dog he'd once seen. The fat man directly next to him in the line had meat grease on his filthy shirt and his belly hung over his roped up britches. He figured he couldn't miss a target like that. As they moved around him he got another look at the two females, their faces and hands were coated in dirt, which probably had never been washed. He saw all this in the time it took to answer his own question.

"Well partner, you're a darn poor dancer and I'm getting dizzy, so I think I'll just forget about that drink and leave."

"You ain't goin' nowhere, boy." The bony man spoke through his grin revealing several missing and broken teeth. "We gonna take your things and then eat yuh alive."

Spence held a steady eye on the dirty man. "Now, that ain't very neighborly . . . *boy*."

The man's eyes opened wide as he threw back his head and laughed. "*Neighborly*. You're funny. We ain't your neighbor. No, we gonna cut yuh up and eat yuh."

Spence shook his head, "Now, how are you figuring on doing that when you're dead?"

The man let out a maniacal howl. "There you go bein' funny again. That's a good'n, since you the one's gonna be dead."

The howl confirmed in Spence's mind the manner of people he was dealing with here. All four circling faces held the same amused expression. They had done this before with other men and had enjoyed the game. They had never met Spence Logan.

Spence grinned back knowing exactly what he was going to do. "Is that a fact?"

He was sure they did fully intend to kill him and probably would eat him to boot, they looked like cannibals. The words of his father came back to him now as they did every time he found himself in a bad situation. "Boy, trouble follows you like winter does summer. You need to settle down and stop giving it something to follow." He didn't listen then, and here he was, still not listening.

The lunatic then slid a long knife from his belt and rotated the point toward Spence's belly. "Ever see an Arkansas Toothpick up close? We use 'em to cut up funny men like you."

Spence studied the knife and then raised his head to look into the wild eyes of the man who held it. "Yup, that's a Toothpick alright, seen 'em before."

"You're funny boy; I wonder if you taste funny too?"

One of the women shouted out, "Stick him Bodie, stick him."

"I aim to. Which piece do you want?"

Spence knew it was time to put an end to the game while he still could. He paused for a pair of seconds and then grinned, "If you think that was funny, here's another one. Try this one on for size."

At the last word, he smoothly pulled his Colt and shot the man between the eyes. Before the others could react he shifted the gun to the right, thumbed back the hammer and gut-shot the fat man. He gripped his big belly and fell to the floor like a sack of oats. He moaned out loud as the laughs turned to screams and curses with the remainder of the crowd scattering and hitting the floor for cover. He fired a couple more shots at their diving backsides splintering slivers of table over them and scoring a hit on one. With only one shot left he quickly turned and ran out the open doorway.

Shoving the gun back in his holster he scooped up the trailing reins and swung himself up on the big roan's back and kicked him into a gallop. He snuck a peek back over his shoulder and caught a glimpse of the people running around like a bunch of chickens, no one seemed to be mounting up to follow him though which suited him just fine. He wasn't in any mood to be chased across the desert by a bunch of cannibals. He kept the horse running west for another five minutes plowing through the sage before bringing him down to a walk.

He looked back over his shoulder and smiled. He patted the roan's neck and began to laugh. "Did you see the look on that ol' boy's face when I came up with the Colt? Walter, it was worth the seeing, I'll tell you what. He wanted funny, well I gave him funny." He rode on for a moment still holding the mischievous grin, "But I reckon he didn't see it as being all that funny."

The roan shook his head as if to disapprove. Spence frowned, "You too? You sound like my old man, I can hear him now." Lowering his voice he mocked, "'Boy, trouble follows you like winter does summer.'" He let out with a loud laugh. "And you know what Walter? It always will. That reminds me, I best refill this gun for the next trouble I come up against."

As he rammed the paper loads into each cylinder he spoke to Walter, "You shouldn't be so judgmental partner; I did it for you you know. I could handle being killed and eaten by a herd of lunatics, but the idea of them crazies having a fine horse like you was unbearable, so I shot him to save you."

Walter flicked his ears back and turned his head to the left, casting a quick glance at Spence. "Yeah, I thought so. Makes you think a might better of me, doesn't it?"

Spence Logan had been drifting around the high desert since he was seventeen, almost ten years in all. He had left his Sacramento home lured by a sign he saw posted in a store window calling for all skinny, wiry young fellows who were expert riders to hire on with the Central Overland to run the mail across the country. They were calling it the Pony Express. He was all of that and to boot they paid twenty-five dollars a week to do it. It was a fortune to a boy who rarely in his life had two pennies to rub together. He signed on and before he knew it, he was in the Utah Territory running the leg from Cold Springs Station to Buckland and back every week.

The Pony Express, or Pony as they liked to call it, had only lasted a year and a half; just until the last telegraph line was spliced linking the East to the West. His big paying job ended there and so did the excitement. He rode shotgun for the stage on a few runs after that, but his thirst to see what was over the next mountain was stronger and he moved on. Maybe one day he would find a place that suited him; however, for the moment staying free and moving was the most important thing in his life.

Checking his back trail a time or two he concluded that the lunatics must have had enough. Lacking pursuit from them, he relaxed into a leisurely pace and let his mind wander back to the days when he rode the Pony. He realized that if he kept riding in the direction he was traveling and reined Walter a little more to the south, he'd be at the old Cold Springs station in an hour. There was nowhere he had to be so he decided to see how the old place looked.

It had been an interesting time on the high desert. About the time the Pony ended, the Utah Territory split into two territories with the western most being called Nevada. Gold and silver were being discovered all through the Sierras and settlers were pouring in. The telegraph was all the way to California and the railroad was working its way toward it and in all that country between St. Joseph and the Sierras, the Indians were none too pleased.

The Paiutes were on the warpath through the northwest corner of the Territory and Cold Springs Station was right in the middle of it. He recalled how lucky he had been not to be there the day the Paiutes hit the station and killed the Station Master. He grinned to himself, his pa wasn't always right, that was one time when it was good luck that followed him.

He knew his father and the others in his family considered him just a saddle tramp, a man with no better purpose in life then to wander around the mountains and deserts. How many times had he heard the preaching from his brothers and sisters that he should settle down and stay put like them? Well, working in a store or being owned by some boss like they were wasn't what he had in mind. They liked that little tight circle of safety around them and never ventured out of it. They had no idea what lay out there beyond their carefully controlled lives. The last time he'd heard their old song and dance was five years ago when he visited his folks and he hadn't been back since.

He had no need for the protection offered by a town or anyone else; his Colt was all the protection he needed. Besides, finding himself in a dangerous spot only added salt to life's stew. He grinned to himself and spoke out loud, "Like finding myself surrounded by lunatics with big pointy knives." Bursting out with a laugh he added, "I like that, salt to life's stew. I sure salted their stew, didn't I Walter?" The blue roan flicked his ears back and shook his head. Spence frowned, "Oh, who asked you?"

He was the youngest, and the black sheep of the family although he really didn't care. He asked nothing of his family and owed them nothing and he wanted it kept that way. They could keep their perfect, safe little lives in Sacramento. He had no intentions of telling them how to live and they didn't need to be telling him how to. He liked his family – liked them three hundred miles away with a mountain range between them.

Unknown to them he did have an occupation, although his family wouldn't see it as such. He was a Mustanger. He followed the wild horses back and forth across the desert and sage flats of the Territory and on up into Oregon. When he wasn't catching horses, he was making a few bucks here and there busting broncs. One here, a couple there, it all added up. It kept him free and in spending money of which he didn't need much.

He wasn't a tramp. A tramp was someone who was too lazy to work for a living. He wasn't afraid to work; he just had a problem with staying in one place too long or working under orders. If he saw the same scenery for more than a few days in a row, it made him restless. That's why the Pony had appealed to him so much, it was fast riding, dangerous, and just plain exciting for a young man. Best of all it kept him on the move. He was proud of the fact that grass didn't grow under Spence Logan's boots.

He made acquaintances along the way, but had no desire or need for friends. He wasn't averse to having friends; he just didn't need anyone along to keep him company. He had an easy way about him, quick to laugh and see the humor in most situations like the one he had just shot his way out of.

Most people, like his brothers and sisters, would have died from fright to find themselves in such a spot. To him it was exciting and maybe a little funny; actually he thought it was a whole lot funny. He remembered the expressions on the lunatics' faces and started laughing all over again. Maybe he was as crazy as that saloon bunch. He liked people as a general rule and was willing to help anyone if they needed it, but if they wanted a fight he was more than happy to oblige them.

Walter was all the friend he needed, even if the big roan didn't always see things his way. The blue roan had some Morgan in him and showed it in his heavy square build. He had been a four-year-old when the Pony Express gave way to the telegraph. The last ride he had made was on Walter. He loved the horse and bought him from the Company when he headed out.

The horse had no name when he bought him. He named him Walter, he wasn't sure why, he didn't know anyone named Walter, he just liked the name. Most people would look at him like he had a screw loose on his brain hinge and want to know why anyone would name a horse Walter. He'd just shrug and smile and say something brilliant like, "cuz."

Walter was twelve now and stood a full hand higher at the withers than most of the horses men rode and two more than the mustangs he caught and sold. Had The Pony continued, Walter would have soon been too big to stay in the string and would have been sold off. As it turned out, Walter's new life had found him rounding up more mustangs and covering more miles than any ten other horses put together. Walter demanded nothing from him, never preached at him about his life, and was always willing to listen. The feeling between man and horse was mutual; Walter liked the man as much as the man liked him. Should any man ever try to take him like that time in Eureka, he would meet the business end of Spence Logan's Colt.

He vividly recalled that day in Eureka. A wealthy mining man had taken a shine to Walter and made him a hundred dollar offer for the horse, naturally he had refused it. The man was not accustomed to being refused his way and he insisted to the point of demanding. Eureka was full of rough characters and shootings were commonplace. A wise man tended to his own business; however this was not a wise man.

The man was growing irritated at Spence's refusals and his temper was taking over his reasoning. He kept raising the offer until he shouted that only a fool would refuse two hundred dollars for a horse. Spence was growing equally irritated at the man's insistence and nasty nature and explained to him one more time that there wasn't enough money in all the mines in the Territory to buy Walter.

That's when the man made his biggest and last mistake. With a curse he angrily grabbed a hold of Walter's bridle and shouted, "By God, no two-bit saddle tramp is going to refuse me what I want, I'm taking this horse." The mining man died in the water trough where the bullet that ripped through his heart landed him. Nothing was said; stealing a man's horse was a killing offense and the men watching only shook their heads at the mining man's stupidity and walked away.

One memory gave way to another as he left the reins slack and let Walter walk slowly through the sand, winding his way between the sage plants. He liked the feel of Walter's easy walk, more than once his rocking gait had put him to sleep. Sleeping wasn't the best habit to get into out in this country, but sometimes a man just couldn't help it. Opening his half-closed eyes he made out the stone structure that eight years before had been the Cold Springs

Station.

The building was bigger than he had remembered; the thick stone walls were still standing, but the door and shutters were gone. Sunlight streamed through the openings in the walls dimly illuminating the interior. It seemed strangely quiet with only the sound of the wind blowing through the cracks in the stone walls. The place never was the same again after the Station Master had been killed there, so maybe it wasn't so strange.

He stepped out of the saddle and walked slowly up to the opening in the wall. The memories flooded back over him as he could see in his mind's eye a skinny, tough kid throwing the mochila over the saddle, toeing the stirrup and blasting out of the station like a Fourth of July rocket. Now, it was just the wind and memories, the glorious days gone.

Looking up, he studied the wires running into the distance drooping between the poles and twisted around the wooden pegs on the cross pieces. A young man's glory had been ended by something as quiet and unexciting as wires that sent messages across the country. It was hard to imagine such a thing, words running along a wire, it was something to ponder.

He was educated, having gone the eight years of school his father required of him. He read when he got the chance; however, books were never a favorite pastime for him. He remembered reading about the history of Europe and the founding of the United States. He wondered if one day the Pony would be remembered as history. Would Cold Springs Station, Buckland, and Fort Churchill become places where people came to visit, like Concord, Lexington, and Bunker Hill, to remember what went before? If so, he had been part of that history and he had something to tell his grandchildren about. Maybe things like words running along a wire was something he should understand, it was history in the making.

Looking back down he considered how quickly the

weeds and sage had taken the station over. Nature had a way of reclaiming what men had built and then abandoned. He stepped over a fallen stone to enter the enclosure and jumped back as a rattlesnake slithered out of his way. He felt an involuntary shudder shoot through his body, he hated snakes. He decided to just look in and leave it at that, no telling how many of that critter's relatives were in there with him.

The past was gone and there was nothing he could do about it. Things changed and sometimes that was good. A Winchester was better than a Hawken, the new brass cartridges were superior to cap and ball, and paper loads. Maybe a telegraph wire was better than the mail being delivered by men on horseback – maybe. Only time would tell.

Walking back to where Walter stood three-legged dozing in the sun, he flipped the off-side rein over the roan's neck and mounted. He took a last look around and moved him toward the stage road. He decided to follow it for a while, maybe he'd head for Virginia City. For as long as he had been running around this country he had never gone up to see the wild town that boasted over a hundred saloons and the wealth of kings. He wasn't much on crowds and had always avoided the bigger towns, maybe it was time to go there and see what all the shouting was about.

The stage road continued to the south but would soon turn back to the west and head on into Carson City. Before he had a chance to make any progress along it, the sound of hooves and rolling wheels caused him to pull the roan up and move him off the road. The red coach rumbled toward him with six stout horses pulling with little effort. The thick coat of dust and white alkali stuck to the bright paint, but not enough to hide the unmistakable markings of the Wells Fargo Company. They were now the primary mover of mail and passengers from east to west. Wells Fargo had bought out the Overland, who had controlled the run when the Pony Express came to its end.

The driver cracked the long, thick reins over the horse's backs and called out to them to *get up*. His attention was suddenly taken from the road to Spence. Spence thought he recognized the man, he wasn't sure due to the distance, there was something all too familiar about the man handling the reins. The expression on the driver's face indicated that he had the same thought about him. The shotgun rider to the driver's left looked anxiously around when he felt the driver start pulling the team to a stop. Spotting Spence, he raised the shotgun and pointed it toward him as the stage moved past him in stopping.

Pushing his foot against the brake lever and pulling the team to a full stop, the driver brought the coach to a rocking halt. He turned in the seat and looked back over his shoulder at Spence. Spence moved Walter along toward the stage, he cast a quick look into the coach and saw that it was empty, only the boxes tied down on the top and bags stamped U.S. Mail were being carried. The driver and Spence stared hard at each other for several seconds while the shotgun rider held the double barreled 12 gauge on him. He wasn't quite sure what was happening, no one seemed alarmed, so he watched and wondered.

The driver leaned toward Spence and squinted, "Spence? Spence Logan, is that you?"

Spence studied the man, trying to picture him without the thick red beard. It was the eyes he suddenly recognized. "Gallagher? Shawn Gallagher, you Leprechaun, is that you?"

"None other!"

Gallagher poked the shotgun man with his elbow, "You can put that scattergun down, this here's an old pal of mine." Handing the reins over to him, Gallagher climbed down from his seat.

Spence dismounted and stepped toward him. The two men stopped and stared at each other, and then they mutually thrust out their hands. With a wild and rough handshake the two men greeted each other. "Shawn, how many years since I last saw you?"

"Oh, it's been more'n a few. What are you doing for a living these days?"

"I'm a Mustanger. So when did you start driving for Wells?"

"I've been on the Virginia City run for almost five years now. Drive into Utah and California some too." He gestured with his head toward the stone walls, "Looking at the old place?"

"Just happened to be in the country and thought I'd take a look. Haven't seen it since I left in '61. We had some good laughs there, didn't we?"

"That we did. We were smart young bucks then, weren't we? Riding fast and living for the danger and no man could tell us nothing. I heard you stayed on here even after the Paiutes killed the old man."

"Between here and Buckland, that and Fort Churchill when the Army took over. What about you? I figured a smart fellow like you would end up being the Governor after you were moved to Carson City. So what happened?"

"When the Pony ended, I stayed on to ride shotgun for the Overland. I quit for a time and lived in Placerville, then went back to driving for Wells out of Virginia City. Pays good, but not like when we rode the Pony. No one gets paid a hundred dollars a month any more, not unless you own a mine in Virginia City."

Spence nodded, "I rode scattergun for a bit too, but you know me, got to keep moving. So, how is that up there in Virginia City? Is it everything I hear about it?"

Shawn let out with a hearty laugh, "Depends on what you heard about it, it is one heck of a town though. Gold dust covers everything like alkali does out here, money flows as fast as the liquor. Shootings, fights, you'd like it. Its Spence Logan's kind of town." Then he paused and winked, "That is, if you're still the man I once knew you to be and you ain't gone all sissified or anything."

Spence grinned, "What do you think?"

Shawn laughed again. "Well, I see you're still packing a Colt."

"Got a new one actually. I used to carry a Navy thirty-six caliber; this here's a forty-four." He pulled the revolver from the holster and handed it to Shawn. "It's an Army Colt. I hear tell Remington is coming out with a forty-four that takes five brass cartridges just like the Winchesters use, no more loading like these. I'll be watching for one of them."

Shawn looked over the Colt and then handed it back to Spence. "Nice gun. Hey, did you hear about the shooting up north? Seems them crazies in that outhouse they call a town tried to rob the wrong man and got shot to pieces."

"How did you hear about that?"

"A fellow on the road told me, he had passed through there a couple hours ago and there was blood all over the place and one of them crazies had a bullet hole between his eyes. They was all excited and carrying on about it. Sounds like something you'd do."

"They said they were going to cut me up and eat me, I didn't figure to let them."

Shawn laughed and slapped his knee, "That *was* you? I knew it, I knew it . . . you ain't changed a bit."

"Hey, I was just passing through, minding my own business and stopped for a drink. Wow, I sure walked into it, what a bunch of crazies! They figured to kill me and take Walter and all I had."

Shawn looked at him curiously, "Who's Walter?"

Spence pointed at the roan, "He's Walter."

"Who in the heck names a horse Walter? Never mind, tell the story."

Naturally, I couldn't let a fine horse like *Walter* fall into the hands of that scum. The one with the hole between his eyes pulled out a Toothpick and wanted to know if I'd ever seen one up close, so I showed him my Colt up close. I don't think he liked it all that much though."

Shawn was now laughing even harder, "You do know they're all inbred don't you? None of them's ever left that stinking hole. That's why they're all so odd."

Spence chuckled, "That wasn't too hard to figure out, guess I cut into their brood stock a bit."

The two men stood laughing for a minute before Shawn asked, "So, where to now?"

"Actually I was planning to head for Virginia City, never seen it and figured it was time." Spence grinned, "But, now I'm not sure if I should. You make it sound like an awful scary place, shootings and fights." Spence gave an exaggerated shiver. "Shawn; you think it's too rough a place for me?"

The Irishman was back to laughing hard, "Spence, I think *you're* too scary for *them*."

"Well, in that case I guess it's safe for me to go. Any mustangs around there for me to catch? I could use a few bucks."

"What? You're not gonna dig for gold like the rest of them up there? Men are walking in there with one silver dollar in their pockets and building million dollar mansions a week later."

"Not me old friend, I'll stick to the horses, crawling into a black hole under the ground doesn't sound too appealing to me."

Shawn gave Spence a sly grin, "Well, there are *other* ways to make your fortune there."

Holding up his hands Spence chuckled, "I know all about those *other* ways, bouncing at the end of a rope isn't any more appealing to me than crawling into a hole."

"You don't have to kill or rob anyone; just find some rich old widow and sweet talk her a bit. They'd fall head over heels for a handsome young buck like you." Shawn threw back is shaggy head of red hair and roared with laughter.

"Thanks, you're just full of good ideas aren't you Leprechaun? Besides, if there's so much fortune to be made, how come you're driving a stage?"

"You ain't the only one who doesn't care for black holes or rich old ladies."

"Is that right? I always thought Irishmen were natural miners and silver-tongued devils who swept women right off their feet?"

"No sir, not this Irishman. Well, I'd better get this mail on the road or I'll get fired and have to end up competing with you for one of them rich old ladies. You look me up when you get to Virginia City."

"Sure, maybe we'll go hunting for buried treasure together or some crazy thing like that."

Climbing back up on the seat of the coach he waved at Spence. "We just might."

Made in the USA
Charleston, SC
28 November 2014